# WHERE THE SKY USED TO BE

Zelda Leah Gatuskin

with illustrations by Linda Mae Tratechaud

Part Title Illustrations by Linda Mae Tratechaud © 2011

Cover and book design by Studio Z, Albuquerque, New Mexico

Printed in the United States of America
First Printing, 2011
ISBN: 978-0-938513-43-8
Library of Congress Control Number: 2011933380

AMADOR PUBLISHERS, LLC
Albuquerque, New Mexico
www.amadorbooks.com

*In loving memory of*
*Big Sarah, Little Sarah,*
*Sadie, Greta, Elma, and Muffin*

**ALSO BY ZELDA LEAH GATUSKIN**


*fiction*
THE TIME DANCER
CASTLE LARK


*creative non-fiction*
ANCESTRAL NOTES
TIME AND TEMPERATURE


*poetry*
BUT WHO'S COUNTING?


*children's*
ZELDA'S COSMIC COLORING BOOK

# WHERE THE SKY USED TO BE

## CONTENTS

# PART I

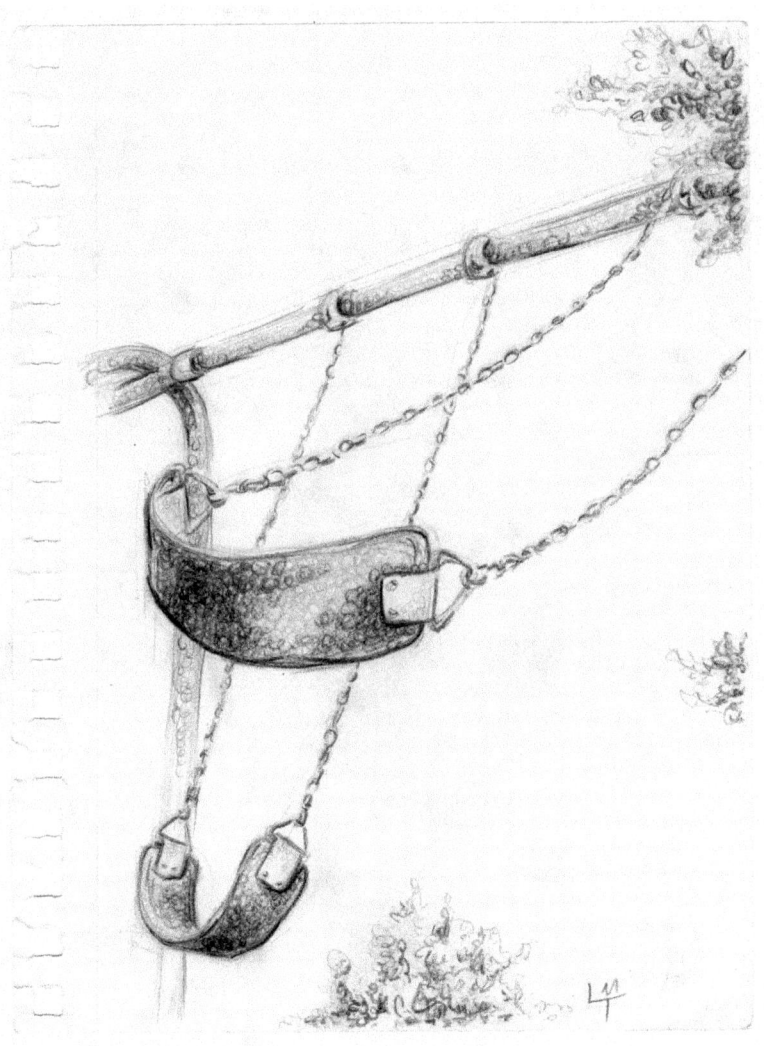

# CHAPTER 1
## CLOSE CALL

Lydia sees herself from above through the eyes of the gull wheeling overhead, hears its shrieks blending with those of her mother. A burly man looms over her and mashes her chest. She is gasping and vomiting water. Familiar and unfamiliar hands lift her head, roll her to the side. Her eyes are her own again, her face so near the sand that she becomes aware of individual granules and each pinprick glint of sunlight reflected from their minute surfaces.

*Like stars...*

"Lydia, sweetheart..." These are her mother's arms. Lydia continues to count stars in the sand.

"Lydia, what happened? Can you talk? It looked like you passed out, you just stopped swimming—you're such a good swimmer."

Lydia retches again and slimes the cosmos. She dare not look up. She feels her father's warm hand on her back.

"That's it. Get it all out. You'll be good as new in a minute."

"She'll be good as new in a minute," he repeats to his wife, as if the words had the power to make themselves come true.

"It looked to me like she blacked out. What if she had a seizure? I want to go back to the States immediately! We've got to get her in for some tests."

At this Lydia pushes herself away from the gritty galaxy, sits up and offers a weak smile. Her voice still works, though it hurts to speak.

"Really, Mom, I just got a big gulp of water and couldn't get my breath back. Don't freak, okay?"

Mrs. Overmyer smiles through her tears. The lifeguard, who has been hovering nearby, stoops down to wrap a rough blanket around

3

Lydia's shoulders.

"Good girl. I knew you wouldn't give up."

"Did you save my life?"

"You're gonna be okay. Strong body, strong spirit, that's what you've got."

The parents back off to let him conduct his exam. He adds softly, peering at Lydia's pupils and checking her pulse, "You've just got to be strong, that's all. Remember that. Everyone's got an angel watching over them. But you gotta do your part. Be strong. Don't you let that angel down."

*He knows*, Lydia thinks, embarrassed.

When her rescuer has finished looking down her throat, Lydia whispers, "Thank you," with tears welling up. "I'll remember. I promise."

She is grateful to be alive. What she had wanted to do was cruel and selfish. Her parents' stricken faces tell her that, even though they couldn't possibly suspect—

"You won't say anything, will you?" she whispers to the lifeguard, now filling in a form on a clipboard.

He asks, "How old are you, miss?" his attention on the form.

"Fifteen. Sixteen in April."

He scribbles. "Anyone can gulp a wave, especially if you've been swimming hard. Happens. That's why I'm here."

Without another look he stands and summons Lydia's folks. They confer over his clipboard, while little Herbie is at last released from the strong grip of Uncle Steve. He flies to Lydia and tackles her, Uncle Steve and Aunt Jill right behind him.

Bart and Emily Overmyer rejoin the group. The adults pack up the beach things while Herbie and Lydia huddle together, crying quietly. Some other bathers who witnessed Lydia's dramatic rescue from the waves venture over to touch her shoulder and say they prayed. They scurry away with sympathetic looks when they see her mother approaching.

"Sweetheart, they said you don't have to go in the ambulance, but we do have to take you to the hospital for a proper exam."

Lydia hates herself, but she knows now that this is beside the point. The people she loves, love her. They would suffer so much if they knew—if they even suspected. For their sake, she is going to put all of this behind her.

*"It happens."* Things happen. Get over it and move on. And if she doesn't say anything, it can be like it never happened. *How many times do I have to be saved before I see the light?* All she has to do is go back to being the old Lydia, and no one will be the wiser.

Later, sitting in the Cancun emergency clinic between her mother and her aunt, Lydia whispers, "I hope you're not going to make a big deal out of this when we get home, Mom. It's really kind of embarrassing, could we not tell the whole world? I just lost my rhythm out there. It was like a totally freak thing."

Emily shoots a questioning look across Lydia to her sister Jill, who purses her lips.

"I expect you'll tell Claire, anyway."

"Uh, yeah, sure. Why wouldn't I tell Claire?"

"Then you won't mind my talking to Claire's parents, so they can be extra careful the next time they make a trip to Miami. I mean, if even a good swimmer like you—"

"Aw, now see, Mom, that's exactly what I'm talking about!"

Emily and Jill exchange a smile. Lydia seems like herself—a typical teen for whom losing face is *the* worst imaginable experience, with loss of life a distant second.

"I know, I know—you would just *die* if anyone knew you almost drowned," Emily teases.

The women find relief in laughing, and this is how Bart, Uncle Steve and Herbie find them when they come in from the parking lot.

✧

Back in New Mexico, Claire sits on the floor of her bedroom idly flipping through her sketchbook, her door closed, her Alanis Morissette competing with her parents' Rolling Stones. It's the most boring winter break ever. She misses Gram and Miami Beach, and feels keenly the injustice of having to hang around Rio Bueno, alone, while *Lydia* frolics in the waves on *her* family vacation.

Every previous year it was Claire who went off to the beach while Lydia was stuck in town. So why would Mr. Overmyer whisk the family away right when Claire and Lydia were finally going to spend the holidays together? Does he think that Claire's a bad influence on the angelic Lydia?

Claire lingers over a drawing of her best friend, a good one, she thinks. She's captured Lydia's lanky elegance, and the intelligence behind her pretty face. Of course, Lydia was never bored without Claire. She has tons of friends. Claire's been wondering lately if Lydia is beginning to prefer their company to hers—those popular girls— and then there are the boyfriends.

Claire feels she's behind the other girls in this regard. It's not for her lack of interest in guys, but more their lack of interest in her. So she perceives it, disregarding the clear evidence in her sketchbook that she is not much impressed by the local specimens. At any rate, she would rather try out the effect of her budding womanhood on a beachful of strangers than have to negotiate the sucky social life of Roosevelt High. She can only imagine the pandemonium lithe Lydia is causing on the beaches of Cancun right now.

Claire sighs, leans over and clicks off the CD. Her parents win. They have to have their rock-n-roll while they work, and they are sworn to work right through Christmas. They need to turn the business around, or the family will have to forego a summer vacation also.

*I should call someone*, Claire thinks. *I wish I could call Lydia!*

She can't think of any other friends to call. She has some numbers, wouldn't be rejected on all fronts, but there's no one else she feels okay being around away from school and Lydia's charmed sphere. Maybe there *is* something wrong with her. Maybe she *is* a bad influence—too artsy, anti-social, with reckless hippy parents...

Her phone rings, an unfamiliar sound with Lydia away. It startles Claire and makes her feel like someone's been eavesdropping on her thoughts.

"Hello?"

"Hello, Claire? It's Tony. I got your number from the phone tree, hope you don't mind."

"Uh, no." Claire almost chokes trying to mask her surprise. *The new kid!* She turns to her sketches from Drama Club and finds her vampire caricature of him. Black hair, black clothes, black fingernails, pointy ears and teeth.

"You remember?"

"Oh yeah, sure." *I am definitely a loser. This is who calls me?*

"Hey, you know that kid Josh? I thought I might call him. His sets were way cool, but I didn't see his number..."

Claire smiles and relaxes. Josh is the best artist in the school, and a pretty good friend. She wonders why *she* didn't think to call him.

"It's under Antresian. I'm sure he's on the list."

"Oh sure, here it is. Duh. Well, thanks."

"No prob."

"But, uh, you know—while we're both like, hanging out—I mean, uhm, wanna do something? I could get my mom to drop me somewhere and meet you. She's going shopping." He lowers his voice. "I've got some really good weed."

Claire's spirits sink again. *Everyone thinks I'm a head.*

"Don't bring that shit, okay?" she says sharply. But because she's bored too, and figures that since she's already got a rep, there's nothing to lose, she adds, "My folks would let me walk to Prince Street and get something at the cafe."

Tony hesitates a second before saying, "Cool, tell me where."

The meeting is quickly set. Claire puts down the phone, furrowing her brow at the Tony-as-vampire sketch. Then she shrugs her shoulders and writes underneath, *"My first date. Christmas, 1999."*

*Good one, Claire.* She can't wait to tell Lydia.

## CHAPTER 2
## ONE SUMMER DAY

It's that sunny day in June, the one which every summer memory is made of, or should be—that day when bright green caps of newly leafed trees alternate with soft-edged silhouettes of tan- and brown- and pink-stuccoed houses against a brilliant sky of uninterrupted blue. It's that same silent sunny day the girls always find so uncanny, when no one is out in the middle of the day but them, and the elementary school playground is deserted. Only Claire and Lydia brave the sun.

They have swung on this swing-set since they attended the school themselves, from the time their spindly legs dangled over the sand, till now, when their shapely hips strain against the narrow saddles. They have always marveled at what a private place the swing-set is, the way it stands starkly in the treeless, grassless, sun-baked school yard, which itself—and for obvious reasons—stands empty much of the time. The patchwork of low, southwestern style homes surrounding the school is silent as a movie-set, the life within insulated behind fences and landscaping and thick block walls. Over the rooftops of the school buildings the Serafina Mountains impose a stately shape against the sky.

Claire and Lydia sat on the swings one day, back when their feet barely brushed the ground, and discussed the Serafinas. If they looked hard, they could make out the angels in the mountains, and so they figured that the angels could see them in turn. From their high vantage the Serafina Mountains saw the girls make friends that day, and have watched them since—throughout this endless sunny summer day, and that windy spring day, the white-sky'd winter day, the golden autumn day—each season always and forever here in the school yard.

Or so it seemed. Now the swing-set sessions grow few and far between, and Lydia feels like she will jump out of her skin if she is forced to be idle for long. The lazy, playful mood no longer comes over her when she plops into her favorite swing. She must feign a friendly lassitude for Claire's sake, while her thoughts skip from one unhappy subject to another, like a tongue testing all the sore places in a tooth to verify the rot is still there. The Serafinas themselves are a painful reminder. *"Everyone's got an angel....Now don't you let that angel down."* She still hasn't told Claire about last winter.

Claire swings lazily and bemoans, again, her plight since Carl and Brianna started their own Internet consulting firm at home. Not only are her parents around a lot more, but their home-office has breached the boundaries of the den and now occupies half the living room as well. Her perpetually present parents are so excited about working together that Claire ends up feeling like *she's* the one who's in the way. A little guilt-tripping got her a TV for her room, now she's lobbying for the old hatchback her dad no longer needs for commuting to work. She uses it regularly since she got her driver's license, but her folks want her to start paying for insurance, gas and upkeep.

"At least they didn't suggest I pay the expenses by working for *them*. There's only so much closeness a family can take!" Claire pauses so that Lydia can express her support.

Lydia just shrugs as their swings pass. She works as an errand-runner for her dad's custom home business and likes being busy. Busy, busy. So busy she's a blur. She pumps harder on her swing.

Fighting back a bitter feeling of loss Claire slows to a stop and watches her friend fly away from her.

"Anyway," she continues brightly when Lydia's anxious arc settles back to a gentle sway, "Mom's found a summer job for me, something I can do and still take art classes. It's for her friend. All I have to do is take a lunch to Mrs. Ferguson's mother in the nursing home a couple times a week."

"Well, I guess that's perfect for you." Lydia sounds unconvinced.

"Yeah, too perfect. Don't you think it seems weird? I mean, the old lady's already in a home. Don't they give her lunch? I think Mom and Mrs. Ferguson cooked it up just for me."

"And you can't afford to turn it down."

"No, I really can't. I have to try it. Free money, right? All I have to do is go visit for an hour."

"Yeah, nothin' to it," but Lydia's squinty, wrinkle-nosed expression says, *"Yuk!"*

Claire scuffs her feet, kicking up the fine playground dirt and rattling the heavy chains that hold the grown-up girls only a couple of feet above the ground. "Hey, it can't be any worse than babysitting." This is what Claire's been telling herself.

"Well, if you say so."

"Not that *you* would know anything about babysitting," Claire teases. Lydia doesn't even have to mind Herbie, the Overmyer's have Carola for that.

Lydia feels a twinge of irritation. *She thinks I have it easy, not a care in the world.* Then guilt. *But why wouldn't she? I should tell her...* She doesn't, though.

"I remember when Granny Abel was in a nursing home before she died. Mom made me go see her every Sunday, until Dad said it was too upsetting and convinced her to leave me home." Lydia shuffles backward, preparing to launch her swing again, and addresses Claire's back. "It was an awful place, and Granny didn't even know us. Going to a nursing home gives me the creeps. I don't think I'd want to do it even for money." With that, she plops into the swing, pushes off and pumps her legs forward to take to the air. Claire pushes off, too, and again swings gently alongside her friend.

"Well, you were a little kid, and it was your own great-grand-mother, so no wonder the scene freaked you out. But when Gram worked in that retirement home and I'd go in with her, it was fun. The old people didn't bother me, and Gram kept the best arts and crafts room. I got to play with all the paints and clay and stuff. It was cool."

"Gram's an artist and so are you."

"Going to be, maybe."

"Are," Lydia insists. Gram has made a big impression on Lydia, too. During her visits to Rio Bueno, she takes the girls out for afternoon teas and excursions to Santa Fe. "But I remember what

Gram said when she retired, don't you?"

Claire sighs. "Yeah, that working around old people depressed her."

"And you don't think it's gonna depress *you*?" Lydia is depressed just thinking about it.

"It's only a few hours a week. And it's only one old lady," Claire insists uneasily.

"When do you start?"

"I'm supposed to go out to Westcare Manor with Mrs. Ferguson on Friday. Then I'll start going out there on my own on Wednesdays and Fridays, and I'll have to go every day when the Fergusons take their vacation in August."

"I guess summer school will be over by then."

"Yeah."

"So, tell me about her." Lydia tries to sound interested. She still isn't entirely clear as to the point of these visits to the old lady, and she suspects that Claire isn't either.

"Well, she's blind."

"Oh great, Claire, this gets better and better. What else?"

"She wasn't always blind. She only went blind when she got old, gradually, and she lost her memory around the same time—from a stroke, I think. Isn't that awful? I can't imagine."

"No, me neither, and I don't want to!" Lydia walks her swing around in little circles, twisting the chain so that when she picks up her feet she'll spin back fast in the other direction. Once she's accomplished this classic move, she makes a motion to leave. "I think you're really noble to take the job, I really do—ugh, it's too hot. Let's go." She mops sweat from her hairline.

Red splotches of heat rash have formed on the backs of Claire's arms. Over by the school, the blacktop of the basketball court sends up wiggly heat vapors.

"Noble, huh? And I thought I was doing it for gas money." They turn in unison from the swing-set and head toward Lydia's house. "Hey, Lyd, get this, the old lady has a nickname. Are you ready?"

"What?"

"Muffin! Mrs. Ferguson calls her mom Muffin!"

"I love it! When she was young, do you think she was a Cupcake?"

That cracks them up. "Cupcake" is Claire and Lydia's private joke—their code word for ditsy, overly self-conscious girls of any age. They don't use it as much now. Their tom-boyish style has given way to certain Cupcake-like vanities of their own, and it's no longer as amusing as it used to be. But, in the context of Mrs. Ferguson's ninety-year-old mother, thus far only a decrepit figure in the girls' imaginations, "Cupcake" is funny all over again. The laughter feels so good, once they start they can't stop. Their voices echo in the school yard as they round the corner and the Serafinas wink out of view.

"Yoo-hoo! Anybody home?" Mr. Overmyer's traditional entrance is greeted by his young son's traditional squeal of welcome.

Up in Lydia's room, Claire marks a place in the magazine she's reading and gets up. "Guess I better go."

"C'mon, you can stay—

"Hi, Dad! We're up here!"

"We?"

"Me and Claire."

"Hi, Mr. Overmyer," Claire sings out at the same time.

A chilly silence, then, "Of course," followed by an unenthusiastic, "Hi Claire."

The girls hold their breath until they hear Mr. Overmyer's footsteps and Herbie's prattle fade into the depths of the house.

"Dad's decided you're a bad influence on me. I can't say anything, it just makes it worse."

This has been coming on for a few years now, with the girls' increasing independence. They have tried to ignore it, or make a joke of it, but right now Claire finds the injustice hard to swallow.

"Is that why he's not filling the pool this summer? So I won't hang around?"

"No!" Lydia is taken aback. "No way! He's trying to do his part for water conservation. Wants to make a show of it, anyway. To get in good with the new guy on the water commission."

Claire rolls her eyes. Lydia feels like a jerk. She can't bring herself to tell Claire about the "accident" in Cancun. She intended to do it right away, but by the time they got back to Rio Bueno, she had decided to put it behind her—to put everything behind her. She may have secretly hoped that her mother would tell Ms. Yost so it would filter down to Claire, and then she would *have* to tell. But for once Lydia's mother had respected her privacy, and now five months had passed with nothing said. As for the pool, Emily and Bart readily acknowledge there's more to the decision than conservation. *"Herbie is at such an active age..."* They've had it drained and securely covered.

"Dad thinks we smoke pot," Lydia reminds Claire, to get her off the subject of the pool.

"Well, why wouldn't he? I bet he smoked it." The girls have had this conversation before.

"If he did, he won't say. At least Mom's honest about it."

"Hey, my folks still think I don't know they smoke."

"So—you got any?" Lydia has an idea for a diversion, a little "plot" with which she and Claire might amuse themselves through the long pool-less summer.

"You're kidding, right?"

Claire began pilfering her parents' stash when she was about twelve, but the girls quickly decided that marijuana wasn't for them. They disdain smoking in general as a filthy habit, and when they tried baking the stuff into cookies and brownies the gritty confections made them sleepy, and only slightly more giggly than usual. Claire supposes her parents smoke marijuana to relax, the way other people do coffee to perk up. She doesn't disapprove of their habit as much as their lying about it. She herself tries not to do things she'll have to lie about, because she's a lousy liar.

"Please tell me you're kidding."

Lydia enjoys provoking Claire, and she doesn't mind goading her father, either. All the excess concern and oversight since Christmas has been getting on her nerves.

"Oh, I don't plan to smoke the stuff," she explains, "I just thought

I'd hide a baggie in my desk. If Dad searches my room, I want him to find something, so I can bust him. It would serve him right."

"That is the worst idea I've ever heard!"

Lydia shrugs, but a wicked smile plays around her lips. "Okay then, how about oregano?"

"Ha! Now you're talking!" Claire and Lydia slap palms. "Call me later, 'kay?"

"Yeah, later"

Claire skips down the stairs and makes a noisy exit for Mr. Overmyer's benefit.

# CHAPTER 3
## THE GAME BOARD OF LIFE

In Claire's neighborhood on the other side of the school, the streets are longer and the houses smaller than in Lydia's cloistered cul de sac. Claire likes the infinite variety of porches, driveways, fences, walls, flowers, trees and weeds which line her route. There are yards with dogs and yards with birdbaths. Some amateur gardeners lean toward roses, others go heavy on the marigolds and mums. Xeriscapes of gravel with little islands of yucca, red hot poker and pampas grass alternate with well watered, closely clipped lawns. It's like a quilt in which every family fills its piece of patchwork with an arrangement of their own design.

And if her neighborhood is a patchwork quilt, Claire's decided, then her town is a life-sized game board. One rolls the dice or picks a card and then hops from this colored square to another. Some squares have significance, other squares are only places you have to pass through to get somewhere else. There's School and the Mall, the Library, the River. There are squares to avoid, too, especially after dark. Sometimes you draw a winning number and get to jump to a really special square, like the Country Club or the Lodge on Serafina Peak. With the new mobility afforded by having her driver's license (like plucking the Automobile card from the deck), Claire has been able to advance farther and farther across the board.

The sprawling metropolitan area of Rio Bueno, New Mexico lends itself to Claire's metaphor. Its streets are laid out in a careful grid surrounding a spacious central plaza, Old Town, now overshadowed by the high-rises of the neighboring business district. The rail tracks, running parallel to the river, bisect the city into east and west sides, and old Market Street delineates north from south, creating four

15

quadrants. *Boxes within boxes,* Claire thinks, imagining Rio Bueno from a bird's eye view. As one swoops closer and closer, one sees the four quadrants fracture into a grid of main boulevards, and then the smaller streets appear, and the little neighborhood side streets, and finally the alleys and driveways and the crazy quilt of front yards and back yards.

Of course, the most important square is Go, the place you start from. It's also the place you go to collect your prize. On Claire's personal game board that square is located at 541 Chamisa Road, and although landing on that property will not bring rewards of play money, failing to do so at frequent enough intervals will certainly land Claire in Jail. She hurries up the street. Porch lights flicker on as she passes, as though she is Dusk's personal herald.

"Sorry I'm late!" Claire slams through the kitchen door and hears her parents' excited voices. They approach from the direction of the den, babbling about the newest job. Claire supposes they haven't even missed her. She washes her hands and considers what she can fix for supper.

"Oh, honey, forget that! We're going out to eat!" Claire's mother, Ms. Brianna Yost, rounds the corner and confronts the open refrigerator door.

Claire's head pops into view, and then the rest of her, as she steps back and lets the door swing shut. She eyes her parents suspiciously. They've hardly eaten out at all since the firm of Stanley-Yost was established, though they've kept the local pizza delivery place busy enough. When she sees that her mother is sincere, Claire really is sorry she's late.

"Let's go, I'm starved." Carl "Stan Man" Stanley shoos his wife and daughter toward the door.

"Me too. Where we going? Should I change? Want me to drive?"

"Appreciate the offer, but we'll take your mother's car, and I'll drive. Brianna, please don't let her change."

"Hmmm, go brush your hair, honey. And put something on over that tank top. We're going to Reginald's."

"Reginald's! Why didn't you tell me?" Claire dashes past her parents.

"Aw, Brianna, I'm starving."

"Here, have some crackers. This *is* our new client. In fact, maybe you should change your clothes."

"Thanks a lot. I'll wait outside."

Reginald's is a popular place. It takes up much of the first floor of one of the stylish east side office towers that stands in convenient proximity to Ladera Mall. Nouveau Continental cuisine is served up with attitude by a wait staff trained to be crisp and condescending. *The Reginald* of Reginald's is from New York City, and the success of his establishment rests on his talent for making the locals feel like yokels. Everyone loves being put down by Reggie. He prides himself on keeping his menu utterly uncompromised by southwestern cuisine, and eschews anything remotely resembling a hot pepper. Those who want a floor show with their meal have only to request a side of green chile, and Reginald, upon being informed by one of his servers, will come storming out of the kitchen to perform his Dance of the Outraged Chef, sometimes to be followed by a strenuous oration on The Decline of the Culinary Arts.

The Stanley-Yosts feel uneasy making their entrance in the middle of a Reggie classic—Capsicum is a Crude Way to Impart Heat—but a lanky hostess bumps Chef Reginald out of the narrow aisle with a bony hip and ushers them to a table. He has taught her well. Claire admires the languid walk which suggests that this black-garbed wraith is so detached, she even bores herself. She drops menus in front of them and strolls away.

A young man appears, also dressed from head to toe in black, also slim as a rail.

"Tony! I didn't know you worked here." There's no point pretending she doesn't recognize him.

"Oh. Hello, Claire," he says crisply, in a tone that discourages further conversation.

In contrast to the hostess, Tony's manner is efficient verging on frenetic. Claire imagines black coffee running through his veins as he pours water, rattles off the specials, and makes snappy asides about having heard Reggie's speech a thousand times already.

*He's really good at this.*

Claire is surprised to see him working at all. During their quasi-date last winter break, to which Tony showed up obnoxiously stoned, he revealed that Roosevelt High was his fourth transfer in two years. He has a "condition" which has been diagnosed variously as ADD, ADHD, Bi-polar Disorder, Anxiety, and a personality something-or-other. The way Tony described it, Claire wondered how the doctors could possibly know for sure what was actually wrong, after trying out so many drugs on the kid. Tony had to go to the Counselor's office every day to get what he called his "pill du jour." She felt for him, but school is too cruel a place for a freak like Claire and a ghoul like Tony to pal around without causing their status to plummet further. In the halls and classrooms of Roosevelt High, the two, by tacit agreement, rarely speak.

Encountering each other at Reginald's, the teens maintain their cool. Claire admires Tony's aloof manner and adopts one of her own. She says nothing more to him, and ignores her parents' questioning looks, turning her attention to her surroundings instead. Claire's glad that she changed into her black jeans and a black t-shirt. Light streaks have come out in her bouncy auburn hair, and her face is ruddy from sitting in the sun. She feels pretty good about herself, even the fact that she's nowhere near as thin as Reggie's typical employee. She figures she must look at least eighteen, if not twenty, and watches the other diners surreptitiously to see if any of the men look her way.

A bill is brought to the nearby table where Reggie's been holding forth, and he wraps up his lecture. He pats the shoulder of the man who takes the check, then makes his way over to the Stanley-Yosts.

"Brianna, Carl, so glad you could make it!" Claire's dad jumps up so Reggie can pump his hand. Reggie kisses her mom's hand and hers, when she is introduced, then he scoots in next to her and starts talking about the website her parents are going to design for him.

Claire is surprised at what a regular person he is, not at all the pompous jerk she's just seen and heard in action. When Tony breezes by to take their order, Reggie asks for a cup of coffee for himself while the Stanley-Yosts deliberate over their menus. He's as nice and normal to his employee as he can be, but the young man never drops his long-suffering smirk or insolent eye-rolling. Once Tony's badgered the order out of them, he dashes off with an air of exasperation. Reggie smiles proudly. "That Tony is a kicker. I've taught him everything I know about waitering."

Claire snickers and thinks about how everything's an act, a big show. Even if you make something of quality—like Reggie's food—you have to create an elaborate package to get anyone to take notice. Claire's not sure how she feels about this, or what it will mean to her intended career as an artist. Will she end up creating art, or merely making packages?

Reggie sits with the Stanley-Yosts through the entire meal, drawing attention to their party. Claire observes how her parents bask in the glow of Reggie's self-made celebrity, and feels cheated. This dinner is all part of their business day, and she's just along for the ride. They talk about the Internet, site design, marketing, the restaurant trade. Their conversation is not especially interesting to Claire. *Boxes within boxes,* she's thinking, *right down to the websites with their frames and sidebars and icons.* She concentrates on the gourmet dishes and the curious youths staffing the dining room. Her passion is for real life, not the virtual world of image and information.

Eventually the adults tire of themselves and turn to their young companion. Claire is drawn out about her painting. She quickly discovers that Reggie is as opinionated about fine art as he is about cuisine. She responds in kind and shares some of her previously private observations: How a painting is always trapped within its frame, and video and computer art are trapped in the same way, and how you can make bigger and bigger paintings or bigger and bigger TV screens, but the art is still bound to be stuck in a box—and that's why, however different it is, it all starts to look alike.

"And then you end up with shit like I saw on TV the other day," she concludes, "where there's a TV report showing a website showing pictures in an art gallery—boxes within boxes within boxes!"

The harsh judgment Claire seems to be heaping on their stock and trade is not lost on Carl and Brianna. Fortunately, Reggie doesn't take Claire's comments as an indictment of her parents' design services, but joins in with some observations of his own: Perhaps such great painters as Mondrian and Kandinsky had come to the same conclusion as Claire, and so chose to employ the boundary as a design element itself, to utilize the geometry of the canvas in their paintings—

And off they go. Over dessert, Reggie engages Claire in a discussion of how painting has evolved since Cubism ("Everything's a mixed media mess now," Reggie asserts) and how it will change in the age of computers ("Nothing can replace the feeling of putting paint on canvas," Claire assures him), while her parents, having nothing to contribute, sit quietly and marvel at their daughter.

Later, on the way home, Claire's mom hands her a credit card to use when she goes shopping for art supplies for her summer classes. Claire decides that going to dinner at Reginald's was like landing on a lucky square. Some of Reggie's successful packaging has rubbed off on her.

# CHAPTER 4
## LUNCH WITH MUFFIN

Claire thinks that Mrs. Ferguson is a lot like Gram, so she feels pretty comfortable with the older woman. Mrs. Ferguson is artistic like Gram—she does calligraphy and paintings on silk. Gram has always treated Claire like an equal, and so does Mrs. Ferguson, who talks to her frankly about "Muffin" as they drive out to Westcare Manor.

"I can't tell you what a lifesaver you are. It's a bit much for me to go out there seven days a week, but when I see what a difference it makes—"

Claire turns to study Mrs. Ferguson's face. She seems to be on automatic pilot, following the road but seeing something else. Her eyes are a little red and puffy behind her prescription sunglasses. Her mood shifts between relief and anxiety.

In addition to sensing Mrs. Ferguson's serious doubts about whether Muffin and Claire can manage without her, Claire detects a touch of guilt—as if by surrendering her mother to Claire two days a week she is shirking her responsibilities. Only, it's not Mrs. Ferguson's job to give Muffin lunch every day. That service is included in the nursing home's hefty fees.

"How long have you been doing this?" Claire asks.

The note of disapproval is not lost on Jo Ferguson. She shoots a look at Claire.

"Oh, believe me, it's still a lot better than having her on the East Coast and spending months of my life out there doing nothing but dealing with her and my poor father."

"Oh, well, yeah, I guess so." Claire can't imagine it.

"I brought Ma out last winter. Pop cared for her at home until his own health went. A few years ago no one would've believed he'd be the first to go, but Ma was impossible. It killed him. I knew it would."

Claire figures that kind of devotion must run in the family, Mrs. Ferguson is nothing if not self-sacrificing. She mentally withdraws her suspicions about this being make-work for her, because it is obvious that Mrs. Ferguson does need help with these visits.

"Ma had already been in a home for two years before Pop died. It was a horrible place, but he could be near her. Once Pop was gone, there was no reason for her to stay. It took a while to find something local. I figured getting Muffin here was the end of the hard part, that once I had her nearby, things would be okay—

"Look, here's Cottonwood Boulevard. I'm going to take a left at the light and go over the bridge and straight on up the hill."

"Got it." Claire finds the intersection on Mrs. Ferguson's artfully drawn map, then turns her eyes to the road. "So, what happened? Did Muffin freak out when you moved her here?"

"Did Muffin freak out?" Mrs. Ferguson laughs sadly. "Ma has been freaking out pretty regularly for about five years, except when they had her sedated. What happened here is that soon after she moved in she got sick, lost a lot of weight, and even lost her will to put up a fuss. That's when I knew she was in trouble. It seemed like she was giving up. I couldn't exactly blame her, but I wanted to be sure. First of all, I could see that the lunches they serve there—lunch is their big meal of the day—are not to her taste. And then there's the fact that she's blind and has to be fed. Well, the noise of the dining room throws her into a frenzy, and one aide has to feed six residents. I asked them to take lunch to her in her room, but no one had time to sit there and feed her."

Claire is having trouble following all this but she nods vigorously. Mrs. Ferguson seems relieved to have someone listen, someone who is about to see the situation for herself.

"I figured I'd take some homemade food and sit in the room with Muffin and see if she would eat. If she was really determined to starve herself, that would be the time for her to show me she meant it."

"But she liked your cooking, huh?"

"It was amazing! She started getting stronger and hungrier, and even a little calmer. We got into a routine, and I'm there every day, so I can see what's going on and try to get the staff to make things more routine for her. The squeaky wheel gets the grease, and believe me, I make noise. Otherwise, well, you know how these places are."

Claire doesn't, and is not looking forward to finding out.

Mrs. Ferguson pulls into the Westcare parking lot beyond a lawn so green Claire wonders if it's real. A low building presents itself, as blocky and undistinguished as TechTel, the nearby microchip factory.

"Oh, and I think you should call me Jo, or Josie," Mrs. Ferguson says as she reaches into the back seat and grabs a little cooler. "Ma won't know who you're talking to if you call me Mrs. Ferguson."

Inside the building, Claire is almost knocked over by the smell of the dining room. It smells like everything she hates—overcooked pot roast, cabbage, lima beans. She follows Jo around the corner, and passes a long line of residents, rolling in wheelchairs or shuffling behind walkers, as they make their way to lunch. She tries not to look at anyone and feels self-conscious. Lots of elderly eyes stare at her hungrily, as if her youth alone could nourish them. Jo says "Hi" to a couple of folks. The aides are too busy to pay them any mind at all. It's a relief when they pass the last of the stragglers, cross the deserted nurse's station, and enter one last remote hallway. Muffin waits in the last room on the left. They hear her before they get there.

"Someone help me! Get me out of here!" a surprisingly strong voice demands. Claire has to smile as she hurries to the room behind Jo. She can think of situations when she's felt like that. Next time, maybe she'll shout it out like Muffin.

"I'm here, Ma. What's the problem?"

"Who's here? Josie, is that you?"

"It's me, Ma."

"It's so cold in here. I'm hungry. Can't we go now?"

Claire stares at the old woman, and tries to digest what she sees, which is not at all what she imagined. The name Muffin somehow conjured the image of a cuddly creature, but the real Muffin is gaunt and angular. Her grey hair is cut so short she has a cowlick, her ears are immense. The long face is a little lopsided from stroke, filmy blue

eyes are wide open and unseeing. She's wearing a faded yellow
sweatshirt and grey polyester pants. Her white sneakers pump at the
footrests of her wheelchair like she might bust out of the chair and
make a run for it. Her hands are translucent and blue veined, bony
fingers rest uneasily like unearthed roots upon the padded tray attached
to her chair. Claire feels anxiety harden into a knot in her stomach.
What has she gotten into?

Jo fusses over her mother for a minute, gives her a reassuring
squeeze of the shoulders, buttons her sweater, and pulls down the
pantslegs which have ridden up over her knees from all that foot
pumping. Jo coos and Muffin quiets now, as she senses something
more than her daughter's ministrations.

"Ma, I brought someone to meet you today. Remember, I said I
would?" Jo straightens and makes room for Claire to come closer.

The rheumy eyes turn in Claire's direction, then look right at her.
Claire could swear that Muffin sees her. She wants to hide. She feels
entirely inadequate.

"Ma, this is Claire. Claire, this is Muffin."

Claire can't think of anything to say. How on earth is she to relate
to this unhappy old woman? She knows she has to say something or
do something—a winning smile will do her no good in this situation.
She decides she'll try a touch on the hand.

"Ma, is it okay if Claire calls you Muffin?"

"Well, I guess so."

Claire reaches a forefinger toward a frail wrist but never quite
makes contact. "Thanks," she blurts out, "and you can call me
Cupcake."

The long face folds its wrinkles upward into a big smile. "Oh, ha
ha, oh," she laughs, "I never heard that one before!"

"The thing is, I really *felt* like a Cupcake. You know, like I was so
*stupid*—just some dumb kid who doesn't know anything."

"So? Sounds like Muffin doesn't know what's going on either. That
kinda makes you even. Maybe you'll have better luck with her than the
staff, or Mrs. Ferguson."

"Jo. She told me to call her Jo or Josie."

"Cool."

"Yeah."

Claire and Lydia are on the phone, each using their own personal line in their respective bedrooms on opposite sides of the elementary school. It is after midnight.

Lydia has been out with Matthew. The Friday night date has become fairly routine, and Claire senses that her friend is getting bored. After the usual obsessive build-up through the week, Lydia's report of the event itself was terse—the movie was okay for a noisy guy flick, bumped into a few school friends afterwards at Pizzazz Pizza, dad flicked the porch lights during the good night kiss—when Lydia suddenly changed the subject to Claire's visit to Westcare Manor, Claire imagined a big X beside Matthew's name. Lydia has been running through boyfriends at a rapid rate.

"So, you think she really got the joke about Cupcake?"

"I don't know how she took it, exactly, but it really cracked her up. That's when I knew I'd be okay with her. I mean, she can't be that out of it if she can still get a joke."

"Yeah, really. You gotta have some sense to have a sense of humor." Lydia is proud of herself for starting the Muffin-Cupcake gag, which broke the ice between Claire and Muffin. She wouldn't mind being included in Claire's "Muffin Project," as long as she doesn't actually have to go into the nursing home.

"What happened during lunch?"

"Oh, you wouldn't believe the lunch Jo packed! Little bitty servings of salad and fruit, yogurt—Jo calls it 'lemon pudding'—and a perfect sandwich in quarters with the crusts cut off. It's just like at Reginald's—presentation is everything. Jo describes exactly what Muffin's going to eat and makes it sound so good, she can't possibly refuse. I sat on the bed and we tried to have a conversation that Muffin could follow. She wasn't really into it, but after Jo got a little food in her, she seemed kind of content. After lunch, Jo took off Muffin's shoes and socks and rubbed her feet with lotion."

"Oh, gross! Do you have to do that?"

"Jo said I didn't, but I could tell Muffin was enjoying it. I don't know—it seemed like a special thing between Jo and her mom."

"Maybe she wouldn't want you to do it."

"Maybe not."

The girls fall silent. Lydia is thinking about her Granny Abel—how inadequate they must've been when she most needed them. Claire is half asleep.

"I have to work tomorrow," Lydia says, "guess I better go."

"You know, your schedule sucks."

"Tell me about it. I've hardly had a chance to use my new telescope."

*It's not the job keeping you so busy, it's the boyfriends*, Claire thinks, but says only, "I can't believe your father makes you work while *he* takes Saturday and Sunday off!"

"Hey, that's the only good part. Everyone's a lot nicer and more relaxed when Dad's not around. I think they're figuring out that they can be normal around me—that he drives me crazy, too."

"I guess weekends are big for showing custom homes."

"Totally. It's like a circus out there. You're lucky you don't have to visit Muffin on Saturdays," Lydia is aware that Claire's route to Westcare Manor passes through prime Overmyer Homes real estate. "What are you doing tomorrow?"

"Mom made me promise to work in the yard."

"Then take your easel out there and work."

"Oh, you are full of good ideas! Speaking of which, did you do that thing with the oregano?"

"Yeah. They haven't found it yet, but they accused me of eating pizza in my room!"

"Hey, that's *good*. Now they'll think you have the munchies."

"Ha! I'll start leaving candy bar wrappers all over the place."

"Perfect." Claire and Lydia yawn simultaneously and audibly.

"Okay, say Bye."

"*Bueno* bye."

"*Bueno* bye."

Claire turns the phone off and tosses it on the floor beside her bed.

It lands gently on a tangle of dirty clothes. Before turning off the reading light and sliding into the sheets, she surveys her room. It is crowded with her possessions, which fan out across floor and furniture in semi-organization: newly laundered clothes, once-worn clothes, twice-worn clothes, grungy working-around-the-house clothes, smocks and dropcloths, art supplies, art supplies in use, art projects in progress, art projects complete or abandoned, a large formation of school papers stratified by semester, an assemblage of colorful crates overflowing with books, disks and videotapes. On the dresser, broken toys mingle with make-up and jewelry, the windowsill is lined with spent still life props—dying flowers and desiccated fruit.

Claire loves her room, but the visit with Muffin has made her look at it differently tonight, as she imagines spending her whole day in a room no bigger than this. *Imagine living ninety years, and then having to boil down everything you own to what will fit inside a wardrobe, a dresser and a nightstand.* Claire couldn't do that now! She reminds herself that this is not exactly Muffin's experience, and snaps off the light, thinking, *If you were blind, it wouldn't really matter how small the room was, would it? Or could you feel the walls pressing in? And if you were blind, not having a lot of stuff would make things simpler. And if you couldn't even remember all that stuff you once had—*

Claire finds little consolation in this thought.

*Imagine you've lived your whole adult life and now you can hardly remember it!*

Tears spring to Claire's eyes. She's let her imagination run away with her again, and again she has over-simplified Muffin's condition.

*Muffin knows who her family is, and Jo says that she remembers a lot about her childhood.*

Claire scans the shadows of her lair. Already the artifacts of her childhood, youth and adolescence are embedded in her memory—she doesn't need the light to see them. What does it mean to all of her hopes and dreams that after another sixty, seventy, maybe eighty years—years she hasn't lived yet—it could all come right back down to this—this place, these memories, this person she is right now? She can hardly order these thoughts, they are so mind-boggling.

*Imagine that seventy years have passed, but you are remembering* this *like it was yesterday.*

She can almost do it. She doesn't have to try to make up all the things that would or could happen in those seventy years. She must only imagine that the years have all flown away, like shreds of dreams, and she is old remembering being young. Because this is what she will remember, this is who she will be, always, the person she is right now.

This is hardly a comforting thought. Claire remembers her trips to the nursing home in Miami with Gram, how the old ladies mostly talked about their fathers or grandmothers and things that happened very long ago. It seems to her that their memories had peeled away, the most recent to the oldest. It will be the same for her. She can look forward to being only herself, pretty much as she is right now.

No, it is not, in the smallest hour of the morning, an especially pleasant thought. Claire makes a deal with herself, with the girl who may be the only sure thing at the end of a long and fulfilling life— *Hopefully long and fulfilling!* If, instead, her fate is to die tragically young, then her promise to herself will be even more important.

"*Now* can so easily turn into *Forever*," she whispers to the shadows. "It's time to stop saying I'm *going to be* an artist and *be* one already."

# CHAPTER 5
## ON BEING AN ARTIST

Claire can say one thing for Lydia's cruel work schedule—it forces her to manage her own social life. Her sphere of friends has shifted to the "art crowd" from school—those mostly misfits who hang out in the Fine Arts wing. A bunch of them are enrolled in the summer scholarship program at the U, along with their artistic peers from other high schools in the area. Claire misses spending time with Lydia, but finds that she doesn't miss the Mall, Pizzazz Pizza, Planet Cool, or the twenty-screen cinema. These kids plan to spend the summer seeing art films at The Palace on College Avenue and eating in the little ethnic places surrounding the U. They'll have fun passing themselves off as university students, toting their portfolios and paintboxes around campus. They gravitate to each other in this unfamiliar setting, and so a ragged clique of individualists is forming. No one really counts themselves "in," they are just—together.

As the summer progresses, a sub-group of the non-group will expand their range beyond the hub of the university. These are the kids enrolled in the Community Art-Reach Mural Association course, who will be painting murals in a notoriously "bad" neighborhood side by side with local youths. This exciting and slightly scary prospect causes the CARMA art students to band together immediately. Claire knows four of the kids well, and a couple of others in passing. She's making friends with everyone else quickly, even before class starts, since they've all arrived way too early on this first day.

Two girls show up after the teaching team has already started class. They command everyone's attention when they saunter in carrying huge paper cups of soda from a Big B. One of them slushes her ice around noisily—maybe a little nervously, Claire detects. These two are dressed in the same black-from-head-to-toe outfit as almost every other

29

teenager in the room, except that their black shoes are higher heeled, their black clothes are shinier, their black hair is coifed taller and their black eyeliner is heavier. Their lipstick is the color of dead roses. If any two girls look like they come from "the wrong side of the tracks," these two do. Claire admires their in-your-face display.

Call-me-Brodie, the sociologist, makes a big deal of welcoming and introducing Laurie and Angela. Claire feels mortified for them when Brodie comes right out and announces that they are from the Cesar Chavez area, where the mural will be painted. No wonder the pair have taken the offensive. Doubtless they've been recruited for the class by their community elders or maybe Brodie himself. Even Call-me-Sherry, the artist of the teaching team, squirms uneasily when Brodie resumes his introductory lecture, "Murals and Positivism: To Light the Eye is to Light the Soul."

*Well-meaning but clueless,* Claire decides. She and most of her fellow students are sketching and doodling under the guise of taking notes. Claire draws a caricature of Brodie with his foot in his mouth. She leans back and holds up her pad so that the guy behind her can see it. His name's Andrew, and he goes to Eisenhower High. Unfortunately, her humor is lost on him. He and the two fellows flanking him are passing a pocket mirror back and forth, which they use to observe Laurie and Angela sitting in the last row. Claire supposes the girls look sexy in a tough, untouchable sort of way. She doubts that any of the young men in the room will have the nerve to go up to them after class.

Claire observes that Call-me-Sherry is an entirely different sort of urban guerilla. Sherry is the only woman in the room not wearing black, though her olive fatigues and t-shirt can hardly be called colorful. Her arms are sunburnt, and a paint splattered baseball cap shades her face and hides her eyes, leaving the lively blond ponytail that sticks out in back to express what goes on underneath. Sherry sits up front and presents her profile to the group as she listens, or pretends to listen, to Brodie's talk. The ponytail sways ever so gently from side to side as if saying, *"no, no, no, no."* Claire elaborates on her cartoon and adds Sherry as a soldier carrying a giant paintbrush instead of a rifle. *"An artist is a warrior,"* she writes to herself in the margin. *"She paints the world the way she sees it and the way she wants it to be."* Aware of the furtive glances being cast toward the back of the room, Claire adds, *"And she paints herself into the picture exactly the way she wants to be seen."*

When the lights are dimmed so that Brodie can finish with a slide show, which is actually pretty interesting, attention shifts from Laurie and Angela. There are pictures from cities all around the country showing mural sites before and after, and how the exciting, monumental artworks have transformed their bleak-looking settings. The last set of slides contains local shots of several completed murals and multiple views of the intersection at Merchant and Soldiers with the brick building they'll be painting this summer.

Sherry jumps up, flicks on the lights and grabs a stack of papers from the desk. "Here's a map of where those local photos were taken, in case you want to go and see some of the murals for yourselves. This other sheet shows two approved alternatives for the east wall of the Old Mercantile. Study them. We need to decide what we're doing quick—we're on a really tight schedule. Wednesday we'll go see the building in person and talk about these options. We'll leave from right out front of the Fine Arts Center at exactly one-forty-five. Don't be late." Sherry looks back at Laurie and Angela and all eyes in the room follow—*"The Stiletto Sisters"* Claire decides, scribbling in her book.

They sneer on cue, and Laurie says icily, "How about if we meet you?"

Claire watches Shelly's face. A tiny ripple of annoyance seems directed more at herself than at Laurie. It passes instantly, and Shelly smiles agreeably. "Great. Anyone else who wants to meet us there, tell me now, please." In Claire's imagination, Shelly raises her friendly smile like a gleaming shield which repels all negativity—the poison barbs of Laurie and Angela fall against it ineffectually with little plink-plinks. *The confrontation ends in a draw.*

"Watcha doin'?"

Claire slams her notebook shut and looks up. Josh is standing over her. Everyone else has gotten up and is ambling out. "Just doodling."

She gets up and watches the subtle choreography of the exit scene. As she predicted, Laurie and Angela are maintaining a wide buffer zone. They carefully ignore the few friendly smiles being cast their way from afar, while a couple of boys seem caught in their orbit but unable to spiral in. Andrew is one of them. Dori, to her credit, steps through the invisible force field. Claire can tell from her body language that she's breaking the ice with the time-honored subjects of nail color and shoe styles. The trio departs in animated conversation. Claire looks at Josh and sees that he's been observing the same scene. She wonders what he thinks of those two. *Probably just imagining what they'd look like on a canvas.*

"I'm not sure I can get here in time on Wednesday," she says as she gathers her stuff.

"Want a ride?"

"No, that's the thing. I'll be coming from the west side."

She's glad to have the excuse, because the eagerness in his voice has given her a fluttery feeling, followed by a wave of irritation. She and Josh have been friends for a long time, and she has always steadfastly ignored any hint that he might want to be her boyfriend, but these days she can't spend any time alone with him without feeling like it's turning into a date. It's not because of the way he acts—because he's always acted like he has a crush on her—but because of the new way she feels. Maybe she really likes him that way, or maybe it's simply that she wants to have a boyfriend, and Josh happens to be handy.

If Claire were to be honest with herself, which she usually is to an almost painful degree, she would have to say that Josh is too easy a conquest. He doesn't present a true test of her feminine powers. It is a shameful, Cupcake-like thought and she shakes it off only to have it replaced by another: *What about Andrew?* He's visible out in the hallway, leaning against the wall with his buddies, exchanging pleasantries with everyone on their way out of class as if he were a king in a receiving line of dignitaries. *C'mon, look at how full of himself he is. And all the girls making eyes at him. You're not gonna play that game, are you?*

Claire conducts this self-scrutiny with a detached part of her mind, while she updates Josh on her summer job—the Muffin Project. She's only been an Artist, in her own estimation, for two days, but it's already made a world of difference in her level of confidence. That and meeting Reggie. *An Artist is in control of the whole show. Even things we have no control over can be expressed and transformed through art.*

Of course, Claire herself is only a beginner—an Artist in word and deed, but still a rather bad one. She loses her objectivity at the most critical moments—like when Josh puts his arm around her shoulder on their way out and that little thrill shoots through her again, and she's not sure if it's caused by Josh's touch or Andrew's eyes following them down the hall.

They part ways in front of the Fine Arts Center. Josh is parked on the other side of campus, and Claire is parked on College Avenue. She spins out from his loose embrace and tries for a casual farewell.

"See ya Wednesday."

"You don't have any classes tomorrow?"

"Yeah, I do. I'm taking Figure Drawing. Nine to noon. Nude models and everything."

Claire regrets the word nude the minute it comes out of her mouth, but Josh is genuinely blind to her discomfort. Without meaning to, he reminds her that he's the best and most serious artist in their school—and that that's why she likes him.

"I took that class last summer. Percy Hartshorn's really good. I'm taking his painting class this year."

"What kind of painting?"

"A little bit of everything, starting with watercolor. It's a follow-up to the class you're taking. The focus is on working from the model."

"Cool." Claire is starting to feel normal with him again, but he doesn't let it last.

"So, you've got Drawing in the morning and I've got Painting in the afternoon. Wanna meet at the Roadrunner for lunch in between?"

"Well, I imagine I'll go over there for a while, anyway." If Claire is to be honest with herself, which she seems hopelessly compelled to be, she must acknowledge that *not* going to the Roadrunner after class tomorrow would amount to avoiding him. Hanging out at the Roadrunner at noontime is one of the chief attractions of taking classes at the U. In fact, when she thinks about it, agreeing to meet Josh there seems unnecessary. Nonetheless, there is that little quiver in the pit of her stomach again when she says, "I'll wait for you," and Josh gives her a huge grin and a little bow before loping off across a not-to-be-walked-on lawn.

Claire strolls through campus toward College Avenue in a daze, trying to figure out when Josh grew tall enough to drape an arm over her shoulder like that, and when his spotty peach fuzz had turned into such an attractively scruffy little beard. No wonder two of her friends had wanted to be fixed up with him. She'd given it her best effort, and Josh had gone out with one and then the other, drawing his enjoyment mainly from being able to talk to Claire at length about their dates afterwards. Since her girlfriends wanted to do the same thing, Claire was quickly bored with the whole business. Each time Josh got the message that Claire was tired of hearing about his relationship with this girl or that, he gave up seeing them.

The WALK signal lights up and Claire crosses the street and turns left. She is constructing images of Josh and Andrew side by side in her mind's eye. A commotion at the pay phone on the next corner breaks her reverie.

"But he's too drunk to drive! Don't you understand? He's been drinking in that bar all afternoon!"

Claire sees with horror that it's Angela crying into the receiver. Laurie is hovering protectively, staring down curious passers-by and scaring off any prospective good Samaritans with an occasional loud, "What are *you* staring at?"

"How *can* we talk sense to him?" Angela wails, as Claire approaches. "We're not even old enough to go into the bar! The man let us in once, but he says we can't be in there or he'll lose his license!"

Laurie grabs the phone from her and shouts into it, "And if Eddie fucks up he's gonna lose *his* license and then we're *all* gonna be up shit's creek, you hear me?! Now, you *dolo*, you go across the street and ask Mr. Pena to please come get us. We can't wait for Eddie, I'm telling you! He's just going to—keep drinking!" She slams down the receiver, having been cut off in the middle of her sentence, then she casts a furious eye at the young woman hovering nearby.

"I'm in your mural class," Claire hurries to say. "My name's Claire and my car's around the corner. Why don't you let me give you a ride?"

"Why, so you can brag about how you saved the poor *dolas* from their drunken cousin?"

Laurie looks like she could strangle Claire for being present at this public humiliation. She has the stylish clothes and slouchy bearing of a movie star. Angela wears her fashion armor with equal confidence, despite a broad frame which might be unfashionable in the 'zines, but is strikingly voluptuous in person. Neither girl is particularly tall, but they are imposing. Once again, Claire admires this daring duo. With their makeup dripping from sweat and tears, they look even more like Amazon women of legend. She strikes an equally stubborn pose, conveying that she has no intention of abandoning her sister warrior princesses.

None of them is aware of the havoc they are wreaking on the traffic flow of College Avenue, where drivers are slowing down to get a better look. The young women have learned to ignore the whistles, catcalls and car horns that follow them when they walk along a busy street. Claire and Lydia have never figured out what's behind these displays—*Do guys really think women are attracted to such Neanderthal behavior?*—but this is not the question on Claire's mind at the moment. She's only anxious that they be on their way so she can get home before she's missed. The surrounding clamor of impertinent and impatient motorists registers as the quickening beat of war drums—the two princesses, warriors though they be, have stayed too long on enemy soil and must be returned quickly to their tribe.

Angela and Laurie feel it too. "We have to do *something*," Angela hisses at Laurie, who takes a deep, shuddering breath. Then Angela tells Claire, "We really could use a ride, if it's not too much trouble."

"Yeah. It's decent of you to ask," Laurie concedes, seeing the concern in Claire's eyes.

"We better get your cousin home, too." The three minors cast disgusted looks at the dark entrance of the bar on the corner. "They haven't seen me before," Claire muses, "maybe I can get in and talk to the bartender for a minute before anyone cards me." But she doesn't move. Laurie and Angela don't encourage her. They just stand there and stare at the bar entrance.

"He's gotta be out of money by now," Angela grumbles.

The door swings open, and a gangly, dark-haired man staggers out, as if he'd been waiting for exactly this cue. He freezes at the wall of outraged womanhood which greets him. "Ready to go, girls?" he mumbles contritely, swaying in a nonexistent breeze.

"You bet we are!" Angela grabs him by an elbow, and Laurie takes the other. "This nice girl from our class is going to give us a ride." They steer him around the corner as Claire jogs ahead to show the way.

"But my car—" she hears Eddie plead.

"That's not your car. That's your Momma's car. And now Aunt Vi is going to have to drive back here with someone tonight and get it, you idiot! Now get in here and behave." Angela shoves Eddie into the back seat of Claire's dad's car and climbs in after him. Laurie settles into the front seat beside Claire and gives her directions.

It takes half an hour to crawl through the rush hour traffic which has accumulated around the U. Eddie is snoring noisily before long. The girls don't speak. Claire blares the radio to cover their awkwardness. Singing along to the songs together is almost like having a conversation.

"I'm getting my license next week," Angela announces when they are nearing her house. "Then this bozo can beg *me* for a ride."

"That's great." Claire snaps off the radio and pulls up to the curb where Laurie indicates. "Listen, could you do me a favor and call my folks to tell them I'm on my way?" She scribbles a number on a scrap of paper and hands it to Laurie. "I'm really late."

"You wanna come in and call?" Laurie asks reluctantly.

"No thanks. It would be better if you called for me and told them I was on my way already."

"Okay." Laurie takes the number and helps Angela get Eddie out of the back seat. She leans into the car again. "You know how to get back? Just turn around here and go up to the light and take a right."

"Yeah, I know."

"And lock all these doors, girlfriend. Brodie wasn't kidding about this neighborhood." The thought of calling Claire's parents to tell them that their daughter has been driving around Cesar Chavez has filled Laurie with foreboding as well as a belated wave of appreciation. "Thanks, Claire. I hope you don't get in too much trouble. Maybe I should tell your momma that we live on the east side."

"No, just tell 'em the truth. They're very liberal." Claire grins, and Laurie cracks up.

"Yeah, we'll see about that!" She pushes the lock and slams the door. "*Bueno* bye!" Claire hears the trio call as she makes her u-turn. She waves to them before she rolls the window most of the way up.

The solitary drive home seems to take forever. Although Claire made sure to memorize every intersection, the route looks entirely unfamiliar in the long shadows of a long summer dusk. Before her eyes, Cesar Chavez is changing from a lively, normal-looking if run-down neighborhood, to a maze of ominously deserted city streets. An unofficial Curfew of the Day People is going into effect. Amid a serenade of neighborly farewells and slamming doors youngsters, moms and dads are vanishing into the brick row houses. An eerie silence descends. Claire rounds one last corner and, with relief, finds herself on Cesar Chavez Boulevard. Soon she will be in familiar territory. She hears a series of whistled messages coming out of the alleys, in between bursts of rap music and shuddering bass blasting from passing cars. Shadowy forms slip out of doorways, young men begin to gather on the street corners.

*An Artist can always paint herself a little braver than she really is,* Claire tells herself, as she steps on the gas.

# CHAPTER 6
# GROUNDED

Josh and his dad are digging a pond in the back yard. It's almost too dark to see, but a breeze has come up and in this last cool hour of lingering daylight they make good progress. This summer, maybe their last summer, father and son have undertaken a major outdoor renovation. They're making a small pond with trickling water feature—the long-envisioned finishing touch to Mrs. Antresian's rock garden—and building Mr. Antresian's long-desired putting green in the barren expanse beyond. It's an elegant plan. The soil from the pond excavation will be used for grading the putting green, and by doing the labor themselves, they'll save money for the pond liner, pump, sod and recycling irrigation system.

For his back-breaking effort, Josh will get to design and carve the fountain—his first full-scale sculpture in stone. His thoughts are occupied with the design as he wields his shovel, and he's vaguely aware of his father grunting and panting a few feet away. They have vowed to complete the excavation by the end of the week.

Mr. Antresian is thinking that if he'd known that the work of an artist could promote such a strapping physique in a boy, he wouldn't have given Josh such a hard time. Fact is, up until a few years ago, all he ever saw for Josh's future was a pale, wasted, sunken-eyed and frustrated city-dweller. Wasn't that how all those painters lived? Because the way he heard it, a serious artist has to make a name for himself Back East before he can afford to settle down in one of those stylish adobe studios up the road in Santa Fe.

Josh is nothing if not serious, and his talent, obvious early on, only fueled Mr. Antresian's fears that his son would end up in New York City—an effete dandy if he's successful, a derelict "starving artist"

38

otherwise. But when Josh, out of the blue it seemed, tried out for and made the high school track team, Mr. Antresian stopped worrying, and he didn't bother starting in again when Josh quit the team a few months later for the chance to work after school in the studio of a locally famous sculptor.

That's been no picnic. Augustus C De Baca has really been whipping Josh into shape—got him breaking rocks just like on the chain gang. And Josh's devotion to the task and the teacher has convinced Mr. Antresian that his son is going for it. Sooner or later he'll have to find the best of the lot and test himself against them. Nope, no doubt about it, his boy would soon make that pilgrimage to the City. *But just wait and see the butt-stomping my Josh'll give that Big ol' Apple!*

Still, Nick Antresian is not quite ready to admit that his son has *him* beat. He labors on, determined not to stop digging until Josh does.

"Josh, you have a telephone call!" The lilt in Kerri Antresian's voice tells them a girl is on the line.

"Saved by the bell!" Mr. Antresian stabs his shovel into the earth and leans on it. "Too dark to work anyway. Here, I'll take that." Josh hands him his shovel and bounds over to the house, where his mother passes him the phone while gesturing toward his dirt-encrusted feet.

"Hello?" Josh sits down on the back porch and takes off his shoes.

"Hi, Josh, it's Claire."

"Hey! What's up?" After two solid hours of digging, his heart rate finally accelerates.

"I'm grounded."

"What?"

"I'm grounded. I can't meet you at the Roadrunner tomorrow."

Josh squelches the sickening thought that she just doesn't want to see him. She'd've thought of a better excuse if so, because Claire is not a girl who gets in a lot of trouble.

"Say something if you're gonna. Mom's got me on a timer. I'm not kidding."

He can hear the tears in her voice and it's all so out of character it's almost funny. "Sheesh, Claire. When did I last see you? Four, five hours ago? You must've been busy to get in that much trouble."

"Oh, I'm nothing if not efficient— No, actually, I got busted for coming home so late."

"What happened?"

"I gave those girls a ride home. You know, Laurie and Angela, the ones from Cesar Chavez?"

"No! After I split?" Josh angles his neck to hold the phone between ear and shoulder and uses a twig to scrape furiously at the muddy cleats of one shoe.

"I found them at the pay phone in front of the Golden Calf. Their cousin had been in there drinking all afternoon."

"Shit."

"So I drove all three of them home, but the traffic was really bad and I was like hours late. I guess we all hung around the U longer than I thought, and it took a while to get that jerk out of the bar. Anyway, I asked Laurie to call my folks from her place to tell them I was on my way but I guess she didn't. All hell broke loose when I walked through the door."

"Wait a minute. You're telling me that your folks grounded you for helping those girls?" Josh is mentally kicking himself for not walking Claire to her car.

Claire takes a long, outraged breath. "No, I am not being grounded for doing a good deed. I am grounded because I was standing next to a pay phone when I offered to help out and I never thought to call home when I had the chance. I am being grounded for *'not exercising the proper forethought'* and for *'taking matters into my own hands when I should have consulted an adult,'*" she recites in her mother's disciplinarian voice.

"Oh, that's *cold.*"

Josh's tone of sympathy is easing her frustration. Claire's glad she had an excuse to call him. "Anyway, I just wanted you to know why I won't be there tomorrow."

"Well, can I call you? What's the deal?"

"There is no deal. I have half an hour to call the people I need to call, and then Mother is coming in to confiscate my phone for a week.

I can go to classes and directly home. Same for going to see Mrs. Ferguson's mom. Otherwise, I may only go out to run onerous errands for my parents."

"*Onerous*, huh?"

"Yeah. Grocery shopping, taking the cat for her shots, going to the recycling center."

"Harsh, man." He senses an opportunity. "You say you're grounded for a week?"

"Yeah, through Sunday."

"And Monday they spring you, huh?"

"Yeah."

"Well, how about if we go out after class and celebrate? You can tell the 'rents a whole week ahead that you'll be home late next Monday. I'll give you a ride to class and then we can do something afterwards."

"That sounds really good," Claire says, "except the telling my folks part—I'm not talking to them, *period*."

"Can't say I blame you."

"Shit! I gotta go. I still have another call to make."

"Go for it. I'll see ya tomorrow."

"But I just told you—."

"I know, but I'll still see you tomorrow." Josh clicks off with a grin. No law against meeting Claire when she comes out of class and walking her to her car. Then he'll make sure she goes straight home.

Claire presses the speed dial button for Lydia and prays that the line won't be busy, to no avail. Ten minutes later the signal is still beeping in futility when Claire's mother marches in and pulls the plug. She takes the phone and marches out again without a word.

Claire feels like the top of her head is going to pop off, she's so mad. But after a minute, reason prevails. She goes to her desk and rummages around in the drawers until she finds what she's looking for—a length of telephone wire. She plugs one end into the recently liberated jack and the other into the back of her father's hand-me-down laptop. It takes her forty-five minutes to find a file with her father's access codes and run the set-up for the internal modem. After that, it's a simple matter to go on-line to her free e-mail provider. By midnight she's written up the whole saga and sent it to Lydia.

*Like riding a bicycle,* Claire thinks. Her parents' passion for e-mail has made her cool to the technology. She'd always rather talk on the phone than write letters. Gram's the only person she writes to voluntarily—mainly to exchange short notes with sketches and photos of their art projects. But she has to admit that e-mail has its advantages. She's going to enjoy corresponding with Lydia during the coming week, and maybe all summer long, since their schedules are so incompatible.

Detaching the cord and hiding it away, Claire finds she doesn't even feel guilty for her secret transgression, because she considers her punishment entirely unjust. Mainly, though, her thoughts are preoccupied with the newly assertive Josh. Without even realizing it, she agreed to an actual *date* with him, exactly the turning point in their relationship she's been trying to avoid.

Or maybe she's got him all wrong, and this is just Josh being a good bud. She's so tired, she can't think straight. If only she could talk it through with Lydia!

Claire throws herself on the bed and memories of the day's events drift into dreams. Her last cogent thought is, *And that was only Monday!*

# CHAPTER 7
## NICE IS NICE

"What is wrong with the 'net today!" Mr. Stanley's outraged lament rings through the house. It's always something with him and the computer. He rides his system like a cowboy on a bucking bronco. And to hear him tell it, his plastic box of electronics is every bit as ill-behaved as an edgy rodeo beast. Claire and her mom have learned to let the storms roll through. Sometimes, if they understand the problem, they might join in with a background chorus of indignation. Occasionally Claire's mom can offer some help. Usually, though, they don't trouble themselves if they even notice, because whatever it is, it's not their fault.

Except for lately.

"What's wrong is that you never give it a break!" Claire mutters. It's Wednesday morning and she's finally managed to log on so she can receive Lydia's e-mail. There are four messages from Lydia, each longer than the previous, but it still only takes a couple of agonizing minutes for Claire to receive the transmission, quit, and pull the plug.

The other problem is that when her father is *not* plugged into the Internet he tends to wander, and is likely to look in on Claire. She intends to be found painting and nothing more any time one of her parents pokes a nose into her room to see what she's up to. She doesn't want them to see her using the laptop at all, should it dawn on them that she's been e-mailing. All in all, the e-mail has yet to ease the pain of being grounded, since most of her energy is spent fretting over when she'll have a chance to go on-line without being discovered.

*Just be patient.*

Yesterday, Tuesday, was the first full day of Claire's sentence. It was destined to be a bad one, and it was. First, she had been too tired and angry to concentrate on Percy Hartshorn's three-hour lecture on

43

human anatomy. She absently sketched the leotard-clad male and female models, who posed alongside the skeleton Hartshorn had dramatically produced from an old metal locker. "When drawing the human figure, one must always account for gravity," he declared. "We are not suspended from above like this fellow." Here he had thrown open the locker located next to the chalk board so that the skeleton, attached to a rod on the inside of the door, seemed to leap forth, to the gratifying gasps of the assembled crowd.

That crowd was another thing. Claire counted thirty-four art students! She'd assumed it would be a small class, because not that many high school kids had gotten into it. Turns out, though, that the university Art Department encourages entering Freshmen to enroll in the summer course, and many do. The realization that she'd have to come early to get a decent seat had added to Claire's ill temper.

Given that she probably looked as crappy as she felt, maybe it was for the best that Josh didn't find a way to see her yesterday, as he'd indicated he would—but that was a disappointment too, and the source of much second-guessing of her own and Josh's feelings. This she didn't need, with way too much time on her hands and no one to talk to. So she came home and ruined a painting that had been coming along well, because she was actually trying to write e-mail, but kept dabbing at the canvas any time she heard one of her parents in the hall. All of that subterfuge only yielded one brief on-line session, just long enough to receive a message and send one. She wished she could've back-spaced the whole day!

*Today will be different,* Claire resolves. She has a full agenda of approved activities to keep her out of the house till dinner. She expects to see Josh at class, and the Stiletto Sisters also, and hopes to get some answers from all of them. And right now, four new installments from Lydia await temptingly. Yes, today is going to be a much more interesting and productive day.

Her first order of business is to make herself look fabulous. Grabbing the outfit she selected last night, she heads for the bathroom, but not before spreading some magazines and sketches across the desk to hide the folded-up computer. When she's showered and dressed, she saunters into the kitchen and fixes herself a bagel and a cup of coffee. She would like to ignore her father's greeting, but she's required to begin each day by reviewing her plans with one of her parents. Considering, she prefers to have the conversation with her father. She launches right in.

"Morning, Dad. Today's agenda is as follows: At eleven o'clock I'm going out to get gas and then pick up Muffin's lunch from Mrs. Ferguson and then go to Muffin, and then I'm going to have to drive directly down to Merchant and Soldiers because I won't have time to go to the U and find a parking place and meet up with my class to go with them in the van. And I left a message yesterday that I'd be coming on my own, and I definitely know the way since I was just down there the other night. Class is supposed to let out at four, so I bet the van packs up at three-thirty or so, and I'll leave from there and come straight home, so I should be back by four-thirty at the latest, unless I run into traffic."

"No traffic allowed."

He has listened carefully to every word and maintains an appropriately severe expression, but Claire can tell that Stan Man does not take her transgressions or the punishment as seriously as her mother does. It does not endear him to her, since she resents that he always sides with her mom. She knows how much he wants her to smile at him so she doesn't. She wants him to be mad, like she and her mother are—either that or do something to smooth it over—not just play along like it's a game.

"If you leave there any time before four, it shouldn't take you more than twenty minutes to get home."

She has succeeded in provoking him with her expressionless expression. Now she curls a lip. "Yeah, right."

"I mean it. Tell me what route you plan to take. And where are you going to park down there?"

"Is this really necessary?"

"Apparently."

They fume at each other. Carl Stanley is wearing moccasins, sweat pants and an ancient bathrobe. His long-in-back-scant-on-top hair is wild, and there are bagel crumbs in his wiry, greying beard. Claire is radiantly clean. Her tawny hair is drying into loose, shoulder-length curls. She wears tan chinos and a form-fitting lime green top, which makes her father wish for a return of the baggy black "widows' weeds" he likes to tease her about. But today she is not hiding behind a costume. He can see that she is all grown up.

"Not," he concedes.

"Not," she agrees, and goes to get her bagel out of the toaster.

A few minutes later she's heading back to her room with a plate balanced on a coffee mug. She pauses at her father's desk where his Internet connection is humming along. He stops his happy clicking and looks up. She brushes a crumb out of his beard.

"See, the thing is, I really want to stay and talk to Laurie and Angela. I need to find out why they didn't call when I asked them to. And make sure they got the car back all right. And I don't want to embarrass them by saying anything when the other kids are around, so I thought I'd just stay a *few* minutes after and see what I can find out."

Mr. Stanley studies her face and shakes his head gently. "You know, you're just like your mother."

"Oh, please!" Claire turns away in disgust and heads for her room.

"Four-thirty at the latest, young lady!" her father calls after her, and she can hear him chuckling at the keyboard.

*Oh, yeah? Won't we see who has the last laugh.* Claire settles down at her desk and reads her e-mail while she eats breakfast, just like her parents do.

Driving up El Rio Boulevard, Claire starts to feel better. That eternal summer day is taking hold of her spirits. Here it is again—or still—the blue blues of the unclouded sky, the green greens of lawns and trees, the red reds of roses climbing on trellises and peeking over sun-bleached adobe walls. A big roadrunner crosses her path on the way to Mrs. Ferguson's—Jo's house. And in between the fancy estates which line El Rio, horses, goats, sheep, and even llamas graze on the remnants of old farming acreage.

Claire drives north and imagines driving all the way to Canada. Her fantasy is enhanced by the white fluff of ripening Cottonwoods drifting through the air and accumulating on the side of the road like snow. At Cottonwood Boulevard she turns west and crosses the river, leaving the surreal scene behind as the road climbs out of the bosque to the dusty mesa. Now Claire imagines driving all the way to California. On the way back, she'll visit Washington, DC, and Mexico. One of these days she's really going to do it.

Jo's little cooler is in the seat beside her. Muffin is on her mind. She's trying to think of something amusing to tell Muffin. It shouldn't be that hard. Just about everything in Claire's life seems like a joke right now.

Once across the river, nature retreats from the roadsides. Shopping plazas and restaurants again predominate. Next comes TechTel, and then a swath of suburbia. Claire takes the turn onto Dove St. and pulls into the Westcare Manor parking lot well before noon. She opens the cooler and takes out Jo's note. In addition to the day's menu, there is a separate sheet with a long list of "things that might go wrong." They have reviewed these already, but Claire appreciates the reminder. She reads the note twice and puts it back in the cooler, reciting to herself, *air-conditioning, sweater, radio, footrests, nose-blowing, fingers, snuggly pillow...*

As it turns out, everything is in perfect order when Claire arrives, and she wonders if Jo isn't being a little hard on the nursing home. Of course, she's been training them for months. A big sign on Muffin's wardrobe says: *MRS. GRIFFIN MUST WEAR SWEATER EVERY DAY.* Underneath is another sign: *MRS. GRIFFIN HAS LUNCH IN ROOM.* On the cover of the ventilation unit: *NO AIR CONDITIONING, FAN ONLY.* On the little radio: *96-FM ONLY.*

Jo's lovely calligraphic printing takes the edge off these instructions so that they read more like pleas than edicts. Apparently the staff has taken heed. Claire finds Muffin dozing in her chair, sweater buttoned to her chin, classical music playing softly, fan blowing gently. She hates to wake her.

"Hello, Muffin," Claire sing-songs, "It's me, Claire."

"Huh?"

"Hello, Muffin. It's me, Claire."

"Who?"

"Claire—Josie's friend. She sent me with your lunch."

"She what?"

"Jo sent me. She fixed a lunch for you."

"Josie?"

"She brings you lunch every day, remember?"

"I suppose so." At this point, Claire detects a note of disgruntlement, as if Muffin is remembering something that troubles her.

"Anyway, I told Jo I would bring lunch to you a couple days a week so she can do some other things. But don't worry, Josie's making the lunches. You won't have to eat *my* cooking."

Muffin, who has been making a sincere effort to understand what Claire is saying, works her lips into a tiny smile and says, "I'm sure you do fine."

Is Muffin really trying just as hard to put *her* at ease? Claire tosses back, "Hah! You never tasted my cooking."

"Is it that bad?"

"Well, I doubt it's as bad as what they serve here." Pleasantly surprised at Muffin's responsiveness, Claire tries to keep up the banter while she gets organized for lunch. "I came in past the dining room and it did not smell very appetizing." There is barely room to maneuver in the tiny, over-furnished room. "You're lucky you live way down here at the other end of the building."

"Ouch! What are you doing?!"

Claire, tentative and inept with the wheelchair, has plowed Muffin's sneakered feet into the side of the bed. "Oh, Muffin, I'm so sorry!" She backs up and tries again. "I'm trying to move you over here where I can sit near you." Now she nearly falls on top of the poor woman as she leans over her to confirm that there is no serious damage, toe-wise.

"Ouch! Stupid! What's wrong with you?!"

"I'm just a klutz, that's what. I'm really sorry. I haven't had much practice with this, and the room is full of furniture."

Claire has broken into a sweat and wishes she could turn on the air.

She wonders how the aides stand it.

"I don't think you know what you're doing."

"You're right about that. I don't! But let me try again. Here we go. I'm trying to get you near the window so you can feel the sun." Meanwhile, it's Claire's back to the sun and she's melting. The chair won't roll right. She's having to lift it and walk it around. She wants to scream, but Muffin's doing enough of that for both of them.

"Ouch ouch! Stop that, you stupid!"

"Almost there. Oh, duh! I am a stupid! Your wheels were locked!" Claire leans forward and snaps back the brake. "Here we go." Muffin rolls smoothly into position. "Now I've got you where I want you," she teases. "The sun is great today. Do you feel it on your shoulders?"

"Uhm, yes. Feels good."

"Good. Now let's see what Jo packed for you." With relief Claire takes her seat in the shadows and opens the cooler. Everything she needs is in there, including spoons, cups and paper towels. "Wow, this is really nice. Did you teach Jo how to pack such a nice lunch?" Again, mention of her daughter troubles Muffin. And just like last week, Claire gets that feeling of being pierced through when Muffin turns a quizzical, bird-like gaze toward her.

"I don't know who you are."

Now Claire understands. Here she is talking about Jo and using the family nicknames, and it must seem very forward, coming from an absolute stranger. *Better take it from the top.*

"I'm Claire. I'm a friend of Josie's. I came and met you last week."

"I'm sure I don't remember," Muffin says apologetically.

"That's all right. The point is, Josie makes you a lunch every day, but today she couldn't bring it herself. So she sent me. I'm going to come twice a week so Jo can do some other things."

"Oh. You're nice to do it."

"I'm glad I can help Jo out."

"I don't see why. I think I'm crazy."

"I guess it feels that way, but it's just your memory. You're forgetful."

"More like crazy."

"When I forget things, I feel crazy too. Are you hungry?"

"No, not really."

*Wrong question!* Claire doesn't want to contradict Muffin. She's been taught to be patient and respectful with the elderly, and she can't bring herself to treat Muffin like an oversized baby. *Maybe she isn't hungry. She just woke up, after all.* Claire changes the subject. She delivers a short monologue about how Jo and her mom came to be friends, while she opens a little can of spicy tomato juice and pours it into a plastic cup. It's a special cup with a big scoop cut out of one side so that Muffin doesn't have to tilt her head back too far to drink from it. When Claire folds the fingers of Muffin's right hand around the cup and announces the arrival of a "nice, icy tomato juice," Muffin takes it eagerly.

"Oh, that's my favorite," she raves. Then she accepts pieces of creamy tuna salad sandwich with equal enthusiasm.

Jo has told Claire that Muffin won't eat everything, so each time Muffin says she's had enough of something, Claire tempts her with the next treat, and then rotates through the courses again. Claire feels funny having to spoon-feed yogurt and salad to Muffin like she's a baby. Poor Muffin can't see the spoon approaching, and Claire can't bring herself to say things like, "Open up!" or "Here it comes!" Instead, she's opening and closing her mouth like a fish, as if Muffin might copy her. It seems to be a reflex, but it sure doesn't work for blind old ladies the way it works for babies. Eventually, Claire figures out that she only has to touch the tip of the spoon to Muffin's lower lip and her jaw will drop.

So long as Claire doesn't try to shovel the food in too fast, Muffin is very compliant. They get through half of the sandwich, a few spoonfuls of avocado salad, all of the jam-laced yogurt, plus a homemade chocolate chip cookie and another Muffin favorite to top it off—iced coffee. This is a small can of coffee-flavored diet supplement served in a second scoop-nose cup, over ice cubes Jo has provided in a ziplock bag. She's packed a cookie for Claire, too, who raves about how good it is.

Muffin is more at ease now that Claire is also eating. She

demolishes dessert, and Claire believes her this time when she says, "I'm stuffed!" Claire rinses out the cups in the bathroom, then re-packs the cooler, keeping up a steady narrative of everything she's doing, because each time she falls silent, Muffin cries out in confusion. "What's going on? What am I supposed to do now?!"

"You're doing it, Muffin," Claire calls through the open bathroom door, then turns off the water and says kindly, "You've had lunch, and now we'll clean you up a little bit and you can sit and relax."

Claire must now perform the most intimate tasks yet. With a damp paper towel she wipes Muffin's fingers and pats around her mouth. Again it seems like it would be demeaning to treat a grown-up person like this, but it would be even worse to leave her looking all messy. Muffin thanks Claire profusely for cleaning her hands, and Claire remembers Jo's warning that Muffin hates having sticky fingers. She dries those fingers carefully and tucks them into Muffin's "snuggly pillow," a quilted muff that Jo made. Having her hands warm and swaddled keeps Muffin from feeling uneasy about not having anything to do. Jo has left some tapes to go with the portable stereo which must always be tuned to 96-FM. Muffin likes soft jazz in addition to classical. Claire clicks in a Duke Ellington tape and adjusts the volume. Then she takes the hair brush from the nightstand and gently brushes Muffin's short hair—making sure to announce what she's about to do beforehand.

Muffin would be enjoying herself if it weren't for a shadow of guilt. "I don't know why you're being so nice to me," she says accusingly.

"It feels nice to be nice."

It really does. Claire feels better than she has in days. She's completely recovered from that flustered feeling she had at the start of lunch, and so has Muffin. Claire's beginning to see at least one good thing about short-term memory loss—Muffin has forgotten all about the earlier unpleasantness. The horror of her helplessness has given way to sleepy satisfaction.

Claire puts the brush away—everything is within arm's reach in Muffin's cubicle—and pets Muffin's shoulders for a few seconds.

"That feels so good."

"I'm glad. You rest now. I have to go. I have to drive way across town, but I'll see you Friday. That's the day after tomorrow."

"I'm sure I won't remember."

"That's okay. I will. Bye-bye, Muffin."

"Bye. Thank you."

Claire hurries down the hall and out to the car, which is broiling in the sun. She writes a note to Jo and slips it into the cooler, realizing that she still has to drop this back at Jo's before meeting her class. Her note says: *"Everything went fine. Muffin was a piece of cake."*

# CHAPTER 8
## AMAZON ARTISTS UNITE

Claire returns the cooler to its appointed place on Jo's front porch and dashes back to the car. She forgot she would have to do this when she planned her day. Now she'll have to take a more convoluted route down to the Old Mercantile, one which will not take her to Alamo Drive with its many fast food franchises. She wends her way down El Rio, then zigs and zags along the numbered streets of Downtown, working her way south and east. It's slow but interesting going. The heart of town is shadowed by a few tall buildings, bustling with business people, shoppers and merchants. A closer look reveals a dotting of vagrants. She only has to make one u-turn, when she misses the one-way that goes under the railroad tracks. Eventually she's on Cesar Chavez Boulevard and back to her original itinerary. She goes right by Angela's, which is on the way to the Old Mercantile.

Claire gets to the end of Angela's street, where it runs into Soldiers, and is relieved to find a Big B on the corner. She pulls in, too hungry to feel out of place. Besides, every Big B has the same floor plan. Even if she really had driven from Canada to Mexico—and it sort of feels like she has—the Big B's along the way would all look the same.

They don't taste the same, though. When Claire scoots into a tiny booth and bites into the pre-made microwaved burrito, she can't believe how tasty it is. The lemonade is above average, too. She sighs with satisfaction and smiles gratefully across a chips and dips display to the grandfatherly man behind the counter.

"Hey! We thought that was your car! What are you doing here?" The Stiletto Sisters push into the made-for-one-butt bench across from her.

"Eeding," Claire says with her mouth full. She swallows the last of her burrito with a gulp. "Wow, that was good. I was starving."

"And all dressed up, too. Whatchyou been up to?" Laurie eyes Claire up and down as she gets up and gathers her trash. Claire is interested to find out that wearing an actual color qualifies as dressing up. Angela goes over to the counter to order a couple of giant soft drinks. The place is small enough so everyone can hear everything.

"I had to see someone on the west side this morning. I didn't think I could make it to the U in time to catch the van, and I figured since I already knew the way—" Claire looks meaningfully at Laurie. "How come you didn't call my folks?"

"Yeah, well, I'm real sorry about that." Laurie is repentant.

"I told her to call," Angela calls over her shoulder.

"So why didn't you? I'm totally in the doghouse."

"Us too, if that makes you feel any better."

"Not really."

Angela returns and hands Laurie her cup. "You owe me. Let's go before we're late, dontchya think?" The three look at each other as if a word from any one of them would be enough to blow off the whole afternoon. Since they're hip deep in trouble already, why not go for broke? But none of them has the heart to lead the others astray.

"What about my car? Think I can leave it here?" Claire looks at the man behind the counter.

"You think, Mr. B?" Laurie backs her up.

"Yeah, sure. Since you bought something."

"Oh, that's great! Thanks!" They head out. "You still haven't told me why you didn't call."

They can see that no van of art students has yet arrived at the Old Mercantile, half a block over, so they shuffle along from one patch of shade to the next. Laurie studies the pointy toes of her ankle-high, high-heeled booties. "See, the thing is, Claire, you didn't tell me your last name. So I got kind of stuck—like, I didn't want to call up and say, 'Hi, Mrs. I-Don't-Know-What-Your-Name-Is, this is a girl you don't know and your daughter hardly knows, but she gave me a ride home to the neighborhood you wouldn't want your little girl to go to, and now she's on her way home so don't worry about a thing.' And then your mom would say, 'Well, who are you and why did you need a ride home?' And I would say, 'Cause my ride home got drunk in a bar.' See, it doesn't sound so good. But you told me to tell the truth. I mean, I would have called and made something up for you, but you said to tell the truth and I thought, 'You know, it's better to just not call. She'll get home soon and tell them anything she wants.' Me, personally, I would not have told the truth!"

"Well, I told the truth and I got busted, so maybe you're right." Claire laughs to show that she's not going to hold the incident against them. She thinks it's sad, though, that Laurie is so locked into the negative image of her neighborhood. Once again, by the light of day, Claire notices what a normal, lively place it seems—but drab where the row houses and old office buildings block out the sky. Right then she decides to vote for the mural design with the most blue sky in the picture.

"There they are." A university shuttle pulls up and their classmates tumble out. Now Claire finds out what it's like to be the object of so much curious attention. Everyone is watching her cross the street in the company of the Stiletto Sisters. This is how Claire continues to think of her new friends even though she's learned they are really cousins. She slushes her ice around in the bottom of her cup and savors the moment. *Queen of northern Artist tribe is greeted by Amazon sisters of the south.* The striking trio sashays over to the steps of the Mercantile where everyone is gathering. All eyes are turned on Claire, whose lime green top glows like neon between the shiny black outfits of Laurie and Angela.

"Did you get my message?" Claire asks Shelly, who is looking stern.

"Yes. But I hope you won't make a habit of this."

She sounds just like Claire's mom—implying but not saying that these streets are off limits to her. Is that because Claire is too delicate, or because the area is too rough? Either way, it's insulting. "I have to come straight from the west side on Wednesdays," Claire says lightly. If Shelly has a problem with that, she's going to have to spell it out.

"Don't worry, we'll protect her!" Angela pipes up. Shelly turns red and walks away. "I hate that bitch," Angela hisses.

"Really?"

"Yeah, she's so stuck up. Brodie is much nicer."

These comments leave Claire reeling. *Brodie? But he was so condescending!* She watches Shelly and Brodie huddle for a minute before they call the session to order. She supposes they both must be pretty quirky to spend their summer painting walls with a bunch of teenagers. *Quirky. So what does that make us?*

"Okay, let's get started!"

Everyone who isn't already seated plops down on the steps.

*"Hmm, hmm, hmm!"* That's Laurie under her breath.

*"Nice!"* That's Angela, whispering in Claire's other ear.

"Hi." That's Josh, settling at Claire's feet.

Brodie starts in with a shorter version of the talk he gave on Monday. The kids wonder why, until people from the neighborhood begin straggling over. Each time a group gets close enough, Brodie gives them a big welcome and explains about the mural. Shelly hands out the designs, and invites everyone to stay to vote for their favorite. Soon there's quite a crowd. Brodie shuts up and Shelly leads a visual survey of the area.

Following Shelly and Brodie's lead, the CARMA students get talking to the onlookers, inviting them to comment on the designs for the wall, and encouraging folks to come back next Wednesday to help paint. It's easy for Laurie and Angela to talk to their classmates in this situation, with everyone meeting everyone. They begin to enjoy their roles as the unofficial ambassadors of Cesar Chavez. Meanwhile, Claire's finally able to have a talk with Josh.

"If you saw me yesterday, I didn't see you," she teases.

"Sorry about that. I was gonna meet you after class but Gus called in the morning and asked me to help him. I barely got to class on time myself."

"That's okay. I was a mess yesterday."

"Tomorrow for sure."

"You really don't have to do that, Josh. I mean, we're seeing each other now, right?"

"Yeah, I guess. And everyone else."

Claire realizes that not only has she been seen with the two baddest girls in class, but she is now in the company of one of the cutest boys. Many eyes are still on her, Andrew's among them. "So, which design are you going to pick?" She reminds herself that she's an Artist, not a Cupcake.

Josh shuffles his papers. "This one—with a few revisions." He's picked the same drawing as Claire, but added corrections to it in red pencil.

"You're not!"

"Well, I thought I might as well show her. I mean, what is with this corner here? If she'd angle the cornstalk to the left, it would lead the eye back into the mural instead of shooting it out to Soldiers Street somewhere."

"Oh boy. I can't wait to see what she says to this." Claire shakes her head and hands the page back to him.

Josh shrugs. He's studying the graffiti-filled brick wall. "Well, I owe it to this corner to try, anyway."

The Muse has him in her grip again. Claire slips away to talk to some other kids. Then she, Laurie and Angela regroup, and Claire enjoys letting them tease her about Josh. They agree that they'll meet every Wednesday at the Big B.

Shelly and Brodie start herding people onto the shuttle. Josh stops for a minute to wag a finger at Claire and to tell her to go straight home. "See ya tomorrow," he tells her. He wishes Laurie and Angela, "Good evening, Ladies," and jogs over to the van.

"Hmm, hmm, hmm!" hums Laurie.

"Nice!" Angela seconds, as they escort Claire back to her car.

## CHAPTER 9
## DEJA BOO-HOO

Once she's glugged down two glasses of iced tea, and exchanged her wilted outfit for the moo-moo Uncle Forest sent her from Hawaii, Claire is bursting to talk about her adventure-filled day. But this would amount to rewarding her parents for isolating her from her friends. No, she must hold out. This is just like that TV movie, where the hostage starts to identify with his captors because they are his only human contact. Fortunately, Claire has not been subjected to the same level of deprivation, and still has her wits about her.

It's a nice dinner that they cooked together, and in between commending themselves for it, Stan Man and Brianna are sending friendly probes across the table: "Everything go all right with Muffin today?" "How'd the car do?"

Claire answers in short, barely polite sentences. The more hurt they act, the angrier she gets. It's just like them to make a big stink about something and then feel bad about feeling bad. No way is it her fault that they feel bad! She still doesn't think she did anything wrong. And if she *was* inconsiderate, which just seems ridiculous that her mother would think so, and think that Claire should have been thinking about *her* of all things when she was *trying to help* those girls! Well, if she *was* inconsiderate, she still doesn't deserve such a punishment. A whole week without phone privileges! It's not fair! She should at least be allowed to call her best friend, they never get to see each other anymore!

Claire works herself up into such a state that she can't taste or swallow the food. She stares at her plate, puts her fork down and asks to be excused.

"Go have dinner in your room if you can't stand our company," her father says evenly.

"No thanks, I don't feel like eating." She nearly knocks over her chair in her rush to get away from them.

A tide of soapy water roils in the dishwasher. Claire's sobbing begins to subside. Brianna Yost has been crying too. Carl Stanley dries his hands and takes the Sports section out to the back yard where he can watch the cactus blooms fold up for the evening, and escape the flood of feminine emotion.

He understands both sides of the week's conflict all too well. A daughter's ideals meet a woman's reality. Claire is ready to explore new worlds, and her mother is afraid—for good reason. It seems like every few months there's a big story in the papers about an increase in rapes at the U, gang violence, purse-snatchings, car-jackings and hold-ups. Of course they've talked to Claire about how to stay out of dangerous situations, but maybe their daughter's too trusting, too good-hearted.

If so, it must be their fault. Carl and Brianna tried so hard to give Claire a bright and hopeful outlook. They named her Light. They involved her in their diverse activities and introduced her to people of all ages, incomes and nationalities. Sometimes they had to get over their own hang-ups to do the correct thing, to raise a daughter who doesn't have a prejudiced bone in her body. Now they feel there are some things that Claire should know about the world and the spectrum of imperfect people who inhabit it. You'd think she'd know everything, watching all that sick stuff on TV. But the truth is, no one gets it from being told or reading a book or seeing a movie.

Claire's social education was founded on respect and reason, not fear. Her parents pride themselves on setting a good example of a man and woman living as equals, a couple of complementary pieces in the puzzle of life. This is not the way Brianna was raised. Her mother—Claire's Gram—considered men to be the enemy. Mrs. Davis Yost McCormick Dreysdale is of the opinion that one half of the human population is naturally selfish, mean, and out of control, while her half of humanity—"womanity"—exists to be the civilizing force for the brutes. Women's lives depend on it, seeing as how the alternative is to be traded like a commodity and hunted like prey. She has mellowed over the years, in large part due to her fondness for her son-in-law, and in larger part due to her decision not to marry again after the fourth divorce. Meanwhile Brianna and Carl have been careful not to poison their daughter with either a fear of men or a sense of superiority. What was so in the past need not be so forever. *They* believe that history is history, and the future is Now.

But did they sell Claire short with their optimism? Did they gloss over certain realities, just because they *shouldn't be*, for Claire or any young woman? Did they let their ideal of a world where no one has to live in fear make the real world—where a little fear is a healthy thing—more dangerous?

Carl knows why Brianna is afraid. She could never forgive herself if she felt she had let Claire fall victim to crime or abuse. As for himself, he only wishes it really were in the power of parents to discipline the danger out of their children's lives.

Claire brushes the pile of soggy tissues into the trash and picks up the latest issue of *Art Forum* magazine. There's no point trying to write e-mail or go on-line, even though Stan Man is safely occupied in the back yard, because she knows what's coming. She can practically count the heartbeats to the moment her mother will tap on the door, then stick her head in and say, "May I?"

Claire will be interested to hear what her mother has to say, because for the life of her, she still can't figure out what she did to earn such a harsh punishment. It's killing her not to be on the phone with Lydia this very minute—at last report, she was planning to break up with Matthew. Claire is desperate for the next installment. And Lydia doesn't even know the half of what's going on with the Stiletto Sisters or Josh, or anything about Claire's first session with Muffin. The thought of trying to write it all down, even if she could find the uninterrupted time to do it, is exhausting. Their schedules make it hard enough for the friends to see each other, it is absolutely cruel to cut off all communications.

*And imagine how mad I'd be if they had really done it!* The e-mail, though inadequate, is a small victory. Claire bolsters herself with the knowledge of it when the tap-tap comes.

"May I?"

"It's your house."

"Oh, brother."

It's at these moments, when Brianna Yost feels most obliged to be reasoned and mature, that something comes over her and she can't take herself seriously. She looks at the weepy-eyed Claire and it's herself on the bed and her mother at the door and one of the ghastly step-fathers in the back yard. It dawns on her that not a one of those deadly earnest battles changed her mind about anything. Mainly, they provided painful affirmation of the flaws of her elders. She can almost smell the cigar smoke wafting through the window.

"What are you doing?"

"Making sure your father hasn't taken up cigars." Brianna has moved to the window and is staring out. "Mom's third husband always smoked a cigar in the back yard when she and I were fighting. For a second, I could swear I smelled him out there."

"Fighting stinks, all right."

"So," Claire's mother takes a deep breath and sits down on the bed, "what are we fighting about?"

"You tell me. I thought you'd be proud of me for helping Laurie and Angela, and instead you threw me in the dungeon. I mean, wouldn't you want someone like me to help me if I was in a situation like that?" Claire thinks this is clever, but her mother is not amused.

"The only way you're going to get into a situation like that is if you start hanging around with those girls."

"Ouch! Will ya listen to yourself, Mom?" Tears gather in Claire's eyes. "That was really mean."

"Was it? Their cousin was drunk, wasn't he?"

"I probably saved lives, not letting him drive," Claire mumbles.

"Look, we've been through this. What you did was fine. I just really needed you to call." She's tearing up again, too.

"So, if I'd called, what would you have done?"

"Well, I probably would've sent your father down there to see what was going on," Ms. Yost admits with a thin smile.

Claire relives the scene in front of the Golden Calf. "I guess I wouldn't have minded having him there," she admits in turn.

Brianna Yost delivers the lines she's been practicing for two days. "You're getting very close to being on your own, Claire. Won't you let us be here for you while we can?"

Claire is unmoved. "Yeah, I guess. But what about my friends?"

"What about them?"

"Is it really fair that because I didn't call you when I was supposed to, I can't call *anyone* for a week? I mean, couldn't we have had this conversation without me being grounded?"

This question is right out of Brianna's own script. She hates herself as she offers up her mother's old retort, complete with the sad sigh, "I guess we'll never know."

"Am I still grounded?"

"Yes."

"But why?"

"I got scared, Claire, I got really scared. Maybe you feel you've learned your lesson, but I'm not comfortable with this yet. I need you to stick close to home until I find a way to deal with this anxiety."

"Oh, great. So how come you let me sign up for the mural thing at all?"

"Going with your class and adult supervisors is different."

Claire shakes her head and thinks, *Like there aren't any adults in Cesar Chavez!* But instead of saying something snide, she tells her mother why Laurie didn't make the phone call on Monday night. "You know, it's bad enough that you think what you do about where she lives, but I think it's awful that she thinks you're right to think it. I admit, it looked like it could be a scary place at night. But isn't that because everyone clears out and acts like it's a war zone? They're just people. And, like *we* don't know anyone who drinks too much?" Claire stops short of accusing several of her parents' friends of being drunks and druggies.

"Yep, I can almost smell that cigar smoke," Brianna Yost says, getting up. "It's like my whole life as a teenager is flashing before my eyes."

"So, am I still grounded?"

"Yep."

"What about the phone?"

"I'll think about it." She goes over to the door and looks back at Claire. "Are we done here?"

"Yes, Mom. You're excused." They smile the truce smile at each other. "And you can tell Dad it's safe to come in."

# CHAPTER 10
## READY OR NOT

Nudity is nothing new to Claire. Her parents practiced it regularly around the house until she was eight, after which her father donned boxer shorts. Her mother will still streak from the bathroom to the kitchen for a clean glass, or to the laundry room for some towels, but she stopped hanging around naked a long time ago, too. As a baby Claire was always carefully clothed against the New Mexico sun. But later, school breaks brought expeditions to see Gram in Miami, where she'd been slathered in sunscreen and allowed to romp naked in the waves. Even as more modesty has been practiced around the house over the years, skinny-dipping and nude hot-tubbing have remained favorite family vacation activities when occasion permits.

Yes, Claire's parents have succeeded in conveying that nature is beautiful and bodies are natural, so bodies in their natural state are beautiful. Groovy—if only either of them had an ounce of fashion sense! The truth is, how she looks *in* her clothes causes Claire more anguish than who might see her without them. Nonetheless, she does not envy the pale young woman who stands legs wide and arms akimbo on a pedestal in the well of the crowded studio.

Every space is taken in this theater-in-the-round affair, which has tiered seating and space in back for easels. Claire came early and got a seat with a good view, but now she wishes she had taken a place in the back where no one could see her sketches. She has never taken a class like this before, and the grotesque forms which flow out of her charcoal make her feel as exposed as the model herself. She doesn't know what she's doing! For an hour Hartshorn had the model move from pose to pose while the class drew stick figures, and then scribbly stick figures all over their big newsprint—to get the feel for the body's arrangement of bones and joints. Now the model is holding a long pose and Claire, who's pretty good at small cartoons and sketches, is uncomfortable with so much time, paper and flesh. She's having trouble making the connection between Hartshorn's lesson and how she's going to fill the page with the form of that woman. Everyone else is scratching away like they're determined to draw every last pubic hair before the bell sounds.

Claire flips over another giant page and starts again. This is the last pose of the day, and there aren't many minutes left. She makes herself forget about everything that Hartshorn said. She blocks out the sounds around her. She narrows her eyes and studies the model. What does she see? With sudden decisiveness, she draws a pyramid near the bottom of the paper—the space behind the model's legs. She draws more shapes—the diamonds made by those arms-akimbo, and two rectangles, each with one concave side, on either side of the head. With the edge of her charcoal she shades in these background areas, and a white silhouette of the model rises like a ghost out of the newsprint. Claire sketches in the brow, nose, chin, shoulders, how the hands rest on the hips, the navel, kneecaps, ankles.

The timer sounds and Claire puts down her charcoal. She feels like she's been in a trance. The model is tying a kimono around her waist and heading for the door, a cigarette between her lips.

"Awesome. Hey, Greg, check it out."

"Way cool."

Claire doesn't suspect that the two students behind her are talking about her drawing. She flips her pad closed and one of them jabs her lightly in the back to make her look over her shoulder.

"Nice goin'."

"Oh, thanks. It took me a while to get started." She flips through her false starts to prove how bad she is.

"Uhm, monstrous," Greg teases.

"That's about right, three bad drawings for every good one," his friend assures her. They clatter out with their portfolios.

Claire sees that Josh is waiting for her under the Dean Leighton Memorial Cottonwood in front of the Fine Arts Center. As she takes in his lanky frame, muscled arms and curly brown hair, she can hear Laurie's appreciative *hmm, hmm, hmm* in her head. The guy is cute, and nice to boot, and he's crazy about her. So why is she so resistant to getting involved with him?

"Back to black, huh?"

"Hides the charcoal stains." She lets him take the big clipboard from her but hangs on to her tackle box. *So he noticed the lime green top, did he?*

"Where to?"

"I parked by the library."

"Yeah, good lot if you can get a space. Let's walk through the rose garden."

"I suppose I can smell the roses, as long as I don't stop."

"No mercy, huh?"

*"We'll see."* Claire imitates her mother. "No, not yet."

"How was class?"

Claire tells him.

"Drawing from a model is like giving a performance—you only get that one chance. It's now or never. I like the energy. It's like painting outdoors and trying to beat the sun. No slacking."

Claire thinks about this for a minute as they wander down a rose-lined path. She turns to her friend. "That's you in a nutshell, Josh. No slacking." And she thinks she knows why she's been keeping her distance.

Maybe he doesn't read her mind, but he hears the question in her voice. He puts his arm around her shoulder like he did the other day and says, "I have time for stuff other than art."

Claire slides an arm around his waist. "Yeah, right."

"I mean, I could make time." He's leans his head close to hers as they leave the roses behind.

"I bet you could!" Claire pulls away. She's wearing black, it's noon and about ninety degrees, and this boy is *hot*. "Whew!" she fans herself with her hand.

Josh looks at her sheepishly. "We're still on for Monday, aren't we?"

"Definitely. These three-minute conversations are killing me."

"Me too." They find the car and put her things in the trunk. "I better pick you up around one-fifteen, then."

"I'll be ready." *Not!* Claire thinks. It is broiling in the parking lot and Josh hovers close as she unlocks the door and gets into the car.

"I'll call you Sunday night anyway."

"If my line is busy, you'll know I'm back in action." *Idiot!* Does she ever regret that line the minute it's out of her mouth! She starts the motor. "See ya Monday."

"See ya Monday." Josh slaps the top of the car and strides away. *mmMonday mmMonday mmMonday,* he hums to himself.

Claire has a nap before cooking dinner. Contrary to what she implied to Muffin, Claire's a good cook, sometimes an inspired one. Tonight's *Fettucini Alfredo* is a success in more ways than one—all that appreciative slurping of pasta precludes serious conversation. Afterwards, while her folks are cleaning up, Claire's able to send e-mail and receive the latest from Lydia, then she joins Brianna and Stan Man in the den for their favorite Sci Fi series. Everyone is being sweet to each other.

Claire is confident that her sentence will be commuted once she and Lydia carry out their plan. Tomorrow, after Claire has gotten back from seeing Muffin, Lydia will simply come over. It's only natural, since Friday is her day off and she'll be wondering why she hasn't heard from Claire all week. And Claire can't believe that her mom would turn Lydia away. Once visiting rights are reinstated, they can mount their campaign for return of the phone.

Friday's lunch with Muffin goes swimmingly well. In fact, Muffin is aboard ship when Claire arrives and finds her wheelchair parked beside the nurse's station.

"She was upset and kept calling for someone, so we brought her out here," the nurse explains. "Now she's on a boat."

Claire can see that. Muffin sways gently with her face turned upward, as if she's smelling the sea breeze.

"Hello, Muffin, it's me, Claire. I brought lunch from Josie."

"Oh, how nice."

"I'm going to take you down to your room now." Claire is careful to unlock the brakes. She sets the cooler on Muffin's tray and gives her a smooth ride down the hall.

Back on dry land, Muffin wants to know exactly who Claire is, and Claire realizes that there was not much point in working up new material on the drive over. She and Muffin are going to have a conversation nearly identical to the one they had Wednesday. As Claire sets up for the feeding, she explains again about Josie's lunches, and how she will be delivering them two days a week. Muffin again declares that it is a nice thing for Claire to do, but she can't imagine why anyone would bother. Claire again remarks about the vicious odors wafting from the dining room, and how superior Jo's lunches are to what is being served down the hall. As Muffin eagerly accepts her "nice, cold tomato juice," Claire reminds her that all is the work of her marvelous daughter. And as mention of Jo again causes a cloud to cross Muffin's face, Claire offers some self-deprecating comments about her own cooking, which again elicit a smile of understanding from Muffin.

"I'm sure it's not that bad," Muffin tells her, between bites of a cheddar cheese and green chile sandwich.

"Oh, you should've seen the mess I made last night!" Claire answers, not untruthfully, because she did make a mess.

"What was it?"

"*Fettucini Alfredo.*"

"What? I never heard of such a thing."

"It's pasta—" Muffin's eyebrows crinkle. "You know, like spaghetti, but flat, and the sauce is creamy with Parmesan cheese and butter."

"Sounds like a mess."

"My point exactly." They laugh. Claire breaks out a tiny tub of "mandarin oranges with lemon pudding."

So long as she keeps talking, Muffin eats heartily. But when Claire falls silent, Muffin becomes confused and restive, deciding she is "full" after every bite. Desperate to keep Muffin listening and eating—without boring herself to death—Claire tries out the anecdotes she has prepared for this occasion. She begins to describe her summer schedule and her crazy first week of classes, featuring the exploits of the Stiletto Sisters.

"...so then I hear this commotion on the corner, and I look over and it's those two at the pay phone—"

"Oh stop that! I don't know what you're talking about!" Muffin exclaims. She is sincerely annoyed.

Claire catches her breath and feels the sting of a tear in her eye. *It's not personal, it's not personal,* she instructs herself, and regains her composure.

"No, of course it doesn't make sense to you, Muffin. I'm sorry. It's just stupid stuff anyway." Claire repeats the story of how her mother and Muffin's daughter came to be friends, and Muffin, feeling once more in familiar territory, steadies herself. The waters calm.

Graciousness, Claire decides during this third visit, is Muffin's natural state. When she is rude, it is due to feeling afraid and confused. But when things are put right, she quickly rights herself. Claire's visual mind places Muffin in her boat, anchored by an inner strength that holds fast below the turbulence of changeable seas.

After lunch, Claire does not hesitate to give Muffin's hands, lips and chin a thorough, gentle cleaning. *She's not a baby, she's a lady. She would never want to look a mess.* Muffin's thanks prove the truth of these thoughts. Claire shakes the cookie crumbs from Muffin's sweater, and offers Stan Man's line, "You know it's good when you get it on ya."

Muffin chuckles and tells Claire how nice she is to do everything. Today, Claire does not have to rush off to class. She brushes Muffin's hair and then softly rubs her shoulders, which makes the old woman purr like a kitten. When Muffin's head rocks forward, Claire whispers good bye and slips away.

✧

Lydia arrives at two-thirty, as planned. Claire lets her mother answer the door and waits in her room. Soon she is being summoned.

"Claire, you have a visitor!"

"Am I allowed?" she calls back, coming down the hall.

"Just this one."

She rounds the corner and she and Lydia throw themselves into each other's arms with cries of joy. Ms. Yost retreats and they rush to Claire's room.

Throughout the afternoon the voices of Claire and Lydia rise and fall in a non-stop duet, dipping low when the subject is personal, exploding in delighted hysteria at secret jokes. In either case, the language which lilts through the house is not one Ms. Yost and Mr. Stanley can interpret, or care to. It babbles on like background music, subtly lifting their spirits. When the girls go to the kitchen for snacks, they pad through the house barefoot without ever breaking the rhythm of their prattle.

There is so much to catch up on—Muffin, Josh, the Stiletto Sisters, Lydia's impending break-up with Matthew, her new crush on Trent, not to mention—until back in the safety of Claire's bedroom—the "pot plot." Lydia puts Claire into hysterics when she describes her parents' reaction to the candy wrappers and fast food cartons she leaves prominently discarded around the house.

"You should see how they inch over to me and kind of *sniff*," Lydia makes her nostrils wide and inhales in short, silent bursts while tears run down Claire's cheeks. "And Mom is keeping a real sharp eye on my waistline! She even tried to get me on the scale in front of her—some lame thing about donating blood, and you have to weigh a certain amount."

"Oh god, that's too much!" Claire splutters. "Now they're going to think you have an eating disorder!"

"Yeah, I was afraid we were getting a little off the track. So I've started burning incense in my room like I'm trying to cover the smell."

"You are sooooo cruel."

"Well, it was so boring without you! And at least this way, you're not getting the blame. I mean, we haven't seen each other all week."

"Oh, jeez." Claire wipes her eyes and takes a deep breath. "You know this is gonna blow up in our faces, don't you?"

"Probably. But we're not doing anything wrong!"

"Oh, yes we are. We're making the 'rents worry. That's a punishable offense in this house."

"But not a *high* crime!"

"Oh, good one!" Claire eyes Lydia's waistline. "So, where is the food going?"

"I don't know. I pick the wrappers up at work—"

Even as they are discussing fast food, Claire's mother does her tap-tap thing and invites Lydia to stay for pizza. Lydia declines. "But I could come back after supper," she offers meaningfully.

"That won't be necessary. I'm going to let Claire have her phone back. She can call you."

"Thank you, Ms. Yost!" Lydia is sincere, but Claire's display of gratitude is forced. She's flashing on that hostage-captor thing: *First they take away something you really need, and then when they give it back it's supposed to seem like a gift.*

"'Preciate it, Mom," she mutters.

"You're welcome." Ms. Yost leaves with a look that says she knows what Claire's thinking.

Over pizza, Claire announces her plans to spend Monday afternoon and evening with Josh. Since they've made no specific plans, she feels comfortable ad-libbing about a tour of the university art galleries and a bite to eat at one of the places nearby. Her parents have known Josh and his family for many years, since they were always running into each other at the same extracurricular activities and art camps. The way Claire presents it, going to class with Josh and hanging out afterward doesn't sound like a date. Not until Stan Man asks when they can expect her home and she says lightly, "Well, I won't stay out past ten-thirty, since I have class Tuesday morning," do her parents raise eyebrows at each other across the table.

"Better make that ten," Claire's father says—just to provoke her, she's sure.

She doesn't give him the gratification. "No prob," she says agreeably. "May I be excused now, and have my phone, please?"

"Of course." Ms. Yost points to the sideboard.

Claire looks inside. She finds her phone nestled behind an assortment of liquor bottles. "Cute," she says, liberating it. "Thanks for relenting," and makes a dignified exit.

## CHAPTER 11
## REBEL TRAIN

Claire's outfit has been chosen after many hours of consultation with Lydia. Above a tight pair of blue jeans she wears an orange top, cut short to ride up above the midriff, and low to drop off a shoulder and reveal the strap of a satiny undergarment. To Claire's relief, her mother makes no comment other than, "You look nice." Her father never even glances up from his computer screen. "Don't forget to go to class," he instructs her.

"Don't worry, we won't. See ya later." Claire withdraws, leaving them to their click-clicking.

Josh pulls up in his sun-bleached Duster and Claire grabs her daypack and goes out before he can come to the house. He leans across the passenger seat and opens the door for her from the inside. "Ready to make your get-away?"

"Yeah. Step on it."

Josh makes a careful u-turn. "Sorry, we're going nowhere slow in this buggy."

"Well, why didn't I drive?" It never occurred to Claire to offer, but there was no reason not to. She makes a mental note, while she leans back and savors the satisfaction of the chauffeured.

"Car runs fine, just not fast. You in a rush?"

"Uh uh." They smile at each other, eyes safely hidden behind sunglasses.

"I called last night but your line was busy."

"Sorry. I was afraid of that." Claire had kept Lydia on the phone for a long time with second thoughts about the wardrobe selection. She hadn't really wanted to talk to Josh last night, feeling they should do their talking in person.

"At least you got your phone back. Thanks for not getting grounded again in the meantime."

"Very funny."

"So, what do you want to do after class?"

Claire shifts uneasily. "Listen, Josh, about class—"

"Hmm?"

"I thought I'd sit with Laurie and Angela."

"Oh."

She feels like she can read his mind, and wishes she couldn't, or at least that she could pretend she couldn't. But it doesn't work that way. He says nothing, while the air charges with his unhappiness.

"I'm not saying I don't want to be seen with you or anything, you dummy," she answers his silence, "I just want to sit with my girlfriends during class. It's the only time we can see each other, and *we* have all evening—I don't have to be home till ten."

Josh has the strangest way of letting his mood shift but not his expression. He stares blandly out the windshield as his electrified aura flips current from mad to glad. "That's cool. You can sit in back and cause trouble and I'll sit up front and cause trouble."

"What kind of trouble?" Josh cracks a grin. "Not the mural design!"

"I drew up my own alternative."

"A whole new design?"

"Hers suck."

"Oh, this should be fun. What is it?"

"You'll see." They fall silent.

"So, what do *you* want to do after class?" Claire throws the question back at him.

*Make you fall in love with me. Run away to Mexico. Lie on our backs out on the mesa and watch the stars come out...*

Tongue-tied, Josh shrugs and concentrates on finding a parking place on the crowded campus.

Laurie and Angela are loitering outside the Fine Arts Center with Dori, who is finishing a cigarette before going to class. Angela greets Claire excitedly, waving her brand new driver's license. Laurie welcomes Josh with a lecherous look to which he seems oblivious. He grabs Claire's hand and squeezes it.

"So, I'll see ya after class."

"Hey, we're coming." Dori squashes out her cigarette, and they all go into the building together. Filing through the classroom door, the girls turn left and Josh turns right, taking a seat in the front row. Claire detects perplexity in Andrew's greeting as she passes his desk. She can feel Shelly's disapproving eyes on her back. She's thinking that she hasn't had this much fun in ages—and still so much to look forward to!

Brodie leads a discussion of last Wednesday's trip to the Cesar Chavez neighborhood. Few neighborhood people actually filled out ballots and put them in the box provided, so the students report on what they were able to glean in conversation. Since more than one student often spoke to the same area resident, they compare notes in class, discovering that some people changed their minds between talking to one person and the next.

"Maybe they were mirroring *your* preferences," Shelly suggests, "and picked the design they thought their interviewer liked best."

"No!" "No way!" The students protest. "Hey, I hadn't even made up my own mind." "Me neither." "Me neither."

There is no clear preference for either of the designs among the students. The picture with the corn maiden in the foreground, and farms, mesa and sky beyond, has slightly more votes than that featuring a multi-ethnic tableau of heroes and heroines, with Cesar Chavez front and center. The corn maiden is prettier, but no one really wants to oust Cesar Chavez.

"So, how are we going to decide?" Brodie stands in front of Shelly's two big drawings. Josh raises his hand. "Josh?"

"Uh, I made up a third alternative." He opens his sketchbook and nods toward the chalk board. "May I?"

"Another alternative, Josh? We don't have time for that." Shelly steps forward, and Brodie takes a giant step back as if he can feel the heat. A deep silence descends. There's something menacing about the quiver of Shelly's ponytail.

Josh turns in his chair so he's speaking to his classmates as well as the teaching team. "If *more* people like this design *better*, then it's worth a couple extra days to get it approved. First of all, more people will get involved in painting something they're really enthusiastic about. And second of all, more people will like it better when it's done. And that's the point, right? I mean, right now it's like fifty-fifty—you can already predict that half the people aren't going to like the mural that much."

"Now that's putting it a little strongly," Shelly snaps. "Maybe it won't be the *first* choice of *half* the people, but to say half won't like it—"

"Yeah, no one feels strongly enough about either design to not-like them," Claire volunteers from the last row.

"Can't we see his design?" Dori chimes in, and several voices second the motion.

Shelly's eyes are shaded by her baseball cap, but Claire imagines them burning red with anger. Brodie steps forward and says equably, more to his associate than the class, "This could be a good lesson in what it takes to get a piece of public art approved in this town."

"Yeah, well, it's *not* going to be a lesson in how to paint murals if we end up spending all our time at City Hall." Shelly and Brodie exchange a long look, then step to their opposite corners, inviting Josh to take center stage. They are a peculiarly well-matched team.

Everyone watches in mesmerized silence. The only sound is the scratching of chalk as Josh holds his sketchbook in his right hand, and with his left draws a large version of his design in a few confident strokes. It is extraordinarily simple. A train traverses a vast landscape. He steps aside so everyone can see his spare drawing, while he fills in the details with words.

"The sky takes up a lot of the space, and is pure blue, like we always see it in New Mexico. The sky is the best part of the corn maiden design. I know that's why she got a few more votes. And in a way it's the most important part of this painting, too. Because it puts the sky back where it used to be, where the building stole it from."

"Right on, man!" Kevin calls out.

"Then there's the whole bottom of the picture, showing the desert in sharp perspective. See, we draw detailed cacti and stuff down here," Josh adds some shapes to his drawing. "Then the desert plants recede up to the middle, getting smaller and more blurry. The train cuts parallel to the horizon, which recedes beyond it into this ghost of a mountain range. We'll get this cool illusion of depth, plus it will be fun to paint. The neighborhood kids can only work close to ground level, since they're not allowed on the scaffolds, and they can learn a lot painting the plants in detail and in perspective. Then our class will do the train, really work up every car, put the names of the lines and manufacturing companies on them—the ones that brought people and goods out here back when the area was first developed. That's the real historical significance of the Old Mercantile and that area. It wasn't named 'Cesar Chavez' until a few years ago—"

"Exactly!" Miranda, a typically quiet young woman, stands up. "If you ask me, both the 'corn maiden' and 'heroes' are just cliches that institutionalize the assumptions everyone already makes about that neighborhood."

"Now you said a mouthful there, girlfriend!" Laurie calls out. Miranda sits down. Brodie and Shelly exchange amazed expressions.

Josh doesn't skip a beat. "Yeah, you said it, Miranda. Both of those murals say, 'Look, we're giving you a picture of the heroes and ancestors of *your people.*' I mean, does our mural have to comment on the race or class of the people living near the Old Mercantile? Even if the images are positive, is that approach really positive?"

Danny stands up. "Yeah, like naming the neighborhood Cesar Chavez in the first place. I remember that one. The Mayor and them acted like it was a big honor. But I always thought it was like naming the place 'Hispanic Town.' I mean, you don't see them naming other parts of town after famous Jews or Greeks or Italians to make a point about who's living there."

"Except for the Dr. Martin Luther King, Jr. Subdivision," Celine calls out.

"No shit!" Paul erupts, "No shit, man!"

Everyone starts talking at once. Josh slides into his chair, flushed with triumph. He can't catch Claire's eye—too many people are milling around among the desks. Shelly and Brodie step into the hall to consult on what to do next. When they return, Shelly slams the door hard, and everyone shuts up and drops into their seats. She gives Josh a thin *"you asked for it"* smile. Brodie beams at him.

Brodie begins. "Very well, group. We will have a lesson in civics as well as mural painting, if that's the way you want it. All of us are going to have to work overtime, of course. First of all, we'll be going back to Soldiers and Merchant to get feedback on this new design. We'll be systematic and document every conversation, making sure the other two designs are presented again alongside this new option. I will try to get us a slot on next Monday's City Council agenda. If we make a convincing presentation and we have community support, we could get approval for Josh's design there and then. But it won't be easy."

"We'll need a new cost estimate." Shelly turns to the class, "Some colors of paint are significantly more costly than others. The second part of today's lesson was going to be a demonstration of how I select a palette and estimate paint volumes for every mural design. Now we need to go through this process with Josh's image, but we're out of time for this session already. So, what Brodie and I have decided is that Josh will stay late today and help me make the drawing that we'll show around on Wednesday—I'm sure he won't mind." Josh shrugs in despair as his classmates call out their sympathy. "On Wednesday we'll all meet here, then half of you will take the new fliers and accompany Brodie to the site to collect responses. The other half will stay here and do the paint and cost calculations with me. I'm going to try to have a friend come in and videotape the lesson so that those of you who miss it can watch the tape. Also," Shelly directs this to Brodie, "I think a little video might improve our presentation to the Council. Do you have anyone who can videotape the neighborhood canvassing?"

"Hey, great idea! I can do that!" Brodie makes a note. "That's it then. Josh, you stay put. The rest of you, meet here Wednesday. Everyone who can, we're going to meet Thursday and/or Friday to get our presentation in order, I'll let you know Wednesday where and when. And if all goes well, we'll be holding next Monday's class in the City Council chamber."

Loud agreement from the class is followed by the scraping of chairs and lively chatter of the group dispersing. Josh is about to be kidnapped by the teaching team. Claire hurries over to them, "Listen, it would still be easier for me to go straight down to the Old Mercantile on Wednesday. Coming from the west side, I can't get here early enough to find a decent parking place."

Shelly shrugs. "Brodie? What do you think? Can the girl gang meet you on site Wednesday?" She jerks her head in the direction of Laurie and Angela, who are loitering out in the hall. "I assume Angie and Laura won't want to drive in either."

"That's fine. Watch for us from the Big B. We'll get there as soon as we can," Brodie tells Claire. He seems stoked by the afternoon's turn of events.

"So, where you off to?" Claire asks Josh with an encouraging smile. His triumph has turned to dejection. He was hoping Shelly would slap his sketch on a copy machine and be done with it, but she has something else in mind. Although she no longer seems angry, Josh conjures a mental image of her drafting up the new flier with a pen dipped in blood—*his.*

"Computer lab," Shelly informs them. "We'll scan Josh's sketch, so we can put it into the same format as the others. Make sure the proportions are right, clean it up some."

"Oh, cool. That shouldn't take long," Claire assures Josh, "I'll meet you down there in a few minutes." Now, as earlier in the car, his wordlessness speaks volumes. She wonders if his sub-speech vibrations are available to everyone or anyone else, or only to her. He trudges after Brodie and Shelly. They act indifferent to his anguish, which Claire feels keenly but does not share. *We'll still have our date, Josh, don't worry.*

She hurries over to Laurie and Angela to tell them that they're on for Wednesday at the Big B, then she walks out with them to get some fresh air before finding her way to the computer lab. A knot of their classmates has formed under Dean Leighton's cottonwood.

"Everyone's really jazzed about the new design," Dori tells them, coming over. "But have you lost Josh?"

"No. Shelly should be done with him soon."

Claire is pretty jazzed herself. The summer day still rules. Everyone and everything is bright, crackling with color, and sizzling with promise. She laughs for sheer happiness and her friends join in. Having a date, a driver's license, a black mini-skirt, a pair of bad-ass booties—there are lots of little things to make a girl giggly under a sun that hangs so high, time seems suspended. Sometimes, nothing is more perfect than anticipation.

# CHAPTER 12
## THE OFFICIAL DATE

Claire and Josh make their escape from the computer lab, emerging from the fluorescent flicker of basement corridors into the warm glow of a lazy late afternoon. The sun's white heat has mellowed into gold. They wander toward the core of the campus, an expansive, landscaped plaza bordered by several rambling buildings in the Mission Revival style. As if of one mind, they stop at the nearest bench and open their sketchbooks. Josh carries his oversized black bound book under his arm wherever he goes, with a thin black marker and mechanical pencil clipped to the spine. Claire pulls her pad from her daypack, along with a set of color pencils in a battered zippered pencil bag.

Their attention is drawn to the play of light and shadow on the pale buildings, the dark window slits, carved wooden lintels and massive, blue-daubed *vigas* that punctuate the textured expanses of adobe. Centuries-old cottonwoods drip young shoots of heart-shaped leaves into the cooling breeze. The silhouettes of their furrowed trunks parade across the paving stones of the plaza. In Claire's imagination, the Serafina Mountains hover over all, blushing in the reflected glory of their sun king, whose loving gaze they have waited all day to meet across the horizon.

Claire draws the fantasy. The face of a trapped princess looks out from the mountains, an army of shadowy ogres crosses the square, the blade of a sword glints in the extreme foreground, as if it might tear through the page. She can draw with precision, but she's never had much patience for rendering the mundane world. Landscapes have a way of re-ordering themselves in Claire's mind into stories she feels compelled to record. Her art struggles between the cartoonish and the surreal.

Josh makes a light sketch in pencil, erasing and revising the lines until he is satisfied with the proportion and accuracy of his composition. Then he inks in the sketch with his marker. He translates color into stippling and cross-hatching, precisely describing shadow and light to tell the exact season and time of day. He adds his initials and the date, then turns to Claire as she hurries to close her sketchbook. "Hey, let me see!"

"Uhm—" She holds the book closed and shakes her head. "It's not very good."

"Hey, don't be so shy." Josh scoots close and puts his arm around her waist. "Not about your art, anyway." *Finally,* he's thinking, *finally, finally, finally.*

"Especially about my art," Claire says, looking pointedly at his masterpiece. He slams the black book shut and sets it on the bench, hating his own talent. Claire flinches. "Do you know you're like a walking mood ring?" she asks him in exasperation.

"A what?"

"A mood ring. It's like it's written all over you all the time exactly what you're feeling, and everyone has to dance to your vibes. It's exhausting."

"A mood ring." Josh's expression is deadpan.

Claire plows ahead recklessly. "Yeah. They change color depending on the mood of the person who's wearing it. My mom has one. Only, you're a little different. You don't change on the outside so much, you just send out these signals—Josh is pissed off, Josh is hurt, Josh is—"

"Claire is just very sensitive," Josh interrupts. A smile twitches at the corners of his mouth. "Really, it's more like *you're* the ring—and I'm the finger."

Claire's jaw drops and her cheeks flush red. "Oh, I don't believe you!" She swats him with her sketchbook.

He grabs the pad. She surrenders it easily, but he's no longer interested in the drawing. He lays it aside atop his own and turns to her.

"So tell me why you wouldn't go out with me. I mean, if you can read me so great, then you knew I wanted to date you. You must've known, or you wouldn't't've been so good at screwing up every opportunity for me to ask you out. And I don't get it! We've been friends forever. Friends. That means we like each other, right? We have things in common. Don't have to feel all weird with each other, we can just be normal. You try to fix me up with other girls—I don't even think they're your friends, they're nothing like you—while you flirt around with guys you don't even know just because—I don't know—you think they're cute or something?"

Claire is fairly amazed and more than a little flattered. She's never known Josh to be this intense about anything but art.

"*You're* cute."

"Huh?"

"We're out, Josh. Right now. You asked and I said yes. This is our date. Hel-lo-o?"

"Aw shit." Josh puts his arms around her and kisses her.

There are kisses, and then there are kisses. Claire and Josh's first kiss is one of *those* kisses. Claire feels stupid—stupefied. She's never had her mind go blank, yet feel so *awake*. The few times she's ever made out her head was full of voices—an entire team of inner announcers calling the plays and offering analysis. She was too busy trying to decide what to think about the situation to feel more than a suffocating tension.

But she would not call this "making out," even if she still did have access to her vocabulary. There is no groping and slobbering. Josh has simply absorbed her language into his warm mouth where they are having a very private, wordless conversation.

Claire teases his lips with hers. There is a flavor here she hasn't tasted before.

There is a picture with no caption.

Josh holds her securely, his right hand tangled in her hair, his left hand under her shirt, burning its imprint into the skin of her back. They are falling, or floating—dancing, perhaps.

Is there a reason she postponed this moment for so long? Oh, yes, and she knows it now. She wanted to find herself for herself before she lost herself to love.

*Shhh. Don't say Love!*


"So, do you feel weird yet?" Claire wants to know. They're walking the long way around to College Avenue, avoiding the bustling, neon-lit street as long as possible.

"No. With you? No way." Josh has never felt more confident. Claire's kiss has put the seal of approval on a long-nurtured intuition. He squeezes her hand. "Hey, you don't feel weird, do you?"

"Uhm." She doesn't want to admit that her whole life has just changed, that she's only now getting the whole sexual subtext of Prince Charming waking Sleeping Beauty with a kiss. Something is alive and moving within her. A revolution against her formerly all-dominant brain is brewing in the southlands. "I think I'm just hungry," she tells Josh.


The Ethiopian restaurant serves everything for two on loaves of round, spongy flatbread. It isn't cool to request utensils. Josh shows Claire how to tear off chunks of bread and use them to scoop up the spicy chicken and vegetables swimming atop it. The flavors are complicated and musky. With her first taste she realizes she is starving and digs in.

The place is busy, the tables minute so that young legs must entangle themselves beneath. To the couple's relief, the proximity of the tables is not conducive to intimate conversation, and they don't attempt one. In spite of the footsies it's like Josh says—they can be *normal* with each other. After all, they've only eaten a few hundred meals together already, brown-bagging it in the Art Room year after year. Soon they are engaged in an excited discussion of Josh's mural design, and the furor he caused in class.

"I think, deep down, Shelly kind of likes your train. She's probably mad she didn't think of it herself, and Brodie just loves the whole *dynamic*." Claire mimics a Brodie gesture of enthusiasm.

"He's a piece of work, all right. Do you think it's like a *tactic*—his being a complete nerd—to make people get together?"

Claire laughs. "You mean, he gets people signing on to his projects just because they feel sorry for him?"

"Yeah. They can't bring themselves to burst his bubble."

"It's funny how you end up liking him."

"Can't figure her out, though."

Claire detects Josh's smoke signals of distress. Shelly really got under his skin in the computer lab. "Shelly? She's just an artist," Claire says lightly. "Off on her own trip."

"Y'think? Wonder what she does besides murals. *Computer* stuff?"

Claire has to take a swig of iced tea to hide her smile. Shelly had tripped Josh up, asking him to edit his image on the computer.

"Anyway, thanks for rescuing me. I'd probably still be there, fixing one *pixel* at a time."

Claire rolls her eyes. "You know, most folks would *rather* edit on the computer than have to draw it over."

"I could've drawn it twice in that amount of time," Josh huffs.

"I know, you're not most people."

He shrugs, then bumps Claire's knee lightly with his. "You're right. I'm luckier."

Their conversation progresses to the Stanley-Yost Internet scheme, then the Antresian landscaping project, and from there to sculpture, Figure Drawing, and Painting. But it stops dead when Claire asks what Josh intends to do after graduation. It's the obvious follow-up to their discussion of his painting class with Hartshorn and his job in Gus's studio. But it raises the specter of their being apart when they've just gotten together. Josh grumbles something about needing to go to New York, he supposes.

"You know who you should meet? Reginald!" Claire rescues him for the umpteenth time.

"Reginald of Reginald's? I heard he was a stuck-up jerk."

"He can sure act like one, but that's all it is. An act. He's really a nice guy, and he knows all about art. I bet he has a bunch of connections in the City."

Josh raises an eyebrow. "Y'think?"

"We should go there and I'll introduce you. The food is really good."

"Okay. Next paycheck."

"Next *both* our paychecks. That's in a couple weeks for me," Claire calculates.

"Okay. But in the meantime, see ya tomorrow? Between classes?"

"We can meet at the Roadrunner."

"And later? What're you doing?"

The waiter brings warm hand towels, the check, and a welcome interruption. Claire doesn't get why Josh is so intense. *We see each other all the time as it is,* she tells herself. *Plus, if it's really love, it's not going to disappear overnight, right?*

*Shhh! Don't say love!*

Claire cleans her face and fingers, remembering Muffin. She smiles to herself as she imagines how she'll describe this exotic meal to her cloistered friend. Surely she can get a laugh out of her, or at least a shudder at the idea of everyone eating off the same plate.

"You're awesome, Claire. I swear, light shines *out* of you."

She looks up, a little embarrassed that her mind could drift away so swiftly. But Josh isn't really thinking about *them* at that moment, either. He's thinking about painting. *Just normal!* She graces him with a Mona Lisa smile and thanks him for a wonderful meal.

Josh goes to the register to settle the tab. Claire grabs her spiral pad and hurriedly flips to the sketch she made earlier. Not bad, but too cliche—*a trapped princess, a sword to the rescue? C'mon!* Finding a brown and a green pencil, she quickly revises the figure in the mountains, whose long blond tresses become a mop of brown curls above a high-collared, green cape. Claire adds a short beard and mustache to turn the mountain captive into Josh himself, and signs *C. Stanley-Yost* in fancy script along the sword blade in the foreground. At a loss for a title, she rips the drawing from her book and tucks it into Josh's before she goes to join him at the door.

"Here," she says, handing him his sketch book, "guess we better get going."

"Yeah, the car's a mile away." Josh takes Claire's daypack from her and slings it over one shoulder. She slides her arm through his, and slips a mint into her mouth from a glass bowl by the register on their way out.

How could she ever have thought that dating Josh would be too easy, too predictable? The walk to the car, the ride home, phone calls, sketching sessions, meetings at the Roadrunner, dinner at Reginald's—she sees before her a banquet of anticipation, an entire world as yet undiscovered. Until now she hasn't considered this aspect of love—that it might be so certain and easy, and at the same time so wonderfully mysterious.

*Shhh. Don't say Love.*

## CHAPTER 13
## BREAKFAST MEETINGS

Claire's eyes flutter open at six-fifty-nine a.m. She watches the digital clock unhappily. Seven o'clock, seven-o-one... *Whose bright idea was this?* Seven-o-two. Her phone rings and she grabs it.

"Lydia, I'm pooped," she whines into the mouthpiece.

"And good morning to you, Sunshine! Now throw on a pair of jeans and be out front in ten minutes. You promised!" Lydia exudes the aggressive perkiness of folks who have trained themselves to get up early—and like it. This morning her good spirits are sincere, she's been looking forward to this breakfast date with Claire since before Claire got grounded.

"You're going to look great, and I'm going to look like shit."

"Well that's the idea, isn't it?" Lydia teases. Her, "Be there in ten minutes," is both command and promise.

Claire throws the phone aside, rolls out of bed, pulls on a pair of jeans and pads to the bathroom. She takes off her "Go Organic" t-shirt, washes her face, neck, armpits, dries off and puts the same shirt back on. Back in her room she glances quickly in the mirror as she brushes her hair. Satisfied, she shoves her wallet and keys into her pockets, scoops up a pair of socks and her sneakers. She dresses her feet while waiting grumpily for Lydia on the front porch.

So far, doing breakfast is not as fun as it sounds. Claire would rather be sleeping. Part of her still is. She can hardly open her eyes. *Sunglasses!* She staggers around the house to the carport and grabs her sunglasses from the car. As soon as she puts them on, summer stops shooting daggers at her. She summons a smile for the sparkly morning she would otherwise have missed.

Lydia's car approaches slowly over speed-bumped terrain. Claire saunters toward the curb. "You look like shit," Lydia greets her.

"And you look like the fuckin' Sistine Chapel," Claire says, plopping into the passenger seat. Lydia's trousers with matching sleeveless tunic are printed in a busy gold, blue and crimson design. Her blond hair is pulled away from her make-up with red plastic butterfly clips. She looks over her sunglasses at Claire, wondering if Claire really is pissed off.

"The Sistine Chapel?"

"Yeah, a regular masterpiece." Claire tilts her chin down and looks at Lydia over her sunglasses. They both crack up.

At the Enchantment Cafe around the corner on Prince Street, everyone has their nose in a newspaper or a laptop or a cellphone. Claire can't believe how busy the place is, and wishes she had put on some decent clothes. Lydia informs her that *most* jobs require one to get up early in the morning and go to work.

"Well, I'm never getting one of those," Claire tells her.

They stake out a booth and pounce on it as soon as two suits slam their briefcases shut and hurry off. A middle-aged waitress who calls them Sweetie and Honey takes their order, swiping at the table with a wet rag as she pockets the business men's tip. Pretty soon, Claire and Lydia are jazzed on coffee and plowing through a full agenda of topics in the short time Lydia has before work.

"Sooo, tell me about yesterday," Lydia prompts, referring to Claire and Josh's first day after their first date, the date itself having been duly reported by telephone late Monday night.

"Well, in the first place, I had like these red splotches around my mouth. I was sure it was from his beard, but he said no way and claimed he could hardly see them." Claire twists her face left and right as Lydia laughs and leans across the table to look. She agrees with Josh, but knows better than to say so.

"It's pretty much gone now, but I thought I would die! I wore my tie-dye scarf, and kind of ducked my chin down into it when anyone looked at me." Claire demonstrates as Lydia laughs louder.

"Poor baby."

"Yeah, well, if Mom had noticed—"

"Bet she did!" Lydia says this purely in jest.

Claire freezes with her coffee cup halfway to her lips. "Oh, gawd—you don't think—?"

"Mothers see *everything*."

"Shit."

"C'mon, they've *done* everything too. Otherwise we wouldn't be here. And your father has a beard, remember?"

"Shit."

Lydia plays it straight and even pretends to examine Claire's chin again while uttering a small "tsk tsk." She has her own story to tell, and is as anxious to share it as she is to hear about Claire's new romance. "So, tell me..." she prods.

"He met me after drawing class." Claire happily resumes her tale. "We were supposed to go to the Roadrunner and meet everyone, but I didn't want to. I was mad about my face, you know?" Lydia, who would have solved such a problem with make-up, attempts a sympathetic look. "I mean, it's not like it was all his fault—"

"Hardly."

"But it was his beard—"

"And your poor face—"

Claire shakes her head. "I was so embarrassed! I mean, why should everyone know what we're doing?"

"It's gonna show whether you have a rash on your face or not." Lydia notes that Claire's face has turned bright red just thinking about Josh.

"Hah! He said that too, and he said we had to go to the Roadrunner because everyone was expecting us."

"Plus, he wanted exactly what you didn't—to show off that you two were getting it on."

"Yeah, that. And plus he wanted to eat lunch. So, we went, and no one acted like they noticed anything, or that there was anything weird about us being together. All they wanted to talk about was the mural and Shelly and Brodie, and going to the Palace tomorrow night. Then like half of them had to go to class, and Josh walked me to my car, which was parked behind the Fine Arts Center. And then..." At a loss for words, Claire concludes with an expressive sigh, remembering Josh's kiss.

"I see. And did he call you last night?"

"Yes." Claire's eyes sparkle. Still speechless with satisfaction, she attacks her scone and lets Lydia take over.

"Well, *I* got a phone call *and* a visit."

"Trent?"

"Trent and Matthew."

"What?"

"Trent called, and while I was on the phone with him, Matthew showed up!"

"You're kidding!"

"Uh uh. Dad let him in. Didn't have a clue we'd broken up. Starts bellowing, 'Ly-dia! Your boyfriend's here!' at the top of his lungs."

"Jeez."

"Great, huh? So I get off the phone fast. Matthew's downstairs buttering up Dad. I said I'd go for an ice cream with him just to get him out of there."

"Oh, really?"

"Really."

"And?"

"Oh, he gave me the whole song and dance about how he wants to get back together. I said maybe we could date again, but I didn't want to go right back to the same old routine, and I wasn't promising not to see anyone else."

"Bet he loved that."

"Actually, he was nice about it. We had a really good talk." Lydia goes a little misty. Claire supposes there might be more to Matthew than she thought.

"Will wonders never cease." She's not sure if she dare venture her honest opinion of Trent, in case he really isn't out of the picture. Besides, it might lead to a discussion of Lydia's taste in boys in general, and there isn't time for that now. Matthew is not the worst of them by far.

Lydia's pensive expression breaks into a broad grin. "And then I came home and found the folks ransacking my room!"

Claire lets out a triumphant whoop that rises above the din and lifts a few heads from their paperwork.

"They hadn't been at it for very long, and they closed all the drawers before I got upstairs, but I could hear them! They were definitely snooping."

"What did they say?!"

"Oh, you shoulda been there! *'Thinking of having the house painted. Needed to come up and take some measurements.'*"

"Lame, lame, lame!"

"Way lame. But I let them get away with it. Gave them that look that they're always giving me," Lydia raises her eyebrows and looks down her nose, "and said, *'Whatever you say.'* And then I marched over to my nightstand and pulled a tootsie pop out of a big stash of candy. You could see they'd been in there and messed it all up."

"But they didn't have time to find the other thing?"

"Guess not."

"Oh, that's *too* good!"

"I know. They are acting like *so* guilty. I think I'll ask for that perfume sampler Dillard's been advertising."

"Oh, you are so bad!" The girls click coffee mugs.

Claire feels wide awake and jubilant. Her inner eye paints Lydia as a punky princess who goofs on the King and Queen while driving the swains wild. She admires the brisk way Lydia takes her last sip of coffee, picks up the check, bids her farewell and marches off. Every head turns to watch her model-like perfection. Lydia isn't required to work, but likes to, and graces the world each day with her elegance as she drives around town in her sporty teal Vivaldi. *Gorgeous, but not a Cupcake*, Claire thinks.

While she finishes her coffee, she observes the cafe scene with an artist's eye: the well-groomed but tired looking trio of women over in the corner—spongy, lumpy figures in vivid make-up and colorful polyester suits; the dark blue backs of three cops at the counter, their wide behinds splayed out on too-small red plastic stools. It would take something more than a sketch, she acknowledges, to capture the agitated undercurrent of rustling newspapers, murmured phone conversations and tapped-at keypads.

Claire hasn't been here since last Christmas and her "date" with Tony. That afternoon, they'd been the ones on display. Heads turned when Tony slouched in wearing an enormous battered black trench coat, an abundance of heavy jewelry, and his hair moussed into little spikes that radiated in all directions. He insisted on sitting next to the window, then carried on a non-stop, too-loud monologue about everyone and everything he saw through it. Some of his scathing remarks were pretty funny, others just mean. Claire thought angrily that he was in no position to poke fun. To distract herself from the humiliation of being seen with him, she mentally invented a composite creature—part bat, part porcupine—which she would sketch into her pad when she got home. Later, when she'd shown the drawing to Lydia hoping for a laugh, Lydia had said, "That kid is really hurting inside. He wears a costume because he hates himself." And Claire had felt ashamed.

Now, as Claire drops two dollars on the table for Sweetie-Honey, she realizes that this was the turning point. It was the last day of winter break, and they were finally catching up after Lydia's trip to Cancun. Only, Lydia hadn't wanted to talk much.

Claire crosses busy Prince Street and follows little Bee Balm Lane for half a block, then turns left and walks home on the footpath that borders the irrigation ditch. She's trying to remember that afternoon, trying to piece something together. She keeps hearing that one sentence, "He wears a costume because he hates himself." This morning Claire had accused Lydia of wearing a costume: "You look like the Sistine Chapel." Sure, it was a joke, but it does seem like Lydia is more done-up every time Claire sees her. Her clothes, her hair, her nails, her make-up—Claire had never thought of it as a disguise, and it's not as if Lydia is any less lovely without all the fashion stuff. In fact, it's almost as if she hides her natural beauty behind it.

*Why would Lydia hate herself?*

"Hi there!" A familiar voice startles Claire out of her reverie.

"Oh, Hi, Mom."

"How was the Cafe?" Brianna and Stan Man are having their breakfast on the back patio. They are not far from where Claire walks, but separated by a high, honeysuckle-covered fence. From a certain hump on the ditchbank it is possible to commune with the Stanley-Yost back yard. This is where Claire stops.

"Good food. Really busy."

"Busy morning around here, too."

"What?" Claire asks suspiciously. There's something teasing in her father's voice.

"Why don't you go around front and find out?" Stan Man ducks behind his paper. Brianna busies herself pouring orange juice.

"Ooo-kay." Claire shrugs and walks on. A wave of agitation ripples along her nerve endings. *Too little sleep and too much coffee*, she tells herself. But when she steps from the ditchbank to the sidewalk and turns the corner she revises her diagnosis. Surely that jolt of electricity could only be caused by the nearness of her beloved—because Josh's car is parked in front of her house!

"How long have you been here?" Claire can't remember walking over to the car, or opening the door or getting in. They are wrapped in each other's arms. It seems perfectly natural to be hugging Josh good morning. She flashes on what it would be like to wake up with him, and then becomes acutely aware that she didn't bother to put on underpants or a bra this morning. He is practically seeing her right out of bed.

"Hmmm. You smell like sunshine." Josh buries his nose in her hair and slides a hand down her thigh.

"I was out walking." Claire pulls away from him reluctantly, reminding herself that it's eight-thirty a.m. The street is noisy with cars heading out for the day. Lawnmowers and sprinklers are being put through their paces. "Did you go up to the house, or what?"

"Naw. It was so early, I figured when you woke up you'd come out." Josh smiles sheepishly. "I couldn't sleep myself. And I knew I wouldn't get to see you at class today—"

"So you decided to come stake out the place."

"Your father came out and picked up the paper at precisely seven-twenty-three."

"Wow, that's early for Dad. Guess I woke him up." Claire tells Josh about going to breakfast with Lydia. They entwine fingers and smile at each other. Since they talked for an hour last night, there's not much left to discuss. "I'm really glad you waited," she assures him as conversation dwindles.

"Me too." He reaches for her again, then hesitates. "Shit. Your mom's in the window."

Claire looks over her shoulder in time to see the living room curtain fall back into place. "Guess that's our cue." They kiss, feeling reckless about beard burn and nosy neighbors. When they let go of each other, an ache begins. It is the most pleasant pain Claire has ever endured.

# CHAPTER 14
## ALL THE RAGE

By the time Claire pulls into the Westcare Manor parking lot she's an agitated, sweaty mess. She's late, despite getting up so early, having stupidly forgotten to go to Jo's to pick up the cooler, and not even thought of it until she was already across the river. Going back for it was like swimming against the current, with lunchtime traffic congealing at key intersections. The Enchantment Cafe's strong house blend still kicking around in her bloodstream, Claire then flirted for the first time with the demons of road rage. There she was, hollering uselessly at the traffic lights and the drivers around her, impatient from the guilt of keeping Muffin waiting.

*But Muffin doesn't have any sense of time,* a forgiving conscience offers, calling up an image of the giant, institutional clock in Muffin's room which has read three-forty-four for the past two weeks. *She won't know how late you are, or how early you leave.*

Ah, here is the truth of it: Claire's lateness means she'll have less time to spend with Muffin if she is to keep her appointment at the Big B. It's not Muffin she's worried about, but herself, and her conscience will not let her off the hook as easily for that.

A mad, agitated, sweaty, clumsy mess. She shuts off the motor, trembling, and wrestles the window shade into place. She doesn't pause to read Jo's note, as she usually does, but grabs the cooler and hurries to Muffin.

The air conditioning is a big relief, as are the vacant hallways. Everyone has been herded into the dining room, and the usual chaos is contained therein. Striding down the cool corridors, Claire regains something of her calm cheer. She tells herself that sitting quietly with Muffin for forty minutes is just what she needs.

"Help! Someone help me!"

Claire registers Muffin's distant plea and runs past the empty nurse's station and down the hall.

"I'm here, Muffin! What's wrong?"

"I have to go to the bathroom!" Muffin wails.

"Oh, jeez! I'm so sorry I'm late! I'll go get someone—"

"I have to go to the bathroom!" Muffin's lament is an order now. Claire realizes that Muffin thinks she's the aide.

"I'm going to get someone to help you right now," Claire promises, hurrying back up the hall with Muffin's distraught voice following. There is not an aide or a nurse nearby. She sees a nurse gabbing to an administrator at the end of the hallway beyond the nurse's station.

"Hey! Mrs. Griffin needs some help down here!" she calls angrily. The nurse faces Claire with irritation. The suited man turns on his heel and strides off. "There's no one down there, and she needs to go to the bathroom."

"I'll get someone," the bright white woman snaps and looks around, as if trying to decide in which direction she's most likely to scare up an aide. To Claire's immense disappointment, the nurse does not hasten after her to Muffin's room.

Claire rushes back to Muffin alone, where her impotent presence only adds to the agony. She is there offering reassurance, but she's not *doing* anything, and she can imagine how stupid this seems to Muffin. The longer they wait—one fussing, one making pointless promises—the more Claire thinks she should buck up and escort the poor woman to the can. She tries to guess Muffin's weight, wondering if she would be required to support her entirely or if Muffin can stand on her own, if she can take steps, if she has any particular ailments or injuries, if she would allow Claire to handle her like that.

What it boils down to is that Claire is terrified that she will do something wrong and injure Muffin. She decides she should at least see the process performed by a professional once before attempting it herself. She feels utterly useless. Muffin moans and pleads, while Claire keeps an anxious eye on the hall and repeats over and over again, "Someone is on the way to help you right now, just another minute and the aide will come."

*Except that I'm going to throttle her when she gets here!* Claire wonders if there is a name for what she is feeling now—*Heartless Institution Rage? Why couldn't that nurse have come herself?*

"I'm hungry."

Claire turns her perplexed gaze from the hallway to Muffin. "I'm sure you are," she says after a moment, "I'm running late today. But let's get you to the bathroom first so we won't have to stop in the middle of lunch.

"I'm hungry," Muffin sulks.

"And Jo packed a really nice lunch for you." Claire takes a different tack. "I'll get it ready for you while you go to the bathroom." Claire waves frantically to a young woman who's coming down the hall. When she arrives—PATTI is printed on her name badge—Claire practically shouts, "Muffin has to go to the bathroom!"

"Okay. Sorry I took so long. Someone's out sick today," Patti says with friendly weariness. "This isn't my wing." She wheels Muffin over to the bathroom door. "We're going to the bathroom now, Mrs. Griffin," she tells her firmly.

"I don't have to go."

Claire opens her mouth and closes it again. Now she wants to throttle Muffin. Patti has detached the padded tray from Muffin's chair and is snapping on a pair of plastic gloves. "She really, really wanted to go when I came in," Claire insists.

Patti is unflustered as she wheels Muffin through a wide door into the handrail-lined bathroom. She looks young but has a maternal air about her. "Okay, Mrs. Griffin, here we go."

The door is wide open, Claire perches on the bed where she can see what's going on without appearing to watch. It seems horrible to her that Muffin should be exposed like this and not even know it. *But wouldn't knowing it be more horrible?*

"Ouch, ouch! What are you doing?!" Muffin, who had fallen silent, cries out as Patti reaches around her to secure a wide band, which she attaches to a sort of girdle she wears as part of her uniform.

"We're going to stand up now, Mrs. Griffin, so I can put you on the toilet."

"No! Stop it! Leave me alone!"

"Here we go. One, two, three—"

"Aaaayyyyeeee!" Muffin hollers as Patti pulls her up to standing, pulling back with her hips to let the tension of the tether take some of the weight. Patti dances her around in little bitty steps, and Claire is surprised to see how tall Muffin is. She seems almost monstrous as she continues to holler, and alternately clings to Patti for balance and punches at her to get away. Unflustered, Patti tsk-tsks and chides gently, in between instructing Muffin on how and where to move.

"I'm going to sit you on the toilet now," she says firmly, yanking down pants and plunking Muffin on the pot with one swift motion that sets Muffin howling even louder. Patti releases the umbilical strap and stoops to collect the soiled garments as Muffin's moment of power melts into quivering, crumpled nakedness. "Oh, couldn't wait," she sighs without accusation.

"I don't have to go," Muffin whines.

"I know. Let me clean you up."

Claire gets up and walks out into the hall as Patti reaches for a dispenser of antiseptic wipes. She hears Muffin's protest, "Stop that! What are you doing?" and Patti's calm assurances.

"There, all done. Now you sit there a minute while I get you some clean pants."

"I'm sorry," Muffin moans, and this is the most heartbreaking part of the whole sad scene to Claire—the helpless horror of Muffin's passing realization that she wet her pants. Claire hurries to get the fresh clothes for Patti, since she knows how Jo has things set up.

"Are you her granddaughter?" Patti accepts the cotton panties and polyester trousers while she fishes around in the cabinet for an adult diaper.

"No, just a friend. A friend of her daughter's."

"Help me!"

Patti returns to Muffin.

Claire gulps back an impulse to cry and plops into her usual chair.

All agitation has ebbed out of her, the sense of urgency, of certain things being important. All she wants to do is feed Muffin a good lunch, tell her a story, rub her shoulders, and make her forget this wretched, humiliating episode. Claire has no idea what time it is—perhaps by the time she finishes with Muffin it really will be three-forty-four—and could care less about being late for her own lunch, or Brodie's neighborhood canvassing session. She listens to Patti and Muffin's progress. Muffin lets out a short wail of surprise when Patti heaves her up, but the fight has gone out of her. She shuffles around and plops into her wheelchair without another sound, and even offers a chastened "Thank you" to Patti when the aide wheels her out to Claire, snaps the padded tray back into position, and tells her she's ready to have lunch.

Claire thanks Patti too, then turns her attention to Muffin, who is fading out from exertion and hunger. Only after she has loaded the juice cup into Muffin's left hand and a piece of peanut butter and jelly sandwich into her right, and Muffin is chomping away contentedly, does Claire open Jo's note. After the usual greetings and lunch menu, Jo's artistic script deteriorates into an angry scrawl.

*"I've been asking that someone take Muffin to the bathroom before lunch whether she asks to go or not, but they are not doing it and she might say she has to go during lunch. Please get an aide to take her, I don't think you should try to do it yourself. She is becoming incontinent because they make her wait so long. I think there's been a turn-over with the staff. It seems like she has a different aide every day. There's no routine, and she's more confused than ever. I don't know what I'm going to do! Hopefully you will have a good day, because I have had a streak of bad ones. Please try to make a note of which aide you find on duty there today."*

Claire folds the note, puts it back in the cooler, and gets out a tub of fruit salad to spoon feed to Muffin. They talk only about food, Muffin greeting each course with enthusiasm and Claire supplementing her taste sensations with vivid descriptions of gardens and restaurants and unusual recipes. For Muffin, a good experience overlays a bad one, obliterating it. For Claire, the tide of rage which had engulfed her, then dissipated, now reshapes itself into something more clearly defined. There is an edge to it and a reason for it. For now, she skirts its perimeter, taking sanctuary in the grace of Muffin's contentment. Later, though, she will survey her coalesced fury inside and out, and see if there isn't something constructive, or at least creative, she might do with it.

## CHAPTER 15
## PAINTING IS A PAIN THING


Brianna Yost happily notes the presence of Claire's car as she pulls in under the carport. Sliding out of her gold Lynx, she is crisp and cool as fresh lettuce, her pastel outfit barely rumpled after a day of visiting clients. *With air conditioning all things are possible.* She has learned that every penny spent on making the car more comfortable is well worth it. Today she has met with success and admiration at every turn and feels confident, finally, that the firm of Stanley-Yost is going to make it. Now, maybe, they can make some plans for a summer vacation.

She enters the house eager to tell Carl and Claire about her day. Carl is not in the kitchen where she had hoped to find him making dinner. An eerie silence hangs over the house, and an aroma of paint. *Something has happened with Claire.* Brianna's elation melts into foreboding, as she approaches the office she shares with Carl and hears him speaking placatingly into the phone. A few more steps, and she has both feet planted firmly on the ground and is studying his computer screen while listening to his end of the conversation.

"Well, I understand that Mr. Brodie— Okay, Brodie. I understand that. But this is an art class, supposed to be, anyway, as I understand it, and my daughter came home this afternoon with a burning desire to paint. I simply could not in good conscience insist that she squelch that impulse and go down there to take an opinion poll about the mural." Carl swivels around and rolls his eyes at Brianna. She's squinting at the monitor, wondering what he's been researching. Carl's brow knits and he swivels back, giving all of his attention to the phone. "Well, aren't you an artist yourself— Oh, you're not? That doesn't seem right— I see. Well, maybe this Shelly could call and talk to Claire herself. Given the circumstances, that might be more productive— All right, fair enough. And I do appreciate your concern for Claire. You were absolutely right to call— Uh huh— Uh huh— Uh huh— Yeah. Uh huh— Good bye.

"What a twerp! Fuckin' *sociologist!*" Carl tosses the headset onto the desk and does one complete rotation in his "power chair" before bringing himself to rest. He watches Brianna's face as she connects the dots between his Web surfing, the phone call, and the floating fragrance of acrylics.

"She skipped class."

"Yeah."

"And now you're shopping for a truck."

"We said we'd give her the Sprite, I'm thinking of getting a pick-up for myself."

Brianna plops into her matching swivel throne and stares at her husband. Though he is often utterly "clueless," as Claire would say, there are times when he displays an empathy for his daughter so deep as to make Brianna feel like she's raising two teenagers. What has gotten into the both of them today? How could she have missed so much in a single afternoon?

"I think something happened with Muffin today," Carl volunteers, realizing he will have to bring Brianna up to speed before she will authorize the purchase of a third vehicle.

"Did you ask her?"

"She said Muffin was doing fine by the end of lunch and that she didn't want to talk about it, she wanted to paint. She had stopped at Craft Corner and bought herself some panels and she got right to it." Brianna's face has shaped itself into a mask of maternal dismay. "I think it's fantastic, don't you? She is compelled to paint and she's painting. Whatever heavy experience she had out there, she's using her art to process it! I think this could be a breakthrough for her."

"Skipping class to paint?"

"Brianna, it's summer school, for chrissake."

"I'm really surprised she would stand up her friends, those girls that live down there?" Red warning lights are going off all over the place—Brianna can't believe Carl doesn't see them.

"Oh, Laurie called already. Nice girl. I've also spoken to Lydia, Dori and Josh. It seems Claire has turned off her phone."

Red lights and bells, clanging bells... Brianna Yost leans back and closes her eyes. "Doesn't *any* of this concern you?"

"Oh, you should see what she's painting!" Stan Man tells her. She opens one eye, gives him a very dirty look, and closes it again. "Anyway, I figure we'll get to the bottom of it soon enough. I called Jo, and she said Claire never stopped back with her cooler, so I asked her to come by after supper. If this is about Muffin, Claire's going to have to tell Jo about it. Apparently things haven't been going too well at the home."

Carl Stanley can feel his wife's disapproval easing away. In spite of his flippant attitude, he has done the right thing. "So, how'd I do?" he taunts.

Brianna takes a deep breath, then opens the evil eye on him again. "After supper, huh? And when might that be?" This sends Stan Man stomping off to the kitchen. She scoots over into his chair and resumes his Web session, checking out the latest model pick-ups. *So much for summer vacation.*

Brianna and Carl are finishing their grilled cheese and green chile sandwiches. With potato chips and chocolate shakes, this is the Stanley-Yost comfort meal of comfort meals. Claire is having hers in her bedroom, where they have waited on her in the unintrusive, deferential manner of servants. It seems only fitting, since she is the princess of their kingdom of three, fast approaching her coronation. Once their daughter claims her place in the world—likely as an artist of great distinction—her parents may withdraw into their quiet dotage. They tip-toed in with their offerings and bowed themselves out again, stealing the barest glimpse of the canvases in progress. They are sharing their impressions of these when Jo Ferguson arrives.

Brianna throws open the door and greets her friend with a warm hug. Carl offers to make Jo a chocolate shake. Jo's impulse is to refuse for the simple reason that she would absolutely *love* a chocolate shake, and it doesn't seem altogether responsible to crave something so sinful and then to *get* it. She has just had dinner, coffee and pie—*no ice cream, though*—and chocolate has been a no-no with her for years.

Carl grins at her wide eyes, magnified by heavy glasses. There's something of a graying Orphan Annie about her as she struggles to make the right choice. "C'mon, live it up," he coaxes, "fortify yourself."

"You make it sound so good," Jo admits, and lets Carl take that as a yes. She and Brianna settle at the dining room table while the blender whirs. "How's Claire?"

"Still painting. She's got a whole series going at once in there. The underpaintings are looking very geometric and gloomy."

"Sounds like it might be a portrait of Westcare Manor. I did call to check on Ma before I came over. They said she was doing fine—that is, no worse than usual—

"Oh, thank you, Carl. Oh, a straw and everything!" Jo interrupts herself to sip the house specialty, then drains almost half the glass before she puts it down, laughing at herself. "Wow, that's good."

Brianna and Carl beam at her. They like seeing people enjoy themselves. Watching the worried lines of Jo's brow loosen eases their own anxiety. The medicine of simple pleasures proves itself again. Brianna goes to get Claire.

Jo reaches into the open bag of potato chips, thinking, *What the hell.* She takes another pull from her shake. She's feeling relaxed for the first time in many months—not free of stress but comforted, like she's not in this alone. Her husband has been supportive beyond the call of duty, but he's protective of her too, in a way that makes it impossible for him to completely understand. Jake's instinct is to defend his mate. It's an instinct born of tenderness, only it's hard to be tender when your weapons are drawn. Then there are the kids, busy with their lives on the West Coast. For them to contemplate the sacrifices Jo is making for her mother would mean contemplating a future in which Jo will no longer be supermom and their own devotion will be tested. There are not enough miles in the world to allow one to escape that inevitability, but they are doing a good job of it for the time being.

"I appreciated the talk we had on the phone this afternoon," Jo tells Carl. "Jake gets too angry when I tell him about that stuff. Really, the whole family seems to feel threatened by the amount of time I put into caring for Ma. And if I talk about it constantly too—" She shrugs and leans back in her chair.

Carl's been thinking a lot about Muffin since he and Jo spoke earlier. He says earnestly, "You have to talk about it, this is consuming a big chunk of your life. And it's not a little thing, or a strictly personal thing. The crap that goes on at Westcare Manor goes on everywhere. It's not just your mother, it's all sorts of people—only people who don't even have an advocate like you keeping an eye on them. We treat our elderly like shit! No one wants to hear about that."

"But how come it's so bad?" Claire slips into her usual seat and looks from her father to Jo. Brianna follows her into the dining room, exchanges a satisfied glance with Carl, and starts clearing the table.

"It's the money," Jo tells Claire. "The aides never get much more than minimum wage, no matter how long they stay. How are you going to find good people to do that kind of work for such lousy pay? If you find them, how are you going to keep them? So they have a high turn-over rate. There's no consistency. Every time someone gets some experience they move on. There are simply not enough aides to give the residents proper care."

"Why don't they pay them more?" Claire has actually been thinking about working in a nursing home sometime, if she ever can't get a job in art. She figures there are always openings, and it would be more rewarding than waitressing. But she hadn't considered the pay scale until now.

Brianna picks up where Jo left off, "The work of caring for the elderly has traditionally been done for free—by women and children family members. Women and teenagers still perform much of this labor, which is considered unskilled. Our society can't stomach having to pay for it. The nursing homes don't want to price themselves out of business, but they have a lot of expenses and it's hard to keep the profit margin up. The single biggest line item on their budget is payroll, because employees are so expensive. All the required taxes, insurance, overtime pay and benefits go up in proportion to the staff's wages. And all that money paid out is never considered an 'asset' like equipment or furniture. You better believe management wants to have a high turn-over and low pay, or they'd do something about it." Brianna goes over to the wastebasket and brushes off her hands, as if disposing of this sordid subject with the crumbs.

"So they scrimp on aides, and there's no one to take Muffin to the bathroom when she needs to go," Claire sums up. "That sucks." Jo, Carl and Brianna all nod in agreement but keep quiet while Claire struggles to digest the hard truths of capitalism and elder care. She directs her comments to a paper napkin that she is shredding and reshredding. "I mean, the work is physically hard and sometimes nasty, and must be emotionally draining too, and if you don't do it right— Shit, that's a *person* you're messing with! How can they say it's unskilled? Because you can't get a diploma in kindness?"

"If there were such a thing, half of us wouldn't qualify," Carl says, "we'd be exposed as the social morons we are."

Tears pool up in Claire's eyes and she can't look at anyone. She twists the napkin while the trio of adults waits expectantly.

"The aide, Patti, when she finally showed up, was really good," she tells the napkin, "but I couldn't believe that nurse, and the man in the suit practically ran away. I bet they get paid tons just to sit on their butts all day." Claire sniffles and brings the napkin to her face, but it's only a pile of lint. "I just wish *I* hadn't been so late!"

Jo passes her a fresh napkin from a holder made of seashells. "None of this is your fault, Claire. I hate to see you taking it so hard. Whatever happened today, you know that Ma's forgotten about it already."

Claire's smile is pained. "Oh, she'd forgotten by the time I left. But it made me so mad..." Now, as the details of the visit with Muffin come pouring out, they start to sound insignificant. Not that the slights to Muffin aren't real, but the subject is so mundane. How can this little business we attend to multiple times a day without a second thought escalate into such a source of outrage?

Claire wipes her eyes and nose for the last time and looks around the table, feeling she is in the company of equals—not grown-ups, that other species she has lived with until now, but fellow humans. *We are all equal when it comes to the call of nature*, she muses to herself, *diapers to diapers, dust to dust.* Out loud she declares, "I think all nursing home administrators should have to spend a day strapped into a wheelchair—at least until they pee their pants."

That gives everyone a good hard laugh, and the evening ends with a tension-relieving spate of scatological jokes. A number of rude contributions are all the more hilarious coming from the normally refined Josephine Ferguson.

Claire goes out with Jo to get the cooler from the car. There's a velvety blackness to the night sky, an embroidery of stars, and the scent of honeysuckle is so strong they can almost taste it.

"I wish I could paint that smell," Claire says.

"You know, Muffin always wanted to be an artist."

Jo is unaware of what a thunderous revelation this is to her young friend. She is too caught up in her own emotions to notice Claire's quick intake of breath, her struggle to find words.

"No, I didn't know that. Thanks for telling me. And thanks for coming over."

"Thank you, Claire."

Claire accepts a hug and hurries back inside, eager to resume her painting.

# CHAPTER 16
## BREAKING THROUGH

Art has its boundaries. For the painter there is the canvas—called the ground or the field. The canvas is only so big. Its edges are the boundaries between what is painted and what is not. A frame might be in its future. A wall is certainly implied. But the canvas is where the paint lives, it is the plot of land where the idea is born, raised and buried. Many an artist has longed to see his children get off to a good start with a nice large field to play on—and then settled for a cozy, more affordable number, an 18"x24" or a 16"x20". Canvases are expensive, and so is the paint to fill them.

When Claire stopped at Craft Corner yesterday she had exactly $32.47 to spend, which included some coins she found under the car floormats and change from the fifty her mom had given her for groceries. She bought three primed, 14"x18" stretched canvases and left owing the cashier fifty cents—luckily it was a friend from school—because she hadn't figured on the tax. She could've gotten four 11"x14"s, but they looked puny. She would settle for a triptych. At home she painted one of her canvases brown-black, one grey-green, and the third a pale, dingy yellow. She mixed big batches of these base colors in glass jars, using up tubes of the dull, uninspiring colors she typically avoids—Chromium Oxide Green, Ferrous Black, Naples Yellow, the Umbers. She's got nothing against the colors themselves, but she's found that the inherent milkiness of acrylics doesn't do justice to them. But for this series her intent was to capture drabness with drabness.

Another property of acrylics is that they dry fast. This has given Claire trouble in the past, but she used it to her advantage during her day and night of inspired painting. Measuring out colors by the quarter-cup, she kept the jars and tubes tightly closed to prevent their drying out. Layer by layer she worked the three canvases, allowing each coat to dry so the next would paint over cleanly, light over dark, dark over light. After the base coat came the underpaintings, a distorted architecture of lines making each canvas a cage—one seen from within, one from without, one from above. Another pass with the brush and another added characters and props, first the bare shapes—tucked off to the side, half hidden behind other forms—then sharpened by hard line and vivid contrasting colors. On the brown-black panel, a startlingly pristine white diamond became the useless starched nurse, mocking and remote. The yellowish canvas suggested a maze of soiled walls flickering with the shadows of unseen bogeymen. And the moldy-green ground took the shape of a long, unhappy corridor, at the end of which a tiny yellow rose bloomed in crisp, perfect miniature. Muffin.

The matte finish Claire had in mind from the start proved unsatisfactory. As the work progressed, she added more and more gloss medium to each successive layer. The flatness in general bothered her. Overpaintings five and six involved repainting some of the architectural planes and daubing at the wet paint with a piece of sponge, or drawing a comb through it to make raised stripes, or pressing a piece of burlap against it for a checkerboard pattern.

By four a.m. Thursday morning Claire has brushed one last coat of clear acrylic gloss over each of the panels and is splashing around in the bathroom, washing her brushes and herself simultaneously. Her heavily textured paintings gleam like finely worked enamel. When she looks at them later she will find them peculiarly, morosely, beautiful. Right now, she only thinks to herself that she pretty much followed the plan she had for the series, with the inevitable adjustments along the way, and that's the best she can do. Her eyes won't focus, her arms feel like lead, and her mind is blissfully empty. All of the emotions that had propelled her to paint have now taken shelter in her creation. She returns to her room and crawls into bed, instantly falling asleep under its three-eyed gaze.

"Uh, Claire? You going to class this morning?"

It's Stan Man. Claire feels like exactly a second has elapsed since she passed out. She is pinned to the mattress by weariness. "I'd like to go," she sighs, "but I don't think I can move."

Barely able to make out her mumbled words, Carl Stanley steps across the threshold into his daughter's sanctuary. The gleam of her canvases catches his eye. Try as he might not to look, he has to. They are weird and marvelous. He has the good sense not to comment.

"Shit. What time is it?" Claire has dozed and woken again.

"You can still make it, 'specially if I give you a ride."

A flutter of life. "Oh, would you, Dad?" She opens her eyes and he quickly averts his from the paintings. "I really can't crap out on everyone again today."

"Spoken like a real trooper."

"I'm sure I can get a ride home with someone."

Carl imagines various young men lining up for the privilege. "I'm sure you can. But call me after class and let me know, okay? Now don't fall back to sleep. I'm going to finish my coffee."

That does the trick. As her father clicks the door shut behind him, Claire tumbles out of bed and reaches for a pair of jeans. She stumbles out to the kitchen squinting against the wretched sun, pours a cup of coffee, and takes it back to the bathroom where she tends to her tangled hair and puffy eyes. *Hopeless.* She puts her hair in a pony tail. Returning to her room, she puts on some clean clothes and slides her feet into sandals. In the car she dons her sunglasses with relief and munches the bagel her father has thoughtfully prepared. When they are approaching the perimeter of the campus, she tells him, "You're the best, Stan Man."

"Just going for my Kindness Diploma." Carl doesn't want to blow the moment by letting Claire see how proud of her he is.

"Ha! I'll draw one up for you myself." Claire leaves him with a cream-cheesy smack on the cheek and a promise to call from the Roadrunner after class.

*Plenty of time,* Carl thinks. He takes a left and heads for the truck dealerships.

Claire's late but she doesn't care. She would rather sit in the back today anyway. She stops at the ladies room and brushes her teeth with her finger, takes down the pony tail which she now thinks looks stupid, examines her eyebags once more, and determines to keep her sunglasses on for the rest of the day, indoors and out. Then, to her dismay, she enters the studio to find that Greg has saved her usual front-and-center seat. It sits accusingly empty in the crowded room, Greg's sneakered foot propped up on it possessively. Hartshorn has already started his lecture, and Claire has to do a walk-on in front of everyone. She mutters excuse-me's as she wrestles her big clipboard past knees and tackle boxes, and gives Greg a facetious little "Thanksa*lot*" before plopping into her reserved seat. Everyone turns their attention back to Hartshorn.

When the model, a plump and pretty girl, ascends the pedestal there's an eager rustling of newsprint. Claire feels none of her usual nervousness about drawing the figure. She's simply too depleted to get worked up about anything. The smooth, honey-colored curves of flesh are intensely beautiful to her weary eyes. She sees them as if superimposed against the ghoulish, hard-edged compositions she worked on all night. Never before have the shapes and textures of the womanly form been so perfectly articulated to Claire's eye. Her hand draws them with confidence and precision.

*This is so easy—why have I been making it so hard? You just draw what's there—so much easier than creating it out of your mind.* Claire wears her dark glasses low on her nose and she looks up and over them to see the model. Her hand proves able to work in the shadows, and after a few minutes she hardly looks down at the page at all.

Percy Hartshorn roams the room, occasionally calling for a new pose and resetting the timer. He looks over Claire's shoulder for several minutes, but she doesn't notice. He can smell the molecules of acrylic polymer clinging to her hair. It's a talent he's acquired from many years of teaching, the ability to literally sniff out what media his students have been working in. "You can smell a dedicated artist a mile away," he likes to say, though not everyone takes it quite the way he means it. Something else he's learned is to not make a fuss when a pupil makes a breakthrough. Often they don't even know what they've done, or how, or why it's so good. The last thing they need right then is to think about it too much. "Good work," Hartshorn whispers to Claire as charcoals whisper all around them, but at the end of class he does not put up any of her sketches for critique.

Claire is grateful. She doesn't want to look at them herself. Doing them was enough—feeling drawing happen in a completely different way. She secures her drawing pad and clipboard with a long elastic that keeps the pages from flapping, and waits for class to end with one eye on the door. She's not sure if Josh will come to walk her to the Roadrunner or meet her over there. They talked for about two minutes after Jo left last night. Josh had seemed almost relieved that Claire was in the grip of the Muse. He has projects of his own to tend to, and was hoping to go with Gus to pick out some stone this morning.

"That boyfriend of yours didn't hit you, did he?" Greg's tone is only half-joking and he keeps his voice low. In case it's true, he doesn't want anyone else to hear.

Claire's first reaction is astonishment, the wide-eyed expression of which he can't see behind her dark glasses. Comprehension follows. And then she gets mad. Claire lowers her glasses to the end of her nose and looks at her classmate with bloodshot—not black and blue—eyes. "I was up all night painting," she says dryly. She slides the shades back into place, grabs her stuff and marches out without giving him another look. *Of all the...*

"Tzzzsssssss," Salman makes the sound of water hitting a hot griddle. "Fiery."

"Sal, I think I'm in love." Greg and his friend are entranced by Claire's haughty exit.

"Then what are you waiting for? It looks like Tall-dark-and-handsome has missed his rendezvous."

Indeed, there is no sign of Josh. Greg is frozen with indecision.

"It's now or never, man. Don't let her go off all pissed at you."

Greg races out. He finds Claire on the steps of the Fine Arts Center. She's stopped to take another look around for Josh. When she see's

Greg out of the corner of her eye she starts walking determinedly toward College Avenue.

"Hey, Claire!" Greg jogs to catch up to her and then falls into step at her side. "Really, I'm sorry I cast aspersions on your boyfriend."

"His name's Josh." She keeps walking.

"You know, it was only a joke—" Greg can tell Claire's not buying it, the way she cocks her head ever so slightly. "Well, sort of. It was a joke unless it wasn't a joke. I mean, shit like that happens." Claire draws an exasperated breath, Greg plunges on, "Oh, not to you, of course! You wouldn't go with guys like that. See, that's why I figured I could make the joke—" If only he could see her expression behind those glasses, if only she'd slow down for a minute! He tries again. "Anyway, that's cool about your painting. You must've been really inspired."

Claire stops, mainly because she doesn't want the guy following her right into the Roadrunner, where Josh is sure to be waiting. She turns to face Greg, takes off her sunglasses and surveys him up and down, finding him cute enough in a wiry, freckled way, and endearingly sincere.

"Well, I gotta say," she finally says, "if I *had* had a black eye behind my sunglasses, you would definitely be my hero right about now."

"But since all you've got is a splitting headache from staying up all night," Greg finishes for her, "I'm like the biggest jerk you ever met."

Claire shakes her head. "Uh uh, not at all." She puts her sunglasses back on. "Listen, Greg, I gotta go. See ya later, okay?"

"Yeah, later." Greg prays that Claire won't relate their exchange to Josh. He watches her cross the street before he hurries off to consult with Salman.

Josh is waiting in front of the Roadrunner. They fall into each others arms as if they've been parted for a century. Everyone's inside, even Shelly and Brodie—even Laurie and Angela! They've all shown up to talk about what's happening with the mural, and they've taken over a whole room in the rambling restaurant converted from a half-block stretch of old storefronts. While they wait to place their orders at a long counter, Josh brings Claire up to date.

"There was definitely consensus on my train idea—everyone in the neighborhood hated it!"

"No! You're kidding, right?"

Josh shakes his head. He's amused, but it's no joke. "Hey, ya win some, ya lose some."

Claire's glad Josh is taking it so well, but she's offended that the residents of Cesar Chavez have demonstrated such poor taste. She wishes she'd gone down there yesterday to help represent Josh's design.

"So, now what?"

"Now we've got other problems, and we have to go to the City Council on Monday anyway. Some architect is complaining about us painting on the Old Mercantile."

"What?" There's a great clatter from the overworked kitchen. "Ouch, my head."

"You need to eat." This is Josh's solution to all that ails. He orders two green chile cheeseburgers, french fries and a coke, and Claire orders a breakfast burrito for herself, with a large iced coffee. Once they've settled in among the CARMA crowd, someone passes a clipping from the morning paper to Claire. She reads intently while

115

excited conversation swirls around her.

### LOCAL ARCHITECT OPPOSES MURAL

*Randall Boseman, of Boseman, Mitchum and Shore Architects, a firm which dates back to 1888, the same year in which the Old Mercantile was built, claims that painting the historic brick will hasten its decay.*

*"It's an exercise in futility," says Boseman, "the mural won't last and the brick won't last. What's the point of that?"*

*Meanwhile, fourteen high school art students and dozens of residents of the Cesar Chavez neighborhood have been looking forward to painting the mural, sponsored by the Community Art-Reach Mural Association (CARMA) which is jointly funded by the City and the University.*

*Angela Lucero is both a student member of the CARMA team and a nearby neighbor of the Old Mercantile. When asked about the design for the mural, she described it this way:*

*"You've got the desert, the river, the rows of corn, the train roaring through, the big blue New Mexico sky, Mother Earth, and our blessed Cesar Chavez smiling down on all the happy brown children."*

*Official representatives of the CARMA project could not be reached for comment.*

*The City Council will hear both sides of the issue this coming Monday during their regular weekly meeting. The public is invited to attend...*

"Way to go, Angela!" Claire exclaims, looking up to see where Angela and Laurie are sitting.

"Yeah, way to go, Angela!" Danny calls out, raising a clenched fist in the power sign.

"Whooo whooo, Angela!" The half-dozen conversations which

have been running simultaneously are suspended as the group takes up the cheer.

Angela looks flustered. She expected everyone to be mad at her and can't understand why they aren't. She thinks maybe they're making fun of her. During a sleepless night spent fretting over what the newspaper might print, she'd decided that everything could be blamed on Claire. She says loudly from across the room, "You're the one who should've given the statement, Claire. The reporters showed up just when the van was pulling away and me an' Laurie were the only ones left. If you hadn't bagged out on us, you could've told it to them right."

The room goes silent. Claire's stunned. She figured Laurie was too busy flirting with Andrew to notice her arrival, now she understands why Angela didn't greet her either. She meets Angela's eyes and tells her, "But I think what you said was great."

"No one could have said the *right* thing because the mural wasn't decided yet," Celine says diplomatically.

"But it is now!" Laurie adds with glee, heedless of her cousin's sensitivity on this very point.

"Yeah, all we have to do is draw it up the way Ange' said."

Danny has no problem with the mural as described by Angela, neither does anyone else. They had all been psyched about the train, and when word got around that the neighborhood didn't want it, the original alternatives were even less appealing. They had nothing to take to the City Council, and they still had to make the delicate choice between the corn maiden and Cesar Chavez. Then, in a single stroke, everything changed and changed again. Boseman gave them a new cause to fight for, and Angela gave them a vision—a vision that included Josh's train! The group assures Angela that what popped out of her mouth in response the reporters' questions is exactly right. Somehow she described exactly what the mural should be.

"What you did," Shelly told her—Shelly of all people!—"is you brought in all of the elements we've been considering. Like Celine said, there was no final design when the reporters asked about it. But there was a creative movement in a certain direction—and *you* had a sense of the wholeness of it. *We* were all thinking about making a choice between three things, but you knew—you felt instinctively—they could all be branches of a single thing. That's art, honey. It starts inside you somewhere, not on a piece of paper. And the way you know it's art is that folks get excited about it." She gestures broadly at Angela's animated classmates and the clusters of other diners who have come in to listen. "Look, when we go to that Council meeting Monday, we won't be fighting for a design, we'll be fighting for the mural itself. They could can the whole project, so we want to be unified about the design, and it has to be a knock-out. I think we can do it—just like Angela described. Let's load this baby up with every icon we've got and see if those architects really have the balls to shoot down the American Dream manifest. Hell, let's throw in Susan B. Anthony and Elvis while we're at it!"

"Whooooo ooooooh oooooh!" The room roars.

Claire holds her head and moans. Josh is laughing so hard tears are falling into his plate. Angela is blushing bright red and grinning from ear to ear. People are pounding on tables and shouting out names.

"Ghandi!"

"John Lennon!"

"No, they have to be American!"

"Okay, Cochise!"

"Yeah, Sitting Bull!"

"Marilyn Monroe!"

"Jerry Garcia!"

"Bill Gates!"

"No, he's not dead yet, they have to be dead!"

"Okay, Al Gore!" The place explodes again. And here comes the manager to see what's going on.

Shelly stands on a chair and raises her arms for silence. She's smiling guiltily at Brodie, who seems genuinely disturbed. "Okay, okay! Now that we've got that out of our systems, let's get real. You know if we take it over the top, we're dead in the water—and not just this mural, maybe lots of 'em."

That shuts everyone up. Shelly hops down and grasps the back of the chair as if it were a lectern. "Look, public art is always controversial. That's why we go through Council in the first place. Let's stick to the approved elements and make it as artistic and accessible as we can. The Council's not going to nix the train if the approved things are in there. If our design does not offend, then the debate will only be about the bricks."

"Yeah, what about the bricks?" Kevin wants to know. "Aren't, like, half the murals in the universe painted on brick?"

"Something like that," says Shelly. "And Boseman's right that they don't last. Brick is really too porous to paint on, and the sealants they use on modern buildings haven't been accepted by preservationists."

"Why not, if they make the buildings last longer?" Dori asks.

"You know what we need, Brodie," Shelly tells her partner, "the minutes to the Council meeting where we discussed all this." Brodie nods and makes a note. Shelly goes on, "See, the Council talked about this already. There's a solution to the brick problem and that's to hang aluminum panels over the wall and paint on those. The advantage is that the mural can be moved and preserved if anything happens to the building. You also get a better surface to paint on. It's not completely satisfying to us traditionalists, but there's a lot to be said for it—not the least being that you can have a more detailed design."

"Let me guess," Miranda pipes up, "the Council didn't go for the panels the first time because they're too expensive."

"You got it," Brodie says.

"But now I think we've found a funding source," Shelly smirks, then pauses dramatically like a magician who's about to pull a rabbit out of her hat. "The Association of Architects!" Only Brodie gets it, and he's all smiles now. "See, that's a very prestigious group. If they want to preserve their building and not disappoint some earnest young artists, they're going to have to buy us some panels. It's not going to look very good for them otherwise," Shelly concludes.

Pandemonium breaks out again, in part because half the kids realize they're about to be late for class. Josh gives Claire an exuberant hug and dashes off. Brodie and Shelly quickly pass around slips of paper, which is really all they came in to do, announcing the time and place of the official emergency CARMA meeting they've scheduled for tomorrow.

Claire needs desperately to get home and into bed. She goes over to Angela, who has been treated to several different desserts and iced drinks. "Are we okay now?" Angela beams through a mouthful of rhubarb pie and nods vigorously. "Well, do you think you could give me a ride home?"

Before Angela can swallow and say, "I'd love to," Shelly butts in and says she'll give Claire a ride, she's going that way anyway. The girls exchange alarmed looks, then Claire accepts—what else can she do—and goes to call her dad. *Probably get home faster,* she tells herself as she punches at the pay phone, *Angela's still working on dessert and Laurie's still working on Andrew.*

Shelly drives an old station wagon, heavily bumper-stickered and loaded with tools and cans of paint. It smells like french fries and feels like an oven. Slouching down in the front seat, Claire looks at the notice in her hand and sighs. Their emergency session is scheduled for noon tomorrow. "I just can't do this," she tells Shelly.

"Why not?"

"I have to go out to the West Side."

"What for?" To Shelly, Claire's just another spoiled teenage girl who's too popular for her own good. But when she hears about Muffin, she reconsiders. "That sounds like a job that seems easy but really isn't."

"When it's easy it's easy and when it's hard it's hard."

"Is that why you didn't meet Brodie and the others yesterday?"

Claire sighs hugely. She is so tired. "Yeah, I was running late, and then by the time I finished with Muffin I wasn't in the mood. I stayed home and painted. I painted all night."

"Oh, so that's it." Shelly's curious, but she doesn't say any more. The poor kid seems to be shrinking into a little ball right there in the passenger seat.

"How can you stand it?" Claire asks after a few minutes.

"Stand what?"

"Fighting all the time."

Shelly's puzzled. "Fighting all the time? Oh, you mean like for the murals?" Claire nods. "I don't know. I guess I don't think of it as fighting, I think of it as part of the art."

"Yeah, we're all warriors," Claire mutters, then, "Turn left here, it's down a ways on the right, the one with the blue trim."

"So, how'd the painting go?"

"Okay, I guess. I like to paint. But I don't think it proves anything, or says anything." Shelly creeps down the street, thinking, *Why don't conversations ever get started until they're almost over?* as Claire continues, "I don't know why I was thinking it was so important. It doesn't change anything for Muffin."

"You sure? It changes you. It's part of your evolution as a person. And the way you care for Muffin has everything to do with the person you are." Shelly pulls up to the curb and turns off the engine. "Of course there are more direct ways of dealing with the wrongs of the world than through art, but most of them involve fighting." She smiles at the insight that has just come to her, thanks to Claire. "Painting is really the opposite of fighting. However much quibbling goes on over the murals, I assure you, when the time comes to dip brushes in paint, it will be pure love. Paint doesn't get wrestled onto canvas—it flows, it's stroked—"

*My head is going to explode!* Claire hurries out of the car. Stan Man is watching from under the carport, wiping his hands on an oily rag with Lady Macbeth-like intensity. She slams the car door and leans in through the open window. "Thanks, Shelly, 'preciate the ride."

"No problem, Claire. Just come on down tomorrow whenever you can. We'll be working through the afternoon at this rate."

"Okay, I'll be there."

Claire walks up the driveway as Shelly does a u-turn and zooms off—not fast, but noisily. Her father greets her with a probing look.

"So that was your teacher, Shelly, the mural artist?"

"Yeah— What?" Claire is zonked and extra defensive. She does not like that look Stan Man is giving her. "Her car too trashy for you?"

"Well, she could use a new muffler. But it was the bumper stickers that caught my attention. You read them?"

"Uh uh." *Who cares? I'm too tired!* Claire wags her head in disgust and drags herself into the house and into her room where, lacking a lady's maid, she simply drops her belongings on the floor and throws herself onto the bed fully clothed. Out front, her father shrugs and goes back to maintaining m'Lady's vehicle.

## CHAPTER 18
## OF BLOSSOMS AND BUDDHAS

Sleep has worked its magic. Claire rises mid-morning, clear eyed and fully lucid. Her paintings are lined up on the dresser, three brilliant witnesses to her day and night of passionate effort. She is pleased with them, but not complacent. Painting, now that she has temporarily spent her energy for it, seems a selfish endeavor. What use are these panels to Muffin, who can't even see them? No, the thing to do for Muffin is just that, do for Muffin. But Claire's not sure she knows how—feeding her is really the least of it. This is what Claire finds herself thinking about, as if in a conversation carried over from dreams. She decides to call Jo.

Jo's voice jangles with artificial perkiness as Claire makes small talk, trying to ease into her rather indelicate question. She figures that things with Muffin must be pretty bad, and comes to the point of her call.

"Jo, I was wondering if I should take Muffin to the bathroom myself if no one's around?"

"Oh, no, Claire. Wait for the aide—you're not trained to do that—"

"Well, I wouldn't want to hurt her—"

"Or her to hurt you! She can be very uncooperative."

"Yeah, I guess you're right." Claire's really relieved, even though this means she might have to endure more such scenes as she witnessed the other day.

Jo sounds relieved too. "Claire, I thought you were calling to tell me you didn't want to do this anymore—"

"Thought I was gonna wimp out on you, huh?"

"I wouldn't blame you. It's a pretty depressing scene."

"Oh, I don't know. Sometimes things are under control, and then it's really sort of peaceful to be with Muffin. I was thinking I might read a book to her. It seems like if I don't talk to her constantly she gets anxious."

"Yes, I know," Jo agrees. "And you can only read the greeting cards from the bulletin board so many times."

"It's weird how she never gets tired of them. I don't know how a person can forget so much and still remember so much. Like she can follow a conversation or a story pretty well. And I swear she remembers how things look so perfectly that she doesn't even know she's blind."

"I think you're right." Jo's amazed that Claire has observed so much in such a short time. "If you stick to subjects that are familiar to her, she's still pretty sharp. Her memory's gone, but not her mind."

"So what do you think I should read to her?"

"Hmm, maybe something to do with animals or nature. Let me see what I've got around, and I'll put a couple of books out for you with the cooler."

"Great! I'll be over in a little while. Thanks, Jo."

"Thank you, Claire. Really, I was afraid that after Wednesday you wouldn't want anything to do with Westcare Manor."

"No way," Claire assures her, "I'm going to do an exposé on the place." The words pop out as a joke, but Claire thinks about it while she showers and finds she likes the idea.

Dressed and organized for a busy day, Claire ventures out to the kitchen. Brianna and Stan Man's greetings waft after her as she passes the den, but to her relief her parents hold their positions. They are engrossed in their work. Everything is normal again.

Claire reads more about the mural in the paper while she eats, smirking at the quotes from Shelly and Brodie, who finally had some comments for the press. Regarding Angela's description of the mural, Shelly offered a scripted reply: "We intend to incorporate into the design all of the elements which have been approved by the City Council." Asked specifically about the reference to "happy brown children," Brodie obliged with a classic Brodie-ism: "We want the mural to be as inclusive in its subject as it is in its process."

*What a load of b.s.*, Claire thinks as she swigs the last of her orange juice. *Art is just so much bullshit.*

The phrase rattles around in her mind on the drive to Jo's house. Then, all the way out to Westcare Manor, she tries to understand how she's come to be so down on the one thing that's always given her so much satisfaction. She's not really going to give up on art, is she?

She thinks not. She thinks she still wants to be an artist. But she's no longer sure it's such a lofty occupation. *Humans have always made art, but over all the ages, they still treat each other like shit.* That's what she's thinking. And as if to echo her excretory theme, the Westcare Manor grounds crew is spreading manure when she arrives.

The ironies of that outrageously lush, green lawn are not lost on Claire. As men and machines swarm over it she gets out her sketchbook and writes at the top of a page: *"Lawns for show and not for pleasure."* Below this she draws a Grim Reaper figure pushing a lawnmower with a sack of weed killer slung over his shoulder. Underneath she writes, *"How about a picnic?"*

She leaves the pad with her daypack in the car, grabs Jo's books and cooler, and assumes an armor of impervious pride as she passes the phalanx of sweaty workers. Certainly their eyes follow her, but hers are focused straight ahead. Then, to her dismay, she finds a maintenance assault taking place inside the building as well. She follows an electrician all the way to Muffin's wing. He has loops of metal tubing over one shoulder and a heavy-looking box under the other arm. Every few feet along the corridor leading to Muffin's room, a panel has been taken out of the ceiling. A man on a ladder greets the man with the supplies.

Claire hurries by, finding Muffin in a bad state. She's calling out, "Help me! Help me!" and looks like she's been in a wrestling match with her wheelchair. Her tray is dislodged and hanging off to one side, so that with nothing to support her upper body, Muffin has fallen forward, while at the same time sliding down and nearly out of the chair. This is on account of her footrests being out of position, so there's nothing bracing her legs. Claire knows that sometimes an aide

# WHERE THE SKY USED TO BE

forgets to lower the footrests for Muffin, but today she gets the feeling
Muffin's pumped them out of place herself. Her legs are sill pumping.
And she's hollering. A soprano aria issuing from the radio doubles the
hysteria.

"Muffin, Muffin! I'm here, we'll get this sorted out." *Did I say this
place was peaceful? Yeah, right!* Claire clicks off the radio on the way
over to Muffin's flailing form. "Wow. What happened to you? Have
you been trying to run away?" She sizes up the situation quickly.
"Okay, we're going to get your feet up on your footrests now." Claire
maneuvers one foot into place and then the other.

"Ouch!"

"Sorry, Muffin. There we go."

"Thank you."

*Always the lady!* Claire thinks. She teases, "You were trying to get
out, weren't you?"

"Yes. I can't stand it. I'm so glad you're here."

"Me too." She hates to think how long Muffin might have been left
to suffer otherwise. "Let's get you sitting up straight." Positioning
herself behind the wheelchair, Claire edges her forearms under
Muffin's armpits. "Now you push with your legs and I'll give you a
lift. Ready? One, two, three!" Claire pulls, Muffin pushes. Together
they get her lanky limbs and torso organized. "Hey, we did it!"

"Oh, thank you."

"See, we'll be okay." The tray goes into place easily enough, but
Claire can't figure out the elaborate system of velcro straps that's
supposed to secure both tray and Muffin to the chair. "I don't get how
this works, Muffin, but it'll be steady enough if you don't push on it
too much. You're not going to jump up and run away again, are you?"

"No, I suppose not. I don't know who you are, but you're awfully
nice."

Claire smiles at Muffin's frank charm. Someone quite unique is
housed within that confused and crumpled form. She hopes that
Muffin will soon recognize *her* as a unique being, more than a generic
pair of helping hands and a solicitous voice.

"I'm Claire. I bring lunch for you twice a week."

"Who?"

"Claire. I come twice a week, remember? Jo makes you lunch and I bring it. Aren't you hungry?"

But Muffin is not so easily sidetracked. "Jo?"

"She'll bring lunch herself tomorrow," Claire keeps her voice calm and soothing, but she feels flustered—in over her head. Muffin is growing agitated again.

"I want to know what this place is! What's wrong with me? I think I'm going crazy!"

"No, you are not crazy," Claire tells her with conviction, remembering what Jo said earlier. "You're just, well, old—and your memory's not so good today. You know, everyone has good days and bad days. You'll do better tomorrow, I bet."

Muffin makes a face that says she's not buying any of it. "That's ridiculous! I don't understand this! I just want to know what's wrong with me!"

By now Claire's gotten the lunch ready. She coaxes the cup of juice into Muffin's left hand and a quarter sandwich into the right. She doesn't have a very good grasp of "what's wrong" with Muffin herself, but she'll tell her everything she knows. *Muffin can take it.*

"All right, Muffin, let me try to explain. You're in a nursing home in New Mexico. Jo brought you out here so she could look after you. You know who Jo is, don't you?"

"She's my daughter."

"Yes, and she's a friend of my mom's. So that's the connection."

Muffin maintains her suspicious attitude. "What's wrong with me? I think I'm crazy."

"You don't remember things. Everyone has that trouble when they get older." It occurs to Claire that Muffin has no idea how old she is. Meanwhile, Muffin is so intent upon the conversation, she chews and slurps compliantly. Claire keeps doling out the food.

"I don't know who you are!" Muffin gasps between mouthfuls of stewed plums in yogurt. This is clearly the crux of the problem. Who is this nice lady and how can Muffin not know her? The only explanation is that she must be crazy.

"I'm Claire. I'm helping Jo out over the summer. I'll be a Senior in high school in the fall." She has an idea now of how to set Muffin straight.

"Oh, that's nice." The old lady casts a beneficent blank stare in Claire's direction, suddenly aware that she is in the presence of a tender young blossom.

"And my mom is friends with Jo. They met at the food co-op."

"What are you talking about?" She supposes blossoms speak a different language these days.

"Your daughter Josie, and my mom." Claire stays on course. "Jo is older than Mom—I think she's like sixty."

"Jo?" A glimmer of understanding. "Is she that old?"

Claire smiles. "Yes, and do you know how old *you* are?"

"No." Muffin's voice wavers as if she's not sure she wants to be told.

"You, Muffin, are ninety-one years old."

"Oh, horrors!"

Claire laughs out loud at Muffin's old fashioned cry of alarm. This distress is perfectly sincere, yet of a different flavor than her previous agitation. Claire's made her point.

"It's not horrible, it's cool that you've lived so long. And it's only natural for you to have some health problems and a bad memory. You have a perfectly good reason for being forgetful, and you're not crazy at all."

"I think it's dreadful. Poor Josie."

A shiver goes up Claire's spine. Muffin's comprehension is now so sharp it hurts. As she puts the homemade chocolate chip cookie between Muffin's fingers, Claire leans close and says insistently, "Jo's happy to have the chance to take care of you, like you used to take care of her. I bet you used to bake her cookies when she was little."

"It's good," Muffin says, presumably of the cookie.

Even if Muffin could articulate her thought, the Blossom is clearly too young and idealistic to acknowledge that this is a waste. The old should die and get out of the way. It is simply crass to persist so. Muffin is disgusted with her own rudeness. To compensate, she accepts Claire's attentions without further complaint, until the pleasing feelings of a moist towel cleaning her fingers and face, followed by the gentle pressure of hands kneading the knots out of her twisted spine, make irksome thoughts dissipate into drowse.

"I need to take off now," Claire whispers into her ear. "Is there anything else I can do for you before I go?"

"No. No, I can't think of anything." Half asleep, Muffin means that. She is lost in fog, at sea with no reference point and only a small raft of courtesy to keep her afloat. "Thank you," she says with sincerity, "Thank you for—" clutching for vocabulary, "for the good feeling."

*Yes, Muffin, likewise,* Claire thinks, feeling herself light and buoyed up by Muffin's sleepy vessel. Before she goes, she slides Jo's books, which she hasn't had a chance to look at, onto the shelf in Muffin's wardrobe.

Claire's peace is shattered immediately when she walks up the hall and turns the corner, to encounter a corridor choked with wheelchairs. Half a dozen old ladies assail her as she works her way through the nurse's station. They would all like to have Claire wheel them somewhere. She starts to comply with the most demanding one, and then, seeing that their destination is already the site of a four-chair traffic jam, Claire backs up and parks the woman in her original position. Now the woman is furious, and the others are chiming in more forcefully. Standing with one hand on her hip and the other holding Muffin's cooler, Claire looks severely from one to another.

"Now, look, I am not going to take any of you anywhere. I don't work here and I'm going to get in trouble if I go mixing you all up in the wrong rooms. Just be patient and the aides will sort you out." She weaves her way through the wheelchairs, closing her ears to the insistent whining.

The next wing over is eerily quiet by comparison. Claire's nearly made it to the lobby when she hears, "Honey, please come in here." It's the woman she sometimes sees after lunch, and thinks is so beautiful, the one who reminds Claire of the mahogany Buddhas at the imports store in the Mall. Her skin in burnished brown and her cheeks

big and shapely from smiling. She's alone in her room, sitting in a
wheelchair with a homemade blanket across her knees. A colorful
department store knit turban, with wisps of grey hair escaping, frames
the wide, friendly face that floats over her pillowy form.

The nameplates near the door say "Lettie" and "Marcia." Without
a thought about the time, Claire steps inside and asks, "What can I do
for you?"

"Tell me what that is." Sitting in front of her own bed, the one with
the window view, the woman points to the foot of the bed near the
door. Claire bends down and picks up a single, clean sock and shows
it to her.

"It's a sock. Someone dropped it." She puts it on the bed she found
it under. "That's all."

"You sure are pretty! A regular redhead! Now why don't you sit on
the bed and visit."

Her smile is like the blessings of a thousand grandmothers. Claire
perches on the bed and thanks her for the compliment, though she
doesn't really take it as such. She's not redheaded like some "carrot
tops," and does not consider her freckled complexion the height of
loveliness. But under the Buddha's admiring gaze, she begins to feel
more appreciative of her natural assets.

"Oh, such pretty hair. I wish I had hair like that."

"I bet you've got some really pretty hair hidden under that turban."

"Oh, ho ho!" She laughs like Muffin does, Claire notices, as if
surprised and delighted to find she still has the capacity. "No, I don't
have hair like that no more."

Claire attempts more conversation, but finds it difficult to interpret
Lettie's slurred speech. She would not even know her name if it
weren't for the cards by the door. It seems that Lettie is more aware of
her surroundings than Muffin, but in some ways is less cogent. She
claims not to know anything about "Marcia." She would really like a
roommate, though, she tells Claire—oh, she wishes it could be her!
She insists that she likes to keep her room neat and she tries to be no
trouble at all, by way of selling Claire on the idea.

Claire doesn't doubt that Lettie has high standards for

housekeeping. A happy, yellow-flowered quilt covers her bed, her few possessions are tidy and dust-fee. So Claire sits for some minutes more, smiling, commiserating, nodding at the sentences she doesn't understand. And when the convoluted conversation falters, Lettie can be counted on to bring it back to how pretty Claire is. She's drinking up the young woman with her eyes.

Saying good bye is difficult. Claire feels the wishful pull of Lettie's eyes on her back when she stands up, brushes the wrinkles out of the bedspread and exits into the silent, sterile corridor.

She sketches fast in the oven of her car before starting the engine, drawing the cluster of elderly women in their wheelchairs—a flock of silver-topped baby birds, all mouths and wide eyes, screeching for attention. *They shouldn't have to beg!* Claire turns the page, almost tearing it out in her haste.

*And why do they feel so guilty for being old? Any time Muffin snaps to reality, her first emotion is guilt. Lettie apologizes for not being able to "do" like she used to!*

With quick strokes, Claire roughs out another pair of old women in wheelchairs. She scribbles above one, *"I'm sorry I'm such a nuisance."* Above the other: *"I'm sorry the place is such a mess."*

The car is stifling! She tosses her sketchbook aside and turns the key. She has to get moving before she melts, but her thoughts remain with Muffin and Lettie and all the women they represent.

*Lettie says she's sick and weak from working so hard all her life, says her body's all worn out.* Claire thinks back to Jo's visit the other night and what her mother said about caregivers. *She probably didn't get paid for much of that work. If she had, she'd have a good retirement to live on. What a rip-off!*

By the time Claire arrives at the CARMA meeting, the new mural design has already been sketched out and the elements are being inventoried. She and her classmates will be responsible for providing the studies and detail drawings from which the painting will be made. Josh is taking on the train; Angela and Laurie get to create those "happy brown children" everyone's so uptight about. Miranda claims the portrait of the great Cesar Chavez himself.

"I want to paint Rosa Parks!" Claire announces, hurrying over to the sign-up sheets. Then, satisfied by this show of solidarity with the brave and beautiful heroines of the world, she throws her arms around Josh and becomes a teenager again.

# PART II

# CHAPTER 19
## FIRE SEASON

New Mexico's summer day has turned brown and brittle around the edges by now. There has not been rain since Pow Wow Weekend squeezed the sky dry eight weeks ago. It's not likely to rain for another month yet. The little roadside booths that sprout up this time of year to sell fireworks are doing as much business as they can before their wares are banned. If it stays this crackling dry, Independence Day will come without any rockets' red glare.

Meanwhile, the "water police" are out ticketing folks caught in the act of sprinkling lawns between 9:00 a.m. and 6:00 p.m., when the drops of precious liquid evaporate mid-air before they ever strike parched earth. The rules are not tough to enforce, since yard work and all other outdoor activities become hellish under the mid-day sun. Dawn finds sprinklers spitting, hoses spraying, mowers roaring and hammers ringing. Life is lived in the expansive shadowy foothills of this new season's days, which now replace the single endless day of New Mexico's early summer.

There are other municipal decrees which come with this season of fire. The bosque river trail is closed, as well as several recreation areas in the Serafinas, for fear some careless smoker might spark the tinder box. Therefore Claire and Josh have been stymied in their search for secluded places to make out. They resent the park restrictions deeply, since neither of them smoke or carry matches. They do not perceive themselves as a threat to woodlands. And who would dare tell them otherwise? Still, some wise officials doubtless had couples such as this in mind when they penned their ordinances. For if a flicked cigarette butt or poorly tended campfire pose a hazard, think of the inferno that might be lit by the pent-up passions of youth. Claire and Josh, after little over two weeks of dating, have already reached the ignition point. They are going to "do it" and they both know it—they just can't figure out when and where.

For better or worse, there is no mandated rationing of tears. For better, probably, since Kerri Antresian hates to break any rules. Her household is up at dawn each day conscientiously undertaking their work in the cool of the morning. And more often than not she's apt to get a little weepy while she stands at the stove cooking eggs and tortillas, and looking out the kitchen window into the back yard. Such is the case on this Monday morning.

Sunlight glitters through the shrubby plants of her garden, reflected by water trickling over smooth river rocks and down into the newly filled little pond. A mini spring bubbles up on the east bank in happy abandon, lacking as it does Josh's sculpture and the necessary plumbing to give the water jet some direction. Beyond the shimmering scene, Kerri Antresian's "boys" are pacing off the putting green with rakes in hand, adjusting clods of earth and irrigation heads the way a museum curator would straighten paintings. They are nearly to the point of seeding the quarter acre with the finest bent grass, after which there will be nothing to do but water and wait. And for Josh, sculpt.

*He'll be doing that statue at Gus's shop,* she thinks. *Between Gus and Claire, we'll be lucky to see him an hour a day. Well, at least Claire might keep him in town through graduation.*

Tears gather at the precipice of Mrs. Antresian's high cheekbones. A glass prism twists on its thread over the sink, splashing rainbows across her torso the way the snapping sprinkler shoots droplets of water over the near back yard. Beyond, Nick Antresian, blinded by the sweat that drips from his eyebrows as he attempts to read a level, looks up quickly.

"I imagine your mother's ready for us."

"Breeeeeeeeeeeeakfaaaaaaaaaaaast."

His mom's voice wafts across the yard even before the words are out of his father's mouth. Josh shakes his head. "You guys." He picks up the level and plunks it in the shade with the other tools, then hurries after Nick. As he skirts the pond he slows, his thoughts on Claire and ideas for his sculpture. He hears but does not register the sound of a phone ringing.

"It's for you." Mr. Antresian, eager to dig into his *huevos rancheros*, pushes the phone at Josh when he comes through the door. "I think it's Gus."

"Yo." Josh wanders over to the stove and eats some home-fries out of the skillet. His parents don't allow talking on the phone at table.

Gus launches into an excited monologue about a public art project in Houston. He's going there over the July Fourth weekend to check out the site and see if he wants to enter the competition. Can Josh hang out at the studio and keep an eye on things while he's gone?

"Sure, no prob."

Josh gives nothing away with his expression when he hangs up and joins his parents in the dining room. He devours his food as usual, thanks his mom with a peck on the cheek as usual, and is running late by the time he runs out of the house, as usual. But his brain is not working as usual. Usually he thinks about painting and Claire, sculpture and Claire, the mural and Claire. This morning, though, all he can think about is Claire. Claire and fireworks.

Scaffolding shades the painters, and after noontime the shadow of the building itself brings additional relief. There's a beach party atmosphere—everyone in shorts and tanks, shades and sun hats; coolers of cold drinks on ice; aroma of sunscreen and acrylic. Kevin's set up with his CD player and two shoe boxes, labeled IN, and OUT. He feeds in the discs on a first come first serve basis, occasionally ejecting one that is vetoed by voice vote. Since most everyone is checking in and checking out with Kevin anyway, to drop off and pick up their favorite tunes, Brodie has made him the keeper of the work log, elevating his operation from the sidewalk to a table and chair. Here Kevin reigns as DJ and receptionist, manning a cell phone and a loose-leaf notebook full of sign-in sheets as well as the stereo.

"Well, if it isn't the happy couple."

Claire and Josh saunter over. Josh keeps his arm draped over

Claire's shoulder as she drops a CD into the IN box.

"Yo."

"Hi, Kev."

Their eyes are shaded behind sunglasses.

A great din rises above the blaring Salsa music. Its source is a dozen six- to eight-year-olds who are anxious to paint, and their harried chaperones imploring them not to touch anything. Shelly and Brodie are shouting up at the platforms for Andrew, Celine and Danny to come down and help.

Blessed distraction. Claire looks over at the kids and smiles, shrugging off Josh's arm as casually as she can. "How cute."

"They're only here till noon," Kevin assures Josh. He knows Josh can't wait to get up on the scaffold and work on the train, but he has his orders. "Pick a couple kids and get them working on the Yucca plants. Claire, how about taking the rattler?"

"Great, let me see the detail." Kevin passes her a little color drawing of a rattlesnake, a print-out from Shelly's computer. "Neat." She initials the sign-in book, drops her pack under the table, and goes over to the children, leaving Josh to banter with Kevin.

The kids are too cool. Like Muffin, they command Claire's attention in a way that quiets all competing thoughts and emotions. A slight blond boy with a runny nose, and an even smaller girl with giant brown eyes are put in her charge, and past events and future plans melt away. Pouring paint, picking brushes, holding little hands around brush handles and guiding them from paint jar to wall, this is Claire's entire world. She explains how to make a nice smooth stroke, watch the line, don't go over it too many times, now back to the paint. They look up at her in awe and admiration, and snuggle close when they get a chance despite the heat. If her mind were roaming here, there and everywhere, as is so often the case, she might think how like these babies' expressions are to those of the old ladies at Westcare Manor when they look up at her from their wheelchairs. If the volume of her inner monologue were turned up loud, drowning out the world around her as it so often does, she might be forced to confront the connection between babies and what she and Josh are planning for the Fourth of

July. Indeed, if it were not for the immediacy of wet paint and cute tykes, Claire's brain would by now be up to a full boil with conflicting opinions of the scheme Josh has proposed. Yes, she wants to go all the way with Josh. Yes, she wants to do it in a private, comfortable setting, not in the back of a car. Yes, his studio-sitting for Gus offers the perfect opportunity. But, she doesn't like Gus. She doesn't. She thinks he's creepy. And the thought of doing it in his space, and him knowing about it later, or maybe even before, disturbs her.

Lucky for her she's not thinking about that now. The snake is starting to squirm off the panel as little Damon and Teresa swab in its gold, copper and green diamonds. She gushes that their snake is the best snake ever painted. To her left, Laurie's got her work cut out for her with two rambunctious girls of going-on-nine. The three of them are painting a roadrunner. Beyond Laurie, Angela has a crew working on hummingbirds and trumpet vine. Eddie, their cousin, is alternately helping one and then the other with their broods. He seems to have a lot of experience with kids—the put-upon attitude he showed up with is giving way to smiles and some earnest effort. Claire has trouble believing this is the same young man she first saw staggering out of the Golden Calf. Josh is down at the end. Claire can see him holding up a little boy so he can reach his paintbrush to the top bells of the yucca flower. At the sight, a tiny disturbance ripples the watery place below her navel, but otherwise the serenity of intense activity is unbroken. Teresa's brushed outside of the lines and is crying. Damon has plunged the entire brush and his arm up to the elbow into a tub of green paint....

Josh lowers the boy to the ground to give a turn to the younger brother, who's been tugging his pantsleg. The kids are intense. They hold the brushes in their fists like spears, thrusting the bristles against the brick and pulling downward to leave great gashes of paint. It's a function of their spindly wrists being unable to manage the big brushes any other way. Josh makes a mental note to try it, deciding to use the technique for his Abstract Expressionist assignment for Hartshorn.

He picks up their murky rinse bucket and goes to change it, his helpers tagging along as he explains how they can't keep swishing their brushes in dirty water. He mixes some pale pink for the tips of the yucca blossoms and finds some narrow brushes, a better fit for their small hands.

The time goes by quickly. Because his mind is usually on painting, Josh has learned to reserve a corner of consciousness for all of the rest of life. Today the screens are switched. Off in a corner, observations about kids and paint and murals tick off with businesslike precision, while on the mainstage it's all Claire. She fills his mental canvas, but he finds that he can't think about her the way he thinks about art. She's not a product of his imagination. She's so real and separate, so mysterious. The more he gets to know her the more he knows this. And his thoughts of her, while pervasive, are unformed. He doesn't know what to do about Claire except to love her.

Holding his inner image of her close, even as he casts glances down the bobbing row of painters to catch a glimpse of the real Claire in action, Josh laughs along with the general hysteria. The music is loud, the sun bright, the kids are in high spirits and the mural is a drippy mess. It will take all afternoon to smooth out the lines and blend in the colors. Had the CARMA class painted the same area without the youngsters' help, they'd be done by now. But there's something raw and ribald about this first attack that they would never have achieved. It's as if color had only been invented that morning, and has burst forth from the Mercantile's wall with a big, "Ta da! Look what I can do!" Gargantuan flora and fauna leap to life. The moms and dads and elder siblings collecting on the curb are as thrilled with the project as the young charges they have come to claim.

The art students are left with dirty brushes and open tubs of paint, but soon they have made a cursory clean-up and are backing away from the morning's work to gawk at it with the others. Some are interfering with traffic and setting a bad example for the little ones by straggling into the street. But much of the tie-up is caused by motorists themselves slowing down to get a better look at the emerging mural. Josh leads Claire across the street and under the shade of the bus stop shelter, where they can stand on a bench and admire the work. The voluptuous white-pink bells of the yucca blossom and the boldly tiled diamond-back rattler seem to reach toward each other across a vivid New Mexico Eden—at least that's how it seems to them. Josh squeezes Claire's shoulder and she squeezes his waist.

"Oh, hey. I have a great idea!"

Claire looks up and gets a kiss before she gets an explanation.

"You can pose for my water sculpture."

"But I already posed for the sketches—like eight hundred views!"

"I know." Josh and Claire hop from the bench and back out of the way as a bus approaches. "But if you start coming over to Gus's to pose for me, then no one will be suspicious when you come over for, you know, other things."

"Like any of our folks'll be fooled." Claire takes a teasing approach while her mind works furiously. Should she tell Josh how she feels about Gus? She'd played it cool on her one visit to the studio, but his menagerie of sculptures had made her skin crawl. She can't imagine making love under the gaze of all those unblinking eyes, or in the funky tumble of a bachelor pad futon.

"Oh, to hell with 'em anyway." Josh has already taken Claire's answer as assent. They move on to the opposite corner where their CARMA companions stream in and out of the Big B. "To hell with everyone."

"Spoken like a true artist." Danny has fallen into step beside Josh, so that Claire is spared further comment. And then Shelly pulls up to the curb in her old rustbucket and calls to them from the open window.

"Hey, I'm going to pick up some more paint. If I'm not back by one, start where the kids left off. No one goes up on the scaffolds till I'm back, okay?"

"Well then, get goin' already!" Danny commands. "What're you waiting for?"

Shelly rolls her eyes and roars off.

A small knot of students has formed on the corner to watch Shelly's departure and catch another look at the bumper stickers on her car, now diminishing in the distance. Even after several readings, some of them still make Claire laugh, especially when she remembers that look on Stan Man's face the day Shelly gave her a ride home. *"All men are created equal—poor things." "Explain to me again why I need a man." "I can't even think straight." "Come Out Come Out Whoever You Are." "Conserve water—shower with a friend."*

"What a waste," Andrew sighs. Laurie smacks him playfully as the girls groan and the boys voice their agreement. After initially being put off by Shelly's forceful personality, they'd come to the conclusion that she was "hot"—and the guys who'd been hottest for her were somewhat shaken when the bumper sticker revelation first got around.

Josh had been unmoved either way, Claire notes with approval, as they turn their backs on the good-natured gossip to focus on their quest for burritos. She's got a tight hold on Josh's hand, with their fingers interlaced, and her hesitation about Gus's studio suddenly seems stupid—stodgy. Gus is an artist, and a good one. She doesn't have to like him, like she doesn't have to go for Shelly's lifestyle in order to respect her as an artist.

With a great sense of relief, Claire embraces her kinship to all the kinky, socially unacceptable, obnoxious and opinionated artists of the world. In this community of loners she finally belongs. She decides that it's nice of Gus to trust Josh with his studio, and nice that he couldn't care less what they do there in his absence. Claire smiles up at Josh and tells him so.

# CHAPTER 20
## SECRETS

For some time now, Lydia has had a secret. Claire has been letting it slide because she didn't want the secret to turn into a lie. And she would know if Lydia lied, because she has figured it out—she knows the secret. Since she knows, she could say that this really isn't a secret, never was. But it is something they haven't spoken of.

Now Claire knows. She knows for sure what the secret was, and she knows why they didn't speak of it. She knows because she has her own secret now. It's the way she felt with Josh yesterday afternoon. Even if she wanted to, she doesn't think she could describe it. That's her secret—hers and Josh's. And she can't fault Lydia any longer for breaking their long-ago promise to always tell each other everything. Claire feels respect, even reverence, for Lydia's secret as she does for her own. Now it will be possible to share some things—not everything, but some—now that Claire has joined Lydia in the shadow of a certain secret.

In the school yard the stringy shadows of swing-sets and jungle gyms do little to soften the sun's ferocity. Claire waits impatiently for Lydia to join her so she can share her news. If Lydia would come, Claire would not have to feel so guilty about leaving the mural site early, because she'd gotten there late after seeing Muffin. Her Rosa Parks is virtually done, and Josh has to be left alone to work on his train. It was making her crazy to be so near him and not be with him, so she called Lydia's cell phone from the Big B and took off. Now she sketches lewd pictures in her notebook, carefully turning a page so that they do not appear beside the day's Muffin notes, and thinks about Josh.

Of course they didn't wait for July Fourth. Because once Claire had accepted Josh's plan, it turned out that her wholehearted desire was the only time and place they needed. Before Monday she'd wanted to make love with Josh, but needed everything to be just right. Then, when Josh had it worked out, she was uptight and even the perfect set-up seemed wrong. But somehow on Monday her last line of resistance crumbled—felled perhaps by Shelly's "shower with a friend" proclamation, or the magical images the children had painted on the Old Mercantile. Or maybe it was simply time. She had reached her own personal zenith, and now she would step across the great divide to experience the pleasures of womanhood. So, Tuesday, yesterday, she and Josh met at his house after classes. Mrs. Antresian was taking her late afternoon siesta. Josh took Claire into his room, locked the door, and they laid down too—only they took all their clothes off first. It couldn't be more perfect.

Unfortunately, yesterday's boon of privacy is not likely to be granted again. Security at the Antresian household has already been tightened, because she'd had the bad luck to pass Josh's dad at the corner of the development when she was leaving and he was heading home. Mr. Antresian was on Josh's case the minute he walked through the door, and Mrs. Antresian's too, Josh told Claire today. Apparently, fathers have more reason to be suspicious of their sons than mothers do. Now they can only pray that the Antresians will not share their suspicions with the Stanley-Yosts.

*And so the lying begins*, Claire thinks. She's decided that growing up has less to do with sex than with learning how to lie. It starts with secrets and evolves to lies. *"Secrets are about pleasure and lies are about guilt,"* Claire scribbles under her drawing of a naked couple embracing. Looking up at the Serafinas, Claire is reminded of the drawing she did on her first date with Josh, and then discovered tacked to the wall above his bed. Again she is suffused with pleasure at the mere thought of him. Love is so natural, so easy, so beautiful, it seems to her. She doesn't understand where the guilt comes in.

*The guilt is the evil part*, she decides. *It's evil to make something that's beautiful into something ugly, and to control people by making them hate themselves because they think they're doing something wrong when they're just being normal.* Claire finds that she deeply resents the charade she will now have to play for half the world—the "grown up" half.

"Watchya doin'?"

Lydia arrives at last, surprising Claire out of her reverie. She slams her sketchbook shut, but Lydia has seen as much as she needs to.

"You didn't?!" She stands over Claire, mocking an accusatory tone. Claire nods, grinning.

"Oh, my baby's all grown up!" Still mimicking an older woman addressing a younger one, Lydia pulls Claire off the swing and gives her a big hug. Claire plays along and laughs off the truth of it—that obviously Lydia has been a step ahead, waiting for her to catch up.

They settle onto the swings. Lydia watches their feet draw swirls in the fine dust while Claire brings her up to date. She notices that Claire doesn't reveal the truly intimate details of her afternoon with Josh. Now Claire has a secret—and a lover. *Lover trumps best friend,* Lydia figures.

Though Claire may yet believe that crossing into womanhood will repair the small rift in their relationship, Lydia feels otherwise. Her secret is not what Claire guesses—quite the opposite, and now it seems like the time for telling it has passed.

"So?" Claire has talked herself out for the moment. She waits expectantly for Lydia to take a turn.

"I saw Matthew again last night," Lydia tells Claire.

Claire raises her eyebrows.

"I think we're getting back together again."

"You keep saying that." Claire is noncommittal, taking her cues from Lydia. "How are you going to get rid of Trent?"

"I already told him he's a jerk." Lydia stands up, clearly unwilling to say more. "It's boiling out here. Let's go get some lemonade."

"Uh, sure." Claire feels perplexed that Lydia has failed to reciprocate confidences. To cover, she offers more of her own. "Gus is leaving Josh to watch his studio over the weekend," she reveals as they saunter across the empty basketball courts.

"And you're going to keep him company, are you?"

"As much as I can." Claire glows.

"You and Josh are made for each other," Lydia says. She is sincerely happy for her friend.

They continue on in silence, each young woman lost in her own thoughts. The closer they've come to sharing their secrets, the farther apart they feel. Claire does not intend to give up, though. She's certain Lydia will come around, once she gets used to Claire's new maturity. And in every other regard, their friendship is solid. Claire is eager to update Lydia on Muffin and the mural and to hear about Lydia's latest adventures. But the minute they cross the threshold of the Overmyer home, young Herbert comes bumping down the stairs on his rump singing, "Lydee's in trouble, Lyddledeedee's in trouble!"

"Oh shit!" Lydia bounds past him.

"Oh shit shit shit!" Herbie echoes as Claire follows.

Mr. and Mrs. Overmyer are waiting for them in Lydia's room. They have been sitting on the bed talking, but they clam up when Lydia comes in. They look peeved at Claire's presence, but she doesn't offer to leave—just stands a half-step behind Lydia and looks at the floor. The girls know what's about to go down, or they think they do.

Lydia looks her father in the eye. "What's up, Dad?"

Mr. Overmyer holds up a plastic sandwich bag, gripping the top flap between thumb and forefinger so Lydia can see the contents—something brownish-green and crumbly. "Do you know what this is?" he demands.

"Pot?" Lydia ventures, trying to look contrite.

"No, it is not pot!" her father explodes. "It's oregano!" This announcement has obviously been seething within him, frantic for release. Mrs. Overmyer watches her daughter with an expression of deep concern. Lydia draws in a breath, but holds her reply when she feels Claire tug at the cuff of her shorts.

"Did you hear me?" Mr. Overmyer yells. "Oregano!!!"

"But I thought—" Lydia begins meekly.

"How much did you pay for this?" her father interrupts.

"Uhm—"

"The truth, Lydia," Mrs. Overmyer says warningly.

Claire tugs once, twice, twice more.

"Forty dollars," Lydia mutters.

"Unfrigginbelievable!" Mr. Overmyer bellows and plops on the bed. "And you smoked this stuff?"

"Well, not much of it. It gave me a sore throat." Apparently just thinking about it makes Lydia nearly choke.

"Oh, honey—" He believes her and his tone softens. But now Mr. Overmyer's attention shifts to Claire. He squints at her accusingly and says, "How could you let her get ripped off like that?"

"Daaad!"

"Bart, we agreed—"

As Lydia and Mrs. Overmyer rush to her defense, Claire musters an appearance of righteous indignation. Actually, now that she thinks about it, she really is indignant. The laughter that was ready to bubble out of her goes instantly flat. "Excuse me, but what exactly are you implying?" she asks Mr. Overmyer coldly.

"Bart, we said—" Mrs. Overmyer tries to cut off any reply.

"I'll tell you what I'm implying—" But the honk of a horn below stops him short.

Lydia goes to the window. "It's your dad." Her back is turned to her parents as she shows Claire a remorseful frown. They lock eyes in a swift, silent pledge of unity.

"Oh, great. Thanks a lot." Claire gives Lydia's parents the evil eye and makes a haughty exit.

She flies down the stairs, almost toppling Herbert, so that Stan Man won't feel the need to come to the door.

"Shit shit shit!" Herbie calls after her, as if reading her mind.

# CHAPTER 21
## LONG ROAD TO HERE


Claire and her father have always had their best talks in the car. That's when you can stare straight ahead, watch the road go by, and say what you have to say. You don't have to see how it plays in the other person's eyes. You don't have to let them look into yours. Night is best, the dark gives you permission to follow your own thoughts. Two people train their eyes on the glow of the center stripe and hope they might see the same thing, that there might be a momentary meeting of the minds.

Unfortunately it is not night, and the drive from Lydia's house to Claire's has taken all of a minute. Not a word has been spoken as Carl Stanley pulls under the carport and turns off the engine.

"I didn't even know you'd gotten home until Mrs. Overmyer called and I looked out here and saw your car," he says, by way of opening the conversation. Neither Claire nor her father makes a move to get out of his new pick-up. They roll down their windows. A little breeze scares up the scent of roses and honeysuckle.

"I really wanted to see Lydia," Claire mumbles, feeling confused about what kind of trouble she's in.

"You know, it's been an interesting day around here. Your mother had a call from Mrs. Antresian earlier. She's concerned about you."

Claire leans back in the passenger seat and closes her eyes. "Mom or Mrs. Antresian?" *This is a total nightmare*, she decides.

"Both, and now I guess we can add Mrs. Overmyer to the list." Carl is able to act pretty cool about everything because he knows very little about any of it, only that a variety of Moms are upset with Claire.

"Don't make me go in yet," Claire pleads, eyes still closed. "Let's go for a drive somewhere."

"Lousy time of day for driving, but let's sit here and you tell me

148

what's going on with the Overmyers. I suspect the Antresian business is your mother's domain." Carl tries not to think about *that*. He trains his eyes out the windshield as if they really are taking a drive, hoping this will make it easier for Claire to talk. When she doesn't say anything, he prompts, "So, what's the deal with the baggie that didn't have marijuana in it? I don't even know if I should be mad at you or not." Emily Overmyer had been fairly incoherent on the phone.

Claire glances at her father. He appears to have taken a sudden interest in the recycling heap at the far end of the carport. She keeps watching him as she speaks.

"Lydia just finally got sick of her father being on her case all the time. You know, like if he was looking to bust her, she'd make him happy and give him something to bust her for."

It makes no sense at all now that Claire's said it out loud. Stan Man nods the tiniest bit, and keeps his eyes on the family's embarrassingly high stack of pizza boxes. Claire continues, "So Lydia asks me to get her some pot, and I tell her I can't, of course—"

This is a lie, told out of love. Claire notices how easy it is to tell, too. She doesn't want her father to feel guilty that she certainly could've gotten the pot for Lydia if she'd wanted—all she had to do was raid his stash. No, this would not be a good time to reveal she knows about *that*.

*I must be growing up*, she thinks, moving seamlessly from the white lie back to her honest accounting of the "pot plot":

"We decided that Lydia should put some oregano in a baggie and let her dad find that. You know, that would be even better, because there's nothing wrong with having oregano, and the shame would be on him and his suspicious little mind."

Carl starts to say something but doesn't. He's still not looking at Claire. So she sits forward to finish the tale, also directing her attention to the pizza boxes.

"Well, we put the oregano in Lydia's desk, and when her folks searched her room, like we figured they would, they found it. So the joke's on them, right?"

"Hmm."

"But the weirdest thing is, instead of admitting they were wrong to snoop on her, they didn't get the joke at all. Mr. Overmyer figured Lydia really tried to buy some pot, but got duped into buying oregano—so now he's pissed that she got ripped off. And he's blaming *me* because he's got it in his head that I know everything there is to know about pot, and maybe even put her up to trying it—except that he didn't find any—but somehow I'm still responsible for anything related to pot!"

Claire and her father finally turn to face each other. They're close to getting to the heart of something, and much as they don't want to go there, they are about to arrive at the scenic overview of Truth.

"You really dislike Mr. Overmyer, don't you?" Carl asks.

"Oh, please!" Claire splutters, reaching for the door handle. "He's not *my* father."

"Then what are you getting in the middle of it for?"

"Me? *Me?* You think it's my fault too! How does this have anything to do with me!" Without motion the car feels claustrophobic. She's ready to bolt.

"Stop, Claire. I want you to answer my question. What does Lydia's relationship with her father have to do with you?"

"He's just so down on us, Dad."

"You and Lydia."

"Yeah."

"Mr. Overmyer's down on you."

"Yeah. What is his problem?"

"You're tormenting him?"

"Hey, he started—"

"He's not *your* father, remember?"

They stop for a minute, trying to find their bearings in this previously avoided territory. Then Claire cracks a grudging smile. "Guess I lucked out."

Carl Stanley's heart is so full it almost chokes him. "Not everyone would think so," he tells her. "I'm sure to some I'm the embodiment of an irresponsible parent."

Stan Man's more serious than she's ever seen him. "What are you talking about?"

"You know why Mr. Overmyer suspects you of smoking pot, don't you?"

"Oh, that. Yeah, well—"

"Because your mother and I do. I think we use it in moderation and handle it responsibly. Mr. Overmyer feels differently. He disapproves of us, and I'm sorry he's transferred that disapproval to you—but I'm not surprised."

There, it was out. Nothing to it. Suddenly they both wonder why it's been so hard to get here.

"Okay, so you guys use pot—but guess what? I don't!" In fact, the whole thing seems really stupid. Defiance courses through Claire's veins. "And Lydia doesn't. And if you all want to bust each other for bad parenting, how about doing it in person and leaving Lydia and me out of it? I mean, what a crock of shit—like we're gonna smoke dope because our parents do? I mean, that's as stupid as thinking we *won't* do it 'cause you told us *not* to!" This time Claire pushes the door open and hops out.

"*Touché*," Carl mutters, and slowly follows her into the house. He feels like he's been on a very long ride.

After Carl debriefs Brianna regarding the Overmyer incident, it's Brianna's turn. She tells her husband about the Antresians' concerns. It's something of a predicament for these parents to remember that when they were Claire's age they were experimenting with sex and drugs—probably, hopefully—more so than Claire and her friends. Nonetheless, they're deeply concerned for their daughter. She's spinning out of their orbit, broaching territory where they can no longer protect her, or won't be allowed. For Brianna and Carl, Claire's very innocence and goodness has become a source of danger.

*She's not worldly enough, she doesn't know what she's getting into,* Brianna thinks.

Brianna Yost is prepared to employ any and every rationalization it may take to bring her daughter back under her control. Perhaps it is a survival mechanism of the species, she ponders, which allows parents to overcome their revulsion for hypocrisy in the same way they learn to handle all of the other dirty business of child rearing. She knocks on the door of Claire's room and waits to be invited in, forbidding herself to think about her own teenage escapades. If she does, it will either cause her to soften her resolve—or it will terrify her so much that she might never let Claire out of her sight again!

"Come on in, Mom."

She's been painting while awaiting her mother's inevitable visit. Now she swishes her paintbrush in a jar of water as Brianna Yost sits down on the bed. Claire wipes the brush on a rag, covers her palette with plastic wrap, then pushes some stuff aside and sits on her desk, facing her mother.

"Okay, let me have it."

"I'm worried about you."

"Jeez, Mom, can't you come up with something better than that?"

Claire's forced civility has flared into hostility, which ignites the dry tinder of Brianna's temper.

"Get off your high horse, Claire. You think you're indestructible, but you're not."

"And you're gonna prove it by crushing me right now, huh? Go ahead, beat me down quick before the world does."

"Now where'd you get that idea?" Brianna is floored by the accusation.

"You tell me, Mom. I haven't done a damn thing wrong."

The list of teenage travesties running through Brianna's head is so long she almost laughs. Instead she says, as calmly as she can, "The Antresians think you and Josh are having sex."

"And what's wrong with that?!" This bursts out of Claire with a force that lifts her to her feet.

"I think you're too young," Brianna answers in a measured voice.

"Bull*shit*! How old were you when you started screwing around?"

She's been expecting this, and has a classic comeback ready. "We're talking about you, Claire, not me."

"What's *that* supposed to mean?"

"You need to concentrate on school, and on getting your portfolio together for your college applications. Josh too. Dating for fun is one thing, but this is not the time to get serious and lose sight of your goals."

Claire leans against the desk and wonders when her mother became such an idiot. Or maybe she's being dense on purpose. Claire speaks slowly, as one would to a child, "Josh and I love each other. We want to help each other reach our goals. I personally don't know where I'm going with my art yet, but I do know how beautiful it is to be in love. Why can't love be one of my goals and why should I wait?"

"Romantic love is beautiful. It can also be transitory, heartbreaking and, in this day and age, dangerous." Brianna continues to deliver her pre-scripted lines. In some ways she is happy for Claire, but now is the time to be a mother, not a buddy. "Claire, I want you to be secure with yourself as an individual before you pour yourself into someone else's life. I think you're too young to get serious about Josh."

"Okay, then I'll just screw him for fun." Claire wants to grab her mother by the shoulders and shake some sense into her. Her words do come close to having that effect. Brianna's face reddens. She narrows her eyes at her daughter. Claire kicks herself for crossing the line. *Now I'll be grounded for life.*

"What are you using for birth control?" Brianna snaps, angry and business-like.

"Uhm, condoms." It now dawns on Claire that her mother thinks she and Josh have been screwing a lot. She decides to say nothing to disabuse her of the notion.

"Good. The condoms are your best protection against AIDS and other diseases, and reliable for preventing pregnancy—if you use them *every* time."

"Mom!" Claire thinks that she might be able to turn this to her advantage. "But now that we're having this talk, maybe you can get me a doctor's appointment to get on the Pill."

Brianna looks uneasy. "Only a barrier method will protect you from sexually transmitted diseases," she insists.

"Josh doesn't have any diseases!" Claire is genuinely insulted. Must all these grown-ups judge *her* based on *their* sleazy behavior?

"It may not always be Josh," Brianna says gently.

"Okay, Mom. You know what? I don't want to talk about this anymore. Obviously you're never going to trust me because you know how much shit you got into when you were my age. You slept around, so you think I'm going to. You did drugs, so you think I'm going to. Well, look, I already told Dad that I'm not a dope fiend. And I'm telling you that I'm not a slut. You come in here saying how worried you are about me, and I'm telling you, look, I get good grades, I have a job, I'm going to summer school, I've never had an accident in the car, I'm dating a super nice guy, I'm getting ready to go to college, I don't even have a tattoo or a pierced lip. So what the fuck? What the fuck are you worried about?"

That pretty much does it. Any empathy Brianna might have mustered for Claire has now been obscured by these obscenities. She stands. Claire sits, singed by her mother's acid tone.

"I'm worried about your attitude, Claire, your total lack of respect for people who have been nothing but gracious and generous to you. The Overmyers have gone out of their way to welcome you into their home, and they've been willing to have Lydia over here—in spite of how they may feel about our lifestyle. They know how important your friendship with Lydia is, and I think they see that in general it's been a positive thing for both you girls. So, why would you play that prank on them?" Claire starts to respond, but her mother won't hear it. "And please don't tell me that the Overmyers brought it on themselves, because it is my understanding that you girls did everything in your power to make them think Lydia was getting high." Claire bites back bitter laughter. "It's not funny, Claire. Parents worry. And you do not help your cause by tricking them when the whole issue is about trust."

"But, Mom—"

"Look, Claire, when they acted like they didn't trust you and Lydia, you were insulted. So what do you do? Go out and pull a stunt that proves you're up to trouble—"

"Now, how were we up to trouble, exactly?" Claire wants to know. But Brianna is still ranting.

"Stupid. Just stupid. You think the Overmyers think more highly of either of you now?"

"Well, since they've finally figured out we're not potheads—" Claire tries to defend herself, but her mother's words carry a sting that brings tears to her eyes.

"I'm telling you. It's not about the pot. It's about respect."

"Oh, for crying out loud, Mom—"

"Which you are lacking at this moment! And which you were lacking for the Antresians when you took advantage of their trust and used their home for activities they do not approve of."

"Hah! Obviously they enjoy those *activities* themselves or they wouldn't've had Josh! And by the way, it's Josh's home too."

"You know what I'm talking about."

"Honestly, Mother, I do not know what the fuck you're talking about. I really think you're just pissed at being embarrassed by my friends' parents. But I can't do anything about your shame. That's your problem. I am not ashamed of anything I've done!"

"Fine. And I am not ashamed of grounding you through the Fourth. In fact, I think it will come in very handy. You can stay home and help me clean all weekend, and then you can help with the party on Tuesday." Brianna strides out.

Claire stares at the door in disbelief as it closes on joy. "And Happy Independence Day to you," she hisses, wiping her face on a nearby rag. The streaks of watery acrylic it leaves behind look like war paint.

## CHAPTER 22
## STRANGE SANCTUARY

*At least there's Muffin*, Claire thinks, slipping into her car. She puts on her seatbelt and sunglasses, turns the ignition and backs down the driveway, feeling grateful. This is more than an opportunity to escape the house, she has come to take sincere pleasure in seeing Muffin, especially now that they are reading a book together.

Claire is doing all the reading, of course, but Muffin is indispensable in her role as audience. She follows and enjoys the reading so well that it is a magical experience for them both. And she seems to follow Claire's conversation better too, and to know Claire from visit to visit. They have become friends. In fact, Claire has come to think of her visits to Muffin as a favor Jo and Muffin are granting to her, not the other way around. Today's lunch has provided Claire's second opportunity in two days to get out of the house. Yesterday her sentence had to be suspended for drawing class, though Stan Man insisted on driving her, and here on Day Two her commitment to Muffin has won her another reprieve.

*Exceptions allowed for missions of mercy.* Claire smiles, winding along under the cottonwoods of El Rio to Jo's house. It's a glorious day, cerulean and emerald and only slightly brown around the edges. She allows herself to savor her freedom instead of lamenting its limits. Sun and shadow split the passing pastoral scene into a colorful mosaic. A pheasant startles out from under a hedge and takes flight, swooping up over the car with a cry of alarm. Hummingbirds dart in and out of the bright orange tubes of trumpet vine draping a mailbox and long split-rail fence. Soon she has passed the vineyard and the village post office and is turning down Jo's road.

With relief she finds the cooler on the front porch and no sign of anyone at home. Claire doesn't want to know if Brianna has called Jo to discuss her "worries"—it would be like her mother to do that—but she did call Brodie and Shelly to confirm that Claire had completed the painting of Rosa Parks, and that it wouldn't set the mural back too much if Claire missed a few days. This is the centerpiece of Claire's punishment—to be separated from her CARMA companions and deprived of going to *any* of the painting parties planned for the long holiday weekend. No phone privileges either.

Claire had only a few minutes to talk to Josh after drawing class yesterday. She told him the bad news—that she was not likely to see him or talk to him at all until sometime next week. Josh promised to spend all his time on the fountain sculpture, and finish it, so that once Claire's sentence is served they can spend every minute together.

*Why are they trying to turn us into Romeo and Juliet?* Claire wonders with disgust. Traversing the familiar route to Westcare Manor, she can't help indulging in a little self pity, and a fair amount of self abuse. She should never have made such a big deal about "finishing" Rosa Parks the other day. It wasn't only unwise, but untrue. Claire's been thinking of little things she might touch up ever since. But her parents aren't buying it and neither is Shelly. *I am never going to share anything about my life with any of them ever again,* Claire resolves, *not if they're going to use everything against me!*

The brilliant summer day fades into a blur as Claire fumes. *There really could not be a worse weekend to be grounded. We're going to miss everything!* She'd planned to introduce Lydia to the CARMA crowd this weekend. Instead, they won't even be allowed to see each other. Claire practically cries every time she thinks of the injustice.

But then, she has to save her tears for the worst of the worst—the fact that she will not get to spend any time at all with Josh at Gus's studio—or with Josh, period. She aches for him. There is hardly a single moment when she's not thinking of him. Doesn't her mother know that this is not the way to encourage Claire to concentrate on her portfolio?

*Why are they coming down so hard on us? It's like she knows—* "Dammit, that's it! She knows!" Claire can't believe how stupid they've been. "Of course Mrs. Antresian told Mom that Gus will be away!"

Now Claire's so steaming mad she's talking out loud to herself, and almost misses her turn. She swings into a parking space, shuts off the engine and stuffs some change into her pocket before going inside. She intends to make some calls from the pay phone in Westcare Manor's lobby.

Waves of upheaval and discontent greet Claire at the door, slamming into her with a force that drives her own turbulent thoughts under cover. *What the—?* Not only is there no phone, there is no wall. Has it been only two days since her last visit? The front foyer has been dismantled. The formerly fake-plush decor has been replaced by plywood and plastic. Institutional guts dangle down from open ceiling panels. Yellow tape, such as the police use at crime scenes, demarcates a small lane for wheeling and walking through the construction zone. If there were a phone, she probably couldn't hear well enough over the commotion to use it. A clatter rises from the dining room, a rumble from the line of residents still waiting to file in. The whine of a drill rounds out the soundscape.

Claire, her outrage transferred immediately from parents to nursing home managers, notes that most of the workmen are on break, but this one guy seems to have been left behind with his drill solely to make lunchtime more unpleasant. She advances towards Muffin's room, alarm growing with every step. Furniture lines the hallway. Several of the residents' rooms have been turned inside out in the same manner as the foyer. They had seen this coming—the workmen, the stashes of equipment and supplies here and there, the shifting of furniture and work stations—but now it's an all-out assault.

With relief she finds Muffin's wing quiet, her room intact. Muffin herself is oblivious to the remodeling project, but more than willing to be entertained by Claire's breathless report, delivered during the familiar routine of hoisting Muffin upright in the wheelchair and rolling her into position by the sunny window.

"I think it's only a matter of time before they get to work in here and move everything around," Claire finishes. "I just hope it won't be too upsetting for you."

"Oh, don't worry about that." Muffin doesn't like for Claire to be upset either.

She knows Claire now, though she's never called her by name. She knows her voice, her touch, the way the room sounds when Claire moves through it. She knows Claire has been enlisted by Jo to make these visits, and she knows Claire reads to her. All it takes for Muffin to know these things is for Claire to come into the room and announce herself. In between visits, Muffin sometimes forgets. This doesn't trouble her, because there is pleasure in remembering it all again.

Claire and Jo have been congratulating themselves on Muffin's progress. The regular, well-balanced lunches have contributed to Muffin's improved health and alertness, and there's been some luck with the aides. A young man and a middle-aged woman take turns on the wing. They keep a pattern to the days, so that Muffin is able to regulate herself to the routine of personal care. Then, too, there's Claire, and the reading of books.

Jo doesn't read books to Muffin, though she asks sometimes if Muffin remembers Claire reading. Sometimes Muffin does. Claire tries to get as far along as she can in their short sessions, and always reads to the end of a scene or a chapter. It takes persistence. Claire must manage the book and the food at the same time. She interrupts herself periodically to chat about what they are reading. The way Muffin is able to follow the story and react to it is one of Claire's greatest rewards. She's been working hard on her delivery, so as to bring out all of the nuances of the writing. Occasionally she indulges in a little impromptu editing, but usually she can make the meaning come through in her voice.

So far they're only on the first book, a nature journal by a woman who adopted an injured wild quail. It's cute and sentimental, sometimes so much so that Muffin and Claire laugh at it. Yet the descriptions are careful and vivid. There are a few drawings, which Claire describes to Muffin, but otherwise Claire is "seeing" the action in her mind's eye just as Muffin does. They are equals in the discovery of the story.

Muffin's mind's eye is acute, Claire finds, and her life experiences, which the reading somehow makes accessible, are rich and varied. In fact, Muffin adds to Claire's appreciation of the book because she has first-hand knowledge of the time and place described. That's why Jo suggested it, but Claire's been trying to think of some other books to read. She's eager to move on to something that's not so corny, something that will test Muffin's imagination still further.

There's another thing, too. The little bird is going to die, that much has been foreshadowed. What other way could the story come out? Now that they are up to the last chapter, Claire feels uneasy. Already, in a previous chapter, the aging bird went blind, though only temporarily. Claire wondered if Muffin would relate the aging and decline of the animal to her own condition. But Muffin, who does not perceive herself as blind, was untroubled.

Claire thinks of this as she slips her hand into the narrow closet and feels around for the worn hardback on the top shelf. The door will only open a few inches due to the placement of Muffin's wheelchair, but Claire always forgets to get the book out first. She apologizes to Muffin for jostling her, then settles down to serve lunch. First she reads Jo's menu out loud, and the note to herself. It's about the remodeling project, of course. Claire folds up the paper, noticing how peaceful the wing is. The man with the drill and the noisy residents are hallways removed. For now, anyway, this little room at the very end of the very last wing is a safe haven.

"Muffin, do you remember the book we've been reading?"

Muffin knits her brow.

"It's called *A Bird in the Hand.*"

Big smile. "Yes!"

"Well, we're going to finish it today. We only have one chapter left." Claire makes sure Muffin has a firm grip on her cup of juice, and places a quarter sandwich in the other hand.

"Really?" Muffin begins to munch contentedly.

Feeling the need to prepare Muffin—and herself—for the inevitable conclusion of the story, Claire says, "So, we know how this book is going to end, don't we?"

"We do?"

"Well, if you remember, the quail—named Rosie—has been with the family for three years already. Last week we read about how she had a problem with her eyes and was getting old. So I'm afraid this last chapter, which is actually called, 'Farewell' is going to end with Rosie dying." She holds her breath. No comment from Muffin. "Do you think we can handle that?"

"I think so." Muffin is unflappable, even amused.

Claire rests the open book against the edge of the tray and leans forward as she begins to read.

This last chapter is a short one. Claire reads slowly, in no rush to finish. Mid-way through, she must put the book down to spoon-feed stewed plums, using the time to remind Muffin of some of Rosie's earlier, more light-hearted adventures. She has come to feel comfortable with Muffin, like she can talk to her about anything. However this isn't really so—many topics lead to confusion, but even the confusion isn't so bad. Their trust and fondness for each other bridge great gulfs of communication.

Claire serves dessert, a cup of "iced coffee" and a chocolate chip cookie. "Okay, back to the story."

Muffin is fully enjoying herself, eager for Claire to continue. She finds nothing sad or scary in the approaching conclusion to Rosie's life. First, it is a bird. Not *just* a bird, but a bird nonetheless, and however artfully written about, a bird can merit only so much emotion. And second, death after a long life is not only inevitable, it is a blessing. Surcease of want, surcease of pain. She envies little Rosie, and wishes someone would write an elegant ending to her own episode—before it's too late for elegance, if it isn't already, which it probably is. Too bad the only Author she believes in is feckless fate. So prayers are out. If anyone goes to hell, surely spiritual hypocrites do, and she does not intend to be among them.

This is Muffin's attitude, though by now the words for such thoughts are gone. She doesn't miss them much. The book has words to spare for her. Her brain can borrow them for a while. It makes her feel full, like the food. She is happy when Claire reads.

The telling of Rosie's passing is tenderly philosophical. When the bird's mistress awakes to find the little quail sleeping in her upturned hand as often happened, she thinks of the biblical phrase, "What is that in thine hand?" We all have at hand some tremendous power for good, the author explains, if we would only see it. Rosie, in the way that she raised awareness and appreciation for our wild neighbors and brought delight to so many, was such a force.

Tears well up in Claire's eyes. *Rosie and her human friends are all long gone*, she thinks, *yet here they are still, a "power for good," bringing happiness to an old woman*. And at the same time the words seem to be written especially for Claire, to make her see what a power for good she holds in her hands, which is her relationship with Muffin. It has taught her kindness and patience—for a few hours each week she is lifted out of her self-absorbed thoughts. But best of all there is Muffin herself, a surprisingly complete being in a sadly broken body. To love her seems even more revolutionary than loving Josh. At this thought, a big lump of emotion in Claire's throat chokes off further reading.

"Muffin," she wails dramatically, trying to make a joke of her sentimentality, "this is making me sad."

"Awww," Muffin croons with tender amusement, as if soothing a child with bad dreams. She is not completely innocent to the real source of the Blossom's distress—the parallel between the dying bird and herself. Claire is getting a preview of how it will feel when Muffin dies. Muffin thinks it's just as well to be out of words at this moment. The young can't do anything but feel these things intensely. The old can't do anything but try to remember. Muffin turns her blind eyes slightly away from Claire out of courtesy, because she can tell that the Blossom is crying.

Claire collects herself and reads to the end, voice steady but tears streaming. In two short paragraphs Rosie succumbs to age and is laid to rest. Muffin listens with equanimity.

Claire closes the book, gets up and squeezes past the wheelchair. "I need a tissue," she explains, reaching for one from the nightstand. "These animal stories really get to me."

Muffin chuckles, playing along, as Claire returns to her seat and blows her nose noisily for comedic effect.

"Do you believe that? I'm crying about something that happened fifty years ago!"

Claire's actually crying about something yet to happen, which seems just as silly, now that she thinks about it. But then, there are so many other things to cry about—and the pettiness of them in the face of Muffin's eventual loss is worth another good cry all in itself—so that when Muffin says, "Oh, you go ahead and cry if you want," Claire lets it go and sits on the bed weeping.

Muffin dozes off to the poorly muffled sobs. She wakes to Claire's gentle rubbing of her neck and shoulders.

"Oh, that feels so good. You're so nice. I don't know why you do it."

"It's the high point of my day, Muffin," Claire answers.

"I think you're crazy."

"I think I am too, but not for enjoying these visits."

"Then why?"

"Because I can't get along with anybody." Sometimes Claire tells Muffin about her social gaffs—*my life as soap opera*—so this is not an altogether surprising thing to say. But Claire is surprised Muffin has woken so alert from her mini nap. She chuckles at Claire's confession, which makes Claire laugh too. "Except for you, Muffin. I guess you and I get along okay."

"Then we're both crazy."

"And that's why I like to come here."

The hall begins to fill up with residents, some returning to their rooms around Muffin's, and some displaced by remodeling in other wings. Claire gives Muffin's bony shoulders one last squeeze and says good bye. The old woman is ready for a serious snooze. Her head nods to the side again. "Don't worry, you can get another button," she murmurs to Claire by way of consolation, and drifts off.

Claire stands before the frail form as if consulting an oracle. Perhaps there is a secret wisdom in that garbled speech. Or maybe the message is beyond words.

On the way home Claire is extra observant of the changing landscape, as she savors her last moments of freedom. Thinking of the darkness that engulfs Muffin—and yet doesn't because so many images still reside in Muffin's mind—Claire opens her eyes to the great wide world and lets the scenery stream in. *Be happy in love*, she tells herself. *Be happy for loving Josh, even when you can't be with him. Be happy for loving Muffin, even though she won't be around much longer. Yes, love hurts, but only because it's so beautiful.*

Claire opens her eyes wide and feels herself filling up with beauty.

# CHAPTER 23
## MUTINY

Lydia is also at large on this Friday afternoon, and for the same reason as Claire—to fulfill her work commitments. A number of houses will be showing over the weekend, and she has several errands to run for Overmyer Homes. None of these takes her anywhere near the Old Mercantile, but she is able to zip through her West Side itinerary and then slip down the valley ahead of rush hour. "Thank you," she tells the mysterious force that seems to be clearing the way for her. The traffic lights are all green, cars peel off to make left and right turns, the road opens up for her. What she's doing is mutiny. But it is a righteous mutiny. No doubt this is why the way has been made clear. Traffic continues to favor her through downtown, past which it dissipates completely.

*She* has *to be there*, Lydia tells herself. But the closer she gets to the Cesar Chavez neighborhood, the more uncertain she is of finding Claire at work on the mural. *Why hasn't she gotten the e-mail going again? They must be coming down really hard on her.* Would the Stanley-Yosts actually keep Claire away from her art classes? Have they forbidden her even to see Muffin?

At this point, Lydia wouldn't put anything past them. Both sets of parents have apparently lost it. The level of reprisal is unfathomable in its severity. *There wasn't even any pot!* And in Lydia's case, how could her parents possibly wound her more deeply than to think she's stupid enough to pay forty dollars for a bag of oregano! Certainly it's occurred to Lydia that her dad was yanking her chain, maybe trying to get her to admit she knew what pot was so he could bust her for *that*. Either way, Wednesday's confrontation was a humiliating display from people who are supposed to be her biggest boosters. And as far as the Stanley-Yosts go—she expected *them* to be more understanding. Lydia's always envied Claire for the way her parents support and encourage her interests. Now, in a way, she's more disappointed in Claire's parents than her own. *She* has *to be there.*

Kevin's boom box is heaving out the newest *Scrapper* CD, so that Lydia hears the mural before she sees it. She turns off the air, lowers her window and follows the music to the corner of Merchant and Soldiers. Seeing no parking places on the street, she pulls into the Big B, and then stares at the mural across the street. The scaffolding is still up. It carves the wall into smaller squares, like the leading in stained glass. The colors of the painting are as vivid as stained glass too, and the sun-tanned figures on the scaffolds appear to be part of the composition. The overall effect is so dazzling that it takes a while for the flowers, the river, the train, the children and animals, and the portraits of Cesar Chavez, Rosa Parks, Susan B. Anthony, and Dr. Martin Luther King, Jr. to emerge from the sea of color.

*Oh. My. Gawd.* For a minute, Lydia can't remember why she came. She slides out of the car and locks it, still staring.

"Pretty impressive, huh?" It's Andrew, who's come out of the Big B with Laurie on his arm, and he's looking Lydia up and down like she's more impressive than the painting. Laurie looks her up and down too, with a somewhat different expression.

Reluctantly, Lydia turns from the mural and, with an equally cool sweep of the eyes, sizes up this attractive couple.

"Mr. B. won't let you park here unless you buy something," Laurie informs her with pronounced attitude.

"You must be Laurie." The tone of voice is the tip-off, and the black leather shorts the clincher. Ignoring Andrew, Lydia puts out her hand. "I'm Lydia—Claire's friend? Is she here?"

"Uh uh." Laurie shakes hands limply. "We thought she was sick. Shelly said she wasn't coming."

"She's not sick, she's grounded, and it's my fault. We're both in a ton of shit, but I thought they'd at least let her paint."

Laurie's expression brightens. "Girlfriend, you better come over here and meet Dori and Angela and tell us what's going down." She takes Lydia by the elbow and leads her across the street. "Then we'll decide if it's something for the boys to hear," she adds over her shoulder to Andrew, who is following morosely.

"What about my car?"

"Andrew, please go back to the B and get Lydia a—" Laurie stops and looks Lydia over again, "—a frozen yogurt supreme, mocha-mint." Lydia nods, laughing, and reaches for her purse. "Don't worry, Andy can cover it, cantchya, hon?"

Andrew gets Laurie back by bowing gallantly to Lydia with an ingratiating, "At your service," before leaving them.

"And don't forget to tell Mr. B it's for the girl with the car!"

"That's Andrew," Laurie tells Lydia. "Oh, and here's Dori."

"Sure, I know her," Lydia says coolly. Of all of Claire's art friends, Dori is the one Lydia could never stand to be around.

*But maybe this isn't the same Dori.* Lydia notices that this Dori is smiling and expansive, nothing like the sullen creature who would duck her head whenever she spoke, so that spikes of bleached blond hair hid her eyes. This Dori holds her head high and acts like she owns the place. They all do, actually. Lydia realizes she is seeing the artists in their natural habitat—and all of the ugly ducklings have turned into swans.

Though she doesn't count Claire, her best friend, among the creeps and twerps, floozies and flakes that populate the creative fringe of Schoolville, she knows that Claire does. "The fringe of the fringe, that's where I'm at," Claire's told Lydia more than once. But she's been totally popular since getting into this mural project.

Guilt stabs through Lydia, more guilt than she's felt all day—which has been quite a lot. Now she sees how special this is, how cool everyone is, and what she'd love more than anything is to see Claire here—belonging. Instead she has to confess to Laurie, Dori, and Angela, who has been hastily rounded up and introduced, that it's her fault Claire will be missing all of the weekend festivities. And then she's going to have to talk to Josh. She can see him up on the scaffold painting in the lettering on the train's boxcars.

"Oh, thanks." Andrew appears, hands Lydia a frozen yogurt and is quickly shooed away.

"Okay, spill it," Laurie leads her flock around the corner and out of view.

Lydia tells her tale. By the time she's done, all four of them are laughing so hard they can hardly stand.

"Okay, okay," Angela gasps. "I think I have a plan. First of all, let's simplify the story, and just tell everyone you guys got busted for smoking pot—not for *not* smoking pot!"

"Yeah," Dori concurs. "Shit, man, you don't want to ruin your *reputations*!"

That gets them all going again, until the shifting shadows remind Lydia that she's expected home soon.

"The plan, the plan! I'm going to be so late."

"Oh, right, Lyd. Sorry. Better be a good girl so they'll let you come to our July Fourth party."

"I don't know about that."

"But it's just around the corner from you."

"Hey, cuz, *que movida*?" Laurie wants to know, dabbing at her eyeliner.

"We'll move the party to Claire's house. That's all. I'll tell Danny, we'll spread the word to everyone here, Kevin will get the phone tree going—"

"But her parents—"

"Screw 'em. Claire can't come to our party, so the party's coming to her."

"But her parents are having their own party."

"Yeah, and Claire's doing all the work. So we'll crash it." Lydia, Laurie and Dori look at Angela in awe. "Cool, huh?"

"Well, at least that gives us a little bit of good news for lover boy," Dori says, making a face. They turn to see Josh peeking around the corner.

*If it doesn't backfire.* Much as Lydia admires the girls' guts, she has a sick feeling that she's initiating a chain of events which will lead to even harsher punishments. *I hope it's worth it!* Lydia tries to imagine the Stanley-Yosts' expressions as Claire's friends come to the door, more and more of them, with sodas, snacks and attitude. *Yes, definitely*, she decides, imagining Claire's expression too.

The girl gang fans out to spread the word about the party. Now the buzz around the mural rises even higher, and Lydia feels the tingle of many surreptitious looks. She hurries over to talk to Josh. In a few words Josh lets Lydia know that he's as responsible for Claire's problems as she is, and his social life is also under wraps for the weekend. Lydia quickly explains the plan for July Fourth. He nods. "I'll just say I'm going to Gus's—since Claire's grounded, I can spend all the time there I want."

"I'm really sorry—"

"Listen, Lyd, if you can possibly get a message to Claire, tell her to be ready to split when we come by on the Fourth. If the 'rents kick us all out, we're taking Claire with us." His eyes are like laser beams.

"Ooo-kay." Lydia takes a step backwards. "Later, Josh. I really have to go." She hurries to her car.

The great ones watch as she drives away, their expressions also piercing despite being fractured by scaffolds and ladders. But Claire's Rosa Parks seems to have a special twinkle in her eye for Lydia. *"You go, girl,"* her look says.

Lydia gradually calms herself in the cocoon of her car, crawling along with afternoon traffic. She has succeeded in stirring up still more trouble while failing to make contact with Claire. It's time to plot her next move.

# CHAPTER 24
## JUST SAY IT

The last time she saw Muffin, Claire remembers giddily, she came home to a love letter from Josh! No one said she couldn't get letters or send them—even prison inmates get to write to people. Josh had written her a long letter after seeing her at the U on Thursday, mailed it from the central post office, and it was delivered Friday afternoon, sealed with several layers of packing tape.

A really, really, *hot* love letter—illustrated! It makes her weak in the knees to think about it. Over the course of the weekend she read it easily fifty times. And she has it with her on this rare Monday visit to Muffin, so she can read it a few more times before returning to the house and her life as scullery maid.

Not the least wonderful thing about the letter, when it came, was the idea of it. Claire wasted no time in writing quick notes to Josh and Lydia. She'd noticed the mail truck still in the neighborhood on her way in, so under the pretext of cleaning up the front yard she kept her eye out for the letter carrier to come down the opposite side of the street. When she did, Claire dashed over and handed her the envelopes which would be delivered the next day.

Claire's note to Josh was sealed within an envelope within an envelope within an envelope within an envelope.

Her note to Lydia said: *"Daddy's downloading! I swear he figured out we were e-mailing last time, and he's doing this to spite me. He's been on-line continuously since Wednesday night. Use the shoe."* She used a fake return address so Lydia's parents wouldn't be tempted to peek. The girls would have to revert to childhood methods.

Lydia, who continues to be granted a reprieve for a few hours each day in order to serve the interests of Overmyer Homes, and who drives by Claire's house on her way from and to her own, responded late Saturday afternoon with a message tucked inside the muddy sneaker left by Claire on the Stanley-Yost's side porch after a round of gardening: *New moon tonight. Look for Spica in the west.*

That meant that Lydia was going to sneak over after dark and Claire was to watch for her. Fortunately, Claire's parents were crashed out well before midnight. Lydia popped in through Claire's bedroom window, and the two friends quietly exchanged their most essential information before she popped out again an hour later. Lydia was fairly certain she hadn't been missed. She'd said good night to her parents when she stepped outside with her telescope, and then waited for their bedroom light to go out before leaving the yard. The light was still out when she returned, and she resumed her star watching, finally going to bed around three.

Claire was up late too, painting. Both girls slept in Sunday, and when they woke, found they had their phones back.

"Why, do you suppose?" Lydia asked Claire through the blessed device.

"They must've figured out you came over and, like, what can they do about it? Lock us up?" Claire was thinking about Josh's message that she should be ready to go with him on Tuesday. Could she do it? Would she leave her parents' house without their permission? And if so, could there be any turning back? The girls spoke briefly by day, and then talked late into the night, strategizing for any and every eventuality.

And now, Monday, the Third of July, Claire reflects that she's had a lot of communication for a girl who's grounded. There have been a few—very few—concessions on her parents' part. Letting her come out to see Muffin today is one. With Brianna's permission, Claire and Jo traded Muffin days this week. This way she'll be able to help put the finishing touches on the mural Wednesday, by which time her punishment will have ended. *Assuming I don't screw up,* she reminds herself.

Claire pulls into the Westcare Manor parking lot, her head full of schemes. Trying to bring her attention back to Muffin, she scans Jo's note for clues about what she'll encounter at the besieged Manor today. Things have stayed about the same, Jo reports, the assault hasn't advanced much over the weekend. But a couple of things are missing—Muffin's "snuggly pillow" for one, and a yellow sweater.

Claire goes inside and finds the source of the problem behind a door marked Housekeeping. The door has been propped open to reveal a room *full* of dirty clothes and linens. Full to overflowing. Mythically full, like the mountains of straw the miller's daughter was supposed to spin into gold for Rumpelstiltskin. It's a sight to make the heart sink.

Claire's pace quickens. How is it that she never comes down Muffin's hallway at less than a trot?

"I'm cold," Muffin complains before Claire can announce herself.

"I'm not surprised. You have no socks." She also has no t-shirt under the nubby yellow sweatsuit she's wearing. Claire zips up the jacket to Muffin's chin and raises the collar. She turns down the air conditioning. "Feel better?"

"Yes."

"Good."

"I'm cold."

And the game is on. Claire puts a blanket over Muffin's lap and scours the room for socks—maybe a dirty pair left under the bed— She's about to take off her own socks and put them on Muffin's feet when a tiny woman appears with a cart of clothes and a litany of excuses. Machines broken, people out sick, extra washing due to the remodeling.

Claire marvels that the woman can manage a smile, but she does. She has washed a selection of garments for each resident and now extends a pair of socks to Claire, then tucks the rest of Muffin's paltry ration into the bureau drawer. Smiling. She even takes a minute to tell Claire how nice it is to see family there taking care of their own, and to tell Muffin how pretty her granddaughter is.

They do not correct her, as that would prolong the intrusion. "Alone at last," Claire proclaims when the overburdened worker has moved on to the next room. Muffin smiles her agreement.

Claire updates Muffin on the progress, or non-progress, of the remodeling. She exaggerates a bit, in order to elicit an appalled, "Horrors!" from Muffin. It cracks her up when Muffin says that, and Muffin has caught on. She'll oblige at the least provocation. They talk and laugh all through the delayed lunch. Next time, Claire promises, they'll start a new book.

"Tomorrow's July Fourth," Claire tells Muffin on her way out.

"Oh, goody," Muffin replies, using another phrase that seems to especially tickle the Blossom.

Back home, Claire plops down at the dining room table and starts working in her sketchbook. Like the school yard, this most public place is often the most private. Out in full view of her parents, obviously absorbed by her project, she might be left alone for hours on end. If she's behind a closed door, they'll eventually feel obliged to check on her, but here they tiptoe around, going out of their way not to disturb. She sits and sketches several scenes of Westcare Manor using the deep perspective of animated video games—a nightmarish rendition of nursing home as *Trapped on Planet Goth.* In the final scene, a space-suited Muffin declares, "Horrors!"

Satisfied with her work, Claire stuffs her art things back into her pack, tosses that into her room, and joins Brianna and Stan Man in the office-den. This is the last room to be made presentable. Brianna's timetable has them finishing by dinner, so they'll be ready to start on the food preparation this evening. Claire pitches in happily, knowing that tomorrow many of her friends will be coming to the house for the first time. It's all she can do to contain her high spirits. She's pretty sure her parents' friends will accept, even enjoy the teenage invasion—some will be bringing their own kids of various ages—and so her parents will have to make nice. *It's going to be the biggest and best Fourth of July party ever*, she tells herself. She runs the vacuum cleaner over the drapes—something even Brianna would never think of doing—while mentally trying on a few dozen outfits.

Lydia calls at midnight.

"Watchya doin'?"

"Painting."

"That thing you were working on the other night?"

"Yeah."

"Oh."

"Oh? What'd'ya mean, Oh? You don't like it?"

"Uhm. Not really."

"Why not?" Claire stands back to admire her canvas. Finally she has achieved the right shade of steel grey.

Lydia sits in a lawn chair by her telescope at the far end of the Overmyer back yard, seeing the painting in her mind's eye. "Whatever happened to color?"

Claire laughs. "This from someone who spends all night looking into space?"

"Only when I don't have to get up in the morning."

"I'm just saying that there's no color in space."

"There's no color where there's no light, but space is very colorful under the right conditions."

"Same for my painting. At first it just looks grey, but you see more and more colors the longer you look at it."

"Whatever you say."

"It's supposed to represent alienation."

"Whatever."

"Lydia!"

"Look, I know I know nothing about art, but c'mon, if you have to tell people what a thing represents, why not just write an essay?"

"Duh. I don't want to have to *tell* you it's about alienation, I want to make you *feel* it. And I think I succeeded."

"Whatever."

"*Lyd*ia!"

"I just think that if you have a message, if you really have something to say—and I think you do—you should just spit it out. I'm sorry, but I'm not into that abstract shit."

*Art is so much bullshit.* Claire said it first. Still, it's troubling coming from Lydia. Claire flips open her sketchbook and props it up on the work tray next to her easel. She steps back and compares the grey canvas to the cartoon-like drawings she made earlier.

"You know, you may have a point."

"Really? I was just giving you shit."

"I know. But you're right. When you're right, you're right." Silence. Claire can tell that Lydia's looking through her telescope. "So, should the same principle apply to you?"

"Huh?"

"Like, if you have something to say to me, maybe you should just spit it out?"

Silence. Now she can tell that Lydia's no longer looking through the 'scope.

"I know there's all kinds of shit you're not telling me, Lydia."

Silence.

"What happened with Trent?"

Softly, "I can't tell you now, Claire, not on the phone."

"Tomorrow then. Before the party. Are you coming? Mom said she talked to your mom."

"We're all coming. She invited everyone!"

"Oh, shit!"

"What did you expect?"

Silence.

"Claire, we'll talk. I promise. I'll try to come early. I've wanted to talk to you, it's just— I don't know. It's stupid. I know it'll seem stupid."

"Oh, Lydia, what isn't stupid? I swear I feel like that twenty times a day—that everything that's important to me is either really stupid, or someone's trying to make it stupid or to make me feel stupid about it, just so it *won't* be so important to me, and I can be a slave to what's important to them instead."

A quiet few seconds pass while Lydia digests this. Then she says, "Claire, you really should do more of your painting in words."

# CHAPTER 25
## INDEPENDENCE DAY


Claire wakens in a state of revelation on the morning of July the Fourth. She opens her eyes to watch a future, which has always been hers, reveal itself on the textured plaster of her bedroom ceiling, and wonders why she didn't see it before. "I'm going to be a cartoonist," she says aloud, envisioning a parade of clever characters cavorting in the streaks of sunlight. These are her artistic offspring, waiting to be born.

*I'm going to be a cartoonist!*

Hasn't she always been going in this direction? Remember that comic book she made in Junior High? And the captioned poster for Earth Day last year?

Today truly is Independence Day for Claire. She feels a sense of tremendous liberation. She's no longer adrift, but is in command of her own destiny! She is no longer following in the shadows of more purposeful individuals—Josh, Shelly, Mom and Dad—but will take the lead in her personal parade of one. She is her own person because she knows what she wants.

She lets her eyes move from the ceiling to the room, tidier than it's been in ages, swept and polished. The organization is pleasing, as are the smooth, uncluttered surfaces. It facilitates her clarity of mind—the knowing continues.

She knows what's troubling Lydia. Not the specifics, but the gist of it. The secret—what she thought was the secret— Lydia wouldn't hide *that* from Claire. If it was just sex, and it was fun, Lydia would've told her. But something went wrong—if not with Trent then with someone—something that's made Lydia feel bad about herself and uneasy with guys. *Why else would she go back to mild-mannered Matthew?* Claire is a little bit afraid of what Lydia will tell her, but

176

whatever the details, she'll have to find a way to handle it. That's what friends do.

What else does Claire know in this fleeting time of knowing, even as the bustling activity of parents encroaches on her thoughts? She knows that *they* don't own her. That her obedience to them is voluntary and given out of love. She doesn't owe them anything. She didn't ask to be born. They knew what they were getting into, and they have to understand that her love for Josh is non-negotiable. *They have to. It's not as if it never happened to them.* Right then she hears laughter and their bedroom door slamming shut. They've decided to go back to bed.

She rolls over and reaches for the phone. Josh has been sleeping at Gus's studio, so she tries that number first. After a leisurely exchange of sweet nothings, they talk about plans for the party, and how everyone's going to the stadium to watch fireworks after dark. Claire promises she'll be going along, whether her parents give their permission or not. That's just the way it's going to be from now on.

At eleven-thirty a truck from Toby's Party Rentals backs in under the carport and a crew of four sets up a canvas pavilion that takes up most of the back yard. They unload five long tables and sixty folding chairs, collect a signature from Carl and roar off to their next delivery. While Brianna wonders if they haven't gone a bit overboard this year, Claire thinks how fortunate it is that Toby's "holiday package" was actually a better bargain than hiring half as much equipment.

"When the band starts playing, we'll probably get some of the neighbors dropping in," Stan Man says. "And we can use some of these chairs inside, too." He and Claire are running an extension cord from the house out to a makeshift bandstand they've set up under the tent. "Claire, you should've invited some of your friends."

"Great, now you tell me." The twitch of her head as she looks away to hide a smile suggests utmost disdain.

"I'm sorry we didn't say something sooner. But we didn't think you'd necessarily want your friends here mingling with our crowd."

"Yeah, they probably wouldn't want to come anyway." Claire

honestly can't tell if her father is toying with her because he knows what's coming, or if he's being sincere. Her mother is standing in the middle of the tent turning slowly around and around while she contemplates how she wants things set up. "Mom, let's put one of the tables and some chairs under the carport," Claire suggests, "that'll make it a little more roomy out here." *And give us kids another place to hang out*, she adds to herself.

"Good idea, honey."

They work together for the next two hours and are pretty much ready for a nap by the time the first guests arrive. It's Lydia, with her parents in tow, and little Herbert. She rolls her eyes at Claire as Carl and Brianna welcome the Overmyers with rather forced enthusiasm.

The beginnings of parties tend to be awkward, and this one is no exception. Claire and Lydia want so much to talk but they're saddled with Herbie, while Brianna Yost and Emily Overmyer can barely fumble through a routine conversation. Carl and Bart circle the food-laden dining room table attempting companionable comments on the spread. Fortunately, members of the band soon show up, demand beers, and the men start hauling equipment into the back yard.

The first order of business is to get the sound system connected and loaded with CDs, since Stan Man's buddies are not likely to pick up their instruments until they are well fortified with food and drink. Once the first strains of The Grateful Dead begin wafting from speakers set up indoors and out, Carl returns to rescue Brianna, but by then Jo and Jake have arrived along with half a dozen other friends. The newcomers are working their way around the food table, to the kitchen for drinks, and out the back door to check out the tent. At two o'clock it provides precious little respite from the heat, but everyone must take the tour before piling back into the house.

More and more people are showing up, and it's starting to feel like a full-fledged party. Several young children have arrived and taken Herbie into their pack. The kids run in manic loops through the house, out the side door, under the carport, over to the back yard, around the tent posts and in through the back door.

Reginald appears with a gourmet platter of goat cheese pastry puffs and exotic fruits.

Soon after, to Claire and Lydia's dismay, Tony shows up—with his mom! They overhear Reggie making introductions.

"You remember my firecracker waiter, Tony? Foster. And this is his mother, Anita Foster."

She's a pleasant looking woman, clearly anxious about her scowling son. "I hope you don't mind. You know, my Tony goes to school with your Claire."

Too late to hide. Claire and Lydia see heads turn their way. They go over.

"Hi Tony."

"Hi Tony."

"Yeah, hi." Tony looks like he would like to die—and came dressed for the funeral.

"*I* invited him," Reggie declares imperiously.

"And I'm just the chauffeur, I'm afraid," Mrs. Foster says self-deprecatingly. Something terrible comes into Tony's eyes when she says it.

Lydia drops her cup—"Oh, it's only ice!"—and squats down to gather the cubes, trembling.

Claire notices Tony's expression too, and feels for him. "Sure I know Tony. We've gone out for coffee."

"Yeah. Hey! Ya got any coffee?"

Mrs. Foster starts to say something and then stops.

"Yeah, sure, we can make coffee. Ice coffee would be good. Except, none for Lydia."

"Very funny." Lydia shakes the plastic cup of dirty ice cubes at Claire and sneaks a look at Tony. Smiling, he is a different person. Or what she'd seen in his face was merely a trick of light. *Yeah, duh. Get over it already.* But of course, before she can get over it, she has to tell Claire.

Lydia follows Claire and Tony to the kitchen, while Tony's mom calls out weakly to them, "Decaf, honey, okay?"

After the surprise entrance of Tony and Anita Foster, the Stanley-Yosts don't blink an eye when Shelly and then Brodie show up, each with a girlfriend in tow. Laurie and Andrew skip the front door and wait for the others out under the carport. When Claire, Lydia and Tony come out with their iced coffees, Laurie and Lydia greet each other with the playful jibes of old friends.

Miranda, Danny, Kevin and Celine all come in one car. The kids slip into the kitchen, grab some sodas and reconvene under the carport. Angela and Dori are there, having a good old time with Matthew, who's come looking for Lydia.

Only when Josh shows up, politely ringing the bell, even though the front door stands wide open behind the screen, does Brianna look around for Claire and notice that her home is overrun with teenagers. She sends Josh out to the carport and goes to consult with Carl. Along the way she bids goodbye to the Overmyers, who have clearly had enough, especially little Herbie. Above his blubbering babble—stoked by frenzied play and a lunch of black olives and sugar cookies with red, white and blue icing—Brianna thanks Emily for allowing Lydia to stay a while longer. With relief, she then slips into the master bedroom, a small puff of smoke escaping into the hallway behind her.

The Antresians stop in on their way to another party, stay about ten minutes and hurry off as quickly as they can. Paul brings another carload of CARMA kids. They add their contributions to the dining room table, which can barely hold all the food.

No one knows exactly when Kevin takes over mixing the CDs, but there are no complaints. The band cuts him loose around five. When the kids hear the sound of guitars tuning up, they go out back and move all the tables and chairs which Brianna had carefully arranged. A breeze comes up and cools them as they dance. Folks are spilling out of the house.

The music draws Judy and her friends from across the street, and old Mrs. Candelaria from next door, leaning on her nephew's arm. No one says anything about the uninvited guests. Instead, the grown-ups take turns supervising things in an informal way—breaking up clusters of teens that form in the far reaches of the yard to blow dope or sneak swigs from a flask, interrupting couples caught in a clench in Claire's bedroom. Occasionally a young man has the audacity to grab a beer openly, but before he's had more than a gulp, one of Stan Man's friends takes it from him, saying, "Thanks, Dude," and chugs it down.

In short, it's the biggest and best July Fourth party *ever*. Brianna and Stan Man are aglow with good feeling, exertion, overeating and a fair amount of booze. Around eight, their friends with children start to leave. They're going to watch fireworks, either at the University stadium or out at Patriot Park on the west side. These are the only sanctioned displays during the continuing dry spell—but flares, sparklers, rockets, Roman candles and the occasional cherry bomb are already punctuating various neighborhood festivities, as sirens tune up in the distance. Claire's friends make a point of sticking around to clean up some, and everyone says thanks to her parents before they leave, and gets a formal introduction if they haven't already. Eventually the teen contingent is down to Claire, Josh, Lydia and Matthew.

"What d'you think about us going to see the fireworks?" Claire asks her parents. They're lazing around with their closest friends, trying to work up enough energy to go up on the roof to observe the effervescent Fourth of July sky.

"Okay, Claire, you can go. I appreciate your friends cleaning up so nicely." Brianna looks at Carl for support and he nods. Once the kids split, they can stop sneaking into the bedroom to toke up. "Lydia, did your parents say you could go? Do they know you're with Matthew?"

"I just called them. They said it was cool as long as I'm home by midnight."

Brianna rolls her eyes and hauls herself to her feet. Only after she has talked to Bart Overmyer, Kerri Antresian, and Matthew's step-mother does she release the teens to the night with a sigh of relief.

# CHAPTER 26
## ART FINDS ASYLUM

Gus's studio is a small adobe house located on a scrubby piece of land off of South El Rio. The land has been in the C De Baca family for four hundred years. They farmed it so successfully that eventually they built a big mansion for themselves on Main Street east of the Plaza, leaving the farm to hired labor, and selling off pieces of it parcel by parcel, generation by generation. In time the wheel of fortune turned the C De Bacas out of high society; the house on Main was sold, and Ferdinando C De Baca, Gus's great great grandfather, moved the clan back to what was left of the ancestral plot.

Only the one house still stands, and the old barn out back. Gus keeps all of his salvage and heavy equipment there. In between the two buildings the earth has been scraped down to a flat, hard-packed floor of dirt, now draped with tarps, shaded with wooden lean-tos here and there, and bristling with sculptures complete and in progress. Beyond the barn is a trench where clay has been excavated, a trough for water, several rough wooden frames for bricks of various sizes, some rotting bales of hay, a wheelbarrow, and a dozen small piles of handmade adobe bricks.

Gus makes the bricks as his grandfather taught him. Between creative projects he rests in the easy repetition of rectangles. His hands, jarred and blistered from shaping stone, relax into the warm mash of clay and straw. He can always use a few more bricks. Like his grandfather before him, Gus lovingly mends and amends the little house in a process of continuous restoration. Naturally he adds his artistic touch, as he adapts the space to his needs. From front to back the place morphs from a traditional arrangement of boxy rooms into one big room into a swirling, sprawling semi-enclosed patio peopled with statuary, which merges imperceptibly into the cluttered back lot.

The front rooms of the house have been left intact. The dining area serves as a showroom for Gus's smaller works. The kitchen also functions as an office, and the parlor serves every other function. There's a futon, an easy chair, a portable television and CD player that sit on an old dresser, a bookcase stuffed with art books, and a wall of shelves built right into the adobe to hold Gus's collection of curios—a disorganized assortment of natural and man-made artifacts of every variety. Beyond the parlor, all non-weight-bearing walls have been knocked out to make one big work space which opens onto the courtyard through sliding glass doors. The bathroom, tiled from floor to ceiling in Augustus C De Baca ceramic art, is a late addition. It juts out from the back of the house with its own sliding door to its own patio, around which Gus has built a curvy wall to screen the hot tub from view by all but the stars. In short, the studio is both a functional and comfortable place. This is where Gus lives between girlfriends.

He isn't living here at present, but he is anxious to get to work on some ideas for the competition in Houston. Knowing that Katy will be in her usual panic to get to work on Wednesday, after the July Fourth holiday, he's come straight to the studio from the airport. He'll call her at the office in a little while.

Gus is not surprised to find Josh's car parked on the dirt driveway, but he is surprised to find the front door locked. The phone starts ringing as he reaches for his keys. Maybe Josh locked up and went for a walk, and that's why he's not answering the phone? Gus lets himself in and hears the answering machine click on. He picks his way carefully through the front gallery, listening for the message. When he reaches the kitchen he can see the red light blinking on the answering machine. This isn't the first message that's been left. Not so unusual, but there is a queer air of urgency about that flashing light this morning. And something's wrong with the phone—the speaker's been turned off.

Gus grabs the phone and pushes the volume button in time to hear Brianna Yost's unhappy "Well, good bye," and the final click. He skips through the long messages that have been recorded, all from Mr.

Antresian and Ms. Yost, all much the same: "Josh, Claire, please call and tell us you're okay—" But the last one includes a plea to him personally, "Mr. C De Baca, please call me as soon as you get in and tell me if you've seen my daughter!"

Gus puts the beer can he's been examining back into the recycle box, having made a positive ID on strawberry pink lip gloss. He dials the Stanley-Yost's number and walks with the phone, noticing other evidence of guests. To his surprise he doesn't find Claire and Josh asleep in his futon. They have taken the blankets, though, and left their belongings strewn about. He stops to poke into the sketchbooks, nodding in approval.

"Hello?"

Brianna's anxious voice startles him. "Ms. Yost. It's Gus. I just got in." He crosses the room and flings open the door to the main studio.

"Are they there?"

"Yes." He wishes he could drop the phone to sketch that tangle of legs and arms and blankets, the sweep of Claire's curls across Josh's muscular chest, and the granite sculpture at whose feet they lay like sacred lovers in the temple of their goddess.

"They are there? Are they okay? Can I talk to Claire?"

Gus is mesmerized. He didn't expect Josh to accomplish this much in his absence. And it's good, superb.

"Mr. C De Baca? What's going on?"

"Oh, sorry, nothing. You have to understand, I just got in myself. Don't worry, the kids are fine. They've been making art all night."

Distracted, he clicks off and begins to circle the statue. The organic part of it stirs—four arms hastily arrange blankets, two heads follow his movements with wide eyes. The phone rings.

"Nice work." Gus tells Josh with a nod to the sculpture and then to Claire. He hands the phone to her. "It's your mother."

He resumes his examination of Josh's work while he listens to Claire's side of the conversation. She's doing most of the talking, and he's able to get a fairly good idea of what's been going on in his absence.

"...Mom, I know it was mean to make you worry, and I should've called, and I would've, except I just didn't know what to say—

"Well, I knew you'd figure out that I was with Josh—

"Yeah, well, I feel safe with Josh, and you should know that I'm safe when I'm with him—

"But we weren't in a car accident, Mom, and if we had been, you'da heard about it—'no news is good news,' right?"

Brianna's response to this causes Claire to move the phone away from her ear. Josh and Gus can make out every irate word. The three remain as motionless as the surrounding statues while the spate of fury runs its course. Claire isn't listening, she's trying to find the words that will make her mother understand. "Is it my turn now?" she asks when the blast subsides.

"Please. Speak."

"Okay. It's like this, Mom. This is our *last* week. The last week at the U and the last week on the mural and the last week to see a lot of people before they go out of town on vacation. So, since you grounded me through, like, *the* weekend, and for nothing, really, I just—" she struggles for words, "I just—"

"*You just* what?"

"I just wasn't going there again, okay! I mean, once I decided I was going out with Josh last night, and, you know, that I wanted to *stay* out with him, I just knew I couldn't risk getting grounded again. I can't let you do that to me! I have to help finish the mural and I have to have my critique in drawing class tomorrow, and plus, I had this—like this idea about—about art, my art, and I want to check some things out at the U—"

"When have we kept you from studying at the U?"

"I know, I know. But I don't trust you, okay? You don't trust me, I don't trust you. You say you want me to focus, but you're the ones getting in the way of it. I'm sick of being your little hostage every time you get spooked about something. I didn't come home last night because I didn't *want* to come home last night. I don't want to come home now, and I don't think I want to come home tonight."

"But, Claire—"

"I can't deal with all the emotional shit—"

"Well, ex*cuse* me!"

"Mom, can't I please just get through this week?"

"I think you're trying to punish us!"

"Yeah, well, maybe I am— I mean I'm not *trying* to, but you made me so mad—"

"So now you're punishing us."

"It feels sucky, doesn't it?"

"Yeah, sucky. Proud of yourself?" Brianna's voice no longer rings out. It's now so soft that Claire can barely hear it.

"Mom, I don't want you to feel bad. I really don't. I want you to be happy, and I want me to be happy too. So how about if each of us just does what we need to do for ourselves, instead of going out of our way to make each other miserable?

"Mom?

"She wants to talk to you." Claire extends the phone to Gus and when he takes it—cautiously, as if it might burn him—she pulls the blanket over her head and begins to shake with suppressed sobs.

"Hello?" Gus takes the phone back to the kitchen, leaving Josh to comfort Claire.

"Mr. C De Baca, I am so angry at that girl right now, I think it might be better if she *didn't* come home."

"Please call me Gus. And don't worry about the kids. This is a good place for them to be."

"Is it?"

"Come over this afternoon and have a look for yourself—while they're out. We'll talk. It's okay with me if they stay another night, but only if you're comfortable with it."

"But I can't just cave in like that!"

"Ms. Yost—"

"Call me Brianna."

"Brianna, I don't know a damn thing about mothers and daughters, I'll grant you that. This situation has taken me completely by surprise. But I must tell you that from what I've seen and heard this morning, I think what we're dealing with here is a matter of art. Your daughter is an artist, she needs some space. This I do know something about.

And, you know, she is also a *work* of art. Wait till you see what young Josh has created."

"All right. We'll come out. I'm not sure if I should be grateful to you or pissed off at you, Gus."

"Ah, for harboring fugitives. Let's talk it over in person. When can you come?"

By the time he's given Brianna directions and also talked with Kerri Antresian, Josh and Claire are dressed and ready to head out. They loiter around the kitchen for a few minutes waiting to see what Gus will say. He's huddling over a small sketchpad and a sheaf of contest forms.

"Done in the studio?" he asks without looking at them.

"Yeah," Josh says. "We're going to work on the mural."

"Good. See ya later, then?"

"Yeah. Thanks, Gus."

He looks up. "And you, Claire?"

"Huh?"

"You coming back with Josh?"

"Well, yeah, if that's okay."

"Either that, or you go home."

"I'll come here."

"Fair enough." He returns to his work.

"Thanks, Gus. I really appreciate it."

"No prob."

CHAPTER 27
A BODY OF WORK


Brianna Yost's reaction to Augustus C De Baca's work upon first viewing it *en masse* is similar to her daughter's. *Creepy.*

"They all have the same face," Brianna whispers to Carl, as the two of them survey the figures and statuary. Carl shrugs, finding the display pleasingly kaleidoscopic, and the individual pieces remarkable in their execution.

In the front gallery, the trademark C De Baca figures which have made his name familiar nationwide. They range from one to three feet in height and are either carved from stone and polished to a high sheen, or molded in ceramic and glazed in vibrant colors. There are women and couples dancing the Flamenco or Tango, and groupings of *Mariachis* and other musicians. There are also traditional Native American drummers and dancers. The Stanley-Yosts have admired similar pieces in galleries around town, and they've seen a lot of knock-offs in local tourist shops. Now Brianna feels privileged to be viewing a new series which has yet to make its public debut. Several ceramic Katak dancers stand in a cluster next to a window with the sun falling on them. They are very lovely. Gus eagerly discusses the challenge of interpreting in clay the gauzy costumes and precise positions of this exquisite East Indian dance form.

But Brianna continues to be disturbed that every female face has identical mask-like features. The Tango dancers have steely gazes, the Pueblo women, reverent ones. But on close inspection it is always the same face, cast in a particular mood by the hairstyle, costume, and position of the body. Brianna studies the male figures. They, too, have one face, though they vary slightly more than the female figures thanks to beards and moustaches. Brianna is reminded of Barbie and Ken

188

dolls in the way Gus takes his stamped-out, idealized forms, dresses them up in costumes, and poses them. She's tempted to ask if he really enjoys doing this or only continues because the figures sell. Instead she decides to wait and see what's in the rest of the studio.

Gus leads the way through the kitchen and parlor—where all beer cans have been removed and the futon carefully made up—explaining that he spends a good deal of time at the studio but sleeps at Katy's apartment, which happens to be in a restored mansion on Main street, not far from the old C De Baca place.

"The old families, we're like *los lobos*," he tells his guests. "We cover the same ground generation after generation."

Carl and Brianna nod, knowing a bit about local history and the families that founded the city. Gus opens the door to the main studio and begins to undrape the works in progress. As he does so, it becomes abundantly clear that whatever his family history, Augustus C De Baca isn't afraid to step off the beaten path. They circle the pieces silently for some minutes.

"It looks like you put your dancers through a trash compactor," Brianna blurts out, eliciting the answer to her unasked question, as well as a hearty laugh.

"Yes, sometimes I'd like to!"

She's standing in front of a large, sharp-edged block of marble from which sprouts a tangle of human body parts. Are they breaking free from their encasement in stone, or are they in the process of being compacted, as Brianna suggests, compressed into blocks like bales of hay? In each of the half-dozen sculptures Gus shows them there is this element of tortured humanity either escaping/emerging from an indeterminate mass, or melting/descending into it. Despite their similarities, each work is uniquely disturbing. One, a rugged chunk of sandstone, suggests the evolutionary process. Fossil impressions give way to shell fragments, dinosaur bones, petrified wood, skeletal remains of birds and mammals, human skulls, and finally fleshed-out human heads, limbs and breasts.

"What do you call it?" Carl asks, for lack of anything else to say.

"The Medusa Principle," Gus answers.

"Oh."

The effect of all of the pieces together is rather grisly. One smallish form remains draped, but Carl and Brianna don't ask about it. They've seen quite enough of this series, and allow Gus to lead them out to the patio.

"Ah, the nudes." Carl attempts an air of sophistication. They are surrounded by larger than life naked women, every detail lovingly articulated. He can't help but be impressed by the way Gus has managed to make stone look so squeezable. Brianna, finding her way to a cluster of male figures, is equally impressed at the way Gus can make stone defy gravity.

"This is Katy," Gus announces, his hands on the shoulders of a voluptuous marble form. She is seated in the lotus position with her feminine attributes prominently displayed.

*At least she doesn't have that same doll-like face,* Brianna notices. In fact, she thinks she'd recognize Katy if they met on the street—which is a bit disturbing in itself.

"Pretty."

Brianna glances at her husband. He's not looking at Katy's face.

"I can show you my metalwork if you like, but it's awfully hot out there." Gus waves a hand in the direction of the back lot. Beyond the curvy nudes a menagerie of scrap metal mutants stand in sharp-edged formation. It's a forbidding scene, with the sun glinting and heat vapors wavering. The trio stares for a minute and then retreats to a shady niche near the house.

"You sure work in a lot of different styles," Carl remarks.

"Well, I can't resist junk. That's where that stuff back there comes from. Can't let myself collect it if I won't do anything with it. Otherwise, it's all body parts—at rest, in motion, dressed and undressed, evolving and de-evolving."

Brianna decides this is the time to broach her concerns about Gus's art and by extension his character. Should she entrust him with the oversight of her daughter?

"I notice that you refer to body parts and not people."

Gus answers, "And I notice you are extremely observant. But don't psychoanalyze me, okay? I'm a superficial guy. I'm interested in surfaces. There's not a thing going on behind these sculptures—it's rock all the way down, like my own hard head.

"Now, your daughter's different," he continues, his answer having stopped Brianna short, as if she really had run into a stone wall. "I've only seen a few of her drawings, and we've barely had a chance to talk, but I can tell she's of a more cerebral nature. Surfaces are not going to be enough for her. Desire will not be enough. How good it feels when you get the consistency of paint just right will not be enough. Claire—like you, Brianna—is looking below the surface. Why is she an artist? Why is it worth her while, or yours, or anyone's, for her to make pictures? I don't envy her. Art takes practice and practice takes a certain level of surrender—just doing it for doing its sake. That's hard when you can't stop thinking. No wonder she finds her escape in love."

That takes some thinking about. For a guy who talks about everything being on the surface, Gus certainly has a probing way with people. Carl studies the robust, grey-haired artist, figuring him to be a good twenty years his senior—old enough to be Claire's grandfather. Then he lets his gaze sweep over the sculpture-filled patio. Gus's harem is full-figured and mature—not a pubescent nymph among them—indicating a man with a strong but not perverse libido. Since Gus has a girlfriend, and a successful career that probably means more to him than women, Carl's instincts are to trust Gus. The Antresians do. Besides, Claire has strapping young Josh to defend her. He could take Gus out in a flat minute. And, as for Josh, Carl knows that he wouldn't hurt a hair on Claire's head. In fact, Carl would welcome Josh as a son-in-law if it comes to that—though he'd rather not force the young lovers into a premature elopement. While Brianna worried all night that the kids had been in a deadly accident, Carl was more concerned that Josh had taken Claire away to Vegas.

Carl stands up. "Let's go, Brianna, before the kids get back. You spent a summer at the shore with your girlfriends when you were sixteen, and I drove cross country in a van. I can't see how letting Claire stay here a couple of nights could be any more risky. Besides, we could all use a breather."

"And believe me, I won't let this go on for too long. I need my studio." Gus extends his hand. "In the meantime, I promise I'll keep close tabs on the kids."

"And call us, please, later on and in the morning?" Brianna takes this to mean she can impose her rules on Gus.

"Yeah, I can do that." But he feels a swell of resentment, like he's closer to sixteen than sixty-one himself. This visit has set him firmly on the side of the teens. He doesn't dislike the Stanley-Yosts, nor the Antresians, but they all seem pathetic. Like his own parents. If it weren't for the Old Man, and getting to come here when he was a kid to sling adobes around, he'd've gone crazy.

On the way out Brianna asks about Josh's sculpture, but Gus has decided it's not his place to show it without Josh's permission.

"Maybe that's just as well," she concedes coldly. "I'm likely to read too much into it."

Then she forces herself to stop thinking about her daughter living with two men in the midst of all those seductive sexual icons. Like Gus said, whatever ill portents she reads into his artwork, they probably spring from her own overactive mind.

# CHAPTER 28
## CLAIRE CUBED

The first thing Claire does when they get to the Big B is call Lydia.

"How was your date with Matthew?" she asks casually.

"Oh, funny you should ask. We had a very nice time. The fireworks were great. We went for ice cream with your CARMA friends. That was pretty cool. Then we came home and looked through my telescope for a while, and the folks even left us alone, and Matt left at exactly midnight. I went to bed thinking, 'What a hell of a great day it's been!'"

"And then?" Claire can't tell if Lydia is really mad or what. They knew there'd be a blow-up.

"And then your mom called me up at two in the morning, and she called and woke my parents up at like five in the morning. They came and woke me up, to see if maybe you'd snuck in, and to pump me for information. There's been no end to the insinuations and recriminations since."

"Ooh, you're hot today." Claire thinks she can detect a hint of laughter in Lydia's lament.

"Seriously, Claire, they almost grounded *me!*"

"But cooler heads prevailed—"

"Your dad just called and said you'd been 'located' and that everything is fine. I think he talked my parents out of punishing me. It's possible they're tapping my phone, though."

"Are you allowed to see me?"

"I'm not sure."

"Can you come down here and hang out with us today?"

"No, they want me to stay home with Herbie. Carola's out sick."

"Too much partying I bet."

193

"You're one to talk. I'm surprised you're up so early—or didn't you ever get to sleep?"

"Very funny. Gus got back early."

"So that's what happened."

"I wish we could get together and talk!"

"Me too. What about tomorrow?"

"I'll be at the U all day—classes and the library. Then we're finally going to have dinner at Reginald's."

Lydia drops her voice low, hearing her mother on the stairs. "Are you going home or what?"

"Gus said we could stay tonight, and I think we can talk him into tomorrow night too. That's the plan, anyway—big dinner date and another night at the studio."

"Romantic." Lydia sounds more than a little jealous.

"What are you doing later? Can I at least call you?"

"Yeah, let's do that. I have to work in the morning, and I don't think they'll let me out a second night in a row."

"I wish I could get my car!"

"Hah! It's your father's car, and he's probably put it up on blocks or something."

"Yeah, or maybe they've rigged up a net to catch me when I go back for it."

"A Claire trap."

"Shit! I have to get to Muffin on Friday."

"Josh?"

"He'll probably want to stay at Gus's and work in the morning. Later we're going over to the mural. It should be cool—they're going to take down the scaffolds in the afternoon."

"I know. Ange was telling me I should come down. I was all set to ask for the day off until things went insane around here."

"I'm so sorry, Lydia—"

"Wait, I have an idea!"

"Too late, I'm out of change." For the second time a mechanical voice breaks in and asks Claire to deposit more coins. "I gotta go anyway. I'll call you tonight!"

The Big B is filling up. Josh is working on his second breakfast burrito as more and more CARMA kids drift in, bleary eyed from partying all day and most of the night. Their brunch is overlapping with the early lunch crowd and Mr. B is in his element. The mural has been so good for business that he's decided to throw a little party on Friday afternoon. There'll be soft drinks and Kurly Fries on the house, he tells everyone.

Shelly comes in, scans the booths, walks right over to them, evicts Josh with one piercing look, and slides into his seat across from Claire. "I just love getting called in the middle of the night by frantic parents," she tells her.

"Sorry. My mother's a maniac." Claire leans back and looks at Shelly, thinking, *I don't have to take shit from you.* She says, "I suppose you *never* gave *your* mother coronaries."

Shelly sighs. "Does she know where you are, or do I have to call her right now?"

"She knows, but go ahead and call her if you want. I *was* having breakfast with Josh."

Shelly shakes her head and starts to get up, but before she does she says, "When I was your age and I went missing, my parents couldn't give a shit if I came back. I think sometimes they wished I wouldn't."

And the rest of the day goes pretty much like that, with everyone whining at her about how her mom called in the middle of the night, and then going on and on about how nice her parents are, and what cool friends they have, and how big her room is—in short, what a fortunate soul is Claire—until she feels like screaming.

"Get me outta here," she tells Josh after some hours of this.

He has finally climbed down from the scaffold, always the last to finish. Now he'd like to join the socializing and revel in the completion of his work, but she's had quite enough—as he sees when he lifts her sunglasses and peers into her bloodshot eyes.

"Sure, Claire. We'll go back to Gus's. Maybe use the hot tub, huh?" And suddenly it's only about her and Josh, and the rightness of her actions is no longer in question. They leave arm in arm, to a lot of friendly teasing.

Gus is there when they get in, and Katy is expected. "She's bringing take-out," he tells them. "I hope you like Chinese."

With a sinking feeling, they discover that they've ended up right back in the bosom of an overprotective family. On the other hand, it's always nice to be fed.

Claire goes out on the patio and finds a lounge chair to doze in until Katy comes. She brushes it off and pulls it into the shade, aligning it parallel to a reclining marble figure the way she would line up her towel with Lydia's when sunbathing. She's come to feel at ease with Gus's art. She likes the way it's with her in space. Claire lays back with her unopened sketchbook in her lap, feeling the companionable granite presence beside her, and savors her memories of last night.

First they soaked in the hot tub and watched flashes of fireworks decorate the sky above. Then they made love on that well-worn futon. It was even better than the first time in Josh's bedroom, not having to worry about being heard. Afterward they talked about getting an apartment together, how it would be if this were their own place.

Naked, they came out here to wander among the nudes, to pose and play with them. That's when Claire's heart opened up to Gus. In the moonlight she could feel the *souls* of the statues. Josh had laughed when she told him this. "Gus does shapes and surfaces. No inner meaning. That's what he says, anyway."

"He lies," Claire answered. "Or there's a thing he does without thinking, so he doesn't think he does it."

"What's that?" Josh wanted to know, laughing more.

"He gives them something. I can't explain it. All I can say is, they seem to have personalities. Not like the characters they represent— Hunky Guy, Sexy Lady—but like as the art thing that they are— Shit. I can't explain it— Okay, it's like attitude. Each piece has its own special attitude."

She felt foolish by the time she finished, but Josh got it—even better than she did. He had to throw on some clothes immediately and try out the attitude thing on his own sculpture. Claire went back to the parlor and drew the artifacts in Gus's collection, until she missed Josh and went to watch him work.

They felt so free last night—so free from the world and yet so connected to each other. They didn't want the night to end, ever, but they slept in spite of their best efforts not to.

"Claire?"

She opens her eyes. It takes her a second to get her bearings.

"Katy?"

"*C'est moi.* Help me make supper, will ya." She holds up two big plastic bags from China West.

"Yum. My favorite." Claire helps Katy wipe down a table and gather four chairs around it. "You know, you don't look anything like Gus's sculpture of you." Claire looks back and forth between the two. She can see something in the eyes maybe, but otherwise she'd never have guessed.

"That's because I went on a diet and lost twenty pounds as soon as he finished! I know, I know—that statue looks like she could stand to lose forty. But that's because Gus always adds extra flesh."

"Was he mad when you lost weight?"

"Not really. It's not like he has to have his women fat—he just hates to waste good stone."

"Oh, that's too funny!" Claire tours the patio again, seeing the figures with new eyes. "I guess that's why the guys have such big dicks." In such a setting Claire can't feel shy around Katy, who's at least her mother's age and probably ten years older. Taking an instant liking to his girlfriend, Claire finds her esteem for Gus going up yet another notch.

They go inside for plates, silverware and cans of soda, inviting Gus and Josh to take a break for supper. The guys are deep in conversation over Josh's sculpture, circling it all the while, sometimes stepping back for the long view, sometimes moving in close to peer and point at the surface. Josh has titled his piece "Claire Cubed," referring to its geometric, abstract design—nothing like Gus's classically styled nudes. Yet it's distinctly a female form, and even recognizably Claire. When she watches Josh work on it, she has a delicious feeling that the attention he's giving to it, he's really giving to her. Now, seeing Gus run his brown, calloused hand over the granite surface as he instructs

Josh on proper polishing technique, Claire feels a flush come over her. She tries to shake off the sensation as she hurries after Katy. If she didn't know better—if it weren't the most ridiculous thing in the world—if she weren't totally in love with Josh—she would think she had a crush on Gus!

The attention Gus lavishes on Claire at supper—drawing her out about her interest in cartooning and, with Josh and Katy's help, even persuading her to show what she's been working on in the sketchbook—only deepens his impact on her psyche. Standing at the parlor window after the meal, Claire watches Gus walk Katy out to her car and take her in his arms. What a romantic figure, the way he seems so reluctant to let Katy go even though he'll soon get into his own car and follow her home. Katy drives off and Claire quickly retreats from the window. It's time to call Lydia.

Gus needs to talk to Josh, man to man, before he leaves—not about safe sex but safe sculpting.

"I don't want you working tonight," he tells his apprentice, throwing a sheet over "Claire Cubed" to make his point. "You're too played out to do this kind of work. Always know when to stop. If you're working tired, you're gonna hurt yourself or the piece or both. You sand too much off, there's no putting it back, you hear what I'm saying?"

"I guess so."

"I mean it, Josh. Get a good night's sleep. The work is always there waiting for you. You think someone else is gonna come in and do it?"

Having convinced Josh to get some rest, Gus takes off, waving to Claire as he passes the kitchen. She's deep in conversation with Lydia and barely notices. They are discussing plans for Friday.

Josh, relieved of his responsibilities to both "Claire Cubed" and Claire herself, takes a quick shower and goes to bed. When Claire joins him an hour later he wakes only long enough to tell her that the next time he makes a sculpture of her, he'll be sure to put a phone in her hand.

# CHAPTER 29
## CHOICES

The many faces of Claire—while Josh chisels them out of stone, Greg records them in his sketchpad. He's been making surreptitious drawings of her in class for the past two weeks. Greg is fascinated by Claire's moodiness, her changeability from day to day and even moment to moment. It's an alluring yet alarming quality, and makes Greg almost content to worship her from afar. Almost. But he thinks he can detect a solid, serious core beneath all the melodrama, especially when he watches her at work. "The Real Claire" is what he calls his sketch of Claire drawing.

She's in profile, sitting forward with her eye on the model and her stick of charcoal on the page, and she's leaning into it, making a certain stroke really black. You can see her marks on the sketchpad that's propped on a chair, which she straddles, one shapely knee in the foreground. It's one of Greg's best sketches, and he puts it up for his final critique along with his other work. The class whoops it up at Greg's brazen display of admiration for Claire, but Percy Hartshorn reviews the drawing seriously. He agrees that it's one of Greg's better efforts, and uses the opportunity to give a windy speech about the necessity of having a passion for one's subject.

Claire's more embarrassed for Greg than for herself. Everyone's seen her with Josh, so Greg's cause must look ridiculously hopeless. *Which it is, right?* She can't help looking Greg over, though she has no interest in switching boyfriends. *It's like window shopping*, she thinks, *a girl always enjoys looking*. When it's her turn to pin her work on the board, she is conscious of all the guys in the class looking at her. The attention is not unpleasant, and because she owes this flattering moment to Greg, the little flutter of excitement it stirs in her becomes associated with him.

Percy Hartshorn is one male who is unmoved. He's not much impressed with Claire's flamboyant drawings, either. She takes his critique bravely, salvaging what bits of encouragement she can. He acknowledges that she draws with intensity but adds, "If only she would stop trying to reinvent the wheel, and apply the tried and true techniques for rendering the human form, we might see that passion channeled into drawings with real teeth."

Claire stands in front of the room for a moment to accept the polite applause which follows each critique, reclaims her art and returns to her seat beside Greg. "Drawings with real teeth? What does that mean?" she whispers, leaning close to him as she sits. That blows his concentration for the rest of class. He just sits there sketching her.

Other drawings are posted and some—many—are excellent. Looking at them, Claire begins to feel let down. She worked hard in class, but still missed something. Hartshorn's remarks start boring their way under her normally thick skin. He was right when he accused her of trying to skip over the basics. She's gotten used to making it on creativity and talent, to having people tell her how artistic she is. But around other artistic souls—here in Art's own realm—she barely even speaks the language. As the parade of skillful charcoal figures marches along, Claire feels like a backward child. She becomes sharply aware that the career she wants to pursue will demand drawing skills above all else.

After class Claire goes over to Hartshorn and asks what he would think about her taking his course again. He looks at her in surprise.

"I'm sorry if my comments were that discouraging. There's no reason you shouldn't go on to Jane Eastman's intermediate class."

"Thanks, but I feel like I went through most of the class not really getting it. I want to start over. You think they'd let me enroll during the regular semester, if I can work it out with my school schedule?"

Hartshorn looks puzzled for a second, then remembers that Claire's a high school student. "I teach two Beginning sessions in the fall and they get filled up fast, but I'll give you a note for the admissions office and you can try. One's a late afternoon session that you could get to after school. It would help if you acted like you were applying for the program here."

"Thanks, Mr. Hartshorn. I'll pick up an application when I talk to them about the class."

"Oh, one more thing, Claire." While they've been talking, he's registered who this young woman is. "I don't suppose you're the reason that Josh has fallen behind in his painting class?"

Claire blushes but holds Harthorn's gaze. "Not me, but maybe a sculpture of me. See, he's studying with Gus C De Baca too."

"Yes, he mentioned that." Hartshorn seems unhappy about it. "So, you're his muse."

"Right. Not his mother." Claire prickles at the implication that she is responsible for Josh's behavior. "If Josh is screwing up, you should talk to him."

"Thank you, Claire. I will. Now hold on for a minute and I'll write that note for you." He grabs a piece of paper and starts scribbling. "Do me a favor and make a copy of this for me. Just drop it in my box."

"Sure. Thanks, Mr. Hartshorn."

He gives her the page. "Hope to see you in the fall."

During this exchange, Greg has stayed in his seat talking to Salman. They've been watching the door, prepared to split should Josh show up. It seems a miracle that he doesn't. When Claire has finished speaking to Hartshorn and walks purposefully to the door, instead of looking around for Josh the way she normally would, Greg knows that his opportunity has come. He jumps up and falls into step beside Claire with a "See ya later," to Salman. There's no point pretending he wasn't waiting for her. Posting that sketch made his intentions known to all.

"Hi, Greg."

"Hi, Claire."

"Bye, Greg."

"You meeting Josh somewhere?" He's careful to call him by name. Claire hates it when he says "Studly," or even, "your boyfriend."

"No, I'm going to the library." It's too hot to be bothered. Claire saunters along, pleased about how things went with Hartshorn.

"Have lunch with me."

"I was going to get something on the Mall."

"Then can I have lunch with you?"

"Greg—" She's on a mission, and was looking forward to being alone for a few hours.

"Claire, it's our first and last chance to sit down and talk."

Again she finds herself attracted to his sincerity. "Well, okay. I'm going for a veggie burger." She heads for a vendor with a green and white umbrella.

"No, no! Come with me. You've gotta try Leo's. Greek salad, falafel, spinach pie—" He touches her elbow and steers her toward the cart under a yellow umbrella.

At his touch a breath of desire disturbs Claire's composure. She knows—she's pretty sure—that she's picking up on Greg's feelings for her. Her body is responding to his with a prickly energy that feels like attraction. But it can't be the same as she feels for Josh, because she loves Josh and she barely knows Greg. Still, the sensation is kind of fun—pleasant and mildly dangerous.

*It's Josh's fault I'm so horny,* Claire thinks, and the ripple turns into a wave. *Greg knows about Josh, so what's the big deal?* She decides to indulge him, and herself. None of this is about Greg, or Josh, she is simply testing the thrilling power of her own awakening sexuality. Greg stands close to her as they survey Leo's offerings. She permits him to recommend something, but not to pay for it. When a gust of wind comes up, he slides one finger along her cheek to pull a strand of hair away from her mouth while she juggles the falafel with one hand and wrestles her change into her back pocket with the other. Their eyes meet. "I knew this was a bad idea," Claire teases.

Greg does his best to play things cool, which isn't that easy. Claire has always acted so tense around him, but today she's relaxed, even playful. Is he actually going to have lunch with The Real Claire?

"What's at the library?" Greg asks when they're settled on a bench with their food.

"College catalogues. I have to decide where to apply. Besides here, of course."

"You're looking at art programs?"

"Yeah. I want to learn to do comic strips and political cartoons."

"Really? Interesting."

"Yeah. I finally decided. So, how do you like the Fine Arts Department here?"

"You know as much about it as I do. That was my only art class."

"You're kidding! But you're so good."

"Not really. I draw like an engineer. I'm a computer sciences major."

"You're kidding!" Greg has captured Claire's interest with this surprising news.

"That's why I took this class in summer school. No time during the regular semester."

"Why'd you take it at all?"

"It's required for the computer animation classes I'm taking."

"Where you reduce all this to mathematical equations?"

"Yeah, something like that."

"Well, what did you think?"

"About the course? Looking at naked girls was okay."

Claire looks up from her food. They blush in unison. "So you're saying you only drew *me* when we had male models."

"You mad?"

"I don't know. Let me see the rest of the drawings."

"No way!"

Claire knows how protective she is of her sketchbook, so she doesn't press. She says, "You should take another art class, Greg. There must be tons of cute art majors who would enjoy dating a brainy computer sciences guy like you."

"You just don't happen to be one of them."

"You know I'm going out with Josh."

"Right. Muscular, passionate, painter guy. Hard to top that."

"C'mon, Josh and I have known each other forever."

"Ah, childhood sweethearts."

"No. We just started going out this summer—"

Greg doesn't want to talk about Josh. The whole scene suddenly seems idiotic. He bundles up his fast food trash. "I guess there's no point in me asking for your phone number."

Claire feels a twinge of regret. Under other circumstances, she might like going out with Greg. She'd at least give him a chance. "How about if you give me your number," Claire proposes magnanimously, thinking she's letting him down easy.

Greg is elated. He takes a pen from his pocket and writes his number on the cover of Claire's big sketchpad. Then he plants a kiss on her cheek. "I sure enjoyed being in class with you, Claire."

She watches him stride away. Looks at the phone number for a minute. Finds a black pen and scribbles over it until it's illegible, then she mentally scribbles over the cascade of thoughts and fantasies her lunch with Greg has provoked. She doodles "Josh, Josh, Josh," all over them, until her raging libido is securely attached to the proper object of attraction.

Percy Hartshorn tells Josh about Greg, not in a specific way but to make his point: There comes a time in life when a person has to choose.

"Take Claire," he says. "Pretty girl. Smart, too. You can see how the guys would be interested. But a woman who knows her own heart and takes herself seriously is not going to succumb to those distractions. It's the same deal with art. Lots of distractions. At some point you have to stop sampling and settle down. Decide what you want the most and commit to it."

"Who's interested in Claire besides me?"

"Josh, do you understand that you're not getting a Pass in this course?"

When Josh meets Claire outside the Fine Arts building and tells her they can't go out to dinner because he has to turn in six finished paintings by Monday or he'll fail Hartshorn's class, she marches straight back to the drawing studio. Josh follows, knowing that it's useless to protest.

Percy Hartshorn is switching off the lights when he sees them coming down the hall. Before Claire can launch her attack he says,

"What's the matter, Claire? Did I screw up your weekend?" He's had a long day and quite enough of these two. He'd like to go home.

"We just wanted to invite you to come down to the Old Mercantile tomorrow," Claire blurts out, as if inspiration itself is working her tongue. "To see the mural we did with the CARMA class."

"The scaffolding should be down by mid-afternoon," Josh adds, relieved that Claire's decided not to throw a fit. Now if they can make a quick exit—

"It's really great. And Josh had a lot to do with the design. He painted the biggest single element in it—this giant train." Claire digs her nails into Josh's hand, so he'll stop trying to drag her away.

"Is that so?"

"Don't you think you could come see it and maybe let some of that work count for the paintings Josh didn't finish for class? He put more hours into that than the sculpture. But you should see that too, and the ten thousand studies he did for it. You could call it extra credit and count it against the incompletes."

"I could?" Hartshorn can tell from the look on Josh's face that he did not put Claire up to this.

"Well, why not? Josh is so close to done with the sculpture, he can't stop now. Then he can concentrate on your assignments. You know he'd do them over the weekend if you insist, but what's the point? So he can work in a painting factory?"

Percy Hartshorn is used to being told off by students. It's what he gets for encouraging their artistic temperaments. Usually they have some valid points to make, often he is inspired by their ferocity. So he doesn't hold the testy attitude against Claire, but seriously considers her request.

"Okay. I'll go have a look at the mural. Meet me there at two o'clock tomorrow, Josh, and we'll discuss your grade again."

"Uh, sure. Thanks, Mr. Hartshorn."

"Thank your sweetheart, Josh." He points his chin at Claire and hurries off.

✧

Tony's gift to Claire and Josh is to be the perfect server for their romantic meal at Reginald's. He wants them to know he approves. Though if Josh hadn't shown up at the July Fourth party when he did, Tony might've fallen in love with Claire himself, on account of her kindness. He always admired her, even when she was distant with him. He admired that she could be an outsider without being disdained, the way he was. When she made him iced coffee at the party—and not decaf—and never even asked—Tony had felt that admiration begin to deepen.

Then Josh had arrived, and a pang of disappointment, a pinprick of jealousy—but Josh was really the coolest one of all. He introduced Tony to everyone and seemed oblivious to Tony's rep as an outcast. He kind of shamed the Roosevelt kids, who know Tony as the "schizo" who gets called out of class to take meds, into being nice to him.

Josh was always decent to Tony at school, in a remote kind of way. Around Claire and his art buddies on the Fourth he was more approachable, even expansive. So instead of falling in love with Claire that day, Tony fell in love with the couple—Claire and Josh. They are so attractive and talented and nice—he has come to idolize them. The minute he saw them enter the restaurant, he asked Melissa to seat them at one of his tables.

"Ooh-kay, but they're not going to tip worth shit," Melissa warned him, sizing up the young couple, *Too young to drink.*

He doesn't care. He would like to tell them not to even leave a tip. His goal is only to be worthy, not the money itself, but then, he would not want to embarrass either. He offers a slight, not unfriendly nod of recognition, and is brisk and unobtrusive after that.

Claire and Josh sit side by side in the secluded, candlelit alcove and eat freely from each other's plates. What the elegant dishes lack in substance, Josh makes up for with multiple orders of dinner rolls. Each time Josh asks for more bread, Tony emerges from the kitchen with a basket more full than the last time. He even manages to keep Reggie away from them. True, their original idea was to come talk art with the saavy chef. But Reggie held forth on the New York art scene at such length at the July Fourth party, they don't think they can handle another installment so soon. Besides, the lovers have much to discuss.

Josh must repeat his entire conversation with Hartshorn, twice, while Claire decides which part she's maddest about—that Hartshorn is pushing Josh to lock into something so quickly, or that he would gossip about her and Greg. But she is glad for the opportunity to tell Josh about her secret admirer—about how he drew pictures of her in class and followed her to lunch this afternoon. Talking about it, she sees that there's not much to it, after all. If Claire did have a fleeting interest in dating Greg—well, that's all it was, fleeting, and she's not sure she'd even go so far as to call it a true interest.

"I think Hartshorn only brought up the part about other boys to cause trouble—and to be rude!" she huffs. "There's no comparison between me deciding between you and Greg—which is, like, not a decision at all—and you settling on either painting or sculpture. Does he really think you have to pick between them right now?"

"He said that it's not such a big deal if I'm going into 'formal study'—that college is a good place to try out different things. But he told me I better have a plan, preferably a *vision*, if I think I'm just gonna slum around and try to get my work into galleries. Like, who am I as an artist and what am I trying to say— But shit, Claire, it's all just shapes and surfaces, like Gus says. I just *see* it and I have to make it. I'm not trying to say anything!"

"Still, your work says a lot. You'd be surprised. Don't listen to Hartshorn. And don't listen to Gus either. They can teach technique, but what do they know about why you do art?"

Josh smiles and takes her hand. "I love you, Claire. I totally love you."

"I love you, Josh."

She says it all the time now. It's the easiest thing in the world to say. And she wonders why she didn't say it to Greg, why she didn't tell him, "I love Josh, give up." Well, she will, next time. In fact, she'd like to see him again if only to tell him that.

✧

Gus and Katy are in the hot tub when Josh and Claire come in from dinner. Parents have been calling them, and so they are waiting to confirm that the teens are okay and now in for the night. Without a thought to modesty, Gus hops out of the water and starts drying off before his guests can retreat to other regions of the house. Claire slips indoors, but not before getting an eyeful of his furry torso. *Grey—all of his body hair is grey.* She tries to put it out of her mind.

"Come with me." Josh leads Claire out the front door and around to the side of the house. He sits on an old cottonwood stump which has been smoothed by many rumps over the years, pulls Claire onto his lap, and they make out. Hearing Gus's voice in the kitchen, they pretend they don't know he's talking to their parents. Soon Gus and Katy are calling good bye to them, and they walk back around to wave as Katy's car, with Gus at the wheel, backs down the driveway.

They're feeling at home here now, and completely at ease with each other. Without a second thought they go right to bed, though it's only nine-thirty, and tumble about all evening, with an occasional break to make detailed anatomical sketches or to raid the refrigerator.

Claire and Josh know that they're living in a dream from which they must soon wake. Rubbing their two bodies together they spark a cheerful fire, but reality crouches just outside their happy ring of light. Soon it will pounce and try to smother their flame. As if to counteract this inevitability, they stoke their passion higher and higher, until they finally collapse in exhaustion. Sleep begins to steal over them, and with it the low growl of the beast that stalks them.

"I'm out of condoms," Josh murmurs.

"I'm out of clean clothes," Claire sighs.

"I'm sick of eating restaurant food," Josh admits.

After a pause, "I can cook."

"I can take our clothes to a laundromat."

Another pause, then, "I'm out of money."

"Me too."

They fall asleep giggling, feeling safe in each other's arms.

# CHAPTER 30
## A THING THAT HAPPENED

The pretext under which Lydia is able to spend Friday with Claire and drive her to Muffin is this: At the end of the month Jo and her husband are leaving on vacation. Claire is to be responsible for Muffin's lunches for almost three weeks, and Jo wants Claire to find someone to help her, so she won't have to go every single day in Jo's absence. Lydia could be that person, but she has to check it out first, and she has to do it soon because the Overmyers are going up to their cabin in Colorado next week. She must either commit to helping with Muffin when she gets back, or tell Claire and Jo to look for someone else.

Lydia is pretty certain it will be the latter, as she still has a strong aversion to the mere thought of nursing homes. Perhaps this is why her mother thinks that visiting Muffin will be an enriching activity for her and has backed today's plan all the way. Mrs. Overmyer had a chance to talk to Jo at the party, so she knows Lydia's not making something up. And though Lydia is prepared to say that Claire is staying at the home of an art instructor, her mother doesn't ask. It's enough that the Stanley-Yosts are keeping track of Claire—more than that, Emily Overmyer really doesn't want to know.

Lydia finds Jo's house without any problem, and Muffin's lunch cooler in the shade within a walled patio. Jo isn't around, and Lydia quickly heads to Gus's, driving down El Rio in the opposite direction of Westcare Manor. In her mind she practices how she will tell her story to Claire.

Secrets, as most anyone will tell you, take more energy than they're worth. Lydia can't wait to cut this one loose. She is eager to tell all and, realizing this, she feels for the first time since it happened that *the thing* is not going to hang over her forever. She smiles at the sun-splashed suburban scenery rolling by, and tells herself, *This is not going to be so bad.*

She wonders if she hasn't made too big a deal of it. Why couldn't she have simply told Claire on the phone, once she started asking? Lydia sees that this secret that stands between them has taken on a life of its own. Like a third character in their private play it waits in the wings to make an entrance. Lydia wonders if the drama is all of her own creation. *It's just a thing that happened*, she tells herself—has been telling herself for months and months.

The road to Gus's studio is an unmarked gravel lane off Poblanos, as Claire described. Dust lifts into a small golden cloud to accompany Lydia's slow approach. At the end of the lane, a rustic adobe sits on a hump of earth, framed by two cottonwoods. Claire is leaning against one of them, her daypack at her feet. She waves, but waits for the car to stop and the dust cloud to collapse before running over.

"Finally! It seems like forever since I've seen you!" Claire plops happily into the front seat, pushing the cooler aside with her feet. "Oh good, you picked up lunch already."

"Yeah. I can cross the river on Main and take Canal all the way up."

"Ooh, don't do that. El Rio's prettier, and we'll have more time to talk."

"Actually, I thought we'd talk first." Lydia drives slowly down the lane and pulls over before getting to Poblanos, parking under another sprawling cottonwood. She takes off her seatbelt and turns toward Claire. Claire rolls down her window and gets comfortable too.

"So talk," Claire says. There is no need for preliminaries. Everything has been said, except the thing that hasn't.

Lydia plunges in. The shapes and colors and smells of a lazy summer day surround them and are a comfort. Lydia reminds Claire about a boy she dated for a short time, a Senior she met in the astronomy club, Blaine. She takes them back to Thanksgiving of last year: Claire and her parents had driven down to Las Cruces to visit old friends of Brianna's. Lydia and Blaine were going to a party that weekend.

"His brother goes to the U and has an apartment in that complex back behind the stadium. He and his friends were throwing a big bash. I told my parents it was the two brothers' party and kind of let them think it was at their folks' house."

This is one of those clever lies-by-omission the girls are getting good at, but Claire doesn't say anything. Lydia's glad, because she's trying to get through this as quickly as possible. She repeats to herself, *It's just a thing that happened. It's over, so get it over with.*

Claire keeps a bland, encouraging expression on her face. Scenes of all of the worst things that could happen in such a situation want to leap forth from her ever-active imagination, but she holds them at bay.

Lydia says, "I thought it was cool, you know, to be with the older crowd. I really liked Blaine, or I thought I did. He and his friends were smart. You know, they seemed too brainy to be up to trouble like the guys in our class. I trusted Blaine, and I was pretty horny for him. If the shit hadn't hit the fan at that party, I might've gone all the way with him, willingly."

Lydia can see in Claire's reddening face that her friend has guessed the worst. She puts up a hand to keep Claire from speaking. "Just let me tell you, okay?" Claire nods, her eyes locked on Lydia's.

"They said there was nothing but a little rum in the punch. I asked before I drank it. Blaine swore the same, high and low, after. But either he spiked my glass with something weird, or the whole batch was laced. I'll never know. I do know that was not an alcohol buzz. After I drank like half a cup of the stuff, I was totally out of it. I could hardly feel my arms and legs, and the world was swimming. It was really like being seasick. Blaine wanted me to lie down—" Claire huffs. Lydia talks faster. "But I ducked into the bathroom and put my finger down my throat. I don't think anyone could hear me puking over the music. I washed up and sat there for a long time. Blaine must've thought I'd passed out and he started banging on the door."

Suddenly Lydia feels like she could heave again. Every time she thinks about what might have happened that night her body goes into a panic, as if she is facing the threat all over again. Little gremlins race through her nervous system and jump up and down in her stomach.

"But you were sober by then," Claire coaxes, starting to put the pieces together. "Here, drink some water." She passes Lydia the plastic bottle she keeps in her pack.

Lydia sips cautiously. The gremlins retreat. "Yeah, but he didn't know that. I take one step out of the bathroom and he grabs me, like he knows I won't be able to walk, and pushes me back to a bedroom. I'm struggling, but he doesn't get it—that I'm not stoned. He thinks he can do anything he wants with me, and my legs are still kind of rubbery from being sick." Lydia shudders. It's too easy to be back in the scene, back in the fear.

"He thought he could do anything he wanted to me," she repeats, this time using the past tense. "It was so awful—him becoming a different person like that—I was stunned. It didn't seem real. And I pushed a little harder and he held me even tighter. Like he had this plan and was just going through with it and wasn't even paying enough attention to me to see I was not the rag doll I was supposed to be. He was pushing me on the bed before I knew I was going to have to fight to get away from him, but when that sunk in I lost it. I mean, I was like a cornered animal—"

"You *were*," Claire says softly, her own stomach turning flips.

"But it wasn't just fear, it was outrage!" Lydia watches herself from the outside now, and almost feels like laughing. "I started flailing around and kicking and screaming—"

"Did anyone come?"

Lydia goes pale, and silent. Claire regrets interrupting her.

"Lydia?"

"Huh."

"Just tell me, okay? Did he rape you?" She can barely make herself say the word.

Lydia takes a shuddering breath. "No. I bit him and he had to let go a little. Then I called him a dirty rapist, and he jumped away and looked at me and finally figured out I was sober and totally on to him—then I was even more scared because he looked so mad. I barely recognized him." She squeezes her eyes tight shut as if to block out the sight, but that distorted face of rage looms there behind her eyelids, and her ears ring with the noise of drunken male voices in the hallway, heavy pounding on the door and nasty laughter. She doesn't know if those sounds spring from memory or imagination, only that they surfaced after the fact to torment her with "what-ifs" too sickening to speak. Lydia opens her eyes and finds comfort in her friend's blotchy face.

"I was so afraid, Claire, I honestly thought he might kill me."

"But he didn't kill you, and he didn't rape you." Claire leans over and hugs Lydia. The floodgates open.

"No, he didn't," Lydia sniffles into Claire's curls. "No, the sonuvabitch did not."

After a few minutes they pull apart, pass the tissue box back and forth, drink more water, then Lydia swivels around and pulls on her seatbelt.

"I'm gonna drive now."

"Okay." Claire bites her lip, her insides seething.

Lydia, insisting on her own route, braves the traffic on the Main Street Bridge and turns north on Canal Boulevard. Multiple lanes of motorists rush forward to the red lights, wait impatiently at busy intersections and rush forward again. Lydia, settling into the familiar rhythm, is able to finish her story.

"I grabbed a couple of empty beer bottles—those guys are such slobs—and he could see that I'd be more than happy to smash him. It was a stand-off for a few seconds, I guess, and then he actually offered to drive me home. Do you believe that? I said no way. So instead he called a cab and gave me the money to pay for it. I went out the window and down the fire escape, so I wouldn't have to spend another second in that place."

Is it Lydia's imagination, or did he urge her to do that, to keep her away from the others? She'll never know, she never wants to know, she can't let herself think about that part. *It was just the crazy music, that's all I heard.*

"Did he ever, like, apologize?"

"No. He acted like *I'd* played a dirty trick on *him*! We have not spoken since."

"I guess that explains why you didn't go back to the astronomy club after vacation."

"Yeah, but I'll join again in the fall, now that he's graduated."

Claire's trying to remember back to Thanksgiving and the time following. What had she been up to? Why hadn't she noticed the changes in Lydia? *I did notice, but only how my feelings were hurt when Lydia made other friends—I was only thinking about myself!*

"What did your parents say about you coming home in a cab?" She pushes aside the guilt and focuses on her friend.

"I told them that Blaine took me to his brother's apartment instead of his house and I really didn't feel comfortable there so I took a cab home."

"Almost true. So they were cool about it?"

"Yeah, except for the short leash they've kept me on since."

"Is that why you all went to Cancun?"

Lydia tenses, then says, "Yes, they thought I was run down." She wants to tell Claire about the near-drowning but doesn't know how to explain, can't really explain it to herself.

Claire asks Lydia, "Did Blaine ever threaten you or anything? About not telling anyone?"

"I guess he knew I wouldn't tell. Or figured if he came near me again I could get him in even more trouble."

"You must've scared the shit out of him—he must've been humiliated."

"Scared, maybe. Humiliated? I doubt it," Lydia says dryly. "I'm the one who's scared and humiliated. The truth is, I still—I still get scared I'll be attacked again, lured into something. It just comes over me—that tension, bracing to defend myself. I can't get over it. A sudden movement, someone looking at me a certain way. Shit, I'm afraid of dogs now! If I hear about someone getting attacked by stray dogs, then I'm sure it'll be me next. Something's out to get me. I haven't let my tank go below half full since Christmas—I'm terrified of getting stuck on the road. Sometimes I can't even stand people looking at me." Lydia inhales deeply, sucking back a sob and letting out a short, mirthless laugh instead.

Claire studies her friend quizzically. "But you always seem so confident, Lyd. And you always look great. People can't help looking at you. In a way, you've been more together than ever. And some of those guys you dated—I was almost starting to think you'd, uhm." Claire stops herself.

"What?"

"Like you were ditching me. You started running with kids I just can't relate to."

"Yeah. The crowd's the thing. Safety in numbers, you know."

"With that group?"

"I've just been doing all this stuff, like, I don't know, testing, I guess."

"Testing who?"

Lydia bites her lip.

"What are you testing, Lydia?"

"God, I think," Lydia answers very quietly. "But maybe He's testing me."

"Oh, Lyd!"

They ride in silence for a few minutes, digesting all that has been said.

"Lydia—"

"What?"

Claire has to ask. "What about the other girls there?"

Lydia frowns. "I've thought about that a lot. So much is a blur. I didn't notice anyone else from school there. None of the other astronomy guys or their girlfriends. The girls were from the U, that's what I assumed, and it seems like they were mostly drinking beer."

"So, you think the set-up was just for you?"

"I don't like to think about it." *That's the understatement of the year.*

"Either way, those guys should be reported—"

"Claire!"

"Okay, okay. Never mind about that." Lydia looks like she might cry again. "You're right. It's totally over. There's no evidence. And you didn't get hurt." Claire gives her friend a smile, but inside she's fuming. She wants to see those guys punished. "It must be good to know you can defend yourself like that." She's thinking, *You shoulda killed him!*

Lydia reads her mind. "You see why I couldn't tell you?" She's turned onto Cottonwood and is climbing the hill past the TechTel plant. Claire tries to give directions and point out landmarks, but Lydia assures her she knows all the roads. Claire falls silent. "Seriously, Claire, you do see why I couldn't tell you?"

Claire stares at the road ahead, glad they're moving, glad this particular piece of the conversation is taking place with the center stripe as a mediator. Does she *really* understand? It still hurts that Lydia didn't tell her—in fact it hurts even more now that she knows. She feels bad that Lydia did all that feeling bad without her. She might have been able to help, if she'd been given a chance. She sure wouldn't've let those guys get away with it.

"Besides," Lydia ventures uneasily. Claire's silence is unnerving. "Besides, it's just a thing that happened."

Still Claire thinks, seriously, quietly, for so long that it's all Lydia can do to keep silent, but then Claire says, "No, Lyd. It's just a thing that *didn't* happen." She turns to her friend with a smile. "And you *have* told me."

Lydia allows herself to be consoled. They've made a start. In her gut she knows that something *did* happen—how could she be so destroyed over nothing? And she still hasn't told Claire *everything.* She is briefly tempted to tell Claire about Cancun—how she almost— She stops herself. She'd only be telling to make the point, to make Claire feel how really bad it was. But that's the last thing Lydia wants to do—spread her pain around to people she loves. That's why she'll never tell her parents, any of it.

*The lifeguard reported an accident. It's a fact now, on paper.* Lydia decides that for everyone's sake she should just let it be that. Besides, she already feels so much lighter for what she has shared with Claire. She's told the worst part, the *thing* that made everything else go off kilter. And she's finally admitted to being off kilter. That's the main thing.

Lydia pulls into the Westcare Manor parking lot. "Okay, we're here—check me in!"

## CHAPTER 31
## TWO BLOSSOMS


Muffin understands that Claire has brought a friend, another young woman. They made a big commotion at first. It seemed like there were more than two of them, a jumble of voices, lots of bumping around. Now it is quieter. But she can feel them pressing in.

Strange clumsy hands are feeding her. The new girl mumbles. Muffin can't make out any words. She seems scared of Muffin. No, it's Muffin who's scared. And angry. What happened to the Blossom? Wasn't she just here? Or wasn't she ever here? Maybe there never was such a girl. Maybe it was this one all the time, and Muffin just dreamed the other one. "I think I'm going crazy," she says.

"Why is that, Muffin?" Lydia asks, looking guiltily over at Claire. She'd been lost in her own thoughts, half hypnotized by Muffin's methodical chewing.

"I don't know you."

"No, you didn't before today. We just met. I came with Claire. I'm her friend, Lydia."

From her perch on the bed, Claire forces herself to get back in the game. Her thoughts keep turning to that creep Blaine, but now is the time for sweetness, not poison.

"Muffin, you remember me telling you about Lydia," she sings out.

The sound of Claire's voice is a great relief. "I guess so."

"Oh no, what did she tell you about me?" Lydia asks with a laugh.

"Nothing bad!" Claire banters back.

For Muffin, the room seems to brighten as if the sun has come out. Two Blossoms have picked up their golden heads.

"Muffin, don't believe a word she says about me," Lydia pleads with mock distress.

"I can't remember a word she says," Muffin shoots back. "I must be crazy." But she no longer feels crazy. She is reciting a familiar refrain.

"Not remembering is not the same as being crazy," Claire says on cue. "Lydia's my friend who likes to look at the stars."

"She does what?"

"Watches the stars, at night."

"Oh, we like to do that too. From the boat." Muffin beams, and the two Blossoms unfurl their petals toward her. The room is very sunny now. And the light off the water dazzles.

"Wow, stargazing out at sea. That must be awesome! You had a telescope?" Lydia gently wipes the jam from Muffin's fingers before tucking another quarter sandwich between them.

Claire notices and smiles. *She's hooked.*

"Did I have a what?"

"A telescope. You know, a long thing that you use to look at the stars. It makes everything look closer."

"Yes, I guess so." Muffin would like to be agreeable but simply doesn't remember. She'd like it if these girls would take her to the boat, where her husband is waiting. She says, "Sam is sitting there."

Lydia is ready to ask who Sam is but Claire shakes her head. She'll explain later that the subject of Muffin's husband is difficult. If you remind Muffin that Sam died, it's like she's hearing the news for the first time, but it's just as upsetting for her to think he's alive and not coming to see her.

"What do you think about when you look at the stars?" Lydia asks. This also seems like a daring question to Claire, given that Muffin has so much trouble with both thought and sight, but maybe Lydia doesn't expect an answer. She's announcing the "lemon pudding with mandarin oranges" course, as she again dabs at Muffin's fingers with a damp paper towel.

After thanking Lydia profusely for this service, Muffin unexpectedly answers her question. "I think about stars. What do you think?"

Lydia holds the teaspoon loaded with its creamy treat lip level in front of Muffin's face. She looks over at Claire, who nods. "Here you go." Lydia touches the tip of the spoon to Muffin's lower lip and Muffin opens her mouth to accept it.

"Hmm, good."

"Looks good."

"Have some."

"No, that's okay."

"So, Lydia. What *do* you think about when you look at the stars?" Claire can see that Muffin is in good form today. Maybe if Lydia talks a little bit, the Muffin oracle will give her some guidance. "I could never get very interested in astronomy myself."

"No, you're more the astrology type," Lydia quips. Muffin's chuckle surprises her. Encouraged, she explains, "When I look through my telescope, I like to imagine myself being out there with the stars looking back at Earth. From that perspective all our problems here seem small and insignificant."

"Yes, I suppose they would," Muffin allows.

"Or sometimes I think about how long it takes the light from the stars to reach my telescope, and I wonder about all the other light that is out there that we haven't seen yet."

"I'm full," Muffin declares.

"Well, okay. You finished most of it." Lydia covers the container and puts it back in the cooler. Claire has told her that whenever Muffin says she's full, Lydia should talk or read for a minute and then move on to the next course. She continues the astral theme, asking, "Muffin, do you think life exists on other planets?"

"What?"

"You know, do you think there's another place like Earth with plants and creatures and some sort of people?"

"Oh, I hope not!" Muffin is entirely serious, but laughs when the girls do. The Blossoms sway and bend with the roll of the boat. Clouds come and go over the sun. She can sense their moods and secrets. The stars are surely the least of it.

"Do you believe in God?" Claire asks mischievously. Jo has told her that her parents were adamant atheists.

"Not really," Muffin answers diplomatically.

"How about a chocolate chip cookie?" Lydia offers, giving Claire a dirty look.

"I'm full."

"You didn't even leave room for a cookie?" Claire asks.

"And some iced coffee?" Lydia entreats.

"Well, okay. If you'll have some too."

"Jo did pack enough for all of us, I see." Lydia pours the "coffee" for Muffin and distributes the cookies. The conversation gives way to chewing and praise for Jo's baking skills.

"When Jo was little, she thought the stars were holes in—in a—" Lydia and Claire stop chewing and wait hopefully for Muffin to complete her thought. The thought is a picture of a small girl and a twinkling night sky. "Bang. Bangs."

"She thought the stars were holes in—bangs?" Claire tries to help.

"Yes." Jo had straight black hair, with bangs that were always too long. Sam used to tease her about parting the curtain so they could see her face.

"You mean a curtain. The stars were holes in a curtain that the starlight shines through." Lydia feels like her brain has been tickled. Is she learning Muffin's language, or did the thought simply leap from Muffin's mind to her own?

"Yes, a curtain." Muffin beams. Lydia beams. Claire beams. Through the curtain, flashes from the great lantern that blinks in the lighthouse up the coast. Night gives way to dawn. Golden Blossoms bob their heads in time to the waves which lap against the shore. Such a lovely day for a picnic on the boat. She hopes Sam will arrive in time to meet the young people...

"Now we need to check on Lettie."

Lydia doesn't want to but Claire insists. She hasn't seen Lettie since the renovations started. While their rooms were being worked on, the residents were corralled into the recreation room. Now the rec room itself is under repair, and everyone's tucked into their rooms or hanging out in the renovated foyer.

Lettie is fretting over a wrinkle in her yellow bedspread when Claire pokes her head in. "Hi, there! How do you like the new decor?"

Lettie's frowning brown face breaks into a smile when she looks up to see Claire. She has on a red turban and red and gold house dress. A big vase of fairly fresh yellow roses sits on her nightstand. The room itself has been re-papered and re-upholstered in shades of a passive peach color that can hardly hold its own against Lettie's roses, bedspread and caftan. Lettie waves the girls in, then claps her hands together in delight.

"Well, look at you, just look at you! Ooh, that red hair is as pretty as ever. Ooh my, you pretty. That green blouse is so becoming. Girls with red hair should wear green, I say. I always did like that red hair." She is by now gripping Claire's hands, and looking up at her, transfixed.

"Thanks, Lettie. I want you to meet my friend Lydia." Lydia steps forward and Claire gently transfers Lettie to her.

"Hi, Lettie." Lydia squats down and squeezes Lettie's hands. "It's nice to meet you."

"Oh my, oh my. Another pretty one. What are you—sisters?"

Lydia shakes her head, not trusting herself to speak. She is infused with an inarticulate happiness of the kind adored puppies and kittens must feel.

Lettie reaches out and brushes one of Lydia's stray locks with a gnarled finger. "No, you don't have the red hair like she does. You got the pretty golden kind. Step back and let me get a good look at you, Sugar."

Lydia stands and backs up a few steps in the narrow space between the foot of bed and the wall.

"Oooh-ee, look how tall! Like a statue. You look like you could be someone important. Important people is tall. So they look good on the magazines."

Lydia and Claire can't help laughing out loud at that.

"What's so funny?" Lettie demands.

"Everyone looks tall in the magazines, Lettie!" Lydia tells her, which gets Lettie slapping her knee and laughing like the girls have seen people do in old movies but never in person.

"Oh, you are some wildcard, you are!" Lettie wags her finger at Lydia as the giggles keep leaking out of her. "Come on now and sit on the bed and visit." Lydia obliges. "There you go."

Lettie turns to Claire, suddenly serious. "You're a good girl to come see me with your friends," she tells her. "I got a daughter and she don't even come see me."

"Is that so?" Claire's heard this one before.

"Hasn't even got the time o' day for her old lady."

"Then who sent you the roses?" Claire asks, turning Lettie's chair to face the nightstand.

"Some big ol' girl I never seen," Lettie answers huffily. She appeals to Lydia with a martyred look.

Lydia looks over at the flowers and then at Claire, who rolls her eyes. "There's a card with the flowers. Let's read it and see who it's from," she suggests.

"Well, I suppose. Give it here."

Claire hands the card to Lettie who hands it to Lydia. Lydia reads: "'To Mom with Love from Yvonne, Frank, Leena and Little Frank.' Is Yvonne your daughter?"

"One of 'em." Lettie takes the card back from Lydia and peers at it suspiciously.

"And I bet Leena and Little Frank are your grandkids."

"Oh, those two devils!" Lettie looks over at the yellow roses, with a smile this time. "They brought me those flowers!"

"Aren't they pretty!" Lydia enthuses. She and Claire exchange a look over Lettie's head.

"They brought me a necklace too, with their pictures in it. Now I can't find it!" Lettie goes back to pawing the bedspread. "I know I put it down right here."

"You weren't wearing it?" Claire starts looking around on the nightstand.

"I took it off to see it better."

The girls search the room, especially the floor under the bed and around Lettie's chair. They feel around in her wheelchair where they can, afraid to lift her, and politely lift her arms and shake her caftan a little to see if the necklace is in her lap. They are about to search her bureau and nightstand when Lettie reprimands them. "Don't you go doing that now!" She has forgotten both that they are searching for something and the object they seek.

The girls exchange another look. "We were just fixing the flowers," Claire says, snapping off a yellow leaf.

"And the card," Lydia adds, placing the greeting card back on the nightstand next to the vase. They make ready to depart.

"You take care, Lettie. We'll see you next time," Claire announces breezily. She pats Lettie on the shoulder as she squeezes by her chair. "Thanks for spending some time with us."

"Yeah, thanks, Lettie. Really nice to meet you."

The girls slip out before Lettie can protest. She looks about her with vague disquiet, but when her eyes come to rest on the bouquet she smiles.

"Pretty," she says, looking at the roses and thinking of her new friends, "like flowers, those two."

# CHAPTER 32
## LEGACY

Many times Brodie has been called a kook, a fanatic, and a workaholic—straight out and behind his back. He's come to see this as a sign that he's achieving his goals in his post as City Youth Liaison and CARMA co-leader, and to welcome his lot as an object of friendly, usually, derision. If everyone can get together around making fun of him, Brodie figures, at least they're getting together on something. And if a community is angry because their project isn't going well, Brodie happily takes the flak. Because if the neighborhood didn't *want* the project, they wouldn't be pissed. Getting them to want the project and fight for it is Brodie's first task, and when they gripe that his agency has screwed everything up and they could do it better themselves, he knows his work is done.

There's been a surprising lack of contention over the Old Mercantile mural after its initial rocky start. A few complaints about the blaring music from people with offices in the building; a graffiti incident early on; an egg thrown at Shelly's way-out bumper; a couple of run-ins between the CARMA students and neighborhood youths—each episode deftly defused by Brodie, forgiven, and then forgotten. Without such confrontations, the mural would simply be an art project. But in the collision, and reconciliation, of conflicting interests, community spirit is built.

Sipping his free orange soda from the Big B, Brodie reflects that the only thing that hasn't changed in the course of this project is the mural's title. The surface changed from brick to aluminum panels, the design changed, the budget and funding changed, relationships

225

changed, attitudes changed—but the mural's name has stayed the same from proposal to finished painting.

City trucks pull away from the curb with their heavy load of steel tubes and platforms, leaving the work fully exposed save for the cluster of kids crowding in to sign their names under Miranda's skillfully calligraphed title block:

*'Legacy' created by the*
*Community Art-Reach Mural Association and the*
*Cesar Chavez Neighborhood Association, July 1999*

"Awesome! That is just awesome!" Brodie calls from across the street. They all turn and wave for him to come over, shouting that he has to sign his name too.

"But I didn't paint a single stroke," he tells the kids as he crosses over and they start waving paint brushes at him. There is no separation now, he notices, between the CARMA group and the neighborhood group. They are all over him and each other like happy puppies. (Brodie considers dogs the most democratic of species, and dreams of the day when humans will be as blind to color and shape as canines are.) "Really, I'm afraid I'll ruin it," he protests at the continued insistence that he sign. "One of you guys do it for me. Marcos, how about it?" he picks out the resentful young man who threw the egg.

Marcos, reluctantly drawn into activities at the Old Mercantile through Laurie and Angela's cousin Eddie, has since become something of a protege of Shelly's. He looks pleased when Brodie passes him the paintbrush, and with a dozen backseat painters coaching him, he carefully letters B-R-O-D-I-E E-P-S-T-E-I-N, C-I-T-Y L-I-A-S-O-N underneath Shelly's artful autograph.

A cheer goes up. Marcos plunks his brush into the rinse bucket, boasting that he could've done better with a can of spray paint. The group disperses, fanning out to view their work from a distance. Neighbors are gathering in clusters up and down the block, workers are streaming out of the Old Mercantile to see the finished mural.

The three Torres sisters, mothers of Laurie, Angela, and Eddie, with their younger children and several other families, are marching up Soldiers Road with a card table, folding chairs and trays of fresh made *biscochitos.* Lydia pulls up to the curb and parks, seeing a serious traffic jam forming ahead. She and Claire jump out and help the ladies carry their stuff to the Big B, where they set up under the shade of Mr. B's awning. Claire runs over to sign the mural before the last of the painting supplies are cleaned up, while Lydia receives a hearty welcome from Dori and the others.

Josh is across the street under the bus shelter in deep conversation with Shelly, Percy Hartshorn and Gus C De Baca. He waves to Claire and she waves back but doesn't join them. That's one pow wow she wants nothing to do with. Instead, she crosses to the other corner and sits down on a parking barrier next to Celine to stare at their creation.

Words cannot convey the awe and pride with which the girls view the finished mural. They know they worked super hard on it—they have sunburns and paint-stained wardrobes to prove it—but it still seems like magic, the way all the pieces now blend seamlessly into one epic image.

"Legacy's a good name for it," Claire says.

"Yeah, the 'happy brown children' really make it." They laugh. This has been a big joke since Angela was quoted in the paper. No one misses an opportunity to goof on it, but the truth is, those children were the most lovingly painted of all of the mural elements, except perhaps for Josh's train.

"Big block party here tonight," Celine explains, as more neighborhood people converge on the corner, some carrying folding chairs, others lugging coolers, platters of food, and instruments. "You staying?"

"No, I'm going home," Claire answers decisively. She's turned her attention to the meeting of the minds over at the bus shelter, while Lydia's secret—former secret—keeps buzzing around in the back of her brain, waiting for her to take it out and examine it again, in private. Meanwhile her eyes are on Josh. He cuts an incredibly handsome figure, standing with his arms folded across his chest between the lanky, distinguished frame of Percy Hartshorn and Shelly's tanned, athletic form. Gus is shorter than all of them, built like a wrestler. Claire detects that his attention is focused on Shelly. He's looking her over as if trying to imagine how she'd look in an extra forty pounds of sculpted stone.

Claire can still see Gus rising from the hot tub, streaming wet and butt naked, and her skin prickles with a disturbing combination of revulsion and desire. She thinks about Gus's studio full of nudes, and the naked bodies presented like pretty slabs of meat in Hartshorn's classroom—and that day Greg thought maybe Josh had given her a black eye, which she thought was stupid at the time, but maybe wasn't all that out of line. Her mind plays through the extremes of Shelly and her hairy-legged girlfriends, and what Lydia told her about Blaine. Muffin would say "Horrors!" to the whole business, as any parent would. Claire watches Josh and Gus, and thinks how safe she felt with them, and still feels—well, with Josh, anyway—and tells herself she would've known right away if things weren't cool at Gus's studio, and would've gotten out of there. But would she? That's another one that will take some sorting out.

Claire turns her eyes back to the mural and tries to make an objective assessment of her rendition of Rosa Parks. Maybe she put too much of Lettie into it, but only someone who had met Lettie would notice.

"Neighborhood's putting on a block party," Danny announces, settling in between Claire and Celine with a friendly wiggle of his hips. "You staying?"

"I think I better go home and come back, so the 'rents don't have a fit," Celine says.

"I'm just going home," Claire says, "I'm beat."

Her eyes are traveling around the whole mural now. It's about the most amazing thing she's ever seen, even though she's been looking at it for a month. She's thinking about her little gem-like paintings, and the sketches she's been making at Westcare Manor, and the books about cartooning that are weighing down her pack. She's thinking about that mysterious multi-faceted creature Josh calls Claire Cubed, about the bed she hasn't slept in for three nights, and how her parents could be so cool about everything, to not come after her with a net and a tranquilizer gun, which she probably deserved.

Then her eyes rest again on Rosa Parks, and Claire considers how Mrs. Parks was so tired that day she just got on the bus and sat her ass down in the first seat she came to. It wasn't war, it was weariness. She sat her weary bones down and the whole world stood up and cheered for her. *Sometimes victory comes when there's no fight left in a person,* Claire thinks.

"Sorry I can't stay for the block party tonight." Josh is standing over her, reaching a hand down. She takes it and lets him pull her up into a hug. "Thanks to you I'm gonna get a Pass from Hartshorn, but I do have to turn in three paintings on Monday, and all my stuff is at the house. If you want to stay, I'll come pick you up later."

"No. I'm gonna have Lydia take me home."

Josh takes a step back and gives Claire a probing look. "You mad?"

"No. Just pooped." Claire gives him a tired smile. She doesn't want him to think she's mad or regretful, because she's not. Whatever shit other girls take from other guys doesn't apply to her and Josh. Josh has been perfect—she loves him—she knows he loves her. "The mural's done, classes are over, and I think it's time for me to face the music." She squeezes his hand and he leans down and kisses her.

"Okay. Let's go get your stuff." They saunter down the street toward Josh's car, arms around each others' waists.

Two police cars crawl past them going the opposite way, lights flashing to clear the street. Everyone stops what they're doing to watch the cars' progress. They pull into the Big B parking lot, and several cops pop out weilding clipboards and bullhorns. Mr. B goes over to see what's going on. Laurie's mom is right behind him. She's the first one to raise her voice.

"Since when do we need a *permit* to have a party?!"

Brodie's there in a flash, his cell phone to his ear and his arm waving away the angry kids and neighbors who are converging on the policemen. Shelly and Gus are wisely staying out of it. But Percy Hartshorn, in his jaunty summer linens, wades right in. He's a head taller than everyone but the tallest of the cops, reminding Claire of Lettie's comment about important people being tall. Which rightfully makes Anthony, Parks, King and Chavez the most important figures at this gathering. Their giant heads rise many feet above the crowd. The policemen, however, are undaunted in asserting their own authority.

"You artists have all the fun," Lydia teases, coming over to Claire and Josh. "What a scene!"

"Personally, I've seen enough," Josh says. "Let's get out of here. Where's your car, Lydia? We were just getting Claire's stuff."

The three turn their backs on what tomorrow's papers will call "Near-riot at Mural Site."

"Well, at least Brodie's enjoying himself," Claire says, taking one last look over her shoulder. Looks like he's got himself another *opportunity for neighborhood empowerment.*"

The action at Merchant and Soldiers is all over the radio on the way home. Claire figures her parents will be having conniptions in front of the evening news when she gets in. Lydia drops her off and hurries on to her own house. With any luck, the Overmyers won't suspect that Lydia's been down there.

It is eerily quiet when Claire steps inside and drops her bag of laundry in the hall. She can hear the pulsing whir of the evaporative cooler, and Stan Man talking to himself while he taps impatiently at the computer keyboard in the den. But no media. Claire thinks how rare it is not to hear the sounds of a radio or TV. Almost spooky. She tiptoes toward the dining room, trying not to disturb her father.

Brianna is sitting at the dining room table, quietly reading a magazine. This too is unusual, Claire thinks. She's used to seeing her mother in motion—if not actually moving, then emitting a frenetic sort of mental energy. Finding Brianna at rest like this startles Claire almost as much as her own sudden appearance startles Brianna. They find themselves looking at each other with the same surprised expressions.

"How did you get here?" Brianna asks, almost annoyed. She's been listening for the distinctive sound of Josh's car for three days.

This is not the greeting Claire has been preparing herself for, but she takes some satisfaction in catching her mother off guard. "I clicked my heels three times and said, 'I want to go home, I want to go home,'" she answers with a little smile. And then immediately plops down at the table, gets out her sketchbook and starts drawing, because she's just given herself an idea.

Brianna Yost looks on, flabbergasted, while the headachy knot behind her left ear begins to loosen. She opens her mouth to speak, changes her mind, and goes back to reading her magazine. At least she pretends to read. Inside she's fighting down waves of anger and relief, frustration and pride, and all the while the urgent scratching of Claire's pencil on paper fills the air with a sound that has been desperately missed. Carl drifts in, is startled, then transfixed, by the silent drama between his wife and daughter.

Claire's picture spills onto the page in flowing, confident strokes: The imposing Old Mercantile blocking out much of the sky and then replacing it with a painted version—the mural and its many elements—with the mural children at street level dwarfing the actual forms of teenagers and neighbors thronging around the policemen, their cars in the foreground, the Big B to the left with refreshments on tables set up under the striped awning, and in an empty space along the right side of the page, a hot air balloon lifting up and out of the top margin of the picture, its gondola at eye level with the four-headed wizard of great ones, and Claire within, waving farewell with one arm and clutching her sketchbook in the other.

The young artist halts her pencil and studies her work for a long minute, erases, corrects, repeats the process several times, then puts down her tools. She takes a deep breath and speaks, eyes on the pad. "I was thinking I'd like to be a political cartoonist or comic strip artist, and I've been looking into schools where I can study that sort of thing. Pratt looks good, and the Kansas City Art Institute, Mass College of Art, and Rhode Island School of Design—but I'm not sure I'm good enough to get in. And I have to put in an application to the U, so I'll have a better chance of getting into another drawing class there during the regular semester." She looks from Carl to Brianna, who are visibly in the process of shifting gears. Apparently the subject is not to be their daughter's past delinquency, but her plans for the future.

Carl gets up to speed first. "You're not looking at any schools on the west coast?"

"Well, I know there're some good ones. But I don't want to be that far away from Josh."

"I see." The clutch goes in again. Stan Man's run out of steam already.

"Have you written for the catalogues?" Brianna asks. If they could not talk about Josh or the past three days right now, it would be a great relief, she realizes.

Claire agrees. She eagerly tells her mother about the schools and some others she's looked into. Stan Man goes into the kitchen and listens while he starts supper. *It's like she* has *been to Oz and back again*, he reflects, visualizing Claire in her hot air balloon. *Now that she's landed back home, her being away almost seems like a dream.*

They try to keep it that way, chattering through the meal about Stan Man's day and Brianna's day and Claire's day, as if not a thing unusual had happened—not among them. Jo calls to tell them to turn on the TV. They pick up their plates and head for the den. There's a helicopter view of the intersection of Merchant and Soldiers with lots of flashing lights and bobbing bodies, while the announcer refers to a "fracas in the heart of Cesar Chaveztown." Carl clicks the remote and another station has a reporter on the scene. He's having trouble stringing words together, as a salsa band wails behind him. The camera looks over his shoulder to show a police barricade detouring traffic over to State Street. Apparently the celebration is being permitted without a permit. The fracas is only a dance party. The camera pans upward to take in the mural looming above, illuminated by a bank of lights installed on the Old Mercantile's roof.

"Wow!" Carl and Brianna are impressed.

"You should see it in person," Claire tells them, then dashes to her room because she thinks she hears her phone ringing.

Her parents keep flipping channels, looking for more shots of the mural and trying to recognize people they know in the crowd. Everyone interviewed by the mingling commentator praises the mural,

"Legacy... Legacy... Legacy..." Carl and Brianna wish the camera would linger on it long enough for them to pick out Claire's portrait of Rosa Parks. It's unclear at what point in the evening they agree that there will be no punishment for Claire. They don't want to spoil the fun of having her home.

They don't want to risk alienating her again.

## CHAPTER 33
## FALLOUT

At the Antresian home, Josh receives a restrained welcome. Unlike Claire, he has been directly in contact with his parents, phoning them periodically like he always does when he's away. He has taken off on "field trips" and other adventures before without their permission, but never with a girl (that they know of), and he always gets in touch before they feel the need to start calling hospital emergency rooms. Claire has complicated matters, but once the Stanley-Yosts settled down—displayed, in fact, superhuman patience with and trust in their daughter—the Antresians were content to let Josh stay at Gus's under the pretext of working on the fountain sculpture—a work they half-suspect they will never see. Even so, Nick and Kerri Antresian are glad to hear their son's car pull down the driveway this Friday afternoon.

They've been watching the "Mural Melee" on the most melodramatic of the local newscasts. When Josh bounds in they look up and try not to give away their great relief at seeing him. He laughs when he sees what's on and sits down to give them a firsthand account of the situation at Merchant and Soldiers. They flip channels for a few minutes, find other reports that are not so dire, and thus reassured adjourn to dinner. Josh devours his meal enthusiastically, converses with his father attentively, thanks his mother profusely, and then hurries to his room to paint. No word of apology or recrimination has been spoken.

*Everything is going to be just the same as it was*, Nick Antresian reflects, *with Josh respectfully doing any damn thing he pleases*. Nick's not sure he can live with that. Not sure that he's doing the right thing as a parent. He puts the dishes in the sink with a noisy clatter and stalks out the back door, grabbing his putter as he goes. The way he

234

sees it, Josh is getting a good education in what it's like to be an artist, but who among his famous *mentors* is going to teach him what it means to be a man? *It's not just about screwing women, not by a long shot*, Nick thinks, *it's more about* not *screwing them.*

Nick Antresian is a strong believer in self-discipline. Were his son not utterly devoted to his art, he'd have serious concern for the boy. But Josh has some spine, there's no doubt of that, and an ethic of a sort. And Nick can't help remembering his old worries regarding his son's masculinity, the result of his own bias about limp-wristed artists. On that account alone Nick finds he has to cut Josh some slack. Nick Antresian can't deny that he is secretly pleased to see his son demonstrating normal urges.

Nick places a golf ball on the perfectly groomed swath of grass and lines up a putt. He wishes he were at the driving range and could swing with all his force, bashing the ball and his confusion of feelings with it into the far distance. He backs off and takes a couple of pretend swipes at the air. A twinge in his side tells him he ate too much at dinner. Sighing, he repositions himself, and taps the ball gently.

Over the next couple of days, while Josh paints furiously and Claire reconnects with Lydia, something rankles in both households. The sheer audacity of the young people, and the complicity of Gus, weigh on the minds of the much-put-upon parents. The anxiety, disapproval, insult and embarrassment which each felt in varying degrees, and which gave way to other strong emotions upon the teens' return—of relief, mostly—have now drained away, leaving a void which must be filled.

For both the Antresians and the Stanley-Yosts the opportunity to express disapproval seems to have been missed. They weren't experiencing disapproval at the moment their children returned, but they are experiencing it now. Unable to articulate it, a chilly silence descends between parents and teens. Although there was no explosion following Claire and Josh's week of infamy, there is fallout. It settles like a blanket of white ash after a volcano.

A week passes. Claire is becoming used to the queerly aloof demeanor her parents have displayed since her return. She tells herself that they're giving her the space she needs, not punishing her for her defection. But it feels like she's getting the silent treatment, like they're perpetually pissed, especially her mother.

They're out hoeing the garden when Brianna finally blows. She's wrung out of hostility and progressed to melancholia by now, in her internal parade of emotions. Feeling wounded, she's at last inspired to bestow upon Claire the payback which is most deserved—guilt. Across the rows of chile plants, Claire thinks she sees tears mingling with the sweat pouring down her mother's face.

"It's just—" Brianna rakes at the ground and launches in, sensing Claire's eyes on her. "It's just that the whole thing has come full circle. Once upon a time I had to wean you from needing me so much, and now I realize that I have to wean myself from needing you."

"Oh, Mom, you don't need me." It's not the right thing to say, she doesn't even mean it the way it comes out, but she wants to say something to fend off what's coming next.

Brianna looks up, past Claire, to watch the bobbing heads of evening joggers pass by on the ditch. With a big sigh she turns her attention to her daughter.

"You know how much you love Josh?" Claire nods. "Then you're probably able to imagine how much I love your father." Another nod. "But you'll never know how much I love you, or the quality of that love until you have children of your own. It's an animal kind of love, hard wired right into my gut. I know I seem like a modern woman, career oriented, all of that. But since the moment of conception I have *lived* for you."

"Oh gross, Mom!" Claire says, feeling embarrassed and somewhat alarmed. "I think you just talked me out of having kids."

That makes Brianna laugh pretty hard, and the much needed laughter retires her inner drama queen for the time being. She and Claire resume their yard work, resisting the urge to hug.

After this Claire feels more like a new order actually has been established, they're not just faking it. She and her parents are going to be companionable roommates instead of manipulative family members. Brianna will try to be less authoritarian, and she's to try to be less of a brat.

But still, Stan-Man is different. They haven't even had any good talks in the car. He and Brianna are noticeably more lovey-dovey, as if Claire's escapade has released them from a certain level of decorum and responsibility. She feels left out, again.

Of course, *she's* the one who's going to leave *them*, she reminds herself, probably within the year. When she tries to think what to say to them, Claire can't find anything specific to complain about. She's too proud to start apologizing. The silence deepens.

Another week passes. Claire hasn't seen much of anyone but Josh and Muffin. It's so incredibly hot that no one feels especially ambitious or communicative. Parties amount to languid gatherings of sweaty people rolling iced aluminum beverage cans across their foreheads. The movie theaters are doing a great business, but the kids can't afford to go a lot. Claire hangs out at the library instead, reading about her chosen field.

Lots of the kids are taking off on family vacations. Lydia's gone already. The Stanley-Yosts usually save their big trip for winter, when they go down to Miami to visit Brianna's mother. It's unlikely they'll even take a weekend road trip this summer, since Claire is committed to taking care of Muffin when Jo goes out of town, and her parents can't seem to tear themselves away from the new business.

The Antresians have invited Claire to join them on their annual fishing retreat up in Green Creek, but she's declined because it overlaps with her Muffin responsibilities, because fishing sounds horrible, and because she'd have to share a cabin with Josh's young and bratty girl cousins. Josh is acting like he doesn't want to go either, if Claire's not going, but if Claire's not going, his parents are unwilling to leave him here in town with the run of their house. They've offered to pay for a bus trip to New York City, where he can check out some schools and meet a couple of Gus's friends—see what he's really in for out there. It's an easy decision for Josh.

Claire can be excited for him, knowing that the separation will be temporary. Josh will be back to finish school. He's promised to stay through both semesters of Senior year, even if he does have enough credits to graduate early. So, they have close to a year before they have to go their separate ways, if that's what they decide.

*Even then, it won't have to mean it's over. Not at all. If we love each other, we'll have the whole future to work out who lives where.*

This is what Claire thinks, but doesn't say.

Josh feels like he's confronting his destiny. That's not an easy thing to talk about either. He's trapped by his own talent. Everything within him and everyone around him demands that he follow this path. They tell him he has what it takes to be a great artist—talent and discipline, passion and curiosity. "But there's something else," Gus reminds him, "the courage to spend your life walking into the unknown. That's the essence of *creating*—making something that wasn't there before."

*How can walking into the unknown feel so much like destiny?* Josh wonders. He never knows what shape his art will take beyond a few pages of ideas in his sketchbook, but the shape of his life as an artist looms large and unmistakable. If only he could be sure that Claire will be there with him, he would march right into the future without a backward glance. But he can't ask her for a promise like that. That's an unknown, too, something to be discovered along the way.

Sometimes they slip away somewhere and make love. They need to show each other how they feel, because it's getting hard to say it. The words "I love you," now have questions hanging from them, fears and needs beyond anything they care to lay on each other, loving one another as they do. They try to savor being together without letting thoughts of the future interfere. They succeed, but there is a quiet place between them on account of it. Their silences are tender, but unsettling.

July drags on. The temperature broaches triple digits. Dust devils skip along the ditch by day, heat lightning arcs across the evening sky. Everything slows down. No one talks much about anything but the heat.

The Antresians have everyone over for the unveiling of Josh's sculpture. "Everyone" being Claire and her parents, Gus, Percy Hartshorn, and Lydia, recently returned from Colorado. And Shelly shows up, but it's not clear who invited her. The side gate is open, and arriving guests follow the sounds of conversation to the back yard, where yesterday the red granite maiden was installed with great travail by Nick, Gus and Josh. Nick is looking the worse for it. And Kerri is nervous because they're running the fountain mid-day, a definite violation of the water regulations.

The group assembles to marvel at Josh's creation. Each newcomer circles it quietly, staying out of the way of the others as they study the work from every angle. Eyes widen and corners of mouths turn upward. Here and there little giggles and gasps escape. Josh watches the human figures ranging around his sculpted one and begins to enjoy himself. He can tell they like it.

When he can't stand the quiet any longer, Josh clears his throat and commences a short speech he's prepared. First he explains how he's titled the work "Claire Cubed" for its Cubism-influenced form, then he gives Gus credit for suggesting he abstract the figure and simplify its shapes to make his first large project more manageable. Together, Josh emphasizes, he and Gus worked out a design that was both beautiful and do-able.

"And then Josh did it. He really did it!" Gus boasts. "The result surpasses all my expectations!" The admiring crowd applauds both artists.

Nick and Kerri finally relax. They were prepared for an awkward morning, what with having the Stanley-Yosts over, and Josh's overbearing teachers. But the fact is, "Claire Cubed" is so striking a work, so well suited to its site, so magically complete when the water comes trickling out of the kneeling girl's pitcher, that a lot of slights are forgiven on the spot. Such is the power of art.

Naturally Kerri and Nick have thought the statue was very good right along, but it was hard to see it at first. First, they weren't expecting any statue at all, and then what they got was so different looking, they weren't sure how to rate it. It didn't look like Claire, exactly. But they find it looks more and more like her with each viewing. It amazes them. Over the past twenty-four hours they have each in their own way found Josh's work to be a truly pleasing object, whether viewed from the kitchen window or the putting green, or from ground level while gathering marjoram leaves or weeding the garden. Words cannot express how gratified they are to learn that their son's genius is evident to others and not merely an illusory product of parental pride.

Once everyone has admired the statue, the pond, the garden, the putting green and then all of the yard, Kerri Antresian invites them in for coffee and cake. Percy Hartshorn and Shelly decline—and can be seen standing on the sidewalk talking for some minutes before getting in their cars and driving off in the same direction. That gets Claire, Lydia and Josh going good, which wins them permission to return to the garden with their refreshments and ridiculous gossip.

The parents and Gus settle in Kerri's immaculate living room. Alone together, they all feel that something should be said, but no one is willing to start. Gus, reminding himself that he's old enough to be Nick and Kerri, Carl and Brianna's father, and that he's a famous artist to boot, lapses into a genial silence, abdicating all responsibility for the conversation. Brianna doesn't feel it's her place, being a guest, and has already instructed Carl not to broach the subject—unless the Antresians do, though he can't be counted on to obey. In fact he will, because he's not anxious to have that talk either. His feelings are too mixed. What would he say? The host and hostess, meanwhile, having convened the group for festive purposes, can't bring themselves to be so rude as to cause a confrontation—although, again, it seems the perfect opportunity to clear the air. Instead, the air remains heavy with unvoiced thoughts. There are a lot of compliments on the cake.

Among the young people a more comfortable atmosphere prevails. They've laughed themselves out and are drifting into their own thoughts, lulled by the sparkling song of the fountain.

Lydia finds herself looking forward to helping Claire with Muffin, and to seeing Lettie again. Up in Colorado, her thoughts had turned more than once to that missing necklace. And Claire had complained that Muffin's homemade handwarmer was missing, had been for a while. Lydia seems to remember that when her Granny Abel was in the rest home she was always "losing" things too. Her parents often suspected theft, and Lydia feels that same tug of suspicion now. She is hatching another one of her plots.

Josh is thinking about his trip—he leaves for New York in three days—and his host, Gus's friend, Javier Ortiz. They met last year when the printmaker-turned-wallpaper-executive was making a vacation tour of the southwest. He surprised Gus and Josh at the studio, and then insisted they round up Katy and all go to a swanky restaurant for dinner, his treat. When later he invited Josh to "crash at my pad" if ever he was in the City, Josh hadn't really taken the offer seriously. Gus was the one who reminded him of it, and made the first call to Ortiz. Ever since, Josh has felt a growing anxiety about coming off as a country bumpkin among the businessman's upscale crowd—arriving by bus, no less!

Josh has never cared much about his image, or his popularity, or the approval of others. In his small circle, success and recognition were almost guaranteed. He had only to be minimally attentive and civilized, and otherwise his talent carried the day. But he suspects this will not be so in New York. He stares at "Claire Cubed," trying to see it through another's eyes. Is it good enough? Will the photos he took this morning do it justice? The compliments he received today have boosted his confidence a bit, but he reminds himself that these come from friends and family and his own teachers—of course they would say nice things.

Claire also studies Josh's interpretation of her in stone. She feels like she is becoming her statue—taking on some substance, smoothing out rough edges, learning to incorporate her many facets into a graceful form. "Claire Cubed," for which she modeled, has become an admirable model for her. She wants to be that solid. She wants to be that unique. She wants to be that beautiful. But she doesn't want to be that silent. She notices how the small splash and burble of water only accentuates the rugged silence of granite, imagines the adults' meaningless conversation striking impotently against a wall of unspoken thoughts.

Claire knows that *she* wants to say something with her art, something that's about more than art itself. She opens her pad and sketches the statue with a word balloon flowing out of the pitcher instead of water. But before she can write in anything, a great gust of wind comes up, blowing spray from the fountain at them and filling the girls' hair with petals torn from Mrs. Antresian's roses. They jump up and look around in dismay at the quickly darkening sky, as if suddenly finding themselves lost in an unfamiliar landscape.

A change in the weather has come, not stealthily in the night, but galloping in at high noon, to sweep out the old regime with a great cloud of dust. Going...going...gone! The summer day that lasted so infinitely long, that changed so undetectably incrementally, is done. Josh, Claire and Lydia move out of range of the spray from the fountain, but otherwise persist in the face of the blustering elements. In speechless reverence the three let the wind whip through them while they watch the dark clouds gather.

"Turn the fountain off!" Nick Antresian bellows from the back porch, having observed the teens standing around stupidly in the spitting rain for some minutes.

Josh jogs around to the utility shed while Claire and Lydia gather up their plates and glasses.

Good-byes in the Antresian's driveway are brief as a light sprinkle gives way to steady rain. Soon the guests are driving home in a downpour.

# CHAPTER 34
## MONSOON SEASON

When Claire was in the fifth grade she did a report for geography class on the embattled country known alternately as Burma and the Union of Myanmar. In making her many drawings of that kite-shaped nation, each partitioned and color coded to represent topography, climate, agriculture, population and other characteristics, Claire learned what the term "monsoon season" means in other parts of the world.

In New Mexico she experiences a monsoon season that lasts for approximately three weeks of every summer, during which the hot, clear days are interrupted by late afternoon thunderstorms, sometimes torrential but rarely sustained. This amounts to half the annual rainfall. However, Claire remembers that in Burma there are two monsoon seasons, each lasting several months, which combine to bring thirty-five to *two hundred* inches of rain per year!

Every summer when the skies open up and release their hoarded rains, Claire's thoughts return to the charts and graphs of her fifth grade report, the maps she so carefully filled in with hash marks and stippling, the pictures clipped from *National Geographic* of women with their soaked cotton shifts whipping around them as they bend to their work in the rice paddies. Even as she indulges in these images of a far-off land, the local front passes, the showers subside, a brilliant shaft of light escapes the clouds, and an orange sun plummets over one horizon while a rainbow arcs over the other. Monsoon season. Words mean different things in different places.

What does the word Love mean to Josh now that he's gone to New York City? Claire can't imagine what kind of new vocabulary he'll bring home. The long letter he wrote to her on the trip out was carefully observant, with illustrations, of everything about the bus ride—his fellow passengers, the towns, the landscapes, the weather. The pages are so full of the Josh she knows, they make her miss him keenly when she reads them and studies the drawings. She notices the way his style changed to incorporate the jiggliness of that bus ride right into his art. He is so full of talent! Since arriving in the City he's been too busy to write—roaming the museums and galleries by day, hobnobbing at studios, clubs and artists' apartments all night. Yes, he called once to tell her what a grand time Javier Ortiz was showing him, and he sounded different.

Maybe Claire's jealous because Josh is having such a good time without her. That's part of it, she'll admit—the trip sounds like a blast! But also, an old concern has come back to haunt her about Josh—that Art is the most important thing to him. She knows that it is. It should be. She must not ever, ever hinder him. But on the other hand, is she prepared to put her all into helping him? If they stay together, live together or move somewhere together, will she end up keeping house for him, working to support him? How much would *he* give up to help advance *her* career? In Claire's eyes, her own talent is to Josh's what the New Mexico monsoon is to the monsoons of Burma. His abilities are torrential. Hers are mostly wind.

Fortunately, Claire has Muffin to keep her mind off of questions that can only be answered by time. Jo has gone out of town for almost three weeks and left everything in Claire's hands. Claire devotes herself to house-sitting and Muffin, and the days pass. In addition to packing Muffin's lunch, Claire must also bring in the paper and the mail, fill the bird feeders, water house plants, and often water outdoors too when the blustery monsoons have been inadequate to maintain Jo's back yard oasis. Jo's house and gardens are bright and tidy and full of colorful things. How different it all is from Gus's studio. The spaces are as different as the people who inhabit them.

Claire wonders what kind of space she will create for herself when she has a whole house or apartment, instead of a single room, to call her own. It's fun to imagine, to tend to her responsibilities at Jo's place as if it were really hers. She's not sure how much to let Josh figure into the scene. Maybe they are living together and maybe not—this cannot be decided even in imagination. Still, her inventive mind can't help but turn in that direction.

But where was she? Fixing Muffin's lunch from the ingredients Jo has stocked for her, and packing the little cooler. She hurries through her clean-up, eager for the visit. With any luck, they will complete another chapter of the book today.

Claire starts her trips to Westcare Manor earlier now because the drive has been taking longer. A massive construction project on the west side is coming to a head, and the traffic pattern is never the same from one day to the next. Lydia, who knows the roads of Rio Bueno inside out, tells Claire about alternate routes, and these detours add another dimension to the daily drill. As she drives, Claire studies her surroundings carefully. They are to become the background for her new cartoon strip.

In "The Cupcake Comics," as Claire conceives the series, Muffin has become a full-fledged superhero—Granny Granola Super Muffin, now past her prime and consigned to a nursing home. Each episode begins with Super Muffin's trusty sidekick Cupcake gearing up for a new battle against injustice. But Granny Granola insists things be set right at Drear Manor before she'll help Cupcake with any superhero work.

Yes, Claire has undertaken nothing less than an illustrated account of the Muffin Project, in comic book format, for the centerpiece of her college admissions portfolio. She's certain that both her writing and drawing are lacking, but is committed to recording her experience with all of the truth, humor and irony that she can pack into her struggling panels. She spends long hours in consultation with Lydia, who has taken up Muffin's cause with enthusiasm, as well as Lettie's, and is happy to help Claire lambaste the nursing home.

As for the bigger causes that engage earnest but inept Super Cupcake, Claire has found no shortage of issues, either global or local, to satirize. Today, for instance, she is driving directly through the heart of the road work rather than avoiding it, in order to get a good look at the devastation. She is both awed and sickened to see a great swath of what was once the knobby, scrubby skin of planet Earth scraped down to flat, featureless, colorless dust. From this a new shopping mall will rise and acres of parking lot will be paved. This road Claire is now creeping along is slated to be bent into a sharp left turn, so as to take travelers directly to the new mall. Cupcake may have to don her cape and fly to get to Muffin.

Claire considers the artistic possibilities as she bumps over the rutted road and avoids orange barrels. Behind her, mountainous guardian godparents glare down at the human infestation swarming over the West Mesa. Or they will, in The Cupcake Comics.

At the Manor, renovations are moving ahead at full throttle. Muffin's wing is finally being repapered and repainted. Elsewhere furniture is being replaced—new and old line the corridors in a constant rotation. Nothing is left alone. A walking path and gazebo are being installed in the back lawn. The parking lot has been re-paved and re-striped, with a secure area added for the furniture vans and contractors' pick-ups.

The roads, the weather, the Manor—Claire's love life—everything feels unsettled. Muffin's temperament is mercurial too, but perhaps no more than can be expected amid such disruption. Claire can now observe the nuances of Muffin's condition day to day, as well as the doings at the Manor.

*Wonder what it will be today,* Claire thinks, walking briskly up to the front door and confronting the recently posted "Visitors Must Sign In" notice with a sour expression. This is Lydia's doing! Only since Lydia started probing into Lettie's lost things—items that some people say Lettie never had or has hidden or lost herself—has this useless rule been implemented. And it wasn't done to discourage thieves, it was done to discourage Lydia! The new procedure is absurd. For one thing, who bothers signing in when no one's at the desk, which is more often the case than not?

The girls have observed that family members who feel guilty for their infrequent visits eagerly sign in and out. *Like they're registering a good deed in their karma account,* Claire thinks, watching a few lunchtime visitors line up for the book. Meanwhile, laborers and tradesmen are coming and going without a thought to signing the register. Doctors and lab workers are never asked to sign either, or show proof that they are who they are by anything other than their lab coats. Claire has been mistaken for a lab technician just because she carries the small cooler—the same kind in which blood samples are transported. And no one who was visiting regularly before the new protocol ever remembers to sign in unless asked—and *then* they can't remember to sign *out*. Claire mentions this to the receptionist who's flagged her down to come sign the book.

"Oh, a lot of people forget to sign out," the heavily perfumed woman chirps. She then assures Claire, "We just go down the sheet and sign everyone out at five o'clock."

Claire starts to say something, changes her mind, and hurries away. *Won't Lydia love that one!*

Logic seems to have no place here, and orderliness has fallen by the wayside as well. The foyer and front wing are in an uproar. At first Claire thinks that lunch is letting out already, so many people are milling around, but then she sees they are late, and just going in. This is because the paint job has worked its way to the second wing branching off from the foyer. Beds are lining the halls, confused residents in wheelchairs are struggling to get by. One bed holds Lettie's bright yellow comforter.

Claire wonders how Lettie is taking all this, but her first concern is Muffin. She weaves her way through the chaos and, looking all around as she passes the nurse's station, sees her charge parked a short distance down a quiet corridor. Muffin is dozing, slumped in her chair, with an empty cup and crumpled napkin on her tray. Claire feels relief—things could definitely be worse.

"Hi, Muffin, it's Claire!" She puts her hand over Muffin's.

"It is?"

"Yes, I brought some lunch for you."

"Oh, thank you." The sagging form starts to come to life.

"Listen, Muffin, you're parked out here in the hall and they're painting everywhere. Let me see if your room is ready before I wheel you down there. I'll be right back." Claire squeezes her hand and rushes off down the other hallway, dreading the scene in Muffin's room.

More relief. It's about the same as last week, reasonably neat with trim work still unfinished up along the ceiling. Claire drops the cooler on the bed and rushes back to Muffin.

*Always hurrying,* Claire thinks. It's funny, because Muffin's not going anywhere. She endures whatever is going on at Westcare Manor all the time—she has no choice. But Claire feels an urgency to serve her on these visits. In her persona as the novice do-gooder Cupcake, Claire zips down the corridors of Drear Manor leaving artistic swooshes in her wake, her longer-than-in-real-life curls fluttering behind her.

"Okay, Muffin, we're all set. I'm going to take you back to your room for lunch. Put your feet on the footrests."

Muffin complies. She knows the routine and welcomes it.

Claire stands behind Muffin and puts her forearms under Muffin's armpits. "Now let's sit up a bit more," she coaches as she lifts gently.

A push from Muffin, a pull from Claire, and there she is sitting almost straight. Muffin gives Claire a relieved "Thank you."

For the past week Muffin has been listing to the right. Now Claire notices that Muffin immediately begins to lean to the right again. She has likely had another small stroke, but her faculties are about the same—if anything, they are a little better.

Claire parks Muffin by the window in her room. There's more furniture than there should be and less space to set a chair beside Muffin's. While Claire rearranges, they talk about the paint job, Jo's trip, and Lydia—"Suzie," Muffin keeps calling her, and remembers her by the peculiar things she brings to eat.

Lydia simply refuses to have Claire make the lunches for her to take to Muffin, the way Jo did for Claire. She accepted some of Jo's stock of spicy tomato juice and coffee-flavored supplement, and otherwise brings to Muffin exactly what she packs for her own lunch. Muffin thinks the cheese puffs and pretzels are a grand treat, but Lydia's main courses have not been as popular. Claire has to admit, though, Lydia has made an impression.

Perhaps because Lydia was on duty yesterday, Muffin is extra hungry. Without coaxing she accepts her drink and a piece of sandwich and starts to eat. Claire reaches into the wardrobe and brings out their book of the week.

"Do you remember what we've been reading together, Muffin?"

"A book?"

Claire laughs. "Good guess! Do you remember which book?"

"No," Muffin admits good naturedly.

"It's called *The Five Children and It.*"

"Oh, yes." Before Claire can say more, Muffin has remembered. She begins chewing more slowly as if anticipating the enjoyment of listening to Claire read about the Psammead, and the children who pester it for wishes.

This happens to be Claire's favorite book from childhood. Stan Man used to read it to her while she sat in his lap. Now, as she reads to Muffin, she is loving it all over again. She wants Muffin to enjoy the story in the same way—to *get* it—and part of the fun is reviewing the earlier chapters before they start each new one.

"Do you remember the first thing the children wished?" Claire asks.

"No."

"They wished to be 'Beautiful as the Day,' remember?"

"Oh yes, now I do." And Muffin means it, which is very exciting for both of them.

"And in the second chapter they wished for 'Boundless Wealth.'"

"That never works," Muffin interjects.

Claire smiles. "And each time a wish goes bad, they miss lunch to boot."

"Too bad for them."

Muffin has accepted another quarter sandwich but will not take a bite. It is apparent that she will not continue her lunch until Claire starts reading. Without further comment, Claire commences the chapter called "Wings."

It's amazing how a wish as wonderful as wings can turn out so badly. Claire hams it up, and Muffin chuckles in all the right places.

Unlike the nature tales they have read, this story has a momentum to it that's hard to resist. Claire reads right through to the end of the chapter, long after Muffin's sandwich and juice have disappeared.

"So, what happens next?" Muffin asks while Claire spoons out oranges and "pudding."

"Oh, with the children?"

"Yes!"

Now that's a first. Muffin has never been this anxious for Claire to keep reading. Claire has no choice but to proceed with the next chapter, "No Wings." She picks up the book and holds it in her left hand and with her right continues to spoonfeed, eyes sweeping back and forth between the book, the bowl and Muffin's mouth. She's getting pretty good at this awkward process. Once the pudding course is finished, Claire sets up Muffin with her "iced coffee" and cookie, and plows ahead, as there can be no stopping before the children's dilemma is resolved. Miraculously, Claire finishes before anyone charges into the room. She returns the book to the top shelf of Muffin's wardrobe, promising to read another chapter tomorrow.

The session has wearied Muffin, and she half-dozes while Claire cleans up.

"See you tomorrow, Muffin," Claire whispers, patting her shoulders.

"Bye. I'll miss you."

Muffin's been saying that lately. There's no question that she knows who Claire is now. The feeling this gives Claire is bittersweet. Sweet to be appreciated so, bitter to think of Muffin lonely and missing her.

*But of course she forgets, in between.*

Not like Claire, who can't stop feeling the absence of Josh. Only constant activity relieves the longing, drowns out the questioning. So although she, too, is tired after lunch, Claire comes home and gets to work immediately. First some sketches of the roads, notes for a funny bit about the sign-in sheet, and then she wants to do something with books, something to express the magic of being transported in one's mind to other worlds.

"Claire, honey, someone just called for you." Brianna Yost has been watching Claire from the threshold for some seconds. Now her daughter looks up.

"Huh? I didn't hear the phone ring."

"No, I don't doubt it. I've never seen you so absorbed." Brianna thinks Claire looks a little pale, and it worries her when she sometimes sees her daughter rubbing her hand.

Claire smiles. She can read her mother's mind. "I keep wanting to draw things that I don't know how to draw. That's why I pulled all these magazine pictures." She gestures to the glossy pages littering the floor, and resists the impulse to massage her aching wrist. "Who called?"

"Someone from your drawing class. I'm surprised he didn't call your number as soon as we hung up. Where is your phone?" Brianna notices the empty desk unit.

"Buried I guess." Claire finds the receiver in a pile of clothes near her bed. "Hmmm, no charge." She replaces it in the cradle.

"That's okay. I told him to call back on this number if he couldn't get through to yours." At that moment the phone in Brianna's hand rings and she passes it to Claire.

"Hello? Oh, hi, Greg. Yeah, Mom said you were trying to call." Claire walks toward her mother, shooing her out, and Brianna backs into the hall. "That's okay, I was just working on an art project." Claire pushes her bedroom door closed.

Big drops of rain begin to plink loudly on the metal roof so that Brianna can't hear anything from the hall. "Get a life," she chides herself, resisting the temptation to press her ear against the door.

# CHAPTER 35
## I SPY

Do the stars object to being spied upon? Lydia never thought about it until she turned her attention away from them and directed it at Westcare Manor. She cannot speak for the heavenly bodies, but as a human she knows she would not like it if someone were watching her, and that what she's doing is wrong. It's probably illegal too, but she doesn't know that for sure and is not going to make an effort to find out. If she can't get her conscience on board, at least she can have ignorance in her corner.

More importantly, she feels her cause is just. It's bad enough that residents of Westcare Manor are the victims of theft, but the fact that no one even acknowledges that this is going on is scandalous. Lydia feels she has been driven to extreme measures. And it so happens she has an excellent pair of binoculars...

She's tried the direct approach already. A series of Westcare Manor administrators of increasing rank have looked at her evidence and found it insubstantial—nothing more than a list of missing stuff. Lydia considers it a long list, given her short acquaintance with Westcare Manor and how few residents she knows there. Item 1: Lettie's necklace, which Lettie was missing on July 7 when Lydia first met her. Item 2: a pair of good shoes, kept in a box on the shelf of the wardrobe of Nancy, who lives across the hall from Muffin. Nancy is among those who think that Lydia looks important. Whether this is due to Lydia's height, as Lettie asserts, or to her nice clothes and make-up as Claire says, it must be true. Every time Lydia visits Westcare Manor, one or more residents appeal to her for assistance. Likely, the only reason Lydia was admitted to the business offices was because she was dressed better than anyone working there.

254

But back to the list. Item 3: Lettie again! As of last Wednesday, a deck of gilt-edged playing cards in a lacquered box was missing from her windowsill. Lydia even remembers seeing that box and admiring it, though she never looked inside.

Items 4, 5 and 6 were all reported that same day by two women whom Lydia encountered in the back yard, They were smoking cigarettes while hooked up to their oxygen tanks. Lydia was wheeling Muffin along the new path to the new gazebo, with Muffin moaning about being cold, and hollering at every bump, "You stupid!" Above Muffin's outbursts, Hazel and Julia called hoarsely for Lydia to come over. Since Muffin was also begging Lydia to stop, she did. Once Muffin was parked in a splash of sunshine she expressed much gratitude for Lydia's niceness, turned her face upward and dozed off, leaving Lydia free to talk to the women. They wanted Lydia to do something about the thief at Westcare Manor. A ring, a photo in a silver frame, and a small doll had all been "lifted" from their shared room.

Hazel and Julia talked like the characters in old detective novels: "I'd lean on the housekeeper and see if you can make her squeal." "Sure looks like an inside job to me." "If this keeps up we'll have to find ourselves some new digs." Lydia found them irresistible, the way they sported their oxygen units like fashion accessories, and smoked their filterless cigarettes with intense pleasure as if each puff might be their last—as well it might! Aside from this senseless addiction, however, Hazel and Julia seemed in full possession of their faculties. Lydia agreed to help. She made her list of "pilfered" goods, and took it on the rounds of administrators that same afternoon after she had fed Muffin and returned her to her room.

"What's going on with all these missing things?" Lydia wanted to know from each official. "And what are you going to do about it?"

Of course there was a ready excuse for things being "misplaced"—the renovations. Many of the residents' belongings were packed temporarily and then moved into new furniture, and of course this gets "confusing" and things get "lost" but "everything will turn up." On the other hand, the powers that be were hard pressed to imagine that anything was missing at all.

"Old people forget things, you know." "They haven't got good eyesight, you know. It'll turn up." "They're remembering things that are long gone. I bet she hasn't had that ring for thirty years."

Lydia found these responses grossly insulting. The final blow came when she herself was made the object of suspicion. Who did she come to visit on Wednesdays and Fridays? Mrs. Griffin? But her name's not in Mrs. Griffin's file. And neither is Claire's. And there's nothing reported missing from Mrs. Griffin's room.

"Oh, but there is!" Lydia promptly added Item 8 to her list: "Mrs. Griffin's handwarmer." The sweater had reappeared once the backlog of laundry was sorted out, but the snuggly pillow had never returned. She flourished her list dramatically, but the Director was unmoved. He had some questions of his own for Lydia.

"Do you mind telling me what you are doing in all those residents' rooms?... Do you have *any* professional credentials or documentation for this so-called 'job' of bringing lunch to Mrs. Griffin?... Does Claire?... If you girls aren't *related* to anyone, maybe you shouldn't be on the premises at all..."

Lydia was forced to back down before she got herself and Claire permanently evicted. It was agreed that the visits, but not the "snooping" might continue until Jo could be consulted.

That Friday the sign-in sheet appeared.

And another object disappeared—Hazel's perfume bottle. There was no perfume in it, but it was still very dear to Hazel.

Now, more than anything, Lydia needs to know for herself if Westcare Manor residents' personal possessions are being stolen, or if she's been drawn into a series of senile delusions. She clings to the knowledge of Lettie's lacquered box. That's something she knows existed and can no longer be found in Lettie's room. Her idea is to plant something else there and watch to see what becomes of it.

She has found her vantage point after a couple of loops around the neighborhood. From a suburban side street that looks down toward the Westcare parking lot, and a good quarter mile away from the building, Lydia can train her binoculars on Lettie's window. She recognizes it by the glass hummingbird hanging there, and hopes this will not be the next thing to disappear. But the hummingbird is about all Lydia can see—that and the back side of the drapes, which are closed! She cannot count on seeing who comes in and out of the room. However, she can keep an eye on the windowsill—that is where she will plant her decoy.

Lydia puts the binoculars aside on the passenger seat. It's only ten past eleven, too early to go over with Muffin's lunch. She turns on her hands-free cell phone and calls Claire.

"Hey."

"Hey."

"What're ya doin'?"

"You don't want to know."

"Uh, okay."

"I'm parked up the street from Westcare Manor, and I'm trying to use my binocs to see into Lettie's room."

"You're right, I don't want to know."

"Don't worry, the curtain's closed. It was a dumb idea."

"Well, that's going to be a pretty complicated scene to draw."

Lydia laughs. She understands Claire's dedication to her comic books, but she misses her. All she does anymore is visit Muffin and draw cartoons.

"So I saw Greg last night." Claire is sketching even as they speak.

"You did?!" Lydia perks up.

"Yeah. He's a real nice guy. I think you should meet him."

"Me?"

"You'll like him. He's easy to talk to."

"But he's no Josh."

"Way not."

Something in Claire's voice tells Lydia that they did more than talk. "Did you kiss him?"

"Yeah, we kind of made out a little, but it didn't feel right. I mean, besides the guilt and all that. He just wasn't the right—*texture!*" It sounds funny when she says it. They crack up, and Claire puts her drawing aside because she's making a mess of it.

"Wow, how do you tell a guy something like that?" Lydia wonders.

"I thought I'd just introduce him to this knock-out friend of mine and—"

"See if he's the right texture for me!"

"Exactly."

Lydia picks up her binoculars and idly points them at Lettie's window.

"Really, Claire, I like going out with Matthew." Claire makes a mental note that Lydia did not simply say, "I like Matthew," and tucks it away for later, as Lydia admonishes, "Better tell Greg how you feel and get it over with."

"Oh, I think he could tell, but he knows I'm kinda nervous that something may have changed with Josh since he's been gone."

"You are? I can't imagine! Josh is your *slave!*" Lydia insists.

"I don't know if I want that either," Claire says seriously, twirling her pencil.

"So what it comes down to is that you've left poor Greg dangling again."

"Spoken by the expert at such things!" Claire teases. She refuses to feel guilty. Greg appreciated her company and she his, it doesn't have to be any more than that.

Lydia notices a movement and steadies the binoculars on the steering wheel, again focusing on the glass hummingbird.

"Lydia?"

"I've gotta go, Claire. I think that's Lettie's daughter who just opened the curtain. I'm gonna go talk to her!"

"Wow. Okay."

"Later."

"Good luck!" Claire puts the phone aside and goes back to her sketchbook. She turns the page and starts doodling a caricature of Lydia in her dark glasses, behind the wheel of her sports car, with a high-tech earpiece accessorizing her hairdo, and futuristic binoculars on the dashboard. Claire laughs to herself at an idea—a second do-gooding team for the Cupcake Comics based on Lydia and Lettie—"Lemon Meringue and Biscuit."

Lemon Meringue is a pretty fair representation of Lydia as now perceived by Lettie's daughters, Yvonne and Letitia. The tall young woman standing before them is noticed to be first white, then blonde, then rich. Facial features are only now beginning to take distinguishable shape. The voice is still chiming on incomprehensibly.

The familiar cadences of their mother coalesce into sensible syllables before those of the young woman. Lettie knows her, or talks as if she does—"Hi there, Sugar! Oh my, how pretty. Come over here and sit on the bed. You didn't come sit on the bed and visit yesterday."

The stranger responds that she didn't come to Westcare Manor yesterday, and besides, she hears that Lettie hasn't had a bed to sit on lately.

This makes Lettie's daughters laugh along with their mother. Although Lettie's bed has been returned to the room, it is piled high with clothes and other possessions because there is still no dresser or wardrobe. Yvonne and Letitia are making this visit mid-week to see that Lettie's room is restored to normal—or else! As it slowly sinks in that Lydia is not some pretty emissary of the wicked lords of Westcare Manor come to smooth things over, their outrage-blurred senses begin to clear.

"What did you say your name was?" Letitia asks.

And Lydia starts over. She explains about Muffin, Jo, Claire and herself, their visits to the Manor, making friends with Lettie, and her frustration with management over her list of missing objects, which began with Lettie's necklace. Lydia finishes her monologue by telling the two women about her plan to plant something in Lettie's room to entice the thief, whom she will observe through the window— maybe—only if they say okay—using her binoculars.

"My original idea was to use my telescope, but that would be overkill. There's not enough room in my car, I'd have to sit in the back seat to use it."

Standing on sore feet in the middle of the wreckage that is Lettie's room, Letitia and Yvonne, the elder sister thin and the younger heavy like her mother, stare at this pretty blonde teenager who looks like a concocted by her own crazy kids. Well-meaning but foolish, and probably dangerous.

"You wanna spy through our mamma's window with a telescope?" she says, to make sure she heard right.

"Binoculars. And only if you say it's okay, and I don't want to spy on *Lettie*," Lydia is quick to point out, "just on whoever comes in and out of the room."

"Do you do a lot of looking through people's windows with your telescope?" Yvonne's perplexed expression is settling into a disapproving frown.

"Binoculars. Before today I only looked at the sky." Lydia tries not to act as insulted as she feels. If she huffs out now it will only make them more suspicious, and she can't have them talking to the administrator. Her only hope is to make them understand. "Really, I just wanted to help, but I felt funny about it, and that's why I decided to ask first. And it wouldn't work very well unless the curtains were open, or I set the thing right there on the windowsill where I can see it either way."

The sisters exchange a look. Lettie is laughing. The more serious her daughters look, the more she laughs. It's funny to her that her giggly little girls have grown up to be such stuffy old things.

"I mean, Lettie's stuff really is missing, isn't it?" Lydia appeals to them. "The necklace and the box and the playing cards?"

"To tell you the truth, we thought Mamma probably lost that necklace herself," Yvonne admits. "But the box is different. She wouldn't hide that. We do think that was taken."

"But you won't let me help get it back?"

"You seem like a nice young lady," Letitia says. "Good upbringing, I can tell. And we're glad to have you on our side, honey. So we're not going to let you do something that's probably illegal, and isn't very nice no matter why you're doing it, plus it's likely to get you in trouble, and won't do much good anyway. No spying, no telescope—or binoculars. Okay?"

"Okay. I'm kinda glad, actually. It seemed wrong to me too." Lydia feels her face flush bright red.

"You're welcome to keep visiting Mamma, though," Yvonne tells her. "It's so nice that you do that and that you care. Maybe you'll find another way to catch that crook."

"And if you don't, don't worry about it, honey," Letitia adds. "These places are like that. We don't bring much of anything valuable in here. We should've known better about the card box, but she was asking after it."

"Well, okay. I guess I better go see Muffin now." Lydia tries to make a dignified exit, though she feels like running.

Yvonne and Letitia watch her go, their arms crossed, heads shaking gently, and mouths twisted into identical half smiles.

Lettie tells them, "Now you mind what she says. There goes someone important." Then she looks up at her daughters and bursts out laughing.

# CHAPTER 36
## REUNION

"You should see the graffiti in the subways," Josh tells Claire. "It rocks. Nothing like this stuff. It's city grade—all layered over, everyone's over everyone else's. Crowded, busy. Makes everything look like it's moving. And nothing's flat. They paint across the ribs of the subway cars and steel girders under bridges. Man, you should see the tunnels. They would freak if they saw this. This is like a roll of canvas, man."

They are lying on their stomachs on a blanket on the rim of the Gallegos Lateral, an immense concrete channel that carries rain run-off and snow melt from the mountain to the river. This isolated stretch descending into the bosque is a good hike from the nearest road. Claire stares across to the opposite wall of the channel. Smooth and gently concave, it is lined with vivid paintings, the placement of which seems impossible given the recurrent presence of high waters, and a residual pond of unknown depth below. Reflected in this moat against a background of azure sky, the mostly pornographic paintings double themselves into an orgy of color and complexity. It boggles her mind to know that a companion universe lies unseen below them, hidden within the curve of the channel. She refuses to go down and see it, though Josh points out the top of a metal stair and describes how one can drop down to a ledge that runs along between a series of secondary drains. Kids go into those drains all the time to screw and blow dope and hide from the cops. It's really not a big deal—so long as it doesn't rain, Josh tells Claire.

She is content and would not budge right now even if there were an escalator into the channel and *Guernica* painted on the walls. Lying close to Josh while he describes his adventures, sharing their sketchbooks back and forth, cuddling and kissing and talking—this is as close to heaven on earth as Claire can imagine. Being together for the first time in three weeks is still comfortable, yet intensely exciting. It's like their first date, when they knew each other so well and couldn't believe there was so much more to know. Better than the first date, since the awkward parts don't have to be relived.

Was Claire concerned that in some way Josh would never fully return from his travels? In fact he has come bearing gifts, having recorded his experiences in his sketchbook especially with her in mind. He has a story to go with each page. Claire loves listening to him describe his forays into the New York art scene. It sounds intimidating to her, but Josh just kept doing his art, and his talent was noticed. He made some encouraging contacts. She's proud of him and full of hope for his success as an artist.

Was Josh concerned that he would find Claire too little changed by comparison to the upheavals he himself has been through? In fact Claire is bubbling with expansive forces, a work in progress who surprises afresh at every turn. Josh begs her to let him keep some of her Cupcake Comics overnight—he can't talk and listen and read and kiss all at the same time! She'll think about it. He kisses her.

"Some of your drawings are awful," he says as nicely as he can. And she can tell how proud of her he is, and how much he likes what she's doing. If he'd said they were all good, she'd know he was just blowing her off.

"Your standards must be pretty high now that you've been to New York," she suggests.

"Some of the stuff I saw there was beyond awful."

"In what way awful?" Claire eggs him on.

"Oh, where to begin?" Josh starts with a scathing review of "a stick installation" in a Soho gallery and keeps going from there, while Claire laughs delightedly.

Josh finds her giggling delicious and he grabs her again. This time is precious. It's Sunday afternoon and school starts Tuesday. How are they supposed to go back to being kids, to living in the tight little boxes clustered around Go on Claire's game board? It says Go, but it means, Stay.

"Dad and I almost killed each other on the way home," Josh confides to Claire. He'd taken the bus from New York to Denver and then a local down to Green Creek to catch the tail end of the family vacation. "I don't know how I'm gonna make it."

"Your dad's so straight. Probably can't stand thinking about you running loose in the City. He wants to get you back in line."

"I wasn't out of line."

"You know what I mean."

"It's like he's gotten stricter, though. He didn't used to be on my case so much."

"Not until you got a girlfriend. He thinks I'm ruining you." Claire tackles Josh this time.

"You are," Josh says, and pulls a condom out of his pocket. "Ya think?"

Claire starts to unzip her pants but stops as a sharp whistle pierces the air. Some kids working their way up to the channel are announcing their approach. Josh could whistle back to warn them off, but the sudden reminder that this is not their private universe has changed their mood. Claire rolls back onto her stomach again and gazes across at the long, concrete gallery, trying to cram that whole amazing sight into her memory. Josh flops down beside her and nudges her shoulder with his.

"Wanna go get something to eat?"

"Sure." She nudges back.

They can hear the kids getting nearer—voices, and the distinctive clatter of spray paint canisters in a gym bag.

"If I'd've gotten back two days ago, we could've used Jo's house, huh?" Josh laments. He thought they would be back sooner, but his father had other plans.

"I guess, yeah."

Actually, Jo had told Claire with uncharacteristic bluntness not to use her home as a "love nest or party palace." "Oh, absolutely not," Claire promised. But if Josh had been around, how could she have resisted? And when she thinks about it, what would've been the harm? *Just the disrespect to Jo!* Would she have stood up to Josh in order to keep her word? Or perhaps to test him—or herself? What if she had said No? Claire wishes she could talk to Josh about what happened to Lydia, but of course she will not. Not any time soon. Not until they have put much distance between themselves and Roosevelt High.

They gather their things and shuffle down a barren swath, which slopes away from the drain and eventually grows scrubby, merges into woodsiness and becomes the bosque. Three boys of perhaps twelve or thirteen emerge into the open and cut eastward, in search of some empty space on the concrete canvas. Claire thinks they look awfully young to be out on such an adventure. Then she has to smile to herself. Many would think the same about her.

Josh leads the way through the bracken, following paths worn by a steady stream of trespassers. Eventually they break through onto an official Bosque Park path and walk side by side under the cottonwoods holding hands, a typical couple out for a typical Sunday stroll. Neither has said anything for a long while.

"So, how many dates did you have while I was away?"

Claire stiffens, bristles—but does not detect suspicion or jealousy, only an invitation to the truth. She can handle that. The last thing she needs is another secret.

"One. How about you?"

"One."

They stop and face each other a little fearfully.

"You first," Claire says.

"No, you first. I know who it is already. That guy from your class, Greg."

"What can I say? He was persistent. And he was lonely. He called a bunch of times, and then last Tuesday we went out for pizza."

"And?"

"I let him kiss me." There's no use playing games.

"And?"

"I feel bad about it. It wasn't, you know, *right*, like us—I didn't expect it to be—but I felt sorry for him, and curious, and flattered, and kind of bored and lonely myself—" Josh has to kiss her then, the kiss he should've been there to give her but Greg got instead.

"Yeah, that's what it wasn't."

"Is he still calling you?"

Claire groans. "Oh, Josh, I thought I was being nice trying to be friends, but I just led him on, and now I'm going to have to hurt his feelings because even though he knows all about you, it's like he can't get it through his head."

"You want me to talk to him?"

"Uh, no, Josh." *That's all I need!* "I was trying to fix him up with Lydia."

"Has he seen her?"

"No."

"Could work."

"Okay, your turn!" So, Lydia's beauty has not escaped Josh's notice, and neither has some other girl's. Claire tries to make light of it, "Let me guess—you were seduced by an older woman from the East village—spiky pink hair, pierced eyebrow, saggy black dress, no tits."

"I thought you knew me better!" Josh teases back. "I swear I only had eyes for those busty young nannies in Central Park."

"But seriously—" In spite of their jokes, Claire's uneasiness is building. She's told all, now she'd like to hear his side.

"Seriously? It was this art dealer's daughter. He'd brought her with him from Atlanta. Javier set us up, because I was there and she was my age and he had business with the father. So I walked her all around the Village, and we ate Indian food and then went to a dance club."

Claire bites her lip, not knowing whether to laugh or cry—she has never seen Josh dance! Since Josh will not say more without a question, she avoids the obvious, *Did you dance?* and asks instead, "What was she like?"

"Short, perky. A southern debutante who couldn't wait to cut loose in the big city. Teri Ann Hastings." Josh tries to suppress the unwanted stirrings that her memory evokes. Claire is watching him closely. "She had a fake ID and a wad of 'mad money' in her bra—"

"Among other things."

He can't help grinning. "Yeah, she had plenty in there."

Claire starts to be mad, but when she thinks of what she did with Greg she can't be. It's frustrating. "Maybe you shouldn't tell me any more."

"Okay." Josh is a bit too agreeable.

"Did you kiss her?"

He looks into Claire's eyes. "It was the same deal, Claire. I'd been missing you, and she kind of threw herself at me. Yeah, I kissed her, and I copped a feel of those boobs while I was at it!"

Claire remembers Greg's hand on her breast and blushes bright red.

"Hungry yet?" Josh asks. Enough is enough, the conversation is making them both horny, but they have nowhere to go.

"Starving!"

They set a brisk pace to Claire's car, each caught up in a swirl of conflicting thoughts and feelings.

She drives to Prince Street for food. They end up at a place where the waitresses go back and forth on rollerblades and you can either eat in your car, or sit at a picnic table conveniently positioned in front of your parking space with an umbrella over it for shade.

They sit at the table. Not many people are out on this warm afternoon. School or no school, summer doesn't want to end and clearly intends to stick around for a while. But the summer day is not what it was. The shapes are not as simple as they used to be, the lines are not as straight and sharp. Life piles on, the picture changes.

Claire and Josh require pictures, as artists do—many and varied and changing. Therefore, they can't but welcome this maturing of the day. Their separation and reunion has taught them something about love's capacity to be constant against a shifting emotional landscape. A spirit of mutual confidence in a mutual future begins to settle over them.

Claire has to ask. Something even more serious (as it turns out, fortunately) than those misdirected kisses has yet to be discussed. She suspects Josh was going there when he started talking about his dad. She watches him devour his burgers—it doesn't take long—and then asks straight out:

"Do you think you'll go back to New York after graduation?"

She's ready to hear, Yes, No, Maybe or I don't know, but the answer that comes rattles her.

"I don't think I'm staying through graduation."

Claire puts down her fork. "Why not?" She stares at him through liquid eyes, while all that stuff about change and trust and maturity and the constancy of love careens away on roller blades and crashes like a clumsy waitress at the end of the concrete pad. "Where are you going?"

He's clearly excited, and he knows she will be too, once he explains. "Up to Green Creek. Probably not till February or March. I made a deal with Mr. Simms. I'll keep an eye on the cabins and do some maintenance, and he'll let me stay in one. I'll be chopping a lot of wood till it warms up, but it'll keep me in shape. The mechanical work and carpentry will be good training too, and there's an old barn to work in. I can stretch my canvases, and store some of my stuff there. Simms is psyched, 'cause he's getting tired of doing it all himself. He said I should hang my paintings in the lodge and try to sell them. Even Dad kind of likes the idea—except he acts like he's got a quota of ball busting to fill, and he's trying to get it all in before I leave home."

Claire smiles wanly. "I guess he thinks it's his fatherly duty." *What is wrong with this picture?* she's asking herself. *Why does Josh want to go to Green Creek?*

"He's a jackass."

"Josh, did something bad happen in New York that you're not telling me?"

Josh looks at her blankly—he thought they were talking about his father.

"Did someone diss your work?" she asks pointedly.

Now he gets it. "Hell no. They fell all over me. If they didn't like what they saw, they said it had 'promise.' That's what turned me off, Claire. You could smell the bullshit a mile away. I mean, they were sincere, most of them, about what they liked and didn't like. But in terms of being able to help you or introduce you to someone or make something happen—after the first week, I wasn't buying it. The nice

ones were doing it to be nice, the others just want to feel important—
except for a few who are really out to screw you."

"But I thought you liked everyone you met there."

"Well sure, I was getting along pretty good with them. I just think
they're all bullshitters. It's not like it's only New York. It's Hartshorn
and Gus and Shelly and all of 'em. It just seems like you start getting
into this *society* of art, or the *business* of it, and it all starts smelling
like bullshit."

"Wow. I've had that very same thought."

"So you understand about Green Creek."

"Not really. You don't think that *we're* bullshit do you?"

"No way, Claire! Listen," he takes her hand, "The first thing I'm
gonna do is get some decent wheels so I can get back and forth. I'll be
down every other week or so. I'm still going to work with Gus. But the
deal is, I had to promise to get up there as soon as the roads are clear.
Simms has a bunch of repairs to finish before fishing season. Claire,
you could come up and stay with me after school's out."

"And then what?"

"I don't know. You go off to college, I guess, and maybe I come
stay with you for a little while when I'm sick of freezing my butt off
in GC. Pick someplace warm, okay?" Josh thinks this is a grand idea.
He can't understand why Claire looks so irked. "Hey, what's wrong?"

"Have you ever heard the expression, 'Don't hide your light under
a bushel'? Shit, Josh, I can't believe you'd be content selling your art
out of a fishing lodge. What kind of a plan is that?"

"It's my plan—which is, do first things first—I haven't done the
work yet, Claire."

"*You* haven't done the work?"

"No, not like I need to. I knew that when I left. That's the reason to
go to college—to do the work. But maybe that's a reason not to go to
college too. Look, I've been all over the map on this, believe me. Like
that first bus ride—by the time we hit the east coast I thought the only
thing I wanted to do was travel. See everything. Spend a year going all
around the country. Shit, *then* I'd have something to paint.

"Then I got to New York. It was totally electric! Everyone's jacked up and hooked into their own crazy dream. And it's all coming at you so fast, overlapping, a new idea every time you turn your head. I didn't want to sleep or even close my eyes the whole time I was there. Seemed like no one did—the City's alive all night. By the time I left, that's all I wanted to do—move to the City and be part of it. I was sure I'd do it too. Come home, grab you, turn right around and go back."

Claire cracks a smile, but it's a noncommittal one. Josh plows ahead.

"Then I had that long ride from New York to Denver, and there was the real world again, huge and urgent. It came to me that living in the city and traveling around the country were about the same thing—nonstop motion. So when do you do the art? How do you choose what to do it about?

"It comes down to this—What have I done? What do I have to show? I have to do the work, Claire, and to do the work, I have to get away. Art classes are great, but at some point they don't help. I don't want to do assignments anymore. I don't want to put my work up against all those other kids' stuff. It's not that I'm trying to hide 'my light,' I just don't want to get blinded by everyone else's. I'm going to stay in Green Creek until I have something to show that's really mine, or until Simms kicks me out. At least that's how I feel right now."

Claire nods thoughtfully. "Okay, Josh. I get it. I can see how you need that space." Josh will take on the world on his own terms or not at all.

"I really won't be that far away."

She smiles bravely.

"So what do you think about next summer?"

It seems such a long way off.

"Well, I have things I have to do, too. I'm going to hang out here as long as Jo needs me to help with Muffin." She can't bring herself to say, *until Muffin dies*, but the tears she wouldn't allow to fall for Josh are released at the thought.

Josh studies Claire, thinks better of opening his pad to sketch that teary, resolute expression. His Claire can be a rogue one moment, a saint the next. And nothing expresses this wild interplay of trouble making and problem solving better than her own Cupcake Comics.

"Your comics about Muffin are going to blow people away. I can't believe how many cool ideas you've come up with already."

"Oh, I've got the ideas. I just can't draw them right."

"Want some help?"

Claire nods eagerly. "I thought you'd never ask!"

They drive to Claire's house first so she can check in with her parents—*always passing Go, but never going anywhere*—and grab her art stuff. Then they go to the Antresian home, where they can work together in Josh's room so long as the door is open. Mr. Antresian really is being a giant pain, stalking around for no apparent reason but to spy. When Claire is invited to stay for dinner she declines.

Back to Go.

Greg calls. Claire has subjected Lydia to many boring conversations this week in order to avoid exactly this occasion. She has talked with Greg since their date Tuesday night, but the conversations have been uncomfortable for both of them, with Greg struggling to work up to a confession, and Claire zealously preventing him from making it. But tonight she feels brave, and resolved as well, after her reunion with Josh.

"I'm sorry I've been avoiding your calls," she tells Greg as soon as they've exchanged greetings.

"If you would ever let me say what I have to say, I'd stop calling you, you know."

"You would?"

"To ask you out, anyway."

"Really?"

"Though it would be nice to stay friends."

"Are you dumping me?"

The small note of insult and astonishment in Claire's voice causes Greg to howl with laughter. Claire has to laugh too—the way you have to laugh in shock and relief when something trips you up, and you fall on your ass but find you aren't hurt.

"Well, I never!" she goofs on herself, setting Greg off again.

"Do you really think a guy enjoys being with a girl who doesn't enjoy being with him?" Greg asks.

"Well, sometimes you don't know with guys," Claire answers, thinking of Lydia and that creep Blaine—which gives her an idea— "Greg, are you gonna be around Labor Day weekend? You know they're dedicating our mural that Sunday."

"Are you asking me out?"

Now that's as funny as Claire asking Greg if he's dumping her.

"Just come, okay, Greg?" Claire says when they stop laughing. "There's someone I want you to meet."

"Not necessary, Claire. Seriously."

*Shit! I'm blowing it!* Claire recovers, "What I mean is, there's someone I think should meet you." And when Greg doesn't say anything, "You should see the mural, anyway."

"Oh, I've driven by there."

"Have you stopped?"

"No."

"Have you had a burrito from the Big B?"

"No, not that one."

"I'm telling you, you should come."

"I'm hanging up now, Claire."

"Okay. Bye, Greg."

Claire presses the TALK button on her phone twice and listens for the dial tone, then punches Josh's number. This simple act fills her with satisfaction.

# CHAPTER 37
## MUFFIN'S RESOLVE

Every day begins in a panic of terror—disorientation, total darkness, a bursting bladder and shooting pains in places she can no longer name. Her instinct is to scream but she holds back. The situation is so utterly unexpected she keeps quiet and stays alert for clues that might tell her if she is a blindfolded hostage or simply mad.

The effort exhausts her. She succumbs to sleep.

A familiar voice speaking familiar phrases wakens her a second time, as though the first waking were a dream, and it is as quickly forgotten. Touch is alarming at first. But the hands, once associated with that voice, become acceptable. Voice and touch together make a person Muffin knows and can see quite clearly. She is a large woman, middle aged, with strong arms and a wide face that is always smiling. To Muffin, it looks like the lady's face has been stretched wide into a perfect circle from all that smiling. Before Muffin can be irritated by this, the curtains are drawn and warm sunlight pours over her. It is a beautiful day.

There is some awkward dancing about, unpleasantness associated with bathroom duties and dressing. Muffin is angry. She doesn't think Sam would approve of her being treated like this. She calls for him, demands that he be brought to her. The bulky woman—why can Muffin never remember her name—pretends not to hear. Drawing the sunny circle of her smiling face into an O, she coos and babbles, as if Muffin were a pet canary. Muffin begins to suspect that this woman is also insane—a fellow inmate, not a nurse or helper—and she begins to struggle harder.

The woman is strong. Muffin curses her, exhausts herself. She's so tired she can hardly keep going. It's humiliating to have to hang on to this presumptuous and pestering person. They are pushing against each other. If Muffin didn't hang on and push back, this creature would push her right over. What are they fighting about? It's not fair, Muffin's no match for this giantess. In despair and exhaustion she gives up and flops listlessly into the awaiting wheelchair. Morosely she allows the padded tray to be secured in front of her and her arms placed on top of it. She permits her feet to be lifted and set on the footrests.

It is a comfort. Muffin thanks the person who has come to do this for her.

The lady bustles around Muffin, pulling and straightening bunched up shirt sleeves and pantslegs, adjusting the pillow behind Muffin's back, brushing Muffin's hair. When the big, round face comes close, Muffin knows her. Satisfied, the woman stands and maneuvers the wheelchair into position by the window. Muffin is bathed in golden warmth. She makes her own face round with a smile for her helper, then turns it to the sun. She will watch out the window for Sam.

Muffin's vigil is interrupted by a young man bringing the breakfast tray. As he places it in front of her, he makes a joke about her getting a sunburn. He makes this same joke every day. This is how she knows him. She smiles and says, "You'd better bring my hat."

One day he did bring a wide brimmed hat and he put it on Muffin's head, but she didn't like the way it felt, and she didn't like not feeling the sun strong on her face. She made a fuss about it and almost couldn't eat, even after he had taken it away. She doesn't remember this, but he does, and now when she says, "You'd better bring my hat," he just laughs and gets her going on her breakfast. She knows him by his laugh, too.

The man with the nice laugh gives Muffin a sip of juice through a straw. Then he folds her fingers around a scrambled egg sandwich. She hears his cart rumble away when she takes her first bite. Muffin eats hungrily. Everything is yellow.

White. The snap of the crisp sheet being shaken, billowing across the bed, and then being smoothed and tucked in around the edges—that sound is white, pure white.

The splashing-flushing sounds of a bathroom being cleaned are white as well, but sparkling with sea foam green and aquamarine. Muffin sees the master bathroom she re-tiled herself. Sam likes it gleaming. She hopes the girl will do a thorough job.

Muffin howls when she feels herself being wheeled out into the hallway. She cannot abide activities and outings. They consist of bedlam or TV or, usually, both. She knows for certain there will be screaming, because it will be coming from her! She demands to know where they are taking her.

"Nowhere, don't worry."

It's a patient voice. Patient hands check her tray and pillow and footrests, and snap the brakes on the wheelchair. The squeaky white sneaker steps retreat around a corner.

Muffin listens to the housekeepers working up and down the corridor. Vacuum cleaners and sloshing water. It reminds her of a hotel, being on vacation.

Off in the distance some teenagers are playing their loud, awful music.

The maids finish and return Muffin to her place by the window in her room, but they have forgotten about the radio station. Muffin finds herself in the midst of a hideous cacophony. She pumps her feet and pushes at the tray that pins her to her seat. She musters all of her strength and screams. This time she is absolutely certain—she *is* a hostage, and her captors are trying to *drive* her mad.

Try as she might, she can't make herself heard above the horrific noise, but she can hear herself. She calls out without any hope of salvation, but the sound of her own voice provides reassurance. Periodically she falls into exhausted sleep, but it is not the forgetful sleep of nighttime. It is a pestering, nightmarish half-sleep.

Sometimes she finds herself praying, "Dear God, just let me die!"

But then she reminds herself she doesn't believe in a god, and renews her efforts on her own behalf. If she can escape the wretched chair, the room, the noise, then she'll crawl if she has to until she reaches a body of water and can commit herself to the briny deep—just like old Uncle Silas of family legend.

Papa Murphy used to tell that story.

Papa Murphy? Now whatever made her think of him?

A flood of memories drowns the original impulse to suicide. Papa Murphy kept dogs, big ones with silky coats, and they always scared her at first. They were bigger than she was, as she remembers. She'd squeal with a mixture of fear and delight when they bounded over to lick her face. But soon they'd all be settled down around Papa Murphy's rocking chair and he'd be telling his stories.

With a start Muffin realizes that the din has ceased.

Relief! Gratitude! She thanks her rescuer profusely, a trembling anticipation rising in her even before the voice, the words, the movement and touch confirm that this is the Blossom, her daughter's emissary.

Every day Muffin's daughter Josie visits. Sometimes she is not physically present, but she sends lunch. Today the Blossom says that Josie did not make the lunch, the Blossom herself did. But Josie has come, nonetheless. She has entered Muffin's thoughts, and brought with her the interlocking memories of a life. When the Blossom says that Josie and Jake have gone to visit their son and daughter-in-law in California, to see the new baby—and that makes Muffin a great-grandmother—Muffin finds her sense of history complete. The markers fall into place and her perception of the present becomes painfully sharp.

She is an infirm old lady in a nursing home. She is in no position to quarrel or make demands. She should be happy—she is happy for any scrap of kindness. At once aware of her misery and cognizant that help is temporarily at hand, Muffin refuses to feel sorry for herself. If nothing else, she must keep up a good front for the Blossom's sake. None of this is *her* fault.

Besides, the Blossom is her salvation. How pleasant to let the Blossom feed her and tell her stories. The stories have an interesting way of turning into a book they have been reading together, which Muffin finds she remembers well by the time the Blossom actually flips to the page and begins reading, using various theatrical voices. A normal kind of forgetfulness ensues. The forgetfulness that comes when one is entertained, and doesn't have to work at being a person. One just is. One's lifetime of knowledge comes into play, and shows in one's understanding things—one is not required to recite it.

The Blossom makes Muffin laugh. Sometimes she makes Muffin worry for her, foolish young thing that she is, or for Josie, who works so hard taking care of everyone. The laughter and maternal worry are equally effective at keeping the mad, nightmare world at bay.

And the food is always, if not immediately, welcome. Sometimes Muffin has to be coaxed to eat, even when she's hungry, which she often is because more of her morning egg has ended up on her rather than in her. The problem might be a recent renewal of her frequently made resolution to starve herself to death. But that's a hard one to keep track of. She can never remember about the hunger strike consciously, and yet will comply with this secret urge by impishly refusing food. More often, Muffin's mouth simply has unpleasant expectations, a chalky dryness. She's not sure she could swallow, or taste anything. The thought of it repels her. But when she's offered an "icy tomato juice" it sounds like exactly the thing she has been needing. And this is the same with each kind of food and drink that is offered afterward. She may not intend to have even a taste of another thing, but then a taste of something is produced and it proves to be the only thing she would consider consuming. She ends up stuffing herself, with pleasure because of the company, but also with a deep, vague guilt about the full feeling.

After lunch, the Blossom touches her shoulders. Sometimes she brushes Muffin's hair, though there's not much to brush. Josie brushes Muffin's hair too, and tries to brush her teeth, but Muffin resists that. That is simply too much. But Muffin does not resist when Josie takes off her shoes and socks and rubs lotion on her feet. That is exceptionally nice. Nicer than she can let Josie know, though she thanks her continuously. It's a nice thing to do, but Josie shouldn't feel obliged to do it. And it is the same for the Blossom and her shoulder rubbing. It is simply too nice. It is like a dream and often turns into one.

At night, which comes quickly, Muffin cooperates gracefully with the aide. She is given a chance to use the toilet, which she accepts, in fact has been eagerly looking forward to it. The changing into bedclothes naturally falls out of this. The aide, a skinny girl who smells like the cosmetics counter at Filene's, is gentle but businesslike, letting Muffin know it is useless to resist.

Muffin is too awed by the way time has turned itself inside out to protest. She remembers peeling off socks and shoes for a young child, pants and top, giving her a sponge bath, toweling her dry, and asking her to lift her arms while Muffin dropped the little nightie over her head. Muffin lifts her feet, raises her arms, lets herself be handled like a doll, helped up and held up like a toddler. She is helpless again.

No, those were her children who were helpless.

Yes, and before that it was she, it was everyone. This aide needed someone to wipe her bottom once. No one's exempt from infancy, and the ones who skip old age are called *un*lucky. Muffin doesn't feel much like bragging about her luck, but she is vaguely relieved about the aide and her brisk approach. At least the girl is getting paid, it would be horrible for Josie to have to do it.

Muffin tells herself that she will have to tell Josie not to come so often. She didn't raise Josie to be a maid and a servant like the workers at this wretched place. Yes, she is going to put her foot down with Josie and insist that she not come. Not come and not send the lunches. Then Muffin will have no problem starving herself to death.

They are finished in the bathroom. The time went fast while Muffin thought about death. When the aide helps her into bed, a pain shoots through Muffin's hips but as quickly subsides. Her gasp of dismay turns into a sigh of relief. She thanks the aide, and then she asks, "Aren't you going to rub my shoulders?"

The aide has no time for this, but the request is so present and direct, a pleasant surprise coming from Muffin. She pets Muffin's back until the angular old woman, folded fan-like, knees to elbows and heels to butt, begins to snore. This is a restful moment for the aide, who resumes her rounds a bit reluctantly.

Sam is patting Muffin's shoulders and telling her not to be in such a rush.

"But there's nothing to do here," Muffin complains, reaching, searching for his hand.

"No, of course not, you shouldn't exert yourself," her husband instructs her. "You help just by being here."

"I can't imagine!" Before she can recite her list of ailments, he has swept out of the room. She supposes if he can keep going, she can. She will rest for another busy day of "just being here." There's always the chance that one of these nights she will pass on in her sleep. Then poor Sam will be free as well.

The Blossom seems to have shot up overnight. Muffin's brother did this—it's been known to happen—but she thought the girl was too old for that. "I think I'm going crazy," she complains.

After a good deal of tedious questioning, Muffin gets the girl to admit that she is not *the* Blossom. She is the Blossom's friend. Muffin vaguely remembers this, or tells herself she does. It's enough to know that this girl knows the Blossom and seems to know Josie too, and even knows Muffin better than Muffin can imagine how she does. She is so polite and quite tall, and has long hair that Muffin can sometimes feel swishing around. She reminds Muffin of her brother's wife, Suzie.

Muffin, to herself, thinks of the Blossom's friend as Suzie. She can't always think of the name Suzie, but if she thinks of the person Suzie, she can think of this girl and know that they aren't the same person but that this one too is pretty and tall, with long hair like Suzie, and nice and can be trusted. If the girl would simply come in and tell Muffin, "I'm Suzie," then they could skip a lot of the part about going crazy and determining if Muffin can trust her and get on to having a pleasant visit. But the girl insists on calling herself something-or-other that is not Suzie and is hard to remember, and sometimes Muffin doesn't really know who it is until she has a bite of the sandwich.

The Blossom's friend does not make food at all like Josie does and sometimes what she makes is especially good, but other times not. Either way, Muffin's reaction always makes Suzie laugh. She tells Muffin a story about the food, and Muffin keeps tasting all the while to see what the girl is talking about. The green gritty sauce is called pesto and the sour rubbery meat called tofu. What strange, horrible words! Knowing this doesn't make the concoctions the least bit more appetizing, but Muffin nibbles along in spite of herself. She doesn't want to hurt young Suzie's feelings. Besides, the poor girl was up all night looking at the stars.

Suzie is nervous and talks a lot, like someone who's nervous. She can make Muffin nervous, but her visits are rare enough to be exciting and not upsetting. Once Muffin has at last determined it is the Suzie girl, she enjoys the visit.

Sam stops by afterward to compliment her on her good behavior.

"Yes, there are some pleasant people in the world," Muffin concedes, "but frankly I would be happy not to meet even one more of them. That's nothing against them, of course. It wouldn't be nice to say so to a stranger. But I'm going to have a talk with Josie, I most certainly am. No more lunches, no more Blossoms, no more prolonging this foolishness. I mean it, Sam. I've had enough."

"You can go, if you've honestly had enough of them. Just don't pretend you've got to go because they've all had enough of you. They haven't. They'll never let you go."

"Oh, horrors! Don't say that!"

"It's true. You've never let me go, have you?"

# CHAPTER 38
## NO FIVE TIMES


"Just say, 'No five times' when you've really had enough," Claire teases.

"I've had enough," Muffin echoes.

Muffin has resisted every delectable offering from Jo's multi-course meal, and not even the cookie and "iced coffee" will tempt her. She declines genially, and Claire presses the food on her politely. But it is tiring and depressing to keep coaxing with no success.

Claire takes the cup and cookie from Muffin and places them on the tray. She has the other half-eaten courses ranged around her on the bed, where she must perch awkwardly, there being no room to set a chair beside Muffin's. A new suite of furniture has been gumming up the works. There are two night stands now, and a dresser, a bureau *and* a wardrobe.

*Some decorator should've said No at least a couple of times,* Claire thinks, as she folds aluminum foil around two untouched quarters of a beautiful peanut butter, red chile jelly and cream cheese sandwich. She's been returning the leftovers intact to Jo so she can see exactly how much Muffin has—or hasn't—eaten. As Claire packs them she can almost feel Grandmother Stanley's sigh of despair in her own throat.

She tries to shake off such worries. It doesn't make sense to be mad or hurt. Muffin hasn't felt like eating, that's all. Otherwise, she seems all right. She knew Claire as soon as she came in and announced herself, even though they hadn't been together for a week. And when Claire explained how she can only come on Saturdays, now that school has started, Muffin was even more effusive than usual in thanking Claire for her visits.

281

"It's always nice when you come," Muffin said, with so much depth of feeling behind the simple words that Claire wanted to hug her.

"You sure you won't have just a tiny taste of pudding?" Claire asks now, poised to repack the cooler.

Muffin presses her lips into a tight, stubborn line, either too annoyed to speak or fearful that if she opens her mouth Claire might try to shove something in. Claire has to admire her determination.

"I have told you about 'No five times' haven't I?"

"I don't think so," Muffin grumbles, but the gleam in her sightless eyes suggests anticipation.

Claire steps into the bathroom for a damp paper towel.

"That's what we say in our family when we've had enough to eat." While she tends to Muffin's sticky fingers and face, Claire tells the story one more time, more to console herself than to cajole Muffin.

"No five times" started at a Stanley family reunion in Deerwood, Montana one summer when they'd gone to the local dinner theater to see the Melodrama. The steak dinner had more to recommend it than the amateur performance, but even so, everyone enjoyed the play. They adjourned to Carl's parents' house declaiming their favorite lines:

"But I CAN'T pay the rent!" "You MUST pay the rent!" and "No! No! A thousand times, NO!"

The next night, with Grandma Stanley pressing unwanted seconds, thirds and fourths of her home cooking on everyone, they got to wondering how many times NO it would take to make her give up. Surely not a thousand. It was agreed that five should suffice. Since then, when someone says "No five times, Mom," Vivien Stanley knows they mean it and starts to pick up the plates and wrap the leftovers.

Claire and her parents use "No five times" among themselves sometimes when things are getting dicey. Brianna might say it to cut off an argument with Claire. But as often, Carl will say it to Brianna when she gets carried away with some of her business schemes. Claire's options for using the phrase remain limited to the context of food, for when it comes to more serious matters Carl and Brianna find nothing humorous about their daughter saying No to them. Besides, neither a single No nor a thousand will move her parents when their minds are made up.

Increasingly, it's Claire and Muffin who engage in the test of wills that brings "No five times" to mind.

"Now we just say, 'No five times,' and Grandmother gives up," Claire concludes her story. "Sooo, how about another bite of that sandwich, Muffin?"

"No."

Muffin's grin suggests that maybe she does get the joke.

"You sure?"

"No five times!"

Claire gives her a big hug. "In that case, we're done."

She drives home with a lump in her throat. There was a resoluteness to Muffin today, a subtle change that she finds disquieting. A feeling of dread is attaching itself to her young soul and she can't shake it. It's the knowledge of death. Even this deliriously sunny day feels tinged with dark omens, and she soon finds that not even "Home" on the Game Board of Life is safe.

"Mom, what are you doing?" Claire stops at the kitchen threshold. Her mother appears to be hiding behind the refrigerator, or perhaps has been banished to stand in the corner.

"Watching Cleo eat. She eats better when I watch."

When Brianna turns around and takes a step toward Claire, Claire can see the decrepit animal at her feet. The cat has been around longer than Claire has, and has been an "old cat" for much of that time. For the past few years Cleo has done nothing but loll around on Carl and Brianna's bed or under the lilac bush in the front yard. As far as Claire is concerned it's hardly been present, though she is sometimes delegated to put down food and scoop the litter box—chores she refers to as, "keeping up the kitty machine."

Lately, the little machine is running faster. Brianna forces pungent treats onto the unwilling Cleo, who seems to know instinctively that however yummy, the food cannot be properly processed and only puts a strain on her failing system. Claire hasn't noticed that Brianna dumps the litter box every day now and mops up and refills it, but she has seen the newspapers on the floor, that's something new.

"Mom, what are you eating?" Claire turns her attention from the cat back to her mother.

"Oh, a fudgesicle. I think they've been in the freezer since July Fourth. You want one? They're in the door."

"Sure." Claire finds the box in the freezer and takes one. "Come outside, Mom, it's really nice." The house, or at least this portion of it, smells like fishy cat food with an undertone of ammonia.

"Uh, okay. I'll bring Cleo. Doesn't look like she's going to eat any more." With the melting fudgesicle in one hand, Brianna scoops up Cleo with the other and follows Claire out to the back porch. The two women stand in the shade, while the cat jumps to the ground with surprising agility. It saunters off and disappears around the corner of the house.

"I love September in New Mexico," Brianna declares, for summer still spools out endlessly, as though it will never come to the end of its bright blue thread, and the air is spiced with the aroma of roasting chile peppers.

"You don't have to go to school," Claire reminds her.

"Oh, I hated September in Pennsylvania when school was just starting and you could feel that summer was really over. Maybe that's why I love it so much now."

Claire can't explain what it is with her mother today. She seems almost childlike, wide open. Her moods are skipping around like the play of sunlight through leaves. When Claire notices Brianna looking around worriedly for the cat, she makes the connection.

The certainty of coming loss has made Brianna defenseless against her emotions. The same thing is happening to Jo. Perhaps it is intrinsic to the process of caring for the elderly that there is simply no time for putting on false fronts. One sees the door of opportunity closing on confessions and devotions, and not knowing when it will slam shut for good, becomes almost worshipful in demeanor. For those who care, the suffering of others is a judgment, and salvation lies in easing it.

"I can't believe I ate that," Brianna says, looking at the popsicle stick in her hand.

"Oh, so you foist them on me." Claire's almost finished hers too.

"That was my second," Brianna admits.

"You're depressed about Cleo," Claire says matter-of-factly. She drags a patio chair into the sun and plops down in it, wanting nothing more than to spend the rest of the afternoon snoozing. Her mother also pulls up a chair.

"I guess it seems foolish, making such a fuss over a pet."

"She's a member of the family."

"Yeah, we've lived together a long time. How was Muffin today?"

"Speaking of people who eat better when you watch."

Brianna smiles sadly. "It is about the same thing, isn't it? Only, for better or worse, Jo doesn't have the option of simply putting her mother to sleep. That's what the vet told me to do with Cleo."

"But you didn't do it."

"No, not yet."

"Sometimes Muffin asks to die."

"What do you say to that?"

"It's only happened once with me, but I guess she says it pretty often to Jo. I just tried to make a joke of it. I said, 'No dying on my watch!' and then I changed the subject quick."

Brianna smiles and says, "Wouldn't it be nice if we could hold death at bay like that?"

"We kind of do, but I know what you mean— I'll be right back." Claire goes into the house and comes out again with her sketchbook. While Brianna sits lost in her own thoughts, Claire makes a sketch of Cupcake in an authoritative, hands-on-hips pose, with a stern command issuing from her word balloon: *NO DYING!*

Satisfied, she closes the book and then her eyes. Brianna leans back and closes her eyes too. But she can't relax for long. Claire hears her get up and go around to the front of the house calling, "Cleo— Here, Cleo—"

Claire wakes from her catnap feeling like she's been cooking under a broiler. She has, but fortunately not for too long. She retreats indoors to find her mother once more poised beside the refrigerator. This time she's holding Cleo under one arm while offering a spoonful of cat food—just as if she were feeding a baby. The cat sticks out her tongue, takes one lick, and withdraws it, then starts to squirm unhappily.

"Mom," Claire says, taking pity on them both, "I think that was No five times."

# CHAPTER 39
## LABOR DAY SUNDAY

It was not Brodie Epstein's idea to dedicate the CARMA mural on the Sunday of Labor Day weekend. He knows better, and he argued strenuously against it. No one goes to a city ceremony on Labor Day weekend. There are church socials, barbecues and pool parties to compete, not to mention that lots of folks have cleared out of town altogether, among them the Mayor, the President of the University, and architect Randall Boseman, who was instrumental in obtaining funding for the expensive aluminum panels. Nonetheless, the Mayor's office thought it would be a special honor for the CARMA mural to be dedicated on Labor Day Sunday, and since the Mayor's office is footing the bill, they've had their way.

Serving as the Mayor's emissaries this sunny Sunday afternoon, when everyone would rather be at a softball game or a Margarita brunch on the patio of one of Rio Bueno's popular restaurants, is Robert Cringe, the Mayor's Assistant Deputy Chief of Staff, Madge Culpepper, a newly hired Budget Analyst for the Parks Division of the Public Works Department, and Brodie himself, representing the Mayor's pet City Youth Outreach Program.

Brodie likes his job—reaching out to youth is what he does best, but he's critical of the Mayor, who took on Youth as a re-election campaign issue and won on it. All that sloganizing about Our Youth and the need to Reach Out to them seemed designed to take the emphasis off of the true "youth" issue, Education. It's as if the administration had already given up on getting that right. When he thinks about all the tripe they'd have to listen to if the Mayor had come today, Brodie concedes that maybe everything is working out for the best. Cringe can be counted on to give a short, serviceable speech that

287

won't offend anybody. But, for the community's sake, Brodie had wanted a big name to be here.

Unfortunately, a grouchy Dean of Art Education has been sent to fill in for University President Cole. Dean Quintana sits unhappily beside Shelly and visualizes the tricky fourteenth green at the University golf course. Shelly is trying to pick out the parents of her students in the small crowd. It's an interesting game, which should keep her amused right through the speeches.

A pair of draftsmen was the best Randall Boseman's office could do. To their credit, the young men act pleased with their seats on the dais. They would otherwise be laboring over their CAD systems at Boseman, Mitchum & Shore, where ambition knows no holiday.

Josh and Angela have been selected to speak for the CARMA students. They take their places on the dais shyly and endure the catcalls from their friends who are settling into front row seats on the temporary bleachers. Celine and Paul are missed, they were graduating Seniors who left town last month to go to college. Andrew is absent as well. Laurie shrugs when asked, and says, "Guess he blew it off." Apparently they've broken up.

Fortunately, the Cesar Chavez residents themselves welcome the ceremony. The neighborhood has turned out in full force and proudly placed their most respected community leaders on the dais. Their City Councilor, Victor Martinez, will cut the great swag of ribbon which has been strung across the bottom of the mural. Padre Emilio, the parish priest, will give the invocation. Eddie, Marcos and other young painters from the neighborhood have been corralled into the front rows with the CARMA students. Their families and neighbors sit behind them, and pack in to give the benches a crowded feeling.

Brodie takes this all in from his vantage point on the dais. He sits with legs crossed, as relaxed as can be, and gazes out with a benign expression which belies his true feelings. Madge Culpepper, who is supposed to introduce Cringe, tries to catch his eye, seeking a cue to start the ceremony. Brodie looks casually at his watch, then pulls a cell phone from his jacket, flips it open and presses the re-dial button.

"KRB News, Tim Houle speaking."

"We're ready to start the dedication here," Brodie says flatly.

"I'm right around the corner, Brodie, honest. Coming south on Soldiers now. Can you see me? I can see your mural. Hey! Super!"

Brodie swivels around and sees a glint of light in the distance—the satellite dish on the top of KRB's news van. He grunts and puts the phone away. *Boneheads!* He motions to Madge, and she steps over to the podium. While she fiddles with the microphone, a white van parks in a barricaded area across the street. Everyone turns to gape at the TV crew, hoping for a glimpse of Paisley Archuleta, Rio Bueno's most popular newscaster. When they see it's only Tim Houle, they face front again and give their attention to Madge.

"I thought it was a beautiful ceremony," Linda Torres Richardson declares, and everyone agrees. Brodie shuts his mouth and nods. He was about to apologize for the Mayor's absence and various other slights, but it turns out that only he and Shelly feel slighted. From the neighborhood's point of view this has been a successful gathering. Much appreciation is expressed for the city's effort in erecting the dais and the bleachers, providing refreshments under a tent, and then pretty much staying out of the way. Oh, it would have been nice to have Paisley Archuleta working the crowd for interviews right now instead of that goofy Tim Houle, but the politicos aren't missed. The mural and the artists are rightfully the stars of this show. Everyone wants to shake hands with the young people who brought such a remarkable vision to life right here on the corner of Soldiers and Merchant.

Plus, there is one luminary present. His surprise appearance among the crowd causes a stir—it's Chef Reginald of Reginald's restaurant! The KRB News camera is rolling as he makes his way over to Shelly and Brodie to congratulate them on the CARMA effort. An admiring circle forms around them. Reggie, attractively flustered by the attention, reveals that he wants to hire the CARMA artists to paint a mural in his restaurant. Not only that, but he thinks he can find other business owners who would also like to have murals on the inside or outside walls of their buildings.

"Maybe," suggests Reggie, the idea only now coming to him

because of the microphone and the camera and the audience, "Maybe the CARMA program can be expanded to create a small business which the youths can run themselves to provide this service to the private sector." He hardly knows what he's saying, but it sounds awfully good. The city people are nodding and making notes. The kids are ecstatic at the idea of staying together, and painting more murals, and getting paid!

"What a pompous SOB," Tony mutters, standing with Claire and Josh, as usual, at the back of the crowd. He's become their shadow since the start of the semester, their reward for being nice to him over the summer.

They didn't expect to see him here today, but he must've overheard them talking about their plans at school. They know he doesn't have a car. When Josh asked how he got here, Tony smiled slyly and said, "I flew." Which made Claire think to herself, *Well you are dressed like a bat.*

Claire and Josh are intrigued by the prospect of a mural at Reginald's. They try to hear what Mr. Cringe says to Reggie after the news crew goes away, but Tony's running off at the mouth, and getting louder about it too.

"Slick. Real slick. You'll see, the city will be paying for Reggie's mural, not the other way. He'll get his mural for free. But I doubt you guys'll get paid. Wouldn't count on it. He's either just talking to hear himself talk, or he's running a scam."

"So why don't you quit working for him if you hate him so much?" Josh hisses, grabbing Tony by the arm and pulling him farther away from the cluster of Reggie admirers before someone gets mad.

"Really." Claire follows them.

She's looking around for Lydia or Greg. She's not surprised that Greg is a no-show, but what happened to Lydia? This was going to be the first reunion of "the girl gang"—as Shelly has dubbed them—in weeks. They were counting on Lydia being there too.

*Lydia hasn't wanted to do anything fun lately.*

Claire doesn't like it. And she doesn't like what's going on with Tony either. He really hates Reggie, that much is clear—his snide attitude at the restaurant is no act. But he seems to need Reggie too, to need to have someone to hate like that. But he also seems to need for Reggie to like *him*, and if Reggie does something that *Tony* takes as a snub, then he hates Reggie even more!

At least Josh is able to keep Tony in line. When he tells Tony to go get something to eat and keep his mouth shut about Reginald, Tony shrugs and walks off toward the tent.

Claire watches Tony with worried eyes and says, "I sure hope he doesn't turn around and talk trash like that about *us* behind *our* backs. Maybe he hates everyone who tries to be his friend."

"He hates the way he feels," Josh says simply.

It's almost exactly what Lydia said last winter: *"He wears a costume because he hates himself."* Claire shudders. *Why does Tony hate himself?* She's not sure she wants to know.

Knowing Lydia's secret is bad enough, but knowing and not being able to help is worse. In fact, Lydia seemed to be better off before she told Claire. She dazzled her way through the spring semester without missing a beat, managed fairly well through the summer—but this fall Lydia's been different. She still looks great, when she's around, but mainly she's removed herself to the stars, and to Westcare Manor.

*Maybe Lydia just needs the old ladies now,* Claire tells herself. In which case she has helped, since she's the one who introduced Lydia to Muffin and Lettie.

"No Lydia?" Laurie demands, startling her.

"Guess she couldn't make it, but neither did the guy I wanted to introduce her to."

"*Mejita*, you are no *yenta*!" Laurie howls at her own joke and Claire joins in. Josh shakes his head and moves off toward the food. He can tell the girls are going to get wound up. Angela is fast approaching, with Dori sauntering behind.

"I really like your parents," Claire tells Laurie, "and your aunts. You guys have a cool family," she expands her praise to include Angela now.

Angela and Laurie exchange a look.

"What?" Claire demands.

"What?" Dori wants to know, joining them.

"We-e-ell," Angela drawls, "Claire was like, so *thrilled* to meet our folks. You shoulda seen how she blubbered at our *dads.*" Claire starts to blush as Laurie takes over.

"*Si, mi padre!*" She turns to Claire. "You'd almost think she was *surprised* to find out we even *had* fathers—"

"You guys!" Claire is embarrassed, because the girls are right. What made her think there were no "regular" families in the Cesar Chavez community—that all the kids here are from broken homes? So far, the worst family situations she knows about are Greg's and Dori's, and she's afraid even to ask about Tony's. *Nice white families all. Jeez, I am such a moron!*

"What, did she think you were virgin births?" Dori jokes.

The girls carry on in such an unladylike fashion that Shelly comes over to tell them to cut it out. They compliment her in a teasing way on her long summer dress, which is hippyish but not too feminine. Their jibes are interrupted by Kevin's wall of sound. He has re-established his stereo system in front of the mural on a table borrowed from the refreshment tent. No sooner has the city crew cleared away the dais than the kids—and to their embarrassment, many of their parents—are out dancing against the colorful backdrop of the mural.

The bleachers come down next and are loaded into trucks. As far as the City's concerned, the party's over. But the neighbors are setting up card tables and lawn chairs and bringing out coolers and barbecue grills. The crowd is growing, not shrinking. A small police escort assigned to the dedication ceremony is calling for backups. It's almost an exact replay of the day the scaffolding came down.

Brodie whisks his cell phone from his pocket and presses re-dial.

"Tim. Brodie. Listen, you might want to get back down here. Or better yet, send Paisley."

# CHAPTER 40
## LYDIA ABLE

Lydia is sleeping late this morning. She has a Senior Work Pass to take Fridays off, so she can continue to visit Muffin at Westcare Manor. All she had to do was get a letter from Jo and fill out a form and have her parents sign it. To get the letter from Jo, she had to promise to stop free-forming Muffin's meals and pick up the cooler from Jo's porch on her way to the west side, and transmit it to Claire at the end of the day. (Jo can't believe her luck—she packs two lunches and the girls give her two days off in a row!) Lydia's parents were happy to cooperate too, so long as she keeps her grades up and runs an errand or two for her father after she's seen Muffin.

She's sleeping late and dreaming about going to see her grandmother in the nursing home. She's a child again in her dream, and she retraces a route imprinted in her child's memory, viewed through her child's eyes. The walls are paste colored, the hallways long, the turns many and maze-like. At last they step into an ominously darkened room. A camphorous smell makes Lydia feel like she's suffocating, but then it clears. Granny Abel emerges from the shadows—not as the withered, bedridden form everyone expected, but as a mature woman, upright, healthy and lucid! The grown-ups gasp and back away. Lydia runs forward.

*"Granny Abel, Granny Abel!"*

*"What, child, what?"*

*"Granny, show me how to put it back the way it was!"*

Lydia opens her eyes. The house is quiet. She is the only one home. She gets right out of bed because she has to pee. When she's done in the bathroom, she goes into her parents' room and opens the bottom drawer on her mother's side of the dresser.

This has always been her special drawer, the only one she was allowed to look in without asking permission first. Its contents have not changed since the days when Lydia used to sit on the floor in front of it and take everything out and then put everything back again. This morning she reaches for a particular item—a small framed photo of her father's grandmother. She takes it over to the window and examines every detail. There she is—a middle-aged Granny Abel—exactly as she looked in Lydia's dream. Lydia smiles, closes the dresser drawer, and takes the photo back to her room. She sets it on the night stand by her bed. Lydia Abel.

Going out to Westcare Manor does make Lydia feel able. In addition to Muffin, she spends time there with Lettie, Marcia, Hazel, Julia and others, and although she is no longer actively tracking thieves, she has devised a plan to discourage further thefts. Claire and Jo have been enlisted to help—all they have to do is take a peek at Lettie's windowsill every day. They usually do it on their way in, while the room is empty during lunchtime, or if there's time they stop for a visit with Lettie on their way out. Lydia often calls Jo for an update after school.

The truth is, she'd rather talk to Jo than her girlfriends, and she no longer hangs around for extracurricular activities. Lydia hasn't liked school much since the incident last winter. She thought it would be different this year, that she'd get off to a fresh start, but although the source of her discomfort is gone, her discomfort is not. She made herself go to the first Astronomy Club meeting, but found she couldn't go back because the presence of two of Ron's friends made her uneasy. She's still going out with Matthew, a safe and pleasant arrangement for both of them since Matt admitted that he's gay, or thinks he is. They've become good friends, but now that they've confided everything to each other, dating seems dishonest. She avoids the parties and group outings she used to love so much by running errands for Overmyer Homes on the weekends, and otherwise staying busy with her schoolwork. And so, she drags herself through Monday, Tuesday, Wednesday and Thursday in a state of pretend perkiness, which has become very tiring to sustain. All the while she is counting down to this weekly visit to her friends at Westcare. They flatter her and make her laugh, and for all their requests, require nothing more of her than a smile or silly story.

Then, why, as she drives across the bridge on this golden September Friday, does she feel like a total loser? Here she is running away from her peers to hide out with a bunch of old ladies. Will she never get over *the thing*? Will she ever stop feeling like a target around boys, like a fake when she's with her girlfriends?

Lydia wonders if she should go see a counselor at the Rape Crisis Center at the U, like Claire keeps saying. Something did happen, she should either deal with it or forget it. Too bad it's practically impossible to will yourself to forget something. She tells herself, "Forget it!" and it only makes her remember more.

By the time Lydia marches into Westcare Manor, she's made up her mind that she'll go to the RCC this afternoon. She autographs the sign-in sheet dutifully, feeling that she's making a pact with herself, then she turns her attention to the drama around her.

Not everyone at Westcare Manor is old, and they aren't all women, either, though most of them are. Lydia has counted five elderly men living in the front wings she passes to get to Muffin's room—men who are up and about, that is. She carefully avoids looking through open doors at the pallid, bedridden figures who remind her too much of Granny Abel's last days. There's also one young man—way too young, she and Claire have guessed he's about twenty—who sometimes stations himself out front to smoke a cigarette. His right leg has been amputated, and his left leg is in a brace from the knee down. He has a motorized wheelchair, wears black clothes with guy-jewelry, a Mohawk hair-do and dark glasses. Lydia feels grateful that she can't make eye contact when she passes—he's inapproachable behind his shades. But Claire thinks it's clever of him to play up the robo image, to make a fashion statement out of his disability, she's decided to add him to The Cupcake Comics.

Then there's the woman who has some sort of palsy. The girls think she's forty or so, based on her hair, which is black with only a few strands of grey. She'd be pretty except for the constant spasm of her facial muscles, so violent that speech is nearly impossible. Her young limbs are frighteningly out of control, so that she must exist within the confines of a mobile cage that's part wheelchair, part walker. She can ride or walk, with difficulty, but if her flailing arms could have their way, she would fly. Lydia's begun to think of her as an awkward angel crashing determinedly, even cheerfully, through her challenging days. She is cared for with special kindness and sympathy.

Lettie's roommate Marcia is another of Westcare's younger residents. She intercepts Lydia now as she crosses the foyer, and Lydia is reminded of the Granny Abel of her dream. Marcia looks to be middle-aged with still a little color in her hair, and when she comes close, she is surprisingly tall—taller than Lydia. It's not clear what's wrong with her, as she does not appear physically infirm in any way. Marcia makes a good roommate for Lettie because she keeps her few possessions tidy and is never in the way when the daughters and grandchildren come to visit. She can carry on a perfectly sensible conversation but rarely feels the need to say much, and she doesn't get put out with Lettie's loopy talk. Lettie often forgets that she has a roommate, since Marcia spends most of her days sitting in the foyer or outside on a bench.

The girls have seen Marcia perk up a bit during these past weeks. She's been watching the renovations with great interest, and today she wants to show Lydia how the new aviary is coming along. They stand together admiring the wood and mesh construction. A nearby worker, who's been making a racket with a staple gun, looks up to admire them.

"That your daughter?" he asks Marcia. She furrows her forehead and hurries away. "Sorry," he says to Lydia.

"It's okay," Lydia says, watching Marcia's retreat, then she shrugs and moves along.

*It is like a dream.* Between the peculiar residents and the renovations, there's something unexpected or incomprehensible around every corner. Lydia thinks of this again when she enters

Muffin's room, finds the slumping human form amidst the jumble of furniture, and sings out, "Hi, Muffin! It's Suzie!"

Since Jo explained to the girls who Suzie is, she's been wanting to try this.

"Suzie?!" Muffin's reaction is all wrong. She thinks Lydia really is *the* Suzie.

"No, Muffin, it's Lydia. You think I remind you of Suzie."

Muffin looks truly irked. Lydia could kick herself. She decides she can't make it much worse, so she teases, "I brought you a tofu sandwich."

And with that Muffin's expression slowly breaks into a grin, and she says, "That sounds awful!"

"Don't worry. I was only joking," Lydia assures her. "Jo made the lunch today."

Even so, Muffin doesn't eat much of it.

Lydia doesn't press the food on Muffin as insistently as Claire and Jo do. Muffin nibbles politely for her and it seems to be enough. They talk—about star-watching, sailing. Today Lydia even tells Muffin her dream. Muffin is interested, not the least confused. She nods sagely, as if dreaming about one's great-grandmother is a perfectly normal occurrence.

"Do you have dreams, Muffin?" Lydia asks.

"I suppose."

"You don't remember them, I guess."

"Maybe you're one." Muffin grins.

"Maybe," Lydia muses. Dreams and ghosts and being crazy and not believing that the girls who come to see her are real are the recurrent themes of these visits. But today Muffin is the one with a firm grasp of reality, and Lydia's the one who wonders if she sleeps or wakes.

"I'm putting this away now, Muffin, unless you want another bite."

It is Muffin's pleasure to decline.

Lydia's approach to the leftovers is to wrap the sandwich remains and leave them with a note suggesting that Muffin might want to eat some later. She tells Muffin what she's doing.

"I'm sure I won't remember."

"That's okay, I'm leaving this here where the aide will see it."

"Thank you."

"Okay. Bye bye, Muffin."

"Take me with you."

Lydia turns to her, startled. This has never happened before.

"I'm sorry, Muffin, I can't take you out today, but Claire will be here to see you tomorrow."

Usually Muffin registers who Claire is. Today she simply pleads, "Please take me home."

After an uneasy pause Lydia answers, "You are home, Muffin. It's just that they're doing a lot of work around here. It'll be better soon."

"I want to go home."

"Okay, Muffin. I'll tell Jo." And with that Lydia slips out, but is quickly accosted by Nancy from across the hall.

"Can you help me find my room?"

"Sure, Nancy. It's right here." Lydia walks the two steps with her and stops at her doorway.

"I don't recognize it." Nancy peers into the room suspiciously.

"That's because they painted and wallpapered and switched out all the furniture. See, everything's new." Lydia acts cheerful.

"It's not my room."

"Sure it is. Your name's right here by the door— Oh. Shoot." Nancy's name is not on the wall. Even the nameplates have been replaced, and new cards have yet to be installed. "Let's go inside and see if you recognize your things," Lydia suggests.

Nancy follows her. They find a stuffed bear, some family photos and a sweater which convince Nancy this is her room. "I want it back the way it was," she says.

Lydia stares at her for a long minute. "Don't we all."

She puts the sweater over Nancy's shoulders, and settles her in a chair with the teddy bear in her lap. "You'll get used to it." She pats Nancy's hand and then hurries out. A minute later Nancy is out in the hallway again, asking loudly if someone can help her find her room.

Beyond the nurse's station the wheelchairs are lining up with residents returning from lunch. Lydia picks out Lettie's turbaned head and greets her.

"Can you push me to my room?" Lettie asks.

"Sure. I thought I'd sit on the bed and visit."

Lydia's been looking forward to this. But Lettie hardly recognizes her today, and she doesn't recognize her room either, not even the yellow bedspread. Again there is no nameplate by the door, and without this Lettie is certain the room cannot be hers. She won't even permit Lydia to wheel her across the threshold. Lydia goes in and fetches a family photo from the night stand.

"No, that's not me," she says, "that's some other lady. I don't know who-all those people are." Lettie is very annoyed and hasn't once complimented Lydia on her blond hair or her pretty clothes or how tall she is.

Lydia goes back into the room to replace the picture, and while she's there she peeks behind the closed curtain.

"Oh, wow!" The small box which she placed there last Friday, and which Jo reported missing Wednesday and Thursday, is back! If Jo hadn't been checking, Lydia would never know it had been gone for two days. She's glad to see it, a pretty piece of cedar with dovetail joints, red felt lining and enameled copper on the lid. With a nervous flutter in her stomach she leans over and peeks inside. Again, nothing to give away the attempted theft—her note is still there: *"I'm watching you. Return everything you've taken and I won't report you."*

Lydia needs to think about her next move. If the box was returned very recently, she could be being watched herself! She closes the box and lets the curtains fall around it once more, as she returns to Lettie in the hallway.

"Okay, I'll get going," Lydia tells her. "See you next week."

"Oh, no. I won't be here next week," Lettie snaps. "I don't live here. I'm going home right now."

"Okay, Lettie, whatever." Lydia walks away shaking her head. The hallways are full of unhappy, lost-looking residents.

The foyer, while chaotic, is less distressed. Here Marcia and some other residents continue to watch the installation of the aviary. These are the fortunate few who understand what the disruption is all about and can look forward to the completed improvements. In the meantime, they are entertained by the contractors' assault.

Yes, Lydia can see how the upheaval is not all bad, and how eventually things are going to be pretty nice, but it still seems like a lot of needless upset. Since she knows the construction business, she can imagine all kinds of ways the work could be done without causing so much disruption. Relatives could have been notified and given a chance to rescue their family members on the worst days, and could have helped to keep track of their belongings.

*But that would generate a lot of griping and complaints.* Lydia reminds herself that the Manor exists to rescue the healthy from dealing with the infirm.

Out front she finds another cluster of confused souls. They have wandered out while the doors were left open for the workmen, and every one of them thinks a cab or a daughter or a husband is coming to pick them up and take them somewhere. Hazel and Julia will be traveling in the highest style. They wave to Lydia and ask her to check around the corner for their limo.

Lydia waves and hurries to her car, as one willing herself awake from a bad dream. She feels like she's been in a dream ever since she woke up this morning.

She feels like she's been in a dream ever since last winter! Again she asks herself when she will wake and put things right. Maybe she can't put herself back together the way she was, but she could be better—like a building after it's been renovated—and after a while her new self will feel like home again. Lydia tells herself that no one asked Muffin or Lettie or Nancy or the others for permission to turn their worlds upside down. There are bullies everywhere, some of them actually have *good* intentions—but even so, those in their path have only two choices—resist or endure.

Driving to her father's office, Lydia hopes there won't be too many errands today. She's suddenly full of questions for the counselors at the Rape Crisis Center. She hopes she can get there before they close.

Donna greets her and hands a roll of documents across the big reception desk. "Take these to the University Architect's office, okay? And pick up an envelope for your father and take it home to him."

"That's it?"

"That's it. Thanks!" Donna swivels back to her keyboard.

Lydia goes out and stands on the curb for a minute with the roll of blueprints in her arms. The sticky note attached to them is very explicit: *"University Architect's office is on campus in the O'Keeffe Complex, directly east of the Student Union."*

It so happens, the RCC is also in the O'Keeffe Complex. From her car Lydia dials the phone number she's had memorized for weeks. A gentle voice answers. Lydia asks how late they're open, and if she can come by this afternoon, just to talk to someone.

"Of course."

That's all. They didn't even ask for her name.

She points her car east and nods to the distant profile of the Serafinas, grateful that there are some things in life which are not easily undone—mountains and stars and ancestors who are always strong and able in our dreams.

# CHAPTER 41
## WAKE UP!

Work is proceeding on the Reginald's mural. A small vestige of the CARMA crew assembles at the restaurant each day after school and works quickly, allowed only the short time the restaurant is closed between lunch and dinner. It's not an official CARMA project. After all the talk at the "Legacy" dedication, Reggie's idea to create a city-sponsored youth business never got off the ground. Reggie himself wasn't much interested in pushing it—all he wanted was a mural of the New York City skyline on that north wall of the big dining room. He hired Josh to design it, and then was greatly disappointed when Josh and Claire didn't sign up for the painting team.

Claire can't say she was all that unhappy when her parents said no to another activity. She has her hands full with Hartshorn's class, Muffin, and college applications. But it was embarassing to have to tell her friends she wasn't allowed to participate, and she feels like she's letting them down. Josh made up his own mind about limiting his involvement with the project. He's taking an extra class so he can graduate in January, and he's still working with Gus. The busy couple drops in at Reginald's from time to time, but they try not to interfere with the work. They can see that Josh's design is in excellent hands with Eddie and Angela leading the painting crew, which also includes Marcos, Dori and Danny. The five are excited to be splitting a generous fee. Laurie came to paint too, but accepted a waitressing job instead. Often she comes early for her shift so that she can visit with her friends.

It's so much fun to hang out at Reggie's that the kids could almost feel guilty accepting pay for such a privilege—if it weren't for Tony. Reggie's unappreciative protege has been appointed to oversee the

302

painters. He rides to the restaurant after school with Dori, or with Claire and Josh if they're going, and lets the crew in and sees to their supplies so they won't disturb the chefs. On Reggie's behalf, Tony is fanatical about cleanliness and clean-up.

Or maybe it's because "He practically lives at the restaurant," as Laurie whispered to Claire on one of their rare chances to talk in private. Laurie told Claire that when the painters leave at five, Tony eats dinner with the cooks and wait staff. At five-thirty Reginald's opens for dinner and they all run their butts off until ten, then they clean up and split as quick as they can, but Tony still hangs around. She's never seen who picks him up. Tony doesn't have a car—no one knows how he gets to school or home from the restaurant, or even where he lives. Comparing notes, the girls agreed that Tony mostly acts like he would rather not go home at all, ever. Then Laurie, only half in jest, expressed some desire for whatever drugs keep Tony going, as he never seems to tire, despite his demanding schedule.

Claire has been turning this conversation over in her mind as she drives to the U with Lydia. Since then, Dori and Danny have both called her to complain about Tony, who's attaching himself to the young artists of the Reginald's crew in the way he formerly glommed on to Claire and Josh, and still does when they are available. Even when he's being a shit, or taking shit, he wants to be part of the group. Dori complained about Tony slowing down the project with his obsessive "neat freak routine." Danny said that Reggie has been no help. The chef dotes on Tony for looking out for the restaurant so well, so no one has the nerve to give Tony an outright brush-off.

Meanwhile, Tony never misses a chance to regale Claire and Josh about his loathing for these same friends he wants to hang with. Claire can see how Tony would be jealous of these new kids coming under Reggie's wing—if he actually liked Reggie. And she can see how he'd feel hurt that the others are cool to him—if he actually liked them. It's a puzzle, but after a while she simply stopped paying attention to Tony's angry talk. The less she listens, the more she feels she knows him. It's a little like talking to Lettie and some of the other residents of the Manor—they make no sense, but they seem okay somehow, inside. Tony does a good job for Reggie, and so far he's doing pretty well at school.

Claire and Josh have compared notes too. They've decided that Tony must need to blow off steam sometimes because of his mysterious condition or his medication or both. He can say the meanest things about someone and then turn around and be perfectly nice to them, and seem sincere about it. Claire and Josh are just relieved that the others tolerate Tony at all, and that he's no longer *their* constant shadow.

It would be fun to hash all this out with Lydia, especially the juicy subject of Laurie and Tony. Claire detects a poorly disguised interest in Tony on Laurie's part, while Tony is clearly besotted with Laurie. But each time Claire starts to say something to Lydia, she's daunted by the intensity of her companion's mood and unwilling to disturb her private thoughts. They have not spoken during the entire ride.

By tacit agreement, Claire never asks Lydia about her counseling. She's glad Lydia's going, except that it's almost like having the secret between them again—and Lydia seems more unhappy than ever.

Claire pulls into a parking space and turns off the engine. Reaching for the sunshade in the back seat, she glances at her friend worriedly.

"So? I'll meet you in the library when I get out of class?"

Lydia is still dreaming. That is, she's still trapped in her moody fog, unable to let go of *the thing*. Her mind plays on scraps of conversation she's had with Betty at the Rape Crisis Center and on memories which have begun to shift alarmingly under scrutiny. Even as the incident in question becomes more remote, something about it becomes more pressing.

From their first meeting Lydia was convinced that Betty could help. The youngish woman had all the concerned, wise and compassionate ways of a mother without the freak-out response. It was a relief to talk to her. And when they met for a full session the following week, Lydia found the courage to ask the question that had been plaguing her for the better part of a year. Could Betty check the records and find out if

any other girls had reported rapes or attempted rapes at that particular apartment at that party last winter?

Betty had to talk to some of her coworkers about that, and then someone did get busy at a computer and come in with a scrap of paper before the end of Lydia's session. No. Nothing had been *reported* for that location in the past year. Betty emphasized that many, many incidents go unreported.

Lydia was too ecstatic to hear that part. The cloud was ready to lift right then. Wasn't that the worry which had been weighing her down, that due to her silence and shame some other girl had been victimized?

Betty felt that Lydia needed another session. Lydia agreed to come, mainly because it was fun to drive to school with Claire on Thursdays and then drive to the U together, Claire for her drawing class and Lydia ostensibly to use the library—she goes there each week after her appointment. Lydia agreed to another date, showed up, and regretted it from the minute the session started.

This time it was Betty's turn to ask the questions. By the end of the nightmarish forty minutes, Lydia was deeper into the abyss than ever. How long had she been feeling drugged before she went into the bathroom and puked? What was she doing before then? Were any of her clothes torn or messed up? Did she have any bruises the next day? Where? Has she had a urinary tract infection or other health problems?

She answered every question truthfully without hesitation. When Betty said to come back again, Lydia agreed—but from the shadowy, puzzled place. In the week since, she's had many imaginary conversations with Betty—frightened, irate, accusatory, bewildered —and while Lydia's mind probed unhappily into issues she dared not talk about to anyone but Betty, those she dared not talk to have receded into the distance. They speak and laugh, and Lydia duplicates their sounds and expressions while her Self watches from a safe vantage point.

"Where will I find you—astronomy section or colleges?" Claire asks loudly. She wants to take Lydia by the shoulders and shake her.

Lydia doesn't notice Claire's annoyance because she herself is fuming. She says, "Literature, I have to write a paper on Ezra Pound," while the voice in her head screams, *Don't go, don't go! You shouldn't have taken the appointment if it's going to make you so bummed!* But she knows she can't walk away from the counseling while she's in this state. For a while, seeing Betty was making her feel better, and she wants that feeling back!

They put the shade in the windshield, gather their things and walk quickly, parting company at the Duck Pond. To Claire, this late afternoon in late September is a picture postcard image of Indian Summer. The bright blue sky is adorned with sweeps of feather-like clouds, the cottonwoods are crowned in gold, and leafy lace vine festoons the rail fence around the pond in fiery red flags.

To Lydia, the sun glares against an unseasonable misty pall, and all she sees is the slate grey walkway under her feet and then the looming, impishly pink adobe of the O'Keeffe Complex.

Across town, things are not going well at Reginald's. Tony insists that a larger area than usual must be cleared of tables and chairs and draped before anyone may get up on a ladder to paint. The crew is ready to rebel. Reggie is not there to keep the peace, or Claire or Josh.

"Shit man, we won't have any time to paint!" Eddie snaps. "I didn't come here just to move furniture and then move it back again. Besides, using a ladder isn't going to make us more messy. Get real, Tony!"

This inspires Tony to demonstrate all the ways a mishap with the ladder, paints and brushes might lead to calamity in the dining room. For a minute it seems like Tony will be the one to spray the place with paint in his zeal to make his point. Dori and Angela find his act amusing. Their laughter eggs him on.

That pisses off the guys. Marcos gets in Tony's face, "Bug off, you little dickhead, or I'll personally clean this carpet with your ass."

The girls stop laughing and look to Danny to intervene. The thin young man blushes. He doesn't fight. He has no intention of putting himself bodily between the antagonists.

*What would Brodie and Shelly do?* he wonders. The answer is obvious: *A mural!*

Without a word Danny starts moving tables and chairs. Dori and Angela quickly join in. Three to two—and time wasting. Marcos and Eddie defer to the majority. They start stacking chairs. Tony concedes ground too. So as not to be in a position to quibble about how much space is cleared, he retreats to the kitchen.

Laurie's there helping the pastry chef with the night's desserts. Her hair is tied back in a tight ponytail and she's put all her jewelry in her pockets. The starched white apron she wears makes her look almost wholesome. But when she feels Tony's eyes drilling into her, she turns and sneers at him with shiny, blood-red lips, a hard glint in her eyes. Tony holds her stare for a long moment.

"Can I bum a cigarette?"

"Sure," Laurie says slowly, and motions to her apron. Her hands are coated in flour.

Tony steps over to her, plucks a pack of Slims Lite out of the big pocket on the front of her apron, removes a cigarette and drops the pack back in, his touch so deft she doesn't feel the slightest pressure of his hand on her thigh, as she'd expected.

"Thanks."

Tony takes a light from a gas burner on his way to the back door. The pastry chef says something sharp to Laurie. She lets out the breath she's been holding and turns back to her task.

✧

"How'd ya do?"

"Not bad. I need about six sentences to string all the quotes together, a paragraph to wrap it up, and I'm done." Lydia clicks her laptop closed and smiles across the big wooden table at Claire. A pile of books between them attests to her diligence.

"Uhm, you did go to your appointment, didn't you? I mean, you got all that done in an hour?" She means too, *You look in too good a mood to have gone to that session.*

Lydia knows quite well what Claire means.

"I went and we agreed it should be my last one, and it was a little shorter than usual. Hang on a sec while I put these books back."

She disappears into the stacks, leaving Claire in suspense. Weary from her drawing class and perplexed by Lydia, but glad to see her friend in a more cheerful state, Claire waits, immobile, without any books or papers around her, staring blankly ahead. Greg comes around a corner and sees her. He plops down in the chair recently vacated by Lydia, giving Claire a start.

"Sorry to interrupt. Are you channeling your research now?"

"Oh, hi, Greg. No, I'm just half asleep. Waitin' for a friend." *Fate*, Claire thinks, smiling at Greg, *this is fate*. "The friend you missed meeting at the mural dedication." She neglects to mention that Lydia wasn't there either.

"Sorry about that." Greg doesn't say anything more. He's studying Claire carefully. She seems more grown up, more subdued—though maybe that's because they're in a library. They haven't even talked on the phone since the weekend Josh got back.

"So, how are you?" Claire's realizing this too. "How's school? What's Salman up to?"

"Oh, you know. Same ol', same ol'."

"There's Lydia!" Claire waves.

Greg turns in time to see a Venus in modern dress brandish a single book at Claire to indicate it's the last she has to shelve, before she slips down an aisle and out of sight.

"*Really* sorry I couldn't make it."

"Well, here we all are. It's *kismet*."

Lydia comes over, collects her laptop and her purse from the chair beside Greg while they are introduced, and they all walk out together. Greg accompanies the girls to Claire's car, drawing Lydia out about the Ezra Pound assignment and her college plans and anything he can think of to talk about. His comment about how bright Arcturus was the other night wins him Lydia's phone number.

"Now that was one strange day," Lydia says, settling back into her seat and watching Greg's jaunty retreat in the side mirror.

"You seem better than when it started." Claire maneuvers out of the parking lot and watches for a break in the traffic on Leighton Boulevard. Rush hour is a blessing tonight, they'll have more time together. Claire senses that Lydia wants to talk. She eases into the long line of cars, and they settle in for a slow ride across town.

"I guess I'm back to where I was a couple weeks ago," Lydia says, broaching the subject of her counseling for the first time since she told Claire she would be going. "I should've quit while I was ahead, but at least I'm finally done now."

"Can you tell me about it?" Claire's quick to add, "It's okay if you'd rather not."

Lydia has figured something out today in the aftermath of her short session with Betty. Betty couldn't possibly know her as well as Claire does, and couldn't possibly care for her as much. Of course, that's exactly what Lydia wanted in a confidant originally, but there's a point at which professionals have to go places a real friend would not. After all, they get paid to be thorough. They've seen plenty of cases where the victim's memories are unreliable, suppressed or blocked by trauma.

"Betty had me come back last week because she wasn't convinced I *hadn't* been raped, and just made up the story about puking and fighting off Blaine." As Lydia says this she discovers that not only is she no longer angry at Betty, but she's beginning to put *the thing* behind her. She watches the color rise in Claire's face, until her florid complexion blends seamlessly into her auburn hair, all of which are bathed in peach colored late-day light.

"Wow, what a sunset!" Lydia looks from Claire to the pastel-washed panorama of Rio Bueno. Her guardian Serafinas are bathed in the last spray of color issuing out of the west.

Claire's eyes are on the rear bumper of the car in front of her. She casts a quick glance left and right and at Lydia. "I'm really sorry," she says, returning her attention to the road. The sunset, pretty much the same one they have every day, seems a slight reward for all Lydia's been through. What an outrage!

"I'm not sorry," Lydia assures her. "Oh, I was freaked last week, totally. What if she was right? What if I was friggin' *nuts?* Why else would it be so hard for me to deal with? Why else would I feel so *ashamed?* I had to replay everything in my mind. And I wasn't sure I remembered everything right—I was stoned, and then sick, and then really scared—"

"But the point was, you were stoned and sick and scared, *in that order*," Claire jumps in.

"Exactly—exactly! When I got so mad explaining it that I was ready to punch *Betty* out, she finally saw how maybe I did fight Blaine off."

"Hmmm." Claire's mentally sketching the scene with Lemon Meringue and the block-headed Betty. "Did you leave quietly or did they have to put you out?"

"I was still mad when I left. And Betty wasn't very apologetic. She felt like she was doing her job."

"Yeah, right."

"Yeah, well, she did do her job. It was really awful for a while, but I do feel better. She got me to think about the things I was trying not to think about—the things that made me feel so bad."

"Like?"

"Like, what if he had raped me? If I'd been drugged would I even remember? What about the other guys there, what if they— Uch, I still can't even think about that without feeling sick. But those things do happen! And just to even think about it almost happening to you makes you feel like dirt. Like, how could they have such zero respect? How could anyone be such an animal? And girls that go through it—you could see how they'd feel less than human themselves." Lydia shudders. "I could hardly handle what happened to me, the *attempt*. I mean I handled it when it was happening, but afterwards I was so weirded out. I felt dirty. I felt bad about myself because anyone could actually see me that way. I almost— There were times when I wanted to kill myself." If she could admit it to Betty, she can admit it to Claire, at least in the abstract. Lydia plows ahead before Claire can react. "I just don't know how I would ever get over the shame of it."

"Lydia! You're the victim. The shame and all the blame is on the rapist."

"You say." Lydia's veneer of composure fractures a bit.

They ride in silence for a few minutes. Then Claire braves a pointed question.

"Are you sure you're ready to stop seeing Betty?"

Lydia sighs. "No, I'm not sure."

"Are you still afraid?" She turns onto Prince Street. They are nearly home.

"It's not as bad, but, it's not ever very far away—that anxiety. Something happened once already..." Claire starts to interject but Lydia won't hear it. "It did happen—something happened! Not rape, no, not 'penetration'—as Betty would say—but attempted, it was a real assault. The guy planned it, he tried it—he could have so easily succeeded! So I can't ever say again, 'That's so far-fetched, that's paranoid, that'll never happen to me.' Yeah, you can talk about odds, 'What're the odds of it happening twice?' But you know what? They're actually pretty high. Betty told me that. Because your self-image goes way down and you wanna die and the next thing you know, you're taking chances, maybe taking drugs, and hanging out with all kinds of creeps." Lydia looks toward Claire with a grim smile. "Sound familiar?"

Claire nods but says nothing.

"So, yeah, I'm on the defensive a lot. Watching out for what stupid thing I could do to myself, plus for what's out there waiting to get me."

Claire pulls into the elementary school parking lot so they can finish talking. She turns towards Lydia. The last rays of sun cast a soft glow on young faces prematurely creased with worry.

"It happens a lot, doesn't it?"

"Oh, Claire, I was *so* lucky!"

This takes them both by surprise. The laughter it provokes is mixed with tears, but before they can get carried away by their emotions, Lydia's cell phone jingles. She glances at the display before putting the phone close to her face.

"Hi! I'm right around the corner, honest—be home in two minutes," she says perkily. "Oh, okay. I'll tell her." Lydia stashes the phone in her purse. "She was calling because your mom called. They're *holding dinner for you*." She grins at Claire.

Claire clutches the steering wheel with both hands and pretends to pound her head on it, then she looks at Lydia and says sweetly, "Okay, I feel better now," and takes her home.

They part with promises to do something together soon, just the two of them, and Claire drives around the corner as slowly as she can to make her mother wait even a little longer. But she's not really mad. She understands her mother's fears much better now, and she wishes Lydia could share her story as a wake-up call to other young women. The question is—how to do it without identifying Lydia? This is not a subject Claire feels ready to tackle in The Cupcake Comics. Her mind plays on other options all through dinner, after which she calls Lydia, and another plot is hatched.

# PART IV

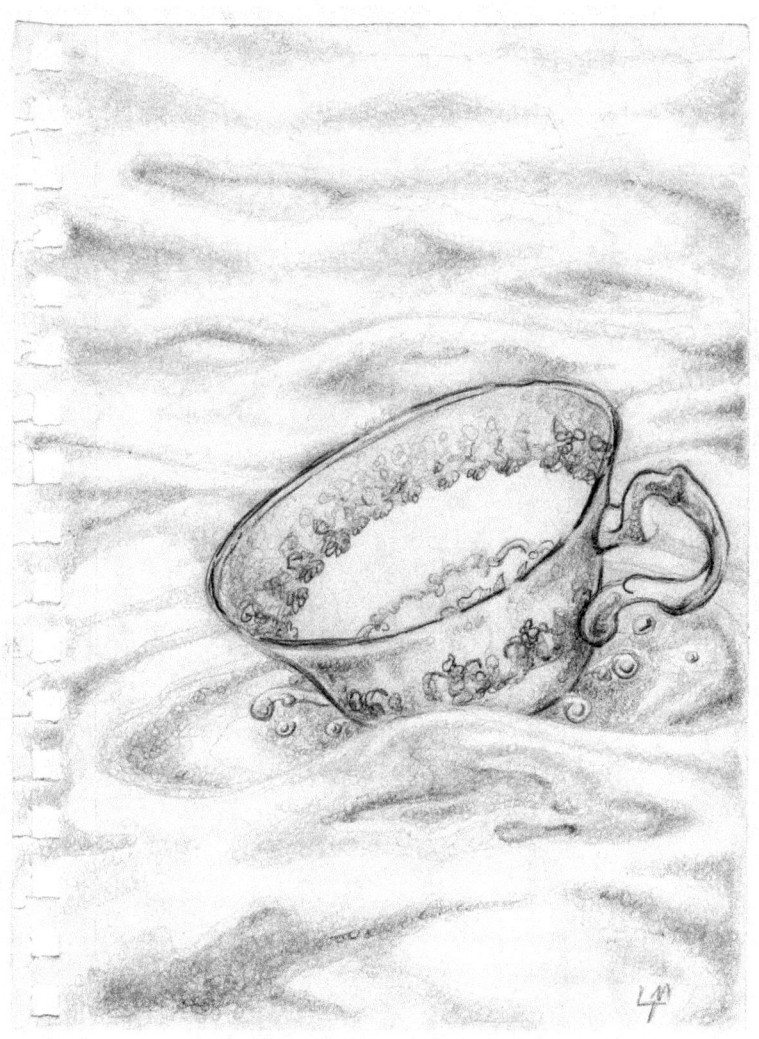

# CHAPTER 42
## RAINBOW DAYS

Sunday morning, the First of October, Carl Stanley wakes late, slips out of bed, and feels the need to don his flannel bathrobe, long buried in the back of the closet. He pulls on a pair of socks and pads into the living room. His first stop is the thermostat, which he studies critically and compares to the clock on a shelf nearby.

Brianna comes in fully dressed, carrying two cups of coffee. "It's about time, don't you think?" she asks hopefully.

"Ten o'clock and still only sixty-five in here. I'd say so." Carl steps over to the big picture window, while Brianna settles on the couch. "You ready?" She nods eagerly. "Should I wake the girls?" She shakes her head.

Carl opens the curtain with a flourish. Sunlight floods the room and with it a spray of rainbow fragments from Brianna's collection of prisms—a dozen dollops of facetted glass hanging from a rod installed especially for them. The brush of the curtain pleats has set them dancing. Without resentment for their long seclusion, they cast the room in magic light. Carl takes a seat beside Brianna. They sip their coffee in the delicious warmth of a sunbeam, while the play of colors makes a kaleidoscope of flesh, fabric and furniture.

When it's time to refill his cup, Carl first wanders up the hall to Claire's room. "Claire, Lydia, don't sleep the morning away," he calls through the door. "It's rainbow time!" A burst of laughter tells him he didn't wake them.

They tumble out of the room, baggy eyed from too little sleep but in high spirits. Lydia knows all about the rainbows at the Stanley-Yost house. She helped Claire pick out one of those prisms as a gift for Mother's Day two years ago. Now they throw themselves into the spectral spectacle with abandon. The sun is fast arcing out of rainbow range, so that Claire and Lydia must stretch to catch the colors on their hands and hair. Stan Man joins the impromptu ballet.

Brianna watches distractedly. She finishes her second cup of coffee and gets up to go into the kitchen, offering to make breakfast. Everyone knows her first priority will be the cat. Lydia accepts a glass of juice but can't wait around for whatever Brianna's making. Claire says she only wants toast. A busy day lies ahead. She figures she can still sneak in a couple hours of sleep before it's time to go over to Reginald's with Josh to see the finished mural.

Lydia goes to Claire's room to finish dressing. She tucks the fat envelope they've spent half the night preparing into her pack, then goes outside where Claire is waiting to give her an extra tight hug.

"You don't have to mail it if you don't want to," Claire whispers in her ear.

"Yes I do," Lydia answers simply, donning her shades.

A chilly night has given way to brilliant sunshine. The stultifying heat has passed, and the pace of life in Rio Bueno is quickening, or feels like it is, with that energizing coolness morning and night, and this shortening of the days, which makes the final months of the year seem to hurtle downhill.

Lydia feels it, driving out of her way so she can drop the envelope in a mailbox before going to church. She's uncharacteristically late, and rumpled. *So what!* She's wasted too much time already maintaining the facade of a former self.

Claire feels it, turning the calendar page and wishing that Josh hadn't told her he would be leaving Rio Bueno before spring. *I had to ask!* Of course she did, and now she must live with the prospect of a final Senior semester without him. This is what comes of being in such a hurry to grow up.

Carl and Brianna feel it too, the speeding up of time, when the girls' voices stop chiming and the rainbows fade. They each think, but neither says aloud, *She won't be here for rainbows next fall.*

For Jo and Muffin time is relentless in a different way. Nothing is happening but Nature. They are leaving things to Nature, but Nature is not doing anything. She is being patient and incremental—and as inevitable as ever. There's no catastrophic event to hasten the unscrolling of Muffin's final chapters, or anything to slow it. Is it October already? Or, is it only yet October? They are adrift in an immeasurable sea, and a stubborn current bears them ever closer to a single island visible on the horizon. They know there is no chance of missing it, but neither is there any way to tell how close they are coming.

Jo does not want to get to the end and wish she had done things differently. Her mother's release will be her own, and she doesn't intend to quit early only to carry the guilt of it into her own old age. Therefore, whatever she can do to make her mother comfortable, Jo will do.

Thinking of Muffin, her mom, the way she once was, Jo invents tempting new combinations of foods and a story to tell with each course. By a trick of spirit involving old memories, wishfulness and love, Jo waves off the dread which often accompanies a visit to the aged. Familiarity helps. Westcare Manor is practically her home away from home, and amid the confusion, frustration and anguish of a typical nursing home day, moments of gaiety and grace flash like rainbows from a prism. There are colors here, and pleasure. Jo doesn't realize how much of that she herself contributes.

On this day at Westcare the new aviary in the foyer continues to delight. Several residents are happily watching the canaries, love birds and parakeets when Jo arrives shortly before noon. She stops and watches with them, greeting Marcia and Nancy personally. For a while the birds are captivating, but Jo feels too strong a sense of irony to linger in front of the beautiful creatures, symbols of freedom, trapped in a pen for the distraction of other creatures similarly held against their will. The birds sadden Jo, but it must be said that the birds themselves appear content. Their clutch of admirers clucks along enthusiastically. They could watch the aviary all day, but they are being called to lunch.

Muffin is more of a water bird—a long-legged heron or egret. Her short hair is ruffled and sticking up like feathers, her aristocratic beak is more prominent than ever against sunken cheeks and eye sockets. Her wings are clipped, knobby knees and elbows jutting uselessly from the confines of her wheelchair. Jo finds this endangered creature in a heavy sleep from which she has trouble waking. Muffin responds to Jo's greetings but won't open her eyes.

"I feel awful."

"I'm sorry. What hurts?"

"I don't know."

"Is it your stomach?"

"No."

"Your head?"

"No."

"Your shoulder?" Muffin is slumped to the right. Jo is shifting her gently in the chair, trying to get her upright so she can eat.

"Ouch. Stop that!"

"Are you hungry?"

"No."

"Do you want some cold juice?"

"Well, maybe."

Muffin takes a few sips and then asks for water. Jo finds a tiny blue plastic cup and a full pitcher on the night table. After Muffin drinks she eats two bites of the sandwich, and she asks for more water. This is all she wants, water. Jo refills the little cup six times. In between she wipes at Muffin's eyes, goopy from an application of ointment, until they will open. Blind though they are, Jo still likes to see her mother's eyes.

Muffin deigns to taste the pears with yogurt, but she's had enough of it after a couple of mouthfuls. She's refused everything else.

Talking does no good. Jo's mention of the new grandson elicits a small smile, otherwise Muffin is unresponsive. Jo babbles on about the family, offering a soliloquy when Muffin won't be drawn into conversation. Nothing distracts Muffin from her despair, and she won't be tricked into eating anything more. Finally Jo gives up, and positions herself to rub Muffin's feet. Muffin even complains about this.

"That hurts!"

Jo's surprised. "I thought the rub would make them feel better."

"No. You shouldn't do it," Muffin snaps, but she sits quietly after this and then dozes off. Jo puts the sock and shoe back on Muffin's foot and prepares to leave.

"I suppose I should rub you now," Muffin mumbles.

"Maybe next time, Ma," Jo tells her and kisses her cheek.

She has to sit quietly in the car for a long while before she can drive home. Her mother wouldn't have eaten any more from a tray of nursing home food with a frazzled attendant to help her, but that single sentence, that fleeting spark of maternal devotion, is enough to convince Jo she must pack a lunch and come back tomorrow.

# CHAPTER 43
## LESSONS IN PERSPECTIVE

Claire feels October slipping away, the better part of two weeks spent and already in the discard pile. Perversely, the more she packs into her days, the faster they go by. She can't stop though, not until her portfolio is complete, and not as long as Jo and Muffin need her, and not as long as Josh is available to go with her to fiestas, football games and other activities once considered un-cool—until she discovered the joys of having a "date." Of course she has to stay up on her schoolwork in order to live this whirlwind life. And the parents pester her so much about college that she's made the applications a priority, if only to get Stan Man and Brianna off her back. Her folks are anxious for an early admissions decision so that, *"we'll know what we're doing,"* as if knowing is the most important thing.

Claire would rather not know, that is, would rather not have to decide quite so soon. Three months might not mean much to her parents at their advanced age, but they represent a significantly larger proportion of Claire's life. She's a new person every day. To make a decision at this stage is like having to freeze herself in time. She begins to understand why Josh is doing what he's doing. Faced with the pressing need to decide what to do, he decided that deciding itself would be his activity, and that he'd go somewhere where he'd be left alone to do it.

*That's Josh. He won't lock himself into anything. He'll freeze time instead.*

Claire watches out the window for Josh's car and freezes time temporarily for herself by dozing off. Her parents are out. Josh has to come to the door to rouse her.

Josh and Gus have been helping Claire with her portfolio, in

320

particular her presentation of The Cupcake Comics, which she really doesn't have the skills or time to finish.

"If you could make it perfect, you wouldn't need college, now, would you?" Gus told her. She'd been so frustrated that day, she was ready to throw her sketchbook into his wood stove.

After that they settled down to make a series of story boards, pasting in Claire's drawings—some carefully inked, some in color—and the thumbnails and studies for others. She thinks the latter look scratchy and awful, but when she slides the boards into the large plastic sleeves of her new zippered portfolio case and pages through them one by one, she sees how the presentation will reflect a good deal of work, versatility and originality. It will have to do! Of course the whole thing will have to be photographed and made into sets of slides to be mailed with Claire's applications. Only after she passes an initial review will she be invited to have interviews and show the original work.

It's rather exciting to think about that. Since Josh essentially decided not to decide about going anywhere, Claire feels there are more choices open to her. She can't follow him if he won't go! She's applying to the U of course, and to schools in California, Florida and Missouri. The Kansas City Art Institute is her first choice. Her folks would like her to be near Gram in Florida. But the University of California is interesting for its size and variety of programs. It's one of the schools Lydia picked out for their astronomy department.

Life is a banquet. When Claire gives up trying to consume it all she finds she can be satisfied by abundance for its own sake. Strangely, her sense of this is strongest when she sits with Muffin, as she did earlier today, in a room whose recent renovations only make it seem more sterile, more impersonal, and Muffin's passing more inevitable—as though her cubby has been prematurely refurnished for the next tenant. The corridor is quiet at the noon hour when everyone has gone to the dining room. Muffin and her visitors are afforded absolute privacy. The clock which never worked has been removed. In this suspended state Claire becomes fully aware of the richness of life and the multitude of possibilities before her. Not that her time with Muffin can be called contemplative. In fact the visits are becoming more demanding, but they are a counterpoint to everything else. They place Claire outside herself, and during her hectic week her thoughts will return to this. When she turns her life into a story for Muffin's amusement—just as when she reframes Muffin as a cartoon character—awkward situations become more manageable.

Riding to Gus's studio, Claire drowses in the passenger seat the way Muffin nods off when set in a splash of sunshine, though the youthful loveliness Josh sees when he glances over at her could not be further from an old woman's brittle, sallow arrangement of bones and flesh. He would like to pull over and draw her like that, her head tilted to the side, supported by the shoulder strap. He'd put a busy strip mall beyond the car window, as a contrast to her relaxed features. He drives along, constructing the picture in his mind's eye. Stopping is out of the question, since it would surely wake Claire. He is as tenderly protective of Claire as he imagines she is of Muffin.

Josh knows Muffin only through Claire's art. He might admit to being a little jealous of Claire's devotion to her, and the time Claire spends rehashing her weekly visits with Lydia, but he isn't immune to the peculiar powers Muffin exerts. If he could talk to Claire about going to Green Creek without her getting so huffy, he'd tell her more about Mr. Simms, not a young man himself, and his elderly parents. They were so excited about the prospect of having Josh around that he had to accept. It wasn't only about his painting. They need him.

Josh looks forward to being useful to Mr. Simms as opposed to simply occupying a desk at school. He looks ahead, not to extended periods of separation from Claire, but to the opportunities they'll have to be alone and on their own when she comes to visit. For his art he can predict nothing but time and canvas. He's eager to begin filling both with works yet to be conceived.

As for Claire, how can she not feel that Josh, though certainly in no rush to say good bye to her, is terribly impatient to start his "real" life? She's been hard pressed not to be insulted, as if a judgment has been passed on her life by extension. *Kid stuff, that's what he thinks.* Her irritation with Josh is one of the things which visiting Muffin helps her escape from, but the vague displeasure settles on her again while she sleeps. She wakes when Josh turns off the engine.

They're parked in Gus's driveway. Claire turns to Josh and says, "You really don't have to help me with the story boards. I know you have your own work to do."

"I don't mind," Josh says, missing the acid tone of her words, or pretending to.

The worst part is that she can't even pick a fight with him when she tries. Claire thinks it's unfair that she is so intensely sensitive to Josh's feelings, while he is singularly oblivious to hers. Morosely she follows him into the studio.

Gus is working. They can hear his tools battering the stone. They follow the sound and stand at the door to the big room, watching quietly. The great slab of pink marble looks impenetrable. It's taller than Gus. Tiny chips fly out from his chisel. The process reminds Claire of archeology, those videos she's seen of workers excavating entire towns with little more than a dental pick and a paintbrush.

"That's you," she whispers to Josh, nodding to the rock, "and that's me." She points her chin at the chisel.

Josh frowns at her and then draws her away from the door and closes it. "You got something to tell me? You saying I'm a blockhead? Well maybe I've been trying to tell you something too."

Having ignited Josh's temper, Claire's own demeanor becomes conciliatory. "I'm just saying we need to talk." She sits down on the futon. Josh glares at her and then sits facing her.

"Okay. Ladies first. Let me have it."

"Oh, never mind!" Now she feels tongue-tied.

"You're mad because I'm going to Green Creek." He tries not to sound like he's mad that she's mad.

"Well, yeah."

"How come?"

"I don't know. I mean, I know I'll miss you, but it's more. It's like you're going to be all grown up, and I'll still be in school."

Josh has to smile at that. "Going to Green Creek isn't going to make me suddenly more grown up than you."

"You think?"

"And besides, how do you think I'll feel when you're in college and I'm not?"

"Like you're a real artist and I'm just a student." There, she said it.

"No way, Claire. No way! You're going to be an awesome cartoonist! Wow—" Josh shakes his head.

"What?"

"I can't believe you feel, like, *less*. I hate that. You know I hate that! I'm so sick of listening to people talk about my talent, my *gift*. So what? You've got ideas, you've got direction. Did you ever think I might be jealous of you?"

"Hey, who said I was jealous?"

Josh shrugs. Claire sighs. The rhythmic tapping of Gus's mallet soothes her. She appreciates the beat emanating from the studio as though it were a song. Now that she's observed the artist at work, Claire has come to understand why Gus's sculptures are so alive—music and movement have gone into the making of them.

"Gus must be as unhappy as I am that you're going," Claire acknowledges. "I'm kind of surprised you'd blow him off. You could skip your last semester and have more time to work with him."

"I'm not blowing anyone off!" Josh erupts. "I told you I'll be coming down here often to see both of you!"

"Okay, okay! Sheesh, I thought you were moving up there to make things simple for yourself, but you seem really stressed. I don't see how this works out the way you want it to—between the chores up there and running back and forth—are you really gonna get that much painting in?" *He's going to be a great artist*, Claire tells herself, *What do you want from him? Don't get in his way*. "I think— I think you shouldn't worry about coming down here all the time—not on my account. I want you to do your art."

"Claire, Claire, it's not a choice—don't make it be a choice between there or here, please?" He takes her in his arms, and she sobs violently for a minute before gaining control of herself. "Listen," he speaks softly, his head leaning against hers, "You gotta understand that I never cared about anything much but art. And, yeah, it's hard for me now. I've got you, and I need to make good on my deal with Gus, and my deal with the Simms. But I think it's doable. I mean, normal people have no trouble with this, right? Having more than one interest, more than one friend?"

Claire pulls away. "Yeah, but only one girlfriend, right?"

"Absolutely."

Claire finally allows herself to listen to what Josh has to say about the set-up in Green Creek. The Simms are aging, and trying to keep a family business and a way of life alive. They've given up on the younger generations, who only want a place to escape to when their city lives become too hectic. Not a one seems to understand what it takes to maintain their paradise.

"Old Man Simms would complain about it even when I was a kid. How folks like us who spent weeks there every summer were more like family—and helped out more—than the 'city mice' who showed up for long weekends and made a lot of trash. I know it was his way of getting us to do chores, but we liked it. That was the fun of being there. I always did have a kind of fantasy about growing up and managing the place and living there all the time."

"Ah, the truth comes out." Claire can see how it wouldn't be a bad life for an artist. *Once you've got your New York and LA agents lined up*.

"Mom and Dad have been going up there since before I was born," Josh continues, "in our case it really was like family. 'Uncle Mark and Aunt Betsy.' When Betsy broke her leg one spring, Mom went up and spent a month with her. I couldn't believe she'd do that, or that Dad would let her. That's when he—we—learned how to use the kitchen. When I was eleven, I got to go up by myself and spend a week before my parents came. I've done that a few times. No way my folks would say no to me spending time there now. I think they even like the idea. I wish you did."

"Well, it's growing on me." As Josh has told his story, Claire's resentment has begun to ebb away.

His promise to come back and take her to the Senior Prom helps too.

# CHAPTER 44
## MASQUERADE

Claire and Lydia learn that their package has hit its mark when they find this essay in the Roosevelt High *Herald*: "POTION WAS NOT ABOUT LOVE, a cautionary tale." By-line: "Anonymous, originally published in the University *Bugle*." The column is accompanied by a lengthy sidebar article by the Director of the Rape Crisis Center containing tips on sizing up dangerous situations, self defense and coping with the aftermath of an assault, plus contact information for the center and other agencies. Of the "cautionary tale" itself, the Director will only say, "It is perfectly believable. We hear about this sort of thing all the time. We trust that the young woman has sought counseling and we commend her for speaking out."

By week's end, article and sidebar have been reprinted in every high school paper in the city, just as the girls had hoped. (The note they sent with the article said that they didn't want to submit it to any particular high school, to protect the student's identity, and they trusted the *Bugle* would pass it on.) Now the story is all over the city papers, as parents get wind of it and stir up controversy. Some are unhappy about the episode, and some are appalled at the word rape appearing in print no matter what the context. Their protests are only bringing more publicity.

The flap doesn't go unnoticed by the Stanley-Yosts. When the essay shows up in the morning paper, they want to know what Claire has to say about it. Claire says it's stupid, the people who really don't want to see that stuff written about should've kept their mouths shut.

"Now the whole city's reading it."

"But what do you think about the story itself?" Brianna presses.

Claire and Lydia have worked out a response to this already. Claire shrugs like it's old news and says, "Oh, we got all of that in Health Ed." She pretends to be half asleep, slurping her cereal groggily. Brianna rolls her eyes at Carl and goes back to reading the paper. Claire is never very responsive early in the morning.

The Overmyers get the evening paper, where coverage is more restrained. If they see it, they never mention the story to Lydia. She wonders if they're being supremely clueless or extraordinarily cool. Possibly they are just shielding young Herbie from an unseemly subject. Whichever it is, Lydia is grateful not to have to go there with her parents. Still, it makes her uneasy to hear the story talked about so much at school and everywhere else. She thinks back to that moment before the envelope left her hand and slid down the mail chute, wishing she could take it back.

*You have to stop wanting to go backwards!* she chides herself. To her relief, there is virtually no speculation about who the "Diane" of the story really is, or the boys. Any reader might guess that the characters have been fictionalized to protect their identities, but no one doubts the fundamental truth of the tale.

It happens all the time. It's called date rape. It is no longer Lydia's shameful *thing that happened*, but a criminal act—one she hopes will occur less often thanks to her courage.

The uproar over the cautionary tale has just about died down when Reggie decides to throw a party to celebrate the completion of the mural. It will be a Halloween Brunch on the last Sunday in October. In keeping with the New York theme of his restaurant, anyone who comes dressed as a character from a Broadway musical will get a free glass of champagne.

The artists themselves are not eligible for drinks, of course, and they've been paid for their work, but Reggie still offers the students a half price deal, if they'll wear any kind of costume at all. He's counting on them to dress up and help make his brunch a festive masquerade. He'll save one of the little dining rooms for the teens, and give Tony and Laurie the shift off so they won't have to wait on their friends. Reggie doesn't want to rekindle any tensions. The mural is a masterpiece, and he wants everyone to feel good about it.

When the day arrives everyone does feel good. Enough time has passed since the mural team disbanded that hard feelings have faded. The mural looks fantastic. They can hardly believe they did it. Everyone is congratulating each other on the painting and laughing at the costumes.

Tony and Laurie, though off duty, have come dressed in their sleek black waitering clothes—pretty much their everyday attire. They stand out as chic and sophisticated-looking against the clownish milieu. Who wouldn't notice how the two have come to be on friendly terms? Claire can see now how Laurie and Tony are kind of alike in the way they both act tough and insulting, but underneath they're rather sensitive and insecure. It doesn't seem so strange for them to have gotten close. Today, of course, they are showing their hard edges, so cool they crackle like ice. They match each other put-down for put-down, and because they're having fun, it's funny, not mean.

Everything changes when a rumor goes around that Tony and Laurie are dating. Celine or one of the other kids not directly involved with the Reginald's mural must have started it. The casual observer might well come to that conclusion, and nothing Angela or Dori or Claire can say dampens the speculation. Despite her friends' best efforts, Laurie catches wind of the talk. She's furious.

"Look, we work together. There's nothing going on!" she says loudly to Kevin, knowing that Tony is nearby. "Give me a break. He doesn't even have a car. What are we gonna do, go to the drive-in on his bicycle?"

Instead of making a witty comeback, Tony pretends not to hear. He stays away from Laurie after that, but Claire catches him watching her morosely.

"I don't think she meant to hurt your feelings," Claire lies.

"Who would want to go out with that bitch anyway?" he says with venom in his voice.

"Now, now." Claire taps him on the shoulder with her magic spatula.

Tony turns around and has to cheer up at the sight of her. Soon he's laughing and monkeying around again. He's even nice to Reggie, but that's his way of being nice to Claire, Josh, and the other kids who have endured his presence, and in their own way befriended him.

The truth about Tony is that though he appears to demand so much from people and can be viciously critical when he doesn't get the response he wants, his grudges are fleeting. He's come to expect nothing but cruelty from his peers, and so it takes very little kindness to encourage him. No one is down on him today, so they are all his friends. And Laurie—well, he's flat out in love with her. He cherishes even her abuse, and the knowledge that he and she *seemed* like boyfriend and girlfriend to some makes him decide to be friendly to her again in order to sustain that impression, and maybe provoke her further.

These teenage dramas are of little concern to Reggie and his guests. The all-you-can-eat gourmet buffet is set up so that diners can view the mural while waiting in line to fill their plates. Perhaps for the first time in Reginald's history, Reggie and his cuisine are not commanding all the attention. The mural is the star of the show. Admiration is expressed for the clever way it conveys the flavor of city streets as well as New York's skyline. A detailed East Side street scene fills the lower half of the long wall with a panoramic skyline floating above. Close and long views are divided by an arcing shape which resembles a bridge.

It's a charming design, inspired by Josh's recent trip to the City. He was a little sorry not to be painting it himself, but he loves the way his friends executed it. They made everything a little more surreal than he would have by bathing the scenes in a southerly light quite different than the east coast haze Josh experienced firsthand. It's like a New Mexican dream of New York—perfect for Reginald's of Rio Bueno. So whenever Josh overhears Reggie bragging about "Josh Overmeyer's design," he makes a point of stepping over to give credit to the kids who painted it.

After the buffet has been cleared away, a photographer from the morning *Ledger* asks for a shot of Reggie with everyone who worked on the mural. Reggie starts gathering the group. Angela sees Tony lurking nearby and calls for him to come over. For better or worse he was certainly part of the mural project.

"Were you one of the painters?" the reporter asks, taking down Tony's name.

Reggie pushes forward and throws an arm around the young man in a belated display of appreciation.

"Tony here was my Project Supervisor."

"He made sure we didn't wreck the place," Eddie clarifies good naturedly.

At this, Tony, fuming within Reggie's embrace, brightens for a split second. The camera clicks.

Another click captures the artists in front of the mural. This is definitely front page material. Josh is dressed like Vincent Van Gogh with a big bandage around his head. Danny makes a superb Salvador Dali with trademark cape and black mustache. Angela, her eyebrows connected with black pencil, is Frieda Kahlo in Mexican ruffles. Dori has her hair pulled back tightly for the severe look of Georgia O'Keeffe.

Eddie and Marcos are wearing their usual clothes, but they explain that they're dressed as "anonymous underground artists of the Revolution."

"Great!" The newsman doesn't ask which revolution. He takes it all down and dashes off to his next assignment. His pictures will appear in the paper captioned: *"Restauranteur with Sidekick,"* and, *"Muralists pay homage to their role models."*

Claire stays well out of range of the camera. She doesn't want to appear in the newspaper dressed as Super Cupcake, in a gold body suit, a pleated paper cape resembling the papers used for lining cupcake tins, and a shower cap fixed up to look like white icing with rainbow sprinkles. On the other hand, the outfit is too good to go undocumented. When the crowd has cleared out and only the kids and a few of their parents are left, she lets Tony prevail on her to pose in front of the mural, "Just like Superman on the streets of Metropolis."

Claire can't resist. She steps in front of the street scene and magically looks larger than life. Tony tells her exactly where to stand, to turn at this angle, to move her legs apart, put one hand on her hip, hold the spatula just so with the other, and stick her chest out. She obeys, seeing the creative fire in his eyes.

Next Tony gathers the amused onlookers over to the side, a few feet away from Claire, and hands around Reginald's oversized menus. Josh, who can see exactly what's coming, stands ready with his own camera. He gives Tony a thumbs up. Tony grabs a menu for himself.

"Okay, everyone, flap your menus!" They face Claire and wave the menus up and down, creating a breeze which lifts her cape. Josh snaps a couple of pictures, then he and Tony switch places and Tony snaps a few for himself. Pretty soon everyone's laughing too hard to go on.

"Way to go, Tony!" "That was fantastic!" "Brilliant!"

They can't laud him enough, but only Laurie's words register. "You should be a director, Tony," she says with genuine admiration.

Her voice rings in his ears long after.

## CHAPTER 45
## MERCY


Jo's note reads: *"Muffin has been pretty negative, depressed and downright ornery. She told me to shut up yesterday, and to go home. She didn't need to see me every day. She's only been eating a quarter of a sandwich. And she's like a broken record: 'I'm sick. I feel awful.' I have just been ignoring the litany. Maybe she'll be better for you girls. Good Luck."*

Lydia thinks this might be a good day to try reading something to Muffin, especially since Jo has provided a book of short stories. The worn paperback, *Three Legends* by Paul Gallico, was left on top of the cooler in typical Jo fashion—conscientiously wrapped in a ziplock bag with an artfully lettered sticky note: *"Muffin might like these."* Lydia gathers it up with the cooler and goes inside, bracing herself for the worst.

Right away the situation doesn't look promising. She must go through the courtyard to get to Muffin's wing because the middle hallway is piled to the ceiling with furniture—again—as another set of floors is waxed. Lydia thinks that whoever orchestrated the renovations must have been trying for some sort of record. How many times has each room been turned upside down? There was the painting and wallpapering phase, then the furniture was switched out—a couple of times before they got it right. Now all of this new furniture must be piled in the hallways again while the floors are buffed.

Westcare Manor is shaped like an asterisk, and Lydia now finds herself at the nexus. Several doors on the opposite side of the courtyard all lead into one large room where rows of wheelchairs are ranged in front of a large, loud TV set. The walls are lined with shelves of books and tables holding jigsaw puzzles and games. A large chalkboard on one wall announces the weekly schedule of activities. A movie this afternoon. Bingo tomorrow. Morning exercises. The hair stylist comes on Thursdays. The aides are hustling in and out, sometimes steering two wheelchairs at once out through the courtyard and around to the dining room. They look exhausted and put out from all the extra running around. They're running late, too. Hungry residents look up at Lydia hopefully, but she skirts around them. She does not like this. It's bringing back bad memories. She tries not to look at anyone, and tells herself to think of the Granny Abel from the photograph, not the one she remembers from the nursing home.

She emerges into Muffin's corridor with relief. But there's yet another project in progress. Carpet is being laid in the hallway. The roll of industrial grade floor covering has been cut and placed. One lone worker remains to secure it. He's doing a methodical job, working his way out from the nurse's station with the rhythmic whsssh-toc, whsssh-toc of his pneumatic staple gun. Lydia skips past him, listening for Muffin's outcry. But in the room at the end of the hall all is in order. The radio is playing softly, Muffin is sitting placidly in the sun.

Lydia sings out, "Hello, Muffin."

"Hello?"

"It's me—Lydia. I brought lunch."

"Oh you did? How nice of you." Muffin rouses herself for a moment, gracious by instinct, but she doesn't open her eyes.

"How about sitting up a little bit more? Shall I wipe your eyes? They look goopy." Lydia fusses over her, feeling unhappy. These visits get more messy and more depressing all the time.

Muffin doesn't want to sit up, or have her eyes wiped, or eat. She tells Lydia not to bother.

"Too late for that!" Lydia bustles around and narrates her actions with fake perkiness. She's putting a pillow behind Muffin so she'll sit up straight, bringing over a chair for herself, pouring an icy cold tomato juice— By the time Lydia puts the cup in Muffin's hand, she seems willing enough to consume it. Lydia puts the sandwich in Muffin's other hand and she eats compliantly.

"Shall I read to you? I have this book of short stories that Jo sent along." Lydia's flipping through the pages, trying to figure out what they're in for.

Muffin is indifferent. She still hasn't opened her eyes, and she's eating in slow motion. Lydia can hardly bear to watch.

"Okay— Do you *mind* if I read?"

"No, I suppose not."

Lydia begins to read "The Snow Goose." The first few pages are all mood. The scene is set on the cold, lonely, grey coast of England.

"Sounds horrible."

Lydia looks up and smiles. Muffin's eyes are still closed, but she is chewing and listening.

"It does, doesn't it? I haven't read this before, Muffin, so I have no idea where this is going. Let's try a little more."

She reads on. Soon they are both spellbound. When Lydia stops to get out the fruit, Muffin says, "You are such a good reader, I just can't believe it."

That's more encouragement than Lydia needs. She reads through the story while Muffin works her way through Jo's lunch. All the while, the whsssh-toc of the carpet layer out in the hall gets nearer and nearer, until the door swings open and the carpet laying proceeds right at Muffin's threshold. Lydia, reading the dramatic scene in which Rhayader is rescuing soldiers from the beaches of Dunkirk with the snow goose circling above, looks up in annoyance.

The carpet guy is kneeling on the ground by the door, smiling up at them with his air gun poised. His expression is flattering and touching. He might be making devotions to Our Lady. Lydia nods, but does not falter in her reading. She completes the story without further interruption, for the worker has decided to rest for a few minutes. He sits back on his haunches, easing the ache in his back, and listens to the ending, then he quietly pulls the door shut and resumes his work.

Lydia and Muffin don't notice the last flurry of whsssh-tocs coming from the end of the hall. The remarkable tale is still working on them.

"That was really good, wasn't it?"

"Yes. Good. Thank you."

"Claire will read another one to you tomorrow." Lydia puts the book back into its baggie. She intends to take it home and read the other stories tonight before turning it over to Claire.

"Don't go to any bother." In a blink Muffin has lapsed back into depression.

Lydia frowns at her. "We don't mind. Really."

"Why am I so tired?"

"You had a busy life," Lydia answers. "Now you're tired. The questions is, Why am *I* so tired?" She starts cleaning up.

Muffin's eyes are closed, but her ears are open. She detects that this is not entirely a joke. "You should lie down and sleep."

"Tell ya what. I'll do that as soon as I get home. Now, how about if I help *you* get back to sleep before I go." Lydia puts her hands on Muffin's shoulders and pets her with a light touch.

"That feels nice," then, without waiting for Lydia to say good bye or for drowsiness to overcome her, Muffin adds, "I'll miss you."

Lydia senses that she's been excused. "I'll miss you too." She bends over and brushes Muffin's cheek with hers. Feeling sad, she leaves.

Lydia concedes that the new rug looks nice, as she retraces her route to the activities room, which she finds filled to capacity with the residents from the middle wing. Lettie is there, wearing a purple knit cap. Lydia squats in front of her to say hello and they gaze admiringly at each other, each telling the other how pretty she is. When Lettie's attention drifts beyond Lydia to the raging game show on the television set, Lydia squeezes her hand and slips away.

In the courtyard, Hazel and Julia are once more plotting their escape.

"Go check out front for the Yellow Cab," Julia wheezes.

"Okay, I'll look," Lydia says agreeably. "But, listen, you two, I've been wanting to ask you about those things that were missing. Were any of them ever returned? Your ring? Or the little doll?"

The elderly roommates look at each other with stricken expressions, and Lydia realizes she's picked a bad time to ask after missing belongings.

Hazel finds the strength to respond.

"Has anything been returned? Why, child, they've pinched every blessed thing in the room!"

✦

Conditions at Westcare Manor are a little better on Saturdays, at least with regard to the facility itself. An effort is made to put things back together and get the place looking nice and orderly for the families who visit on weekends. The residents' care is another matter. The staff is made up of part-timers, the meal schedule is altered, and there are fewer group activities. Weekends at Westcare Manor can be long indeed for those residents who don't get visitors or go home to family.

Muffin is among those who do not take well to changes in routine. The arrival of the young man who tends to her comes as an unhappy surprise. By Sunday she'll be used to him, but Saturday morning is a struggle. When Claire marches in at lunchtime she finds Muffin down and out. She barely remembers who Claire is, and calls her Josie for the first ten minutes. Claire swirls around the room, narrating her actions while she sets up for lunch. Muffin punctuates Claire's chatter with a dolorous chorus of, "Thank you for coming and doing everything."

"It's really okay, Muffin. I'm happy to do it. I haven't seen you since last Saturday." Claire plops down in the fancy new padded chair she's placed next to Muffin. "Wow, that is more comfortable."

"Where were you?"

"At school. Remember Lydia coming yesterday? She said you read a story together." Claire has already taken out the book.

"Oh, we did." This might be a statement or a question, but Muffin has figured out that she is not speaking to Josie. The Blossom is here.

"I'm going to read another one today." Claire pours a cup of juice and places it in Muffin's hand without asking if she wants it. "This is your favorite."

"Oh good." Muffin sips, but she is referring to the story.

Claire eases a piece of sandwich into Muffin's other hand and brushes away a fly that hovers around her cup. Muffin flinches. "Sorry about that. There's a fly in here."

"Yes, it's a fly here all bother!" Muffin blurts out.

"Been bothering you all day, huh?" Claire correctly interprets. "Must've come in from the cold. I'll see if I can get it. Shall I read?"

Muffin nods. Her eyes remain closed, just as Lydia reported.

Claire flips through the Paul Gallico collection and skims the opening of a story entitled "The Small Miracle." She decides to give it a try. It's about an impoverished young street urchin in Italy whose only friend is his donkey. When the animal falls ill, the boy takes him to the shrine of St. Francis in Assisi so the saint will save him. The pious yet insensitive keepers of the shrine are reluctant to allow the wretched child and his donkey admittance.

Between courses Claire reminds Muffin that St. Francis is the patron saint of animals. She figures that Muffin knows about St. Francis the way she does—from images in art and not through religious instruction. Still, this is sufficient to enjoy the story.

"I bet you've seen statues of St. Francis," Claire tells Muffin. "He wears the humble brown robes of a monk, and there are always birds and animals and flowers around him."

Muffin nods. She knows what Claire's talking about.

The story is fairly long, but Claire is determined to get through it in one sitting. Muffin eats well and slowly, listening. While Claire reads about St. Francis and the small boy's faith, that little, fast fly lands right on the open page. All she would have to do is shut the book sharply to catch and kill it. But Claire doesn't want to smear the yellowing pages of Jo's book with fly guts—and it strikes her as inappropriate while reading about St. Francis, friend of all living creatures. She keeps reading. The fly stays on the page until she turns it, and then it settles on the window screen behind her, for all the world as if it's listening. As she becomes absorbed in the story, and the challenge of reading it while simultaneously feeding Muffin, Claire forgets the presence of the fly.

When Muffin has finished eating, Claire takes a break to clean up, then returns to her chair to read the last few pages of "The Small Miracle." They agree it was a touching story.

"And I didn't even get too emotional," Claire says, making fun of herself. "You know how I'll cry at things in books that have nothing to do with me."

Muffin laughs at this. But Claire finds herself marveling again at how these animal stories—they have read quite a few by now—are both so suitable to Muffin's mental state, and somehow always about the frailty and beauty of life and nature. The parallels to Muffin's circumstance never escape her. Does Muffin sense them too?

Claire stands up and begins to massage Muffin's shoulders. Miraculously, after all their moving about, that little fly is still sitting on the window screen.

"Remember that fly that was bugging you earlier?" Claire asks.

Muffin nods, she does remember that.

"Well, I had my chance to kill it when it landed on the book, but I couldn't because we were reading about St. Francis."

Muffin chuckles heartily at this, making her bony shoulders quiver under Claire's hands and proving how well she'd followed the story. And the fly also seems to understand that it has escaped death by the mercy of St. Francis. Claire makes an imaginary promise with the fly that it won't disturb Muffin for the rest of the day.

The weather turns. November settles into its blustery, chill and grey persona. The parking lot at Westcare Manor fills with gold and brown leaves overnight. Jo shuffles through them, positively dreading this visit to her mother. The lowering skies accentuate her foreboding. The Serafinas have been swallowed up in clouds.

Lydia and Claire had such positive reports, but Sunday was nightmarish, as if Muffin had saved up all of her routines for Jo. There was the "I want to die" routine and the refusing to eat routine, the nose-blowing routine, in which Muffin has a tickle in her nose and must wipe and poke at it with a tissue for perhaps twenty minutes at a time. Of course she said she had to go to the bathroom, but there was no aide in sight, and by the end of lunch she'd already soiled herself. Unable to pinpoint the source of her discomfort, Muffin had sunk deeper into listlessness, calling out mechanically from time to time, "I think I'm crazy. I think I'm sick." When Jo tried to make conversation,

Muffin interrupted with another outburst, "I don't know what's wrong with me!" When Jo tried to soothe her by rubbing her shoulders, Muffin didn't say even once that it felt good. She didn't even say thank you.

Jo left with the feeling that her visits have been pointless, and only prolong her mother's suffering. She returns today with bitter resolve. She'll comply with her mother's wishes. She won't pretend any longer that she doesn't know what those are. She'll cease her efforts to delay the inevitable wreck of Muffin's weary vessel on the looming shore, but she will not abandon Muffin altogether. She's changed her mind, not her ritual. The lunchtime visits must continue, she will just have a different attitude about them.

"I want to die!" Muffin hollers.

Jo can hear her from the nurse's station. She strides down the hall. With the footrests up, Muffin has walked her wheelchair several feet across the room and gotten it wedged in between the bathroom door and the foot of the bed. She's slid down, twisted to the right as always, and her head lolls back uncomfortably. "I want to die!" Muffin shouts again when Jo comes into the room.

"Muffin, what's going on? It's Josie."

Startled by Jo's sudden entrance, Muffin asks grumpily but more quietly, "Oh, it's you?"

"Yes, I brought you a little lunch. Let's get you up. You're a mess. Here, you're falling out of your chair," She eases her forearms under Muffin's armpits. "Push with your feet." Jo gets her up enough to maneuver the wheelchair over toward the window. With a little more elbow room, she's able to muscle Muffin into an almost upright position.

"I want to die," Muffin says matter-of-factly.

"We're all gonna die, Ma, whether we want to or not. Why rush it?" Jo is testing her.

"This is a mess for everyone," Muffin replies quite lucidly.

*So she understands her situation. But is there any enjoyment there at all?* Jo pushes Muffin closer to the window. "Can you feel the sun?" she asks, wishing the sun were stronger today.

"I guess. I think I'm going crazy."

"Ma, you've had a bunch of medical problems. One of them is your memory. Forgetting things makes everyone feel crazy, but you're not."

"Then what's wrong with me?"

"You're blind. You've had a series of small strokes. And you're ninety-one years old."

Today this does not come as a surprise to Muffin. "Am I going to die?" she asks hopefully.

"Not today, looks like. We get to have lunch together."

"All right. But don't go to too much trouble."

"It's no problem, Ma."

Muffin doesn't like holding things today. Her hands are weighed down by the juice and sandwich, they lean heavily against her tray and she can bring neither to her lips. When Jo takes the sandwich away, Muffin uses both hands to carry the cup to her mouth. After she slurps from it, Jo guides the cup back to the tray, extracts it from Muffin's fingers, putting the sandwich in its place. At Jo's urging Muffin takes a bite, chews and swallows.

"My nose is sticky."

"Do you have to blow your nose?"

"No."

Josie wipes away a tiny crumb from Muffin's lip. "Is that better?"

"Yes. You're wonderful."

"I love you, Ma."

"I'm full."

"I know you are. You don't have to eat it if you don't want to. Would you rather have some fruit? Or iced coffee?"

Muffin samples both, asks for water, and then dismisses her dutiful daughter.

"Thank you for doing everything."

"Don't you want me to rub your feet?"

"No."

"How about your shoulders?"

"Well, maybe a little."

Jo leaves Muffin sleeping. Instead of going to her car, she wanders out to the gazebo and sits on the damp bench with the wind whipping against her back. It's not a New Mexico day. That's New England in the air, even to a faint ocean smell. In the keening wind Jo hears her own lament for something lost and faint, urgent voices from the past calling Muffin home. She's trying to think of what to tell the girls.

# CHAPTER 46
## NO MERCY

A dreary Friday in December. Everyone's scrambling to line up their party supplies for the weekend. A couple of kids who are skipping class encounter Tony on his way to the Counselor's office. They have an idea between them and pin Tony to the wall. They want to know what kind of medication he's on—will it get them high?

"Just might." Tony plays it cool. He's imagining them both dropping dead from a bad reaction to his *pill du jour*.

"Good, we'll wait here for you. Bring it out."

"She watches while I take it."

"Palm it. You know how."

"What'll you give me for it?"

"Pack of cigarettes."

"Nuh uh."

"Okay. How about we don't beat the piss out of you?"

"How about a toot?" Tony asks audaciously. If they have coke, why would they be hitting him up for pills? *Cause they're idiots and they're desperate for a new high.* "I could see about nabbing two pills for some toot." He happens to have one pill already in his pocket. He didn't feel like taking it yesterday.

They let him go. "In that case," they tell him, "meet us in the library after school."

He nods. The library has become the safest place to deal. Joints, pills in coin envelopes, and tiny aluminum foil packets of coke or crack are bartered or sold for cash as routinely and easily as one might hand a useful book to a friend. No one who's quiet and looking at books gets busted in the library, whereas if any two students stop to chat outdoors under a tree, an entire SWAT team is likely to descend on them. Everyone knows about the library. The funny part is that the kids do find some interesting books, read parts of them, and even get some homework done while they're hanging around to make their deals. Plus, no drugs are consumed in the library itself, as opposed to what goes on under the stadium bleachers.

Tony wants the coke to share with Laurie after work tonight. Since her grades started slipping, her parents only let her work one school night and two weekend shifts per week, so he hasn't seen her since Tuesday. Tony's saved up lots of things to talk about. All week, when anything interesting happened, he thought how he'd tell Laurie about it. In his imagination he sees them running a perfect shift together and then sharing a little pick-me-up out back when all the customers have left—bopping through the clean-up, and then—

This is where Tony's dream always crashes. In his most wildly optimistic moments he can conjure a scene in which Laurie has borrowed Angela's car and invites him to go out with her after work, and they get some really greasy fast food that would make Reggie gag, and then she takes him home and he asks if they can't maybe see each other when they're not working, and she says maybe yes.

A rare and precious fantasy indeed. Generally, the whole scene collapses right there at quitting time, when Laurie's father will come to pick her up and Tony will get a ride with Reggie, who's anxious to go home and screw Tony's mom.

Tony doesn't begrudge his mother or Reggie their comforts, but it seems pretty obvious that the odds of his own father popping back into their lives are nil, so long as Reggie's in the picture. His mom could care less about that action. Reggie's supporting the family now.

*He owns us, but he won't "own" us,* Tony thinks. They are dependent on Reginald, between the money Tony earns at the restaurant and the gifts his mother accepts. But Reggie won't move in officially, and hardly ever goes out with Anita. He doesn't want their relationship to be public. Tony figures Reggie's trying to maintain his image as a footloose bachelor, and all the better if people think he's gay—it's good for business.

*He probably doesn't like Anita enough to be with her full time, thinks she isn't stylish enough.*

Or maybe Reggie really is gay, or bi, or has some sick fetish that he doesn't want to give up. Tony wouldn't put that past him either.

On the other hand, it could be *him*. Reggie won't commit to Anita because he can't stomach being the full-time father of an emotionally disturbed teenager.

Tony fingers the pill in his pocket. It's not too late to take it. Maybe he should. His mind's been cranking on Reggie ever since he palmed it and returned to class. He hasn't heard a word of the lecture. The pill would help him settle down. He has the other one that he can give to those thugs. He doesn't have to get beat up. But now they're expecting two pills, so maybe they'd beat him anyway.

Maybe if they could beat the thoughts out of his head that wouldn't be such a bad thing.

But he can handle it. He can get his head together without pills. Why is he thinking about Reggie anyway? What came before that? Trace it back. Why is he saving the pill? Because he wants the toot. He wants it for Laurie. Just a few hours and he'll get to go to work and see her. He can tell her all those things. Does he remember them? The movie, remember? And the funny couple he waited on last night. And that jock who came in so blitzed for math class they had to boot him, and now the football team will probably lose this weekend.

Piece by piece Tony puts his fantasy back together. When the teacher calls on him he falters, but the next time he's prepared.

The deal goes down after school as planned. Tony thinks there still might be a beating in store for him if those guys don't get high. He says under his breath, "Make sure to wash 'em down with a beer or two." Then he ducks into another aisle, finds a book about sailing, and heads for the circulation desk. The librarian looks at him suspiciously, but she's looking at everyone suspiciously. She can't understand how the place can be so crowded on a Friday afternoon.

Josh intercepts Tony on his way to the city bus stop and asks if they can give him a ride somewhere, Claire has her car today. Normally Tony would jump at the offer but he doesn't this time. He's getting that feeling like he can see through people—actually look at their faces and see inside them to what they're really thinking. This is the gift that the doctors are always trying to suppress with meds. People don't like having their minds read. He can understand that. They're so often thinking hurtful things. Do they think he likes reading all those vicious thoughts? That's why he takes the pills at all. The gift isn't pleasant for him either. But it's special, it's his gift. Right now he can tell that Claire thinks he's a freak of nature and ought not be entrusted to serve food to people. Josh is suspicious. Josh might be on to him about skipping the meds. Josh thinks he's pathetic and needs minding. No, Tony doesn't want to be with them today. "I'll take the bus," he says and sprints away from them.

Laurie is late. Tony and the other waiters do all the set up and pray they won't be a server short on Friday night. Melissa, the hostess, is ready to start calling around to find someone to cover when Laurie rushes in. Tony catches a glimpse of the car that dropped her off. Angela usually gives her a ride, but not today.

There's no time to talk. Laurie goes right into the kitchen and apologizes to Reggie for being late. He could care less that the others did her work. He says, "Well, you're here now, get cleaned up." She disappears into the bathroom. By the time she comes out the first diners are arriving. Melissa doesn't like this crew—too many under-agers, and she has to serve all the drinks. She'd have preferred to call in someone else. Instead, she punishes Laurie by putting the most troublesome parties at her tables—elderly couples who always have discount coupons and don't tip, families with young children, broke-looking college students who will only order appetizers.

The dining rooms fill up fast, and pretty soon everyone is running. There's no time to talk, and when Laurie won't even make eye contact with Tony, his mind starts spinning out of control again. She hates him, she hates him—

He screws up an order and the second chef mocks him, "I can do ten things and you can't even do one!" He scrapes the offending element off the plate and repairs the damage, pops it under the heat for thirty seconds and strides out to the dining room to personally present it with his apologies. Tony's humiliated. Reggie's stirring all the sauces, acting like he hasn't seen anything. But Tony can see into his mind—he knows Reggie's thinking, *The kid's a total loser.*

Reggie turns around and says, "Don't let it throw ya, Tony. Take a quick break."

"Yeah, I guess."

*Why does he always makes me feel like I should grovel? Asshole!*

Tony goes into the employee restroom and takes the coin envelope out of his pocket. Inside is a little square of aluminum foil, and inside of that about a half teaspoon of white powder. It was supposed to be cocaine, but it looks like meth. Tony scoops up a tiny bit with the nail of his pinky finger and sniffs it into his right nostril. He takes one more snort into his other nostril and wraps up the stash. He takes a leak and washes his hands and face and goes back to work. He feels better. He can focus now. He's in total control. Tony's the star waiter again. He covers for Laurie's goofs a couple of times. When she thanks him, he won't even look at her.

They're still not talking when the diners have departed, and the tips have been counted up and the staff is dispersing. Laurie's keeping an eye out for her ride, real anxious to get going. Tony's dipped into the packet again without her and now doesn't think there's enough to share. They've finished their chores and he's waiting around for Reggie, who's waiting around pretending to do some work in his office until Laurie's ride comes and they can close the place up.

"Busy night, huh?" Tony's ranging around the kitchen, fiddling with things, fidgety. Laurie's leaning against the back door, so tired she can hardly move.

"I thought so, but you look like you're raring to go."

"Oh, you know me. Just a ball of fire."

Laurie studies him slyly. "Whatever you're on, you got any more of it?"

Tony beams. Here's his chance to impress her. He pulls the little envelope out of his pocket and waves it at her.

"Ooh, would you?" She puts out her hand. "I don't see how I'll stay awake otherwise."

Tony squints at her suspiciously. "You going out now?"

She tips her head like it's no big deal. "Yeah. Marcos is taking me tagging."

*Of course. Marcos.* Tony pockets the envelope.

"There's a place under the new cloverleaf. Miles of fresh concrete. Tagger's dream." Laurie brightens, thinking about the adventure in store. Her eyes are on Tony's pocket.

"Kinda cold for that, isn't it?" Tony mutters, turning away.

She shrugs and goes back to looking out the glass door.

Tony resumes prowling around the kitchen, fingering knives and skillets, turning the gas burners on and off, unwinding and rewinding the spool of cord used for trussing game. He hates her. He imagines violent punishments for her, but of course he hasn't got the guts to do it. He's too messed up. He's a loser. He can't even do a bad thing well. He can't even score some toot and get her to do it with him. He blew it. Ha! First he blew it and then he blew it! And she's probably blowing Marcos. He hates her. He hates himself.

"Hey! Finally!" Headlights flash outside, an engine rumbles. "Later, guys!" Laurie dashes out.

Tony goes to the door and locks it behind her. Through the glass he sees them in the car, sees their heads come together, then separate. The car speeds off. He turns away. Reggie's standing at the door of his office.

*How long has he been spying on us?*

"You ready?" Reggie asks.

"Yeah, I guess." Tony isn't ready. He takes a towel and starts running it along the pristine counter tops.

"Girls are like that," Reggie offers, sizing up the situation. "If you had a car, she'd be riding around with you right now."

"Yeah, right." He starts wiping things—the can opener, the mixer, the knives—

*If I had a car! If I had a car! If I had a car I'd've driven myself to the interview and you'd've never met Anita! If I had a car, you'd've never given me a ride home, ever! If I had a car, I'd be a thousand miles from here! If I had a car! If I had a car! Yeah, all the girls would be falling all over me. I could go out and screw a different one every night. Yeah, right!*

"So give me a car, asshole. That'll get me outta your life!" This comes out garbled, like the words of a drowning man. Tony's not sure he said them out loud. Reggie's not sure he heard correctly.

"Tony?"

"You heard me, asshole!" He wheels around.

"Tony!!!"

"Aaaaaggggghhhh!!!!!" Tony lunges at Reggie. He doesn't even know he's holding a knife until he throws his fist into Reggie's chest and blood spews into his face, and all he can think then is that it's Reggie's fault. Reggie's fault for having blood, for having the knife, for making Tony hate him so. "You bastard! You bastard! You bastard!" With every curse he stabs again until the pristine kitchen is awash in blood, and the unconscious man's legs buckle and his body, braced between Tony and the wall, slides heavily to the ground.

It's over in seconds.

"You didn't even fight back, you shmuck!" Tony blames him for that too. He throws down the knife, then thinks better of it and picks it up again. Part of his brain has gone blind and he can't see blood. No, most of his brain has gone blind. His vision is down to a tiny pin-prick of focus. He can't see the blood—he can only see molecules. When he reaches into Reggie's pants pocket for keys, he sees only small twisted threads of wool.

His hand closes around the keys. He gets up and backs away, slipping. Sucking noises are coming from Reginald. It's the sound of the blood running out of him, or the sound of labored breath, or both. Tony hears it as the sound of lapping waves. He remembers the book from the library, but not where he put it. He tells himself it doesn't matter. He has a car now. He can read about sailing later. He can't see to read anyway. He feels his way along the counters, holding on tight because he keeps sliding on something wet underfoot.

By the time he gets to the door he can't remember what made him go blind. A blow to the head perhaps. He touches parts of his body. They feel wet, bloody. He has Reggie's keys in his hand. They must've been attacked. Maybe someone he can't see is still there, waiting to finish him off. Reggie's dead, he thinks he knows that much. He should get away. He should get away in Reggie's car and get help. He'll take the knife in case he has to defend himself again.

Tony lurches through the back door and runs blindly to Reggie's car, parked in its usual space in the back of the lot. The keys are a problem. Tony rubs at his eyes and tells them to start seeing again. It's easier out here in the dark. His eyes and head don't hurt so much. The cold is sobering. Look at the keys. It's this one. Look at the lock. There.

✧

"You okay?"

"Just dead on my feet."

"Hey, no crapping out."

"I thought I was gonna get some ice from Tony just now, but he was being an asshole."

"Did you offer him money?"

"No."

Marcos turns the car around. "Let's go see if we can score something. The night is young."

Laurie would rather not. "They've probably left already. Stop and get me some coffee."

"Primitive!" He speeds up. "We're only two blocks away."

She looks out for cops, terrified they'll be pulled over. Marcos' old sedan is out of place in this neighborhood. And so is his face. He's got a gym bag full of spray paint in the back seat and a beer between his knees.

"Please slow down."

"There's no point going at all if we're just going to miss him," he chides her. "How much cash you got?"

"I don't really think he has that much— Look we missed him." Reggie's car is pulling out of the lot as they drive in.

"Looks like someone's still there."

Marcos pulls up to the back door. The lights in the kitchen are still on. The door looks like it's ajar.

"Shit. What's going on." Laurie opens her door.

"Laurie, we gotta get outta here." Marcos thinks he sees blood on the concrete near the back door. "Laurie! Dammit!"

She's out of the car while it's still rolling. Like a kitten entranced by a string she has to follow what her eye sees—until she's standing inside the door and takes in the horror of the blood-smeared kitchen. Marcos comes up behind her and grabs her before she can collapse. Her mouth is open but she's not screaming. She's barely breathing. Marcos' breath is coming hard.

"Let's. Get. Out. Of. Here." He enunciates every word into her ear while pulling her backward, back out into the parking lot. He puts her in the car. She starts to gasp and hyperventilate. She opens the door to vomit and almost falls out. Marcos pulls her back in and rips out of the parking lot, then gets a grip on himself and slows down. "We'll find a phone and call for help," he tells Laurie. She's holding herself and shaking.

"Tony—" She thinks Tony has killed himself.

"What the fuck happened back there?" He's shaking too. "Hey, where's my beer? I put it on the floor over there."

Laurie leans over numbly and feels around for it. She can smell it, and the floor is wet. "Sorry, I guess it spilled." She sits up and dabs her hands on her denim jacket.

"S'okay. I'll buy more here." He could really use a beer to steady his nerves. He pulls up to a pay phone in a brightly lit convenience store parking lot. "You call someone."

Under the street lamp Laurie examines her sticky hands and then her jacket—and starts screaming. She's tracked blood into the car, and it's the pink mix of blood and beer that's soaked her shoes, and is now smeared on her clothes.

"Shut up, Laurie! Shh, shh!" Marcos reaches for her but she flails and bounces in her seat, screaming hysterically.

"Get it off of me! Get it off of me!" She's found a used tissue and is tearing at her hands with it. "Get it off! Get it off!" And she stamps her feet, feels the giving moistness in the carpeting, lets out a violent shriek and reaches for the door.

"No you don't!" Marcos throws the car in reverse and floors the gas. The blood, the beer, the girl—he's a gonner in this neighborhood. He's heading for home now. He'll take the heat from Laurie's dad any day before he'll get tangled up with the cops. They didn't see anything, anyway. They didn't do anything and they didn't see anything. Just blood. Goddamn fucking blood everywhere, and now it's in his goddamn car.

Marcos is stone sober now. Laurie's sobbing. He roars out of the parking lot before she gets the idea to bail out again. The cashier in the convenience mart takes down the car's license plate number and calls the police. It looked to him like the young woman was being kidnapped.

A helicopter splutters overhead, circles around and heads back in the direction of Reginald's. Marcos drives the speed limit. He obeys every signal. The copter gains on them again and fades out. "They must've found it," Marcos mutters, clenching the steering wheel. Laurie is quiet now, and sits rigidly staring straight ahead, as if just looking around will make them more suspect.

More copters are in the sky. They're never out of earshot of at least one. Traffic seems to be light for a Friday night. Marcos and Laurie begin to think about what will happen next as they approach home territory.

"I didn't see a body or anything," Laurie whispers. "I didn't see anything."

"Me neither. And we didn't touch anything but the door."

"It was either Tony or Reggie or both. They were the only ones there."

"Whoever did it stole Reggie's car."

"What about the beer?"

"That's the least of our problems. Why will we tell them we went back?"

"I'll just tell them I wanted to talk to Tony."

"Yeah?"

"I'll make something up."

By the time Marcos pulls up in front of Laurie's house, they feel they've pieced a story together out of the last half hour of panic. Marcos reaches for a towel in the back seat so he can mop up the floor.

"You said that was the least of our problems. Come on in with me now." Laurie feels sick again. Something doesn't seem right on the street.

Marcos feels it too, that's why he wants to clean up. But he throws the towel down and says, "Okay, here we go."

Laurie wipes her feet on the towel before getting out of the car. She walks numbly toward the house. Behind her she hears Marcos slam the car door, then suddenly the street is flooded with light. A big man seems to come out of nowhere to drag Laurie up onto her own porch. She twists her head around to see Marcos caught in the headlights of four cop cars. Men's voices shout at him to lie down on the ground.

"Stop it! Stop it! Stop it!" Her screams cannot drown out their's. Her parents are holding her now. All the neighbors are out on their porches, heedless of the gun wielding policemen.

"Get down! Get down on the ground!" The cops holler while Marcos, bewildered, stands there with his arms in the air.

"I didn't do anything! I didn't do anything!" he pleads.

They rush him and throw him face down in the road, handcuff him and shove him in the back of a squad car.

"He didn't do anything! He didn't do anything!" Laurie sobs. "Oh, god, what is going on?"

Three of the police cruisers, one carrying Marcos, race into the night with sirens blaring. Half a dozen men from the neighborhood pile into two cars and follow at a more temperate pace. Laurie's parents are trying to pull her into the house, but the big cop won't let them. His partner stands on alert out by the remaining cruiser.

"Did you go with that young man voluntarily?"

His big ugly face is right up close to Laurie's while she shivers in her mother's arms. Laurie's dad is looking at the gun in the man's holster and his friends out on the sidewalk and telling himself not to go making things worse.

"I want you to tell me the truth now." He's looking pointedly at her feet.

"Sure I was with him," Laurie mumbles.

"Voluntarily?"

"Yeah."

"Then I'm afraid we're going to have to arrest you as a suspected accomplice to a murder."

Is it their imagination or is he almost gleeful to do it? Laurie's dad squelches his rage and says very calmly, for his wife and daughter's benefit, "I'm sure we'll be able to get everything straightened out at the station. Would it be possible for me to ride in with my daughter? I think she needs to be seen by a doctor. Obviously she's in shock."

The officer thinks these are ideal conditions for questioning the girl.

"We'll go to the station first," he says gruffly. "The wife can ride along."

He cuffs Laurie right there on the front porch with the neighbors watching, and marches her to the car. Laurie's parents exchange some quick words, and her mother hurries to get to the curb before the car pulls away without her. Her husband is soon following in his car.

Across the street, Angela's mother is already on the phone to Councilor Martinez, while Angela stands in front of the TV watching in horror as a white draped gurney is rolled out of Reginald's and into an awaiting ambulance.

# CHAPTER 47
## LIES BUY TIME

When in doubt, make something up. This is Anita Foster's formula for survival. Being truthful wins her nothing. Most of the time she has no useful information whatsoever, and the rest of the time the facts she could supply would only bring trouble. What can she say to satisfy the landlord regarding the past due rent, or the social worker regarding Tony's medications, or her husband regarding extravagant purchases for the household? She has learned that a lie confidently told will buy her time to fix things, or to make up something else to buy her more time to try again to fix things. At any given moment she is embroiled in an elaborate fantasy which she is trying desperately to make come true.

The current fantasy, concocted purely for her own peace of mind, is that Tony and Reggie are on their way home and she will hear Reggie's car pull up at any moment. Or the phone will ring, and they will explain why they are so late and assure her that they're fine and will be home soon.

The phone does ring.

"Hello?"

"Hello, Mrs. Foster? This is Lieutenant Jane Preston with the Rio Bueno Police Department. Were you expecting a call?"

Anita instructs herself never to answer the phone on the first ring again.

"No, I didn't want to wake up my son," she answers calmly.

"Your son Tony? He's home then?"

"Yes. He's not in trouble, is he? What is this about, Lieutenant?"

"There's been an incident at the restaurant where he works. The owner's been stabbed."

Anita gasps, her mind working frantically. She can't think of anything to say. *That's a reasonable reaction,* she tells herself.

"That's horrible," she tells the officer, "I don't know what to say."

"Yes, it's quite a shock. I'd like to ask you a few questions, if you don't mind. And I'll want to ask Tony some questions too."

"Of course. Whatever you need."

If she has to, she'll go to another phone and put on a voice and pretend to be a sleepy Tony. Anita hopes it won't come to that, but anything to buy some time.

"What time did Tony get home?"

"Let's see." Anita steps over to study the city bus schedule which has been stuck to the refrigerator with a magnet. "It was after eleven, almost eleven-thirty."

"That's rather late, isn't it? The restaurant closes at ten." Lt. Preston is frowning at the coroner's report in front of her.

"They have chores to do, but Tony would've been out of there by ten-thirty to catch the last bus. It takes a while to get across town. Poor kid. He was exhausted and went right to bed when he got home. I hate to wake him just to hear this horrible news. Can't it wait till morning?"

*"Cause of death: Stab wound to heart. Time of death: 11:00 p.m. Estimated time of attack: 10:45 p.m."*

The lieutenant mulls this over. *The alarm company investigator was on the scene by 11:20 and our team was there five minutes later. The coroner can't be more than ten minutes off in either direction. If mom's telling the truth, the kid wasn't involved.*

"Does Tony take the bus home often, Mrs. Foster?"

"We give him a ride when we can. I would've picked him up tonight but I'm having car trouble, and my husband's out of town." Anita tells herself it would be unnatural not to express concern and continues, "Will Mr. Wells be all right? Was anyone else hurt? What am I going to tell Tony?"

"Don't tell him anything. Let him sleep. Keep him home in the morning. I, or one of my associates, will be over before noon to question him, and we'll tell him what he needs to know ourselves."

"All right, but what about—?"

"Too early to tell," Lt. Preston lies. She was buying Mrs. Foster's story until she referred to the restaurateur as "Mr. Wells." He was one of those characters who didn't use a last name. The detective is certain that even his staff called him Reggie. "Are you going to be okay, Mrs. Foster? I can send a patrol car over tonight if you feel uneasy."

"No, thank you, Lieutenant. I think I'll try to get some sleep."

Mechanically, Anita writes down the number Jane Preston gives her in case she needs to "get in touch." Then she hangs up the phone, puts on shoes and a coat and goes out to disable her car. There. One lie fixed. She comes inside and begins to scour the house for Reggie's possessions. Everything she finds goes into a black plastic garbage bag which she ties up and puts in the attic. All of the other boxes and bags there have labels on them. She uses a piece of masking tape to make a label for this one too: "Give Away."

Every car that passes is potentially a police cruiser. Anita tiptoes through her darkened house, tidying up. At last she gets into bed. In the glow of the street light outside her window she begins making calls to track down her husband.

By four a.m. it's evident that the only thing Marcos and Laurie had to do with Reggie's murder was to stumble upon the crime scene after the fact and fail to report it. Someone's bloody footprints have been tracked through the parking lot, where the perpetrator is presumed to have stolen Reginald's car.

Laurie and Marcos have independently attested to the fact that both Reggie and Tony were in the restaurant when Marcos picked up Laurie at approximately 10:40 p.m. There's some doubt now as to whether Tony actually is asleep in his bed, and a cruiser has been dispatched to sit watch outside of the Foster home until dawn. Whether Marcos and Laurie believe Tony to be Reggie's attacker or the attacker's second victim is unclear. Marcos says that Tony was Reggie's pet, that's all he knows about him. He doesn't know Tony well, but he can't see why Tony would attack Reggie when Reggie gave him such a good job.

Laurie knows more and says less. She says she's not saying anything until they let Marcos go because it's obvious now that he wasn't involved in Reggie's stabbing, and he didn't kidnap her, and she's not going home until he does. She knows how the police treat the brothers from her part of town, and they're not going to use all this as an excuse to pull that shit on Marcos.

Dolores just about falls over when she hears this. All she wants to do is get her daughter home. But shouldn't justice be on duty no matter the hour? She and her husband go into a huddle and come out saying that they can't force their daughter to talk. They'd like to get her a lawyer now, if it's the department's intention to continue holding her.

This sends the officers away scratching their heads. The problem is that the morning paper is in the can already. Two hundred and twenty thousand copies have been printed, stuffed, folded, bundled and are being delivered at this very moment. A copy of the city edition sits on the sergeant's desk as he contemplates his dilemma. A screaming headline below the fold reads, "POPULAR RESTAURANTEUR STABBED TO DEATH, *Reginald Wells believed to be victim of gang warfare*." A mug shot of Marcos from a previous arrest for tagging is juxtaposed with a publicity photo of the debonair Reginald. The text of the story focuses on the gruesome condition of the restaurant kitchen, the helicopter chase, and the possible kidnapping of a teenage waitress.

Sergeant Padilla pushes the paper away in disgust. For the kid's own safety they can't let Marcos loose until the retractions and corrections have been issued. And there's still the problem of the alcohol and residue of other drugs in the car, not to mention the known gang connections, failing to report a crime, and involving a minor in some or all of those activities.

"Someone get me Father Emilio's number," Padilla barks into his intercom. "From Cesar Chaveztown. Get Baxter from City Legal over here, and get that asshole from the *Ledger* on the phone so I can tell him exactly where to put his late breaking news! Anyone got that?"

A couple of agreeable grunts issue from the speaker on the sergeant's desk. Not long after, a call comes in from Clayton over on the far side of the Serafinas. Reggie's car has been found abandoned on the exit ramp leading into town. Inside—a bloody knife presumed to be the murder weapon, and a pair of bloody shoes presumed to be Tony's. It's cold in Clayton, no one expects the barefoot youth to get far. Local law enforcement officers are going door to door to see if anyone's taken him in.

Padre Emilio shows Laurie the Saturday morning *Ledger*, and carefully explains to her why the police do not want to release Marcos until a more accurate story is circulated. Laurie says that's fine, but she won't talk to them until Marcos is free, and she doesn't know anything anyway. The priest negotiates with the sergeant, and Laurie is released to her parents' custody, while he remains to personally oversee Marcos' treatment and to issue statements to the press on behalf of the family and community. He expects he'll be able to come up with an excellent homily for Sunday during his stint in the city detention facility.

Laurie's parents make numerous calls when they get home. She showers for forty-five minutes. It's dawn when she comes out. Her folks have unplugged the phones, double locked all the doors, closed the shades and curtains and gone to bed. Laurie calls Angela, disconnects the phone again and cries herself to sleep.

Angela calls Claire, who calls Josh. All they know for sure is that Reggie has been stabbed to death, Tony was at the scene before, during or after, and is now missing along with Reggie's car—but tomorrow morning's papers will say that Marcos did it!

Claire and Josh are furious on Marcos' behalf, but secretly relieved that Tony's name is not in the mix yet, not publicly. It buys them a little time to sort out their feelings and think about what they should do or say, if anything. They hardly know what to say to each other.

Claire has a horrible feeling about Tony—a sickening anxiety that the worst has happened. She translates this into a scenario whereby a mysterious attacker goes after Reggie, Tony hides and then gets away in Reggie's car—or the attacker takes Tony away in Reggie's car as a hostage, and Tony is now stranded somewhere and possibly hurt—

"Are you still awake?" she whispers. Josh hasn't made a single sound throughout her hushed narration.

"Yeah."

"Well, what do you think?" A second ago Claire couldn't imagine being more apprehensive, but suddenly she is.

"I don't want to say. I'm worried about Tony too."

They can't seem to say anything about Reggie. His death is beyond comprehension. They say, "I'm sorry," and "I love you," and "See you soon."

Claire doesn't think she'll sleep any more but in fact drifts back into unconsciousness easily. The mind and heart rebel against such news. When her parents show her the story in the paper a while later it's easy to act shocked, like she's hearing the news for the first time. "It's like a nightmare," she says. "There's no way Marcos could've done that."

She doesn't say anything about the phone calls, or Tony, or what probably really happened. Her parents are grey with sorrow, and barely notice that she leaves early for her Muffin duties. The television is on with the volume down, and a ticker is running across the bottom of the cooking show with breaking news about the murder: *"Victim's car found in Clayton. Manhunt for teenage waiter Tony Foster..."*

Brianna looks up to ask Claire if that's her friend Tony, but her daughter's already out the door.

"Did Claire say she was going somewhere on her way to Muffin?"

"Yeah, to see Josh."

"Oh, okay."

They sit listlessly, unable to digest the fragments of news that come across the screen.

"I suppose we should put something up on Reggie's website," Carl finally says.

"We should! But what?" They get busy making phone calls and preparing a memorial page for their friend. Working always makes them feel better. Then a newscaster's head pops up on the TV screen, and Carl turns up the volume. They learn that the murder suspect has been apprehended in Clayton—it's Tony Foster, a Reginald's employee. Brianna and Carl recognize the photo that flashes on the screen. They were present when it was taken. Reggie has his arm around the young man's shoulders, both are handsome and smiling.

Brianna chokes back a sob. "Poor Claire!"

"This is not good!" Carl huffs. He's working up a worry that any or all of them might be questioned about Reggie and Tony, and he feels especially protective of his daughter. He clicks off the TV, as if simply showing an interest in the news might implicate them, and so misses the lurid footage of Tony's mother being taken into custody outside her house for lying about her son's whereabouts.

Over at Josh's house, Claire begs Mr. Antresian not to put on the news because it'll just make her cry. Of course he doesn't want that. She explains about the mix-up with Marcos, and how she has the story first hand from Angela who has it from her cousin Laurie who was with Marcos.

"That's second hand," Mr. Antresian points out, but he's more receptive to this version of events with Claire telling it than he was when Josh tried to explain.

"Well, it's a relief to know that the boy's not a murderer," Mrs. Antresian says, frowning through her reading glasses at the front page of the morning paper. "But what about the beer and the drugs and the prior arrests? If I had known this was the kind of person you were hanging around with, Josh—"

"He's an artist, Mom. We really don't hang around except for when we're doing art stuff. Why don't you ever look at it like I'm a good influence on someone else, instead of someone else is always gonna be leading me astray? I'm not astray yet, am I?"

"Uh, I'll be taking off now. Gotta go see Muffin." Claire gets up and takes her coffee mug to the sink.

Josh is still staring down his parents. "And look at what they did to him! Does anyone deserve that? Being called a murderer on the front page of the paper? For what? Drinkin' a beer? Yeah, I think I'll stop bein' his friend right now." Josh almost knocks his chair over getting up from the table.

"That's enough, Josh." Mr. Antresian stands up too and puts an arm around him. "We're sorry about Reggie and about your friends. It's tough to see people you care about being hurt."

Claire can't believe what happens next. Josh throws his arms around his father and buries his face in his shoulder, muffling an inarticulate outburst that's more like cursing than weeping. Mr. Antresian holds him tight, rocking him like a baby.

Claire slips around them, waves grimly to Mrs. Antresian and goes out to her car. She leans against the hood and tilts her face to the sun, letting the tears evaporate as they form, not thinking about anything.

Josh comes out after a few minutes and spends longer than necessary loading some art gear into his own car. He comes over to stand with Claire.

"Should I come to Gus's when I'm done on the west side?"

"Yeah. If I'm not there, wait for me."

"Where are you going?"

"To the Juvenile Detention Center. I think that's where they'll take Tony."

"Did they find him?" Claire's stomach does a flip.

"Yeah. They just had it on TV."

She turns and looks up into Josh's face. Her brain's doing flips too, flapping around like a bird trying to protect its young. She so doesn't want to know what she knows, what Josh has known all along.

"Tony did it, didn't he?"

"Yeah, looks like."

## CHAPTER 48
## HEAVEN AND HELL

It's always summer in heaven, Claire supposes, with a sparkling blue sky stretching out into infinity. The banks of December clouds that cast their pall over Rio Bueno, showing only their ominous grey underbellies to the mortals below, are here a pristine, plush white carpet. She half expects to see Reggie walking along them, his well shod feet sinking gently into their softness, so that with each step the expensive Italian shoes emerge newly buffed and shiny, the way he likes them.

Yes, leaning her head against the chill glass of the airplane window, she can see him. His look is effortlessly exquisite, from the fresh crease in his trousers to the perfectly folded white handkerchief in his breast pocket, grey silk tie and handsomely coifed, silver streaked hair. His expression is benevolent, at peace. Here is the Reginald she saw day before yesterday at repose in his casket—no slash or stain betraying the violence of his passing—tipped upright and set free to walk among the angels.

Cleo the cat is trotting beside him. She, too, is shiny and whole, rejuvenated. Claire thinks how alike they are, with their passion for grooming.

If she's not careful, she will be seeing Muffin next, striding robustly toward her in canvas shoes, culottes and a jaunty striped jersey—dressed for a sail with Sam. But this is not allowed. Muffin is going to wait for her. She must.

*She must!*

Claire wills herself to envision Muffin in all her frailty. She is waiting—not impatiently—by her window, with a soft winter sun warming her shoulders and phantom images of the ocean filling her sightless eyes. When Claire returns she'll give Muffin a firsthand account of that ocean, not just how it looks, but how it feels when you dive into it and swim through the surf, how it tastes and smells.

*Muffin will like that.*

Only yesterday, Claire and Muffin made a tremendous breakthrough. Claire had insisted on visiting one more time before her parents whisked her out of town. Since Reggie's funeral was on Saturday, she'd gone to Westcare Manor Sunday instead, and found Muffin less agitated, having had a day to accustom herself to the weekend regimen.

Claire made her usual entrance, determinedly putting a brightness in her voice that she didn't feel.

"Hi Muffin, it's Claire! I brought lunch for you!"

Muffin responded with a single word.

"Claire?"

"Yes, it's me!"

It was the first time Muffin had ever spoken Claire's name, though she almost always recognized it. The achievement made Claire's spirits soar. She proceeded to serve lunch with enthusiasm, temporarily forgetting the horrors of the past week.

Yet she emerged from the polished, fluorescent glow of the Manor into a stark winter day wondering, sadly, if that had been Muffin's parting gift. At home she would find a suitcase on her bed waiting to be packed. Her parents would be making distracted but determined circles around the house, anxious to put a period on this hideous chapter of their lives.

Jo and the girls have noticed that Muffin's recent, rapid physical decline has been accompanied by a proportionate increase in mental alertness. She is perhaps stimulated by an inner knowledge of impending death, and has roused herself to make her final farewells.

Claire wishes that she could face Muffin's demise as courageously. She tells herself she will be able to, once she has recharged her batteries with sun and sea. She is run down, emotionally spent. Maybe there's some wisdom to her parents' plan after all, but she's not sure she'll be able to forgive them if Muffin passes in her absence. Superstitiously, Claire did not make much of her good-byes yesterday. She is counting on seeing Muffin again.

While Claire has been thinking about Muffin, Reggie and Cleo have hitched a ride on the wing of the plane. It's a game to them. They are exploring the exciting new possibilities of their afterlives. They are inviting Claire to draw them, trying to make her smile. Can't she see that everything lives again in her imagination, that all wrongs can be righted in her art?

No, she can't. She leans back and closes her eyes. Her sketchbook is safely tucked away in her daypack, which is out of reach in the overhead compartment. She would have to climb across her parents to get it, or ask her father to pull it down for her. But she doesn't want it. For all she cares, her art supplies could be in her suitcase in the belly of the plane. For all she cares, they could be sitting on her desk at home. She only brought them because her mother insisted, *"Just in case you feel like sketching in Florida."* She doubts she will.

Claire hasn't drawn anything except class assignments in a week. Her portfolio is on a back burner, all plans for early admissions abandoned. No one had the heart to demand she keep busy. No one had the heart for demanding, period. If she'd wanted to stay home from school, they'd've let her, but her parents' grief was even harder to bear than her schoolmates' gossip. Because Tony was her friend, Claire half feels like she murdered Reggie herself. The folks don't blame her, of course, but she feels responsible for their pain. She could never tell them that she's already been to see Tony at the Juvenile Detention Center.

She and Josh went because they were so worried about him. How can she explain that they feel too sorry for Tony to hate him, though they hate what he did? Reggie is gone and everyone misses him. But Tony lives, and nobody wants him. Being dead can't be half as bad as making someone dead. Just look at Reggie out there, spiffy into eternity. Meanwhile Tony is locked up, head shorn, clothed in a green jumpsuit, isolated, poorly fed, and subjected to an endless inquisition by lawyers, detectives and psychologists, while the papers debate whether he is sick or sane, a child or an adult, redeemable or executable.

Claire and Josh had a small taste of the criminal treatment themselves simply for making the visit. They were questioned, carded, and searched. Every word they said to Tony and he to them was monitored.

All this past week they waited to be called and questioned about the crime, Tony's state of mind, his relationship with Reggie. But—because Tony's guilt is incontestable, they suppose—no one has been interrogated but the school counselor, the restaurant staff and Tony's parents. Even so, anyone who actually knows Tony is not talking much—Claire and Josh, or the teens and their parents, or the kids that worked with Reggie and Tony. In case they are eventually questioned, no one wants to know anything more than they already know.

At the JDC they met Tony's parents. They recognized the couple from TV. Tony's father had appeared from nowhere to bail Anita out of jail and get her a lawyer. Now they're living together again, presenting a united front. Mr. and Mrs. Foster thanked Claire and Josh for sticking by their son.

"He needs his friends now," Mr. Foster told them, his arm around his wife.

"He won't talk to us, maybe he'll open up to you," Anita said, weeping, but the look that flashed from under her lashes told them this was the last thing she wanted. She took her husband's hand and let him lead her away.

Claire could feel Josh's fury rise and the great effort it took for him to quell it. She kept quiet. They never mentioned the encounter to Tony.

Tony says he doesn't remember, and that he's sorry beyond words, and that there is a monster inside him that deserves to be punished. He doesn't deny that the knife was in his hand, but he says that he wasn't in his body at the time. Claire and Josh believe him, though they know it's not as simple as that.

The last thing Claire intends to do is draw anything remotely related to the incident—plus, her hand hurts. She doesn't do any more with it than she has to. The doctor said she should wear a support around her wrist. Her parents arranged to pull her out of school a week before the start of winter break. They are running away to Miami to see Gram.

In some ways Claire is more unhappy with her mother and Jo than she is with Tony. Tony's violent act was mindless and too horrific to wrap her brain around. She doesn't try to make sense of the senseless, it's struggle enough to live through the aftermath. It's that reasoned, even loving, termination of life that strikes a sour chord for Claire. Was it compassion or convenience that caused her mother to finally make her decision to end Cleo's life only days before their trip? Was it obedience or exhaustion that made Jo rethink her approach to dealing with Muffin?

Brianna said it would be more cruel to leave Cleo in the less attentive care of strangers, or boarded at the vet for two weeks, with no guarantee that she would survive until they got back.

"I suppose you could call it selfishness," she'd conceded. "I wanted to be with her at the end. I wanted to make sure we had her remains to bury in the back yard. And yes, I wanted to enjoy our time in Florida without worrying about her. I'm tired, Claire, so was Cleo, and there was no point making us both suffer more."

But Claire could see that her mother had only managed to double her grief, at least in the short run. And shouldn't a right decision be easy to make—easier than that, anyway? Even Brianna didn't seem all that comfortable with the power she wielded over the animal's life. Is that why she's weeping quietly now, in the seat beside Claire? Or is she weeping for Reggie?

With her eyes still closed, Claire feels for her mother's hand and squeezes it, letting a few tears roll down her own cheeks.

She wishes she hadn't been so mean to Jo when Jo had explained how feeding Muffin would no longer be the first priority of their visits. It wasn't like Jo was suggesting that Muffin be "put to sleep" there and then like an ailing cat. She only wanted to comply with Muffin's own wishes, which each of them had heard expressed clearly and lucidly, and repeatedly. Out of respect for those wishes, Jo would no longer try to trick Muffin into eating more than she wanted. She was going to support Muffin's determination to die, not try to intervene.

"But what if it was legal to actually help her?" Claire asked disapprovingly. Would Jo go so far as to have a doctor end Muffin's life?

It was a mean, pointless question which obviously caused Jo pain. Jo had only shrugged and said, "I'm glad that's not my decision to make."

Fortunately Lydia had been there to smooth things over.

"I guess I never did have the heart to *make* Muffin eat," she'd said. "It's her life, it's her body. The only point is to make her comfortable. We all know she's not going to live forever. No one does. Only God decides those things anyway, no matter how much we think we're in control."

At least Claire had the good sense not to ask Lydia if it was God who put the knife in Tony's hand and made him stab it into Reggie's heart.

Claire thinks that if there is a God, then He-She-It has got to have about the lousiest job in the universe.

And that almost makes her feel like drawing a cartoon.

# CHAPTER 49
## SURRENDER


She has descended from the clouds to the waves, completed her journey from high desert to sea level—to the sea itself. She has tripped through the seasons like an errant tumbleweed to find herself deposited on foreign soil in the false summer of Miami. There's a deceptive familiarity in the stretches of sand—not unlike the expanse of New Mexico's high plains—and the sunny warmth decreed by latitude. The ocean, stretching out to the horizon, might be compared to the limitless skyscape of the west. But the senses, saturated, are not deceived. The lapping and crashing of waves drones in the background. Moisture laden air clings to the skin, films the eyes, weighs heavy in the lungs. It's as if the cloud has followed her to earth. And where once Claire strode strong and determined in the bright blue clarity of a summer day, she now wanders wearily, feeling swaddled and glad for it. Let the light be softer, the edges blur, and memory too. Let desire and despair melt into indistinguishable numbness. Let all hard features be rounded like chips of glass under the relentless washing of the waves. There is only one want now, and it is the most obvious and easiest to attain—the sea.

She's too heavy on land, too singular and identifiable. She's weary of being a distinct item in the universe. It's too difficult, and rather pointless. She is apt to generate her own salty puddle away from her beloved beach, to awake in a pool of sweat or tears or both. She rolls out of bed at uncharacteristically early hours, dons a still-damp swimsuit and stumbles out to the pool to swim laps until movement is detected on the balcony of Gram's condo. Wrapped in a towel, she eats breakfast out on the patio. The adults join her, but she doesn't join

368

their chirpy prattle. She eats dutifully to replenish calories, does not savor the tastes. What would she like to do today, they ask her. Her answer is always the same, Go to the beach.

She offers to drive herself, but the adults won't let her go anywhere alone. Since going daily to the beach is the only request she makes, the only matter on which she asserts herself, she gets her way. Someone is always willing to make the outing. They seem to have worked out a little schedule among themselves. They guard her in pairs or in rotation, giving her a wide berth, not intruding on what they suppose are her thoughts but in truth are her non-thoughts. She is afforded her solitude, and surreptitiously, anxiously watched. Brianna and Carl frame their concern in physical terms. Has Claire taken her vitamins? Has she applied her sunscreen? But it is her state of mind that worries them, her disinterest, her listlessness.

Claire allows none of this to trouble her. She's genuinely indifferent and the easiest thing is to go along. When they nag her about something she complies, when they try to baby her she submits. She is not thinking about them. She is not thinking. They might as well oversee her safety because she isn't personally concerned with it. Not that she feels self-destructive, she is simply in a state of non-resistance.

*This is good,* Claire thinks, as she lies down on her back at the surf's edge and feels her body being absorbed into the wet sand, feels the sand being deposited on her with the ebb and flow of the tide. *This is fine.* She squints up into the clouds and notices how low they are. The sky is right there, above her nose, and the atmosphere presses against her reassuringly, a gauzy shroud. The sand pulls her deeper into itself and the voluminous Atlantic tickles the bottoms of her feet. Her particular features are melting away, the same for her pestering thoughts. She's one with the beach, at peace. To sand and clouds and sea the distinction between a human shape and a seaweed is subtle. Against the enormity of Nature, Claire could as well be a seashell or a lost shoe or a crab.

At the thought of crabs, Claire breaks her watery bond with the beach and attempts to rise, her swimsuit waterlogged and weighted with sand. If she stands it may decide not to come with her. Half sitting, she waits for the next big wave to roll in and crabs her way out to meet it, letting the water wash through her suit. She rises from the spray, slogs forward a few steps, dives in properly, and swims determinedly toward the horizon, until she reaches a sand bar and can stand with the water at chest level. She is surrounded by the ocean on all sides. Blinking the water out of her eyes, she sees her father standing on the beach not far from where she had been lying. She can't see his eyes from this distance, but she can feel them on her. How long has he been watching her? She turns her back and gazes into the infinite distance, bobbing with the waves. Nothing made by human hands mars her view of water and sky. She likes that.

"If you're fated to drown, you could drown in a teacup," her grandmother said the other evening. Gram was quoting her own grandmother, illustrating a particular way of looking at things which—as a rule—is not her own.

"I personally don't believe in fate," she said, "but I can see how it comes in handy when things happen that you can't explain, couldn't prevent, and have no control over. You might as well say it's fate. It happened. No going back. In retrospect everything seems inevitable."

They've been having these sorts of conversations—conversations that revolve around the dire events which propelled the Stanley-Yosts to Florida without actually addressing them directly. The talk is mostly between Gram and Brianna and Stan Man. When Claire is present she listens without saying much, or pretends to sleep, or sleeps. Perhaps the adults speak more openly when she isn't present. She can sometimes hear them talking animatedly after she goes to bed, but she doesn't eavesdrop. Words are much too willful and obtrusive. Words turn into sentences which turn into paragraphs which turn into stories that don't have happy endings. Words involve accusations and explanations and misgivings. They describe feelings which, perhaps, need not exist in their absence.

"Wouldn't you like to use the camera?" Brianna leans over and calls to her as from a long distance.

Claire's lips form a polite smile. She shakes her head. "No thanks."

Brianna points the lens at Claire and snaps a picture, curious to see if the peculiar affliction her daughter suffers will be recorded, or if the camera will capture only the deceptive external glow of health.

"Why don't you call your friends?" Gram offers one evening. "I don't mind about the phone bill."

"Thanks, but I think I'll just go to bed."

"Don't you even want to talk to Josh?"

"We talked the other night. Remember? He called."

It wasn't much of a conversation, since Claire's usually the one who does all the talking, but it had been nice to listen to each other breathe, to feel each other's companionship. Things may not be right with their world, but everything is good between them. Still, Claire thinks she'd better get used to not having Josh around. He reported that he'd completed all his credits, and he's not required to return to school after the winter break.

This and his other news—that Laurie asked him to take her to see Tony, that his parents were promising him a new car for Christmas, that Gus was thinking about proposing to Katy—had threatened to undo Claire's carefully nurtured numbness. All of that was very interesting—too interesting. Any one of those subjects might shock her into action, awareness. "That's good," was all she said, shelving her usual barrage of questions, and foiling all of Josh's attempts to capture her interest.

"You seem so down," he said.

"I am," she admitted. "I keep wondering if I'll ever see Muffin again." Yes, this is a fraction of the troubles Claire is hiding from.

"She'll wait for you," Josh promised, knowing nothing of such things. "And I'm here for you too. At least till March. We'll get to spend a lot of time together."

It was good of him to say it. In turn Claire said, "Well, whatever happens, I'm going to come up and see you in Green Creek over Spring Break." And so they had ended on a hopeful note. Claire is content to leave it at that until she's returned to the comfort of his arms.

"What about Lydia?" Gram tries again, as Claire makes ready to retreat to her room.

"That's okay. Lydia's probably busy with her family for the holidays." She quickly pecks everyone on the cheek and slips away.

Her parents and grandmother exchange worried looks. The girl's behavior is positively abnormal.

At the beach, Claire finds it possible to go nearly blank and to not think anything. It's pleasant when done in a wet, melting way. Afloat in the ocean she can relax completely and let the salt water buoy her. Her spirit rises on a swell of appreciation for the here and now, balancing there precariously, too easily swamped by a stray thought forward or back. In the same way, her body experiences but a modest degree of enjoyment while resisting too much sensation, which would bring discomforts as well—certain kinds of memories, desires and fears. Claire falls into a morbid curiosity about what happens when all of this really does stop, about death, about dying one way or dying another. About what it feels like to stop feeling anything, to stop thinking and knowing and being. But no matter how she tries, she can't get there, either with her mind or without it. The closest she can come is this return to the womb, this bobbing and floating in a saline bath. She feels she has nothing at all to fear. She's obviously not fated to drown. She has surrendered herself to an ocean, and it has proved as benign as a cup of tea.

*"If you're fated to drown, you could drown in a teacup."* Even though she doesn't participate and tries not to listen, the conversations between her parents and Gram sometimes whisper their way into Claire's consciousness. Fate. Drowning in a teacup. Cartoons construct themselves against her will. She stops bobbing, and lets the waves smash over her head as if they might wash away those inner images, and all remnants of desire—

She comes up choking, afraid—she can't breathe—*I fucked up!* Instinctively, she's flexing her legs under water like a frog, forcing her body to spring upward as she coughs hard and finally catches her breath. She opens her eyes and sees her father running down the beach in a panic. Another wave crashes over her, and with it a sudden thought of Lydia. Lydia in Cancun. Lydia just a few weeks after her ordeal with Blaine, and no one to talk to, and her fears, *"You want to die."*

Claire bobs out of the water and waves both arms to show Stan Man she's all right, before swimming determinedly to shore.

## CHAPTER 50
## GIFTS OF NATURE


Despite her parents' remonstrations, Lydia zips up her jacket, puts her cell phone in the pocket and carries her telescope out the sliding glass doors to the back yard. It's a frigid, clear night, just short of the new moon—perfect for star gazing. It also happens to be Christmas Eve.

"I'm going to look for Santa Claus," she told Herbie when she tucked him in. He had no reason to doubt her, or doubt that she'd find him.

She figures she has about as much chance of locating Santa's sleigh as she ever had of retrieving any of those missing possessions at Westcare Manor. It was worth a try, though. She doesn't regret it at all, or the friends she made there—or the enemies. The staff will be glad to have seen the last of her. Lettie and the others will soon forget she was ever there. Knowing that made it easier to say good bye yesterday. There is a grace to forgetfulness, Lydia has learned, it brings the end of longing.

There is a grace to remembering too, she realizes. Remembering painful times that have passed brings strength to push on through new hardships. *And what about the good memories? If you try to block out all the bad stuff, you'll lose a lot of those because the bad and the good are always so mixed up together. Every time someone* cares *that something bad is happening, and shows it, then a little good comes of it, too.*

Lydia puts her eye to the telescope and, as she often does, prays. For Lydia, the heavenly bodies are a scripture truer than any sacred text transcribed by human hands. They are what they are with or without the words used to describe them or the science employed to measure their age and distance. As the darkness of night is required to reveal their beauty, so the darkness of human suffering is the backdrop against which blessings like kindness and compassion are best displayed.

"Lydia, you are like water in a desert," Yvonne told her yesterday. "Knowing you has been a real pleasure for all of us."

"I kind of feel like I should come back and see Lettie sometimes, even though, you know, Muffin doesn't need me anymore. I'm on the west side all the time, doing errands for my dad."

"You don't need to do that, sweetheart. You've got other things to do with your life than to 'sit on the bed and visit.'" She winked and passed the pretty box to Lydia. "I'm really surprised you're getting this back." Lydia couldn't resist peeking under the lid to confirm that her original note was still there.

"It was an interesting experiment, but I don't know what it proved."

"Proved you put the fear of God into someone!" Yvonne hugged her. "And it proved you cared. I can't tell you how much that meant to us—and how many laughs we had over you and your telescope—"

"Binoculars."

"You gave us a whole new perspective on things, made us less resigned to the injustices, you might say."

"I guess Jo taught us that."

"I'm sorry to hear about her mother. I guess we can't really expect she'll get better, but I hope she doesn't suffer too much."

Letitia and her family had piled in then, so that Lydia's good bye to Lettie got mixed in with their greetings, and she could go out on a cheerful note.

*Like water in a desert,* she repeats to herself, focusing her telescope on Saturn. That's about the nicest thing anyone's ever said to her.

It doesn't help her solve her dilemma, though. What is she going to tell Claire? She's been expecting a call from her for days. Jo said not to say anything, to let her enjoy her vacation. But if Claire asks about Muffin, which she certainly will, Lydia won't be able to lie to her. She'll have to tell her that Muffin has come down with the flu and has been put to bed.

The Manor wanted to send Muffin away in an ambulance as soon as she got sick, but Jo found a way around it. She filled out forms naming the attending doctor at Westcare as Muffin's primary physician. Now he can see her when he makes his rounds and authorize any treatments that she needs.

"I'm not letting them do much," Jo explained when Lydia found her standing over Muffin's bedside yesterday afternoon, waiting there to tell her that her services were no longer needed.

"I understand." She forced herself to act as composed as Jo. Really, she wanted to run.

"That oxygen tube to help her breathe easier. Some antibiotics."

"That seems reasonable."

"But no forced feeding. Only what she'll take voluntarily, which has been precious little. A few bites of yogurt, some jello."

"I totally understand. You're the one who knows what's best for Muffin. She trusts you to do what's right."

Suddenly the docile figure erupted with a violent coughing fit. Lydia watched in distress as Jo tried to soothe Muffin with gentle patting and sips of water. How could such a frail form emit such a deep, forceful sound? The energy of the attack indicated there was still some fight left in Muffin, as did her brusque, "Don't bother!" when the coughing subsided and Jo attempted to fluff the pillows.

Lydia would rather not have to describe that racking cough to Claire or reveal that she herself has already said her farewells to Muffin and Westcare Manor. It's only a matter of time now.

Her cell phone jingles and she fumbles for it guiltily, knowing that Claire wouldn't want to be spared anything. But it's not Claire. To Lydia's delight, it's Greg.

✧

Claire has brought a short-legged beach chair to the water's edge and sits like a normal person, letting the waves lap at her feet, instead of surrendering her whole body to the sand. She's in the process of reverting to a human entity. The sea has swallowed her and spit her out again. She thanks it for its healing, but of course it remains indifferent. She will try to remember this when she is back in Rio Bueno coping with all of the feelings she has been hiding from.

She was allowed to borrow Gram's car and come out alone this morning, for the first and last time. They leave tomorrow. Brianna is packing and her father has taken Gram grocery shopping in the rental car. She wants to make a special meal for them tonight. Sitting here, Claire realizes she's ready to go home. She misses her friends, the "girl gang," Josh, Jo, Muffin.

She squeezes back the tears and reaches down to splash water on her face. She doesn't even know if Muffin still lives or not. Jo hasn't called to report any news, nor has Lydia. It might mean there isn't any, and it might mean they simply don't want to upset her. Soothed by the vastness of the sea, Claire pokes around at all the places inside her heart which she's been keeping under wraps. Her love for Josh is still there. Her grief for Reggie remains. Her fears for Tony, side by side with her horror and rage, still seethe. And yes, if she's not mistaken, there's Muffin, Muffin herself—not an emotion but a presence, something living and bonded to her psyche. Muffin lives. Claire can feel her.

One thing which has thankfully loosened its grip on Claire's being is remorse. She has Gram to thank for that. The ocean was a comfort in its way, but lacking wisdom. It settles things with forgetfulness, whereas Gram is just the opposite. She believes in the power of the mind.

"If your problems are all in your head, then the answers are there, too. I think it's nonsense to say we're at the mercy of our traumas, our neuroses, our karma, our astrological influences, our chemistry, or what have you. My golly, we may not be in control of anything else on this planet, but this, up here," tapping her skull, "this is our domain, no one else's. We decide what goes on up here."

The outburst had drawn Claire's attention, as she padded from bathroom to bedroom. She was going to make another early night of it, but found herself leaning against the wall in the hallway listening. Little did she know that the discussion had begun with Brianna saying that she thought Claire should see a counselor when they got home.

"That's being a little simplistic, don't you think, Mother?" was her reply at this point.

"The mind is a muscle—" Gram started, but Stan Man immediately said, "No it's not," to which she said, "Well the brain is a muscle—" but he interrupted her again, "No, it's not."

"All right it's an organ, and it can be in condition or out of condition, and further it can be trained, and if we can learn to spell and add and—name all our body parts—then obviously we can learn to master our thoughts!" Gram spoke quickly so that no one would interrupt. She doesn't like it when her son-in-law gets snooty with her.

"But what about feelings?" Brianna wanted to know.

"You practice meditation, don't you? Feelings can be mastered."

"It's not healthy to suppress one's feelings."

Stan Man said that, and now it was Gram's turn to correct him.

"Oh, that's nothing but psychobabble. Not only is suppressing our emotions healthy, it's necessary a lot of the time, or we would never make it as a civilization. Maybe suppress is the wrong word. I mean just plain get over it. Someone makes you mad—are you going to be mad forever? How healthy is that? You let it go. You let things go."

"Well, that's the point of talking it through with someone," Brianna explained patiently, "So you can let go."

Exasperation. "Well all right, if you say so. But I think we all have our own little guru up here," tapping her head again. "It comes back to the mind. Mind over mind."

They all laughed at that.

"So, what does your inner guru tell you, Ruth."

Claire wondered if her father was reading *her* mind.

"No regrets."

"That's it?"

"Yes, that's my personal mantra—no regrets."

"Wow. You mean it, Mom? How do you do that?" Brianna's a worrier. "Even when you've screwed up?"

"Especially when I've screwed up. Mistakes are what you learn from. You've got to honor your mistakes. Without them you stay stupid."

This is when Claire had to come around the corner in her pajamas and put in her two cents—to everyone's surprise and fleeting embarrassment. How much had she heard?

Enough. "Some mistakes are bigger than others—they change everything." She was thinking of Tony, and her remark was directed at Gram.

"That's true. Any minute might change the entire shape of the future. If you think about it, the future does change with every act, every word. It's scary, but it's also what gives us hope." And because her granddaughter seemed anything but hopeful, Gram continued, "Life's nothing but a grand experiment, Claire. You've got to roll up your sleeves and plunge in. Learn from the failures and don't get too comfortable with the successes. Something's always going to come along and knock you on your behind. You sit there crying in the dirt, you're just going to make mud."

That came close to making Claire cry right then. Her parents were looking at Gram like they might cry too. This would never do. Gram headed for the kitchen for snacks. "And there's always food," she called over her shoulder. "Never fails to make me feel better. Who wants ice cream?"

The thing is, food *doesn't* always make them feel better. Restaurants make them think of Reggie. All kinds of foods make Claire think of lunchtime visits to the Manor. Reminders of everything are everywhere. This beach where Claire has convalesced is itself a persistent reminder of Muffin—of Muffin's fantasy of lolling on a boat with her face turned to the sun. Now the beach also reminds Claire of Lydia's crisis, and her own moment of panic.

*And I'm only sixteen.* Claire considers how such associations of one event with another must pile up over the years. Gram's right. A person better be in control of her mind, which might as well be a muscle.

*Use it or lose it,* Claire thinks, *I mean, really lose it.* She stares out at the swimmers frolicking on the distant sand bar and tries to imagine how she must've looked to her parents, moving as far away from everyone as she dared and just floating there, not leaping and laughing like everyone else, but just floating, and sometimes not even trying to keep her head above the waves. *Almost lost it,* she thinks grimly, standing up. *Almost, but not quite.*

She carries her chair up past the tide level, sets it down, and returns to the water for one last immersion. She doesn't swim all the way out to the sand bar, only far enough to meet the nearest band of waves, where she can leap and laugh.

# CHAPTER 51
## MUFFIN WAITS


Claire knows Muffin is dying because she's more beautiful than Claire's ever seen her, despite the oxygen tube running under her nostrils. Her face is alabaster and her lips strawberry red.

"Hi, Muffin! It's me, Claire."

"Oh, hello," she answers hoarsely, her voice two octaves lower from the congestion in her lungs. She knows Claire, but doesn't demonstrate that she's missed her, or that she's aware Claire's been gone. Talking is difficult, with a compressor running noisily at the foot of the bed and a humidifier burbling. Muffin's shrunken outline is all too visible beneath the single sheet that covers her.

"How about some juice?" Claire asks, determined to act like things are normal.

"All right," Muffin gasps. She's breathing through her mouth, not her stuffed up nostrils, so the extra oxygen is doing little good. She is wearing mittens—Jo warned Claire of this—so she can't tear the tube away from her face.

Claire opens a baby food jar three-quarters full of cranberry juice, and inserts a straw that has been cut in half, noting how Jo continues to adapt to her mother's changing needs. She holds the jar in the palm of her hand and brings the straw to Muffin's lips, using her other hand to tilt Muffin's head up slightly. It is a labor for both of them, but Muffin drinks. Claire does not distract her with a newsy monologue. Her words are soothing nonsense, or taken from their old familiar script.

"How about some 'banana-pineapple delight'? It's your favorite." Muffin accepts one spoonful of Jo's special concoction, and then clamps her mouth tight shut when the refilled spoon approaches again. "Some more juice, then?" Muffin sips and falls back, exhausted.

"Would you like me to read to you?" Claire asks her. She's brought another of her favorite books, *The Boxcar Children*. It was the first chapter book Claire ever read to herself.

"Don't bother," Muffin wheezes.

She has a rattling cough that sends chills up Claire's spine. The oxygen machine makes a racket. There's no point trying to talk. Claire sits by the bed with her hand resting lightly on Muffin's shoulder and reads the book to herself, finding she still loves it. Every so often Muffin cries out weakly, "I want to die!" or, "I want to go home!" or, "I can't do this!"

Claire reassures her each time. "It won't be long now, Muffin," or "I'm here," or "I'm sorry it hurts." She will not let herself add to Muffin's misery by showing how miserable she is. She concentrates on the book as best she can and tucks her sorrow away in between the pages, thinking, *Mind over mind.*

Another attempt with the juice leaves Muffin coughing. "Just kill me," she whimpers as the fit subsides.

*There it is*, Claire thinks. *I wonder if they'd make her sign something before giving her an injection.*

"I know, Muffin," she tells her, "it's very hard. The time will come. We can't make it come any sooner. I'm here with you."

"I want to go home," Muffin says.

Claire remembers that she'd said this to Lydia. She answers, "You are home, Muffin. This is your room, this is where you have been living right along, and we're here with you every day." She goes back to reading, petting and soothing Muffin when she gets restless.

As soon as she thinks Muffin is sleeping, Claire makes a motion to go. She doesn't feel like she'll be able to contain her own emotions much longer. But Muffin stirs, groans.

"Do you want some juice?" Claire offers.

"Just water." There's some by the bed, and she's able to drink a little.

"I guess I'm dying," Muffin says weakly, falling back onto the pillow. There is surprise and sadness in her voice, though this is what she's been wishing for.

"Yes, I guess you are." *Even when we're ready, we're not really ready,* Claire thinks.

Claire slips her hands behind Muffin's neck, and rubs her as best she can. The skin is hot and moist. She touches Muffin's shoulders and head, lays her hands on Muffin's chest, which she can feel rattling with congestion as she breathes. If she could see herself doing these things she would wonder where she had ever learned to behave so. Babysitting? Scenes on TV? She might call it simple instinct, forgetting that there ever was a time when she was afraid to touch Muffin.

Muffin is quiet again. Claire slowly packs up the cooler, writes a note to Jo, who has said she will come in the evening, and puts on her coat.

"I need to go, Muffin."

"Okay." She understands everything now.

"Jo will come soon."

"Thank you for everything."

*Muffin, the most gracious woman in the world.*

"You're welcome. It was a pleasure." Claire takes a step toward the door.

"I love you." Muffin enunciates this perfectly above the gurgling and humming of medical equipment.

Claire stops, frozen in amazement and joy and sorrow. This is even more miraculous than Muffin saying her name. She's thrilled to hear these words. Now she has permission to say them back to Muffin.

"I love you, Muffin," Claire moves close to the bed again and kisses Muffin's cheek.

"Thank you," Muffin says again.

"I love you," Claire says again, and goes out, holding back the tears.

The west side is pretty blanketed in snow. Precision landscaping and rubbly construction sites are unified under nature's woolly cover. It's possible to imagine what the mesa must have looked like before the land was sliced and diced for roads and development. The wetness in Claire's eyes facilitates this trick of perception and imagination. The world blurs, everything is becoming one.

The day, still frigid, is all white and golden and sky blue. If Claire squinches her teary eyes, she can turn the sky into ocean and the snow into sparkling sand. She can imagine herself soaring above it all, now a snow goose over a winter landscape, now a seagull over the balmy shore.

And there is the valley of the Rio Bueno, gridded by her Game Board of Life. She has that bird's eye view of it again, the way she likes to draw it. Only this time she thinks she sees her world from a temporal distance, not just a physical one. She's a winged time traveler observing a former-future world dappled in sunlight and shadow—a place of contrasts, of dread and hope—shifting as swiftly as a cloud blows across the sun, or her own reaching wing disrupts the fall of photons from sky to earth. As she circles high above a path that began from a seemingly endless summer day, only to progress through a week in winter bleaker than she could ever have imagined, memories streak through time to pierce her breast like arrows. But they do not cripple her flight. She is protected by two talismans, one inscribed with Muffin's last words to her: "I love you. Thank you." And the other bearing Gram's credo: "No regrets."

Lydia and Claire have made their farewells and Jo expects nothing more from the two girls. Muffin has fallen into a semi-comatose state, and no "extraordinary measures" are being taken to revive her. New Year's Eve is right around the corner. The teens are planning a party. It's a time for endings and new beginnings.

But Muffin will not be cooperating with the calendar. Her life breath persists out of pure habit, long practice, and simple science. Even in her decline Muffin has continued to build up a large store of psychic fuel, and her human body can survive for some days without a drop of food or water, especially when so little energy is exerted. Strong bonds of love secure her to life, however much she has come to hate her particular rendition of it. Numerous permissions must be granted before all of these threads can be cut. This is far more complicated than coming into the world with the snip of a single small cord.

The teens have their party. Everyone has a party. The numbers roll on the slot machine of measured time. New year, new decade, new century, new millennium. Jackpot! And yet the routine is essentially unchanged. School starts up again. Even Tony is taking classes, having been deemed suitable for the detention center GED program. The Stanley-Yosts return to work. Everyone's back to stuffing quarters into slots—

While Jo continues to make the trip to Westcare Manor each day. While Muffin lingers on. While Claire continues to float above, gazing distractedly at the Game Board of Life, unable to choose a square to land on, to roll the dice and resume play. She is suspended between states of being, like Muffin, like Jo. Compared to this, all of the other kinds of waiting they've done so far don't feel like waiting at all. This is the really doing-nothing-but-waiting kind of waiting.

Jo isn't even permitted to sleep. The night nurse calls frequently. He's not calling to say that Muffin's near the end and Jo should come sit with her. When Jo asks if she should come over, he says no. He calls because he expects Jo to give him instructions to call the doctor or send Muffin to the hospital. He disapproves of Jo's strategy, which is to let nature take its course. His job is to keep people alive, not to let them die. He is responsible and Muffin is unconscious, and doing nothing is not something he's good at.

Jo supposes that it's only fair for Muffin to sleep continuously while she herself must be perpetually awake—between them it comes out right. Thoughts like this help her keep her sense of humor. She can't get mad and instruct the night nurse not to call, since any night might be Muffin's last. Each time the phone rings, Jo feels a little hopeful that it might be *the* call. It doesn't seem right to think that, or to be disappointed when it's only the usual, "Mrs. Griffin's breathing is labored....Do you want me to order a prescription of....No, no, don't rush over."

It doesn't seem right, but Jo only wants what her mother wants. She perseveres. Compared to everything else Jo's been through with Muffin, this isn't so hard. This is merely waiting, and it is very nearly over.

# CHAPTER 52
## NOT FOR NAUGHT

Claire can't sleep. She can't stop thinking about Muffin. Jo called days ago to report that Muffin was in something like a coma. There would be no more lunches, Claire could have Saturday off. But Claire doesn't want Saturday off. She sits up until almost dawn looking at her Cupcake Comics and re-reading her notes and thinking about Muffin. When she finally begins to doze off, there's Muffin again, more like a vision than a dream. At first she's limp and slumped over in her wheelchair, but gradually she begins to straighten, to strengthen, shedding her years. She rises out of the wheelchair in her tennis shoes and the yellow sweatsuit she often wore. She begins skipping, bounding down the corridor of the nursing home. She gives a shout and laughs and the walls fall away. She leaps. She's up in the clouds now—no, those are waves. She's splashing in the surf.

Claire wakes with a start, looks at the clock. Early still. She goes back to sleep.

At noon she rises, dresses, has breakfast, and looks in on her parents. They are busy at their computers.

"I'm going to the Manor," she tells them. It's not a question. They nod somberly and turn back to their work.

Claire drives the familiar route to Westcare Manor. The day is glorious, no signs yet of the snowstorm that's supposedly on the way. The lawns of the nursing home still hold patches of snow from the previous week, while roads and walks and most of the neighborhood yards are dry. She sees Jo's car as she pulls into the parking lot. It seems funny not to be carrying a cooler inside.

No one pays any attention to her until she gets to the nurse's station, where two of the aides that sometimes care for Muffin are taking a break.

"Oh," Mary says uncomfortably, recognizing Claire, "Mrs. Griffin's not really eating. We put a glass of cranberry juice by the bed."

"She's very tired," the other aide says meaningfully. Lupe is from the Pueblo. She's not so reluctant to acknowledge what's happening to Muffin. This is her way of saying that Muffin is ready to go.

Claire thinks it sounds right. She says, "Yes, I've been in touch with Mrs. Griffin's daughter. She's here already."

"Oh yeah," Mary says. "Yeah, I did see her come in."

Claire goes to Muffin's room, where she finds a well-meaning nurse bending over Muffin and explaining to Jo that she can't give Mrs. Griffin any medications when she's in this state—unable to respond or to swallow on command. The doctor would have to order something to be given intravenously.

Jo nods, then shakes her head—yes, she understands. No, she doesn't want to contact the doctor. She looks past the nurse to Claire, more relieved than surprised to see her. Now that Claire has come, the nurse doesn't feel obliged to stay with Jo. She fusses over Muffin for another minute and leaves.

Claire hugs Jo. She steps over to where the nurse was standing and talks into Muffin's ear.

"Hi, Muffin. It's Claire."

No recognition. Muffin is calm, slightly feverish. She doesn't open her eyes, and her hands are resting perfectly still, one over the other atop the white sheet covering her chest. She breathes with her mouth slightly open, taking a huge yawn every so often—more and more frequently as the time passes—closing her mouth and swallowing once after each yawn. Otherwise she doesn't swallow, even when water is dripped into her mouth—which, Claire notices, is turning black and scaly inside. Jo tenderly applies creme to Muffin's lips and lotion to her face and neck, and coos to her words Claire can't hear. She's apparently gotten there just a few minutes ahead of Claire.

Claire gets out of her coat. They pull the new chairs up close to the bed, and Jo begins to talk quietly. Without any urging from Claire, she commences a long reminiscence of her mother's better days, beginning with her impressions of Muffin and Sam from when she was a child.

"They were an incredible couple. Tall, good looking—really striking. They were both so intelligent and well read. Of course Pop was in radio, so he knew everyone. They entertained a lot. I loved to listen to the party chatter, then someone would always get worked up about politics, there'd be an argument—when Sam spoke up, everyone shut up and paid attention—" Claire has only to raise her eyebrows for Jo to fill in the missing information.

"He was News Director for a popular radio station. His hours could be crazy, and it was a full time job for Muffin to take care of him and us, and keep the apartment looking gorgeous—it was a beautiful apartment. You'd never know there were two young children living there.

"And we had to be just as tidy. It was a little unnatural, but Muffin was a perfectionist, and we loved and admired her so much. She had that artistic eye, a way of keeping things simple and elegant, so you hardly noticed it was 'decorated.' She'd do flower arrangements and amazing place settings for their parties.

"She had such a dry, clever sense of humor. I remember eavesdropping on those parties. Muffin would say something, and then everyone would go quiet for a second before laughing uproariously. She never clowned around, it was always something ironic."

"Was she hard to live with?"

Jo shakes her head. "No. She was a lot of fun. Always had something going on—she was an excellent photographer, wrote poetry. Plus she was very athletic, played tennis, bicycled—and of course there was sailing. But the boat was not always a vacation for her. It had to be kept neat and organized and well stocked, so everyone had what they needed, and, again, there were always guests. When Pop retired and it was just the two of them—I think that's when Muffin really started to enjoy it.

"Anyway, for all of Ma's meticulousness, she never made things difficult for the rest of us. The whole point was to make everyone happy and comfortable. Pop always came first, then us kids, then everyone else. Muffin last.

"But she did give herself one day off per week. Pop had to take us for the whole day, and she got to do whatever she wanted. It was always a mystery what Muffin did on her day off, but it was sacred. When I was really little it hurt my feelings, but later I admired her for that ritual. Now I realize that it couldn't possibly have been enough. She should have claimed more for herself. No one would have begrudged her."

Claire's not sure what it all means, but it doesn't matter. Jo's narration is for Muffin's benefit and Jo's own. It is an epic ballad, a recapitulation of the highlights of her mother's better days. It's a way of saying, "You have done much, you have given us everything, and now you may rest." Claire reflects again on Lupe's words, *"She is very tired."*

Claire never asked much about Muffin's adult life. The lost memories were troubling for Muffin and not useful for making conversation. Sometimes Muffin would spontaneously bring forth a snippet from childhood—a pet canary, Papa-someone and his dogs—and later Claire would ask Jo about it and gather a few details to help Muffin's memory along the next time. Of course Claire had wanted to know about the nickname, which seemed so unsuited to this stoic, angular woman.

"That's why it stuck," Jo explained. "Everyone in the family had a nickname, and we thought Ma needed one, too. My baby brother blurted out 'Muffin,' and it was so funny it stuck. Of course it didn't fit her at all. Later on we called her Tough Muf."

Claire remembers this now, as Jo's soft soliloquy flows forth. "Tough Muf." She's fleshing out an image of the adult Muffin—a vibrant and capable woman, highly literate, with a wry sense of humor and a streak of perfectionism. Of course, those qualities were apparent to Claire well before she knew anything about Muffin's history.

The humidified oxygen gurgles loudly. Staff members begin to wander in and out. They come in to take a pulse or an oxygen reading, or simply stand by the bedside speechless and impotent. Claire wonders where they all were when Muffin needed to take a pee these past months, but she keeps that to herself. She pities them. They seem unable to offer words of condolence or sympathy, to acknowledge directly that death is imminent.

Those great big yawns make Muffin look almost childlike. The aides and nurses do remark on how lovely and sweet she is, and make little jokes about how ornery and loud she could be. Everyone there has been the target of Muffin's ire at one time or another, but she didn't fool anyone for long. Muffin was a brave soul suffering through a humiliating ordeal with surprising grace.

The nurse who was in earlier stops by again before going off duty. She, at least, is kind enough to say, "I don't think Mrs. Griffin can feel anything now. I don't think she's suffering."

After the shift change the flurry of visitors subsides. Jo extracts three drawings from the night stand drawer. She's hidden them because she doesn't think the staff would approve, but she knows Claire will understand.

"I've been sitting here the past few days working on these when no one was around," she explains. "I think most people would find it morbid or indecent, or at least disrespectful. I felt funny about it myself, but I had to draw her. It's actually made me feel better. Plus, I have these to remind me. I think it's important to remember this." She passes a page to Claire.

Claire hadn't realized Jo did this kind of art. The drawing of Muffin's hands is quite realistic.

"See how they're resting? Ma could never be idle."

"That's why you made her the snuggly pillow. I remember her asking me, 'What should I be doing now?'"

"Yes, that was Muffin." Jo lays out the other two drawings side by side. They are identical profile views, nose pointed up. One was drawn Thursday morning, and the other was made yesterday.

"I wanted to show how Ma's face is changing, to capture how she's letting go. A camera wouldn't do it—it would be too stark," Jo explains.

The lovingly drawn pictures show clearly how Muffin's face has calmed and smoothed out. Claire looks from the sketches to Muffin. Jo was right about the letting go. Today Muffin is even more peaceful.

"These are really good," she tells Jo. "Was Muffin good? I'm sorry I never tried to talk to her about her art. Well, I did ask once, but it seemed to annoy her."

"I'm not surprised. Her art was a sore subject."

"But why?"

Jo breathes in and out heavily, growing pensive. She chooses her words carefully.

"My mother—I'm convinced of it now, looking back—I think Ma was always somewhat—depressed, I guess. There was an edge to her. A little anger, and a little self-denigration. Like the things she worked at weren't big enough, weren't significant. And sometimes she would just give up. Drop something entirely for months or years, and even try to erase the fact that she'd ever tried it. Late in life she was ruthless in getting rid of things—special things like her school art assignments, and sports trophies and even the photographs."

"I don't get it."

"Think of the times Muffin lived in. Doors were closed to her, or she felt they were. She had so much talent and so little outlet for it. Ma did what was expected and required. She had a lot of pride and did everything well. She could have been an accomplished artist but would never devote herself to it because it made her angry to have to stop to tend to her 'real' duties. My mother suffered for not having been able to fulfill her true potential."

Jo looks over at her mother's spindly form and feels the aura of a forceful personality hovering nearby.

"She was a frustrated woman, Claire. I know this is hard to relate to from your perspective, but she didn't have the opportunities or the acceptance that you take for granted. Her art was a sore subject, like I said—a dream that didn't materialize." Jo slides her sketches back into the drawer.

Claire's first impulse is to reject what Jo has said. It's only one side of the story, after all, Jo's perspective. But it makes sense. With all of those activities and responsibilities, how could Muffin possibly have had time for art? And if she had pursued the art, she'd probably have felt that she was neglecting something else. Muffin was not a "no regrets" kind of person like Gram.

At the thought of her grandmother, a dark foreboding washes over Claire. *If you think this is hard, wait until it's... someone in the family...* She can't bring herself to insert the words Gram or Mom but the mental image is there. The thought has been thought and can't be taken back. Painful as it is, it brings increased awareness, a clearer understanding of what Jo's been through. Claire studies Jo, who watches Muffin, and collects her thoughts.

"The way you described your mother in her prime—" Claire begins, "Well, I can see now how hard this has been for you. Way harder than for me. You always saw her in comparison to that—how strong and smart she used to be—how much more she'd wanted—how perfect she liked everything—and how *not* perfect all of this would seem to her.

"But see, I never knew her that way. So, I think it was more okay with me, how she was. I mean, this is the only Muffin I ever knew, and I still loved her. I still thought she was awesome—a whole person—a really special person. I guess it was wrong of me to want her to hang on, even when she didn't want to herself—it made everything so difficult for you. But, but—"

Here it takes a tremendous effort for Claire to hold herself together so she can finish her thought. She rolls her eyes upward and studies the pattern of the new mauve wallpaper with the fancy ribbon border running around the top of the walls. The colors are insipid, the design uninspired. As she analyzes why the scheme is so unappealing, Claire's tears retreat and the lump in her throat subsides. At least now she knows what the fussy decor is for. Claire turns her attention back to Muffin and then Jo, who waits attentively. Jo has become very good at waiting.

She continues, "I can't even tell you how much Muffin gave me. I mean, it might have looked like she was sitting there being useless. And it's awful to know, now, how that must have felt to her, feeling like maybe she hadn't ever done *anything*—which is obviously ridiculous! Anyway, maybe that's how it seemed, but I honestly don't know what Lydia and I would have done without her, and we're still learning from her and inspired by her. She's even still making art—through you—and me too."

Claire hasn't had the nerve to show the Cupcake Comics to Jo, though she's sure Brianna has mentioned them. Claire sometimes has second thoughts about the series—the way Jo is embarrassed about her drawings. Now, she feels that Jo's drawings have given her permission to continue with her own. In fact, she'd like to make up a little booklet of them to give to Jo. She wants to show her the Muffin *she* knew, Super Muffin. *Maybe that's what she was doing on her days off!* For the first time in many weeks, Claire feels eager to get back to work on her project.

Jo has her glasses off and is dabbing at her eyes. Muffin yawns silently, a great, deep inhale that stretches her mouth wide, ends in a gulp, and then gently releases her face into an even more placid repose.

"Do you think she hears us?" Claire asks. "I hope she can hear us because I want her to know that as far as I'm concerned, not a single second of her life has been wasted."

After a long moment, Jo answers, "Maybe she can hear us, Claire. I hope so. I can't tell you how much that means to me. I'll always think of that when I think about Ma."

They sit quietly for a few minutes more. They've said everything they needed to say to each other and to Muffin. With very little fanfare, just a peck on Muffin's cheek from each of them, Claire and Jo go out together. They've waited so long that Muffin's imminent death doesn't even seem real now, it's more allegorical.

"Are you coming back soon?" the nurse asks Jo, anxious that she not be away too long.

"Yes, I'll be back in a couple of hours."

Claire's fallen asleep in front of the TV after supper. She struggles out of her stupor when she hears the phone ring. Her father answers. It's Jo. He passes the phone to her.

"Claire, I just wanted to let you know that Muffin died about an hour ago, just a few minutes before I got back. They were trying to call me when I came in. They said she went peacefully."

"She didn't wait for you."

"She didn't make me wait for her. It was starting to snow when I left."

"I'm glad I went today."

"Me too. That was nice. Thank you for everything."

"Now you sound like Muffin."

That makes them both chuckle. They say good bye before it makes them cry.

Claire goes to the window and stands beside her parents, watching the snow slanting in, borne by a stiff wind. Cyphers of icy air leak through cracks in the caulking, a chill breath whispering a warning against the frigid night. Snow has already covered road and yards.

"It was good of Muffin not to keep Jo out on a stormy night," Brianna says. "Jo was able to get home before the roads iced up."

"I was thinking that too." Clare shivers. Stan Man puts his arm around her.

"We need the snow," her father says, which is true, but Claire hears another message in his words.

*We need it all—life and death, sun and snow—or the world is not complete.*

Claire hugs her parents good night and goes to her room. She'll call Lydia and Josh tomorrow. She doesn't feel like talking but is neither sleepy nor weepy. Awake and clear eyed, she takes out her neglected sketchbook and sits in bed paging through it, until she comes to the sketch she made of "Claire Cubed," abandoned with an empty word balloon coming out of the fountain in place of water.

What should it say? After all that's happened, what does Claire have to say now? At one time, she had thought it desperately important for her art to have a message. She'd created the Cupcake Comics as a commentary on her world—no, on the world around her. When her own world was rocked, she couldn't bring herself to express that in her art. She couldn't make art at all. It would probably have done her good. That's probably what art is for—a way of getting the mind working on something constructive instead of sinking into illness, or just turning off, which is what she did.

Claire sighs and tells herself that this was clearly one of those mistakes she's supposed to learn from. In the future, she must remember not to abandon her art when she needs it most. *That's it.* With a pencil she roughs out some lettering for the word balloon, then she gets out a royal blue marker—Gram's favorite color—and carefully inks in the words: *Life is a Grand Experiment.*

She inks in the rest of the drawing. Then she flips to an empty page and keeps drawing, and fills the next and the next. She scribbles away, drawing anything and everything that comes to mind. Her eyes give out before her hand does.

Claire drops the sketchbook to the floor and lets her head fall back against the pillow. She turns out the light and stares into the darkness, her thoughts swirling into dreams. Did it go the other way for Muffin, she wonders? At the end, did shapes emerge out of the shadows as mysteriously as they once blurred into blindness?

Maybe so.

When Claire closes her eyes, she herself sees everything.

## NOTES ON THE READINGS

The book called *A Bird in the Hand* in Chapt. 21 is based on the book, THAT QUAIL, ROBERT by Margaret A. Stanger (1966, J.B. Lippincott Company). All other books exist under the titles and authors referenced and are available at most libraries:
FIVE CHILDREN AND IT, by E. Nesbitt
THREE LEGENDS, by Paul Gallico
THE BOXCAR CHILDREN, by Gertrude Chandler Warner

## ACKNOWLEDGMENTS

My heartfelt thanks to Michelle Miller Allen for literary critiques early on, Dani Lee Delaney for the technical polish, and Ashley N. Jordan for "reality checks" and hand-holding at the end. This book was in progress for quite a while, more than a decade, and I am grateful to those who read it in less than a finished state and provided encouragement and thoughtful feedback—Mikey, Eve, Marty, Ariel, KC, Ellen, Frank, and Harry. To my family and friends, my readers and fellow humanists—it's a pleasure to write for you.

www.ingramcontent.com/pod-product-compliance
Lightning Source LLC
Chambersburg PA
CBHW071147020726
47502CB00002B/313